HOMEWARD

LIAH S. THORLEY

Published by Kara Fox Publishing

The right of Liah S. Thorley to be identified as the author of this work
has been asserted by her in accordance with the Copyright, Designs
and Patents Act 1988.

First published 2021 by Kara Fox Publishing, UK and Malta

ISBN- Print: 978-9918-0-0037-1 & Ebook: 978-9918-0-0038-8

Cover design by Pro_ebookcovers
Front cover painting: Samuel Charles Brees (1810-1865) *Flemington
c1856*. H17071. Pictures collection, State Library of Victoria.

For my three times great grandmother, Mary Keeling, whose life choices inspired this novel.

&

For all the intrepid explorers and pioneers that braved the journey to begin a new life in a far off land.

HOMEWARD

Part 1

1

Staffordshire, England.
September 1856

Glass splintered and tumbled. The kettle screeched on the stove. Behind her, legs stopped swinging beneath the table and a child sniffed. Emma pressed her fingers to her forehead and breathed slowly. The steaming suds and starch were making her eyes sting. Outside spirals of smoke pummelled the grey autumn sky and hung over the cottages like a heavy blanket. She watched a dirty pigeon sail past the window and away from them. Reaching into the sink to gather up the broken glass, a sliver sliced into her thumb. Emma swore under her breath. The chair at the table behind her scraped back and a pair of little feet padded towards her.

"It's all right Mam." Gloria wrapped her small arms around her mother's waist, rested her head against her back and hugged her.

The momentary relief the warmth that her daughter's embrace brought Emma was quickly replaced by exhausted sadness. Gloria's skinny body was bony and small for a seven-year-old. Emma considered the meagre cluster of potatoes in the spud tub and prayed they would feed the five of them for two more days. Gloria released her mother.

"I'll help."

Emma turned to look into the pair of large hazel eyes that were peering up at her.

"You're too bonny for scrubbing laundry," she said with a glance at the dry reddened hands of her child, "you've helped enough for today lass," Emma sucked at the thin flow of blood from her thumb. "Fetch me a bit of rag and I'll get rid of this glass." She watched her daughter's dark ringlets bounce away and thought of Jacob. Did he ever imagine how his children looked now, after seven years away from them? Her eyes flickered to the unopened letter on the dresser and she wondered at the contents.

Gloria came back with a tattered bit of torn off fabric. Emma took it and smiled. She remembered the frock it had once belonged to, handed on from one of the neighbours when Gloria had been much smaller. It had been well worn then, and by the time Gloria had grown out of it, it hadn't been fit for anymore use, so she'd ripped it up into dishrags. Emma wrapped it around the glass shards,

"Now go on lass, go play out for a bit."

"Ta, Mam."

"Just be careful..." Emma began to call, but Gloria was already out the door. She shook her head and rubbed at the cramping nerve at the small of her back.

"The laundry won't wait for God to do it," she said to herself and went back to the scrubbing.

*

Damp cloth squeezed through the wooden rolls of the mangle with a creak and sank like a long sigh into the basket below. Emma's back was sending painful warning signs into her hips and the nape of her neck. She needed to sit down for a while but there were still three piles to go. Mrs Craven's pile was just clothes but the lot from The Hall included bedding and towel linen. The thought of working on it after tea made her head hurt, but if it didn't get done she wouldn't get paid on Friday. She set the flat iron back on the stove to reheat and rolled her wrists. There was a click. Emma glanced towards the kitchen door.

"All right, Mam?" Albert's face was smudged with soot and his arms and knees black as night.

"What in Heaven's name have you been doing?" Albert was the fourth child she had brought into the world and older than Gloria by a mere eleven months. He looked down at his knees and grinned.

"We was 'elpin'...

"We were..." she corrected with a sigh.

"Me an 'arry were..." he took extra and somewhat exaggerated care of the 'were', "'elpin' Mr Feldman sweep out 'coal yard before t'delivery." The child had the innocence of an angel on his face. Emma smiled despite her best effort not to.

"You were supposed to be with Mrs Feldman," she attempted to chastise. But she could hardly tell him off for working hard. She opened her mouth to ask if they were being paid, but the lad saved her the breath,

"Mrs Feldman said she'd teach us for free if we 'elped in the yard."

Emma was impressed. If Albert and Harry could earn their lessons, then it was tuppence more a week saved for the food pot. She was determined her children would learn their letters, even Gloria in time, and Sunday school just wasn't enough. Emma narrowed her eyes,

"Then where's the tuppence I gave you for the lesson?"

Albert looked down and scuffed his shoes.

"Albert! What did you do with it?" She was about ready to clip his ears when the boy's mouth twisted into a pout of concession. He dug in his trouser pockets for a moment and then held out his hand to reveal the pair of copper coins. Emma examined his grubby face. His dark eyes shone as bright as the coal he'd been clearing and his smiling lips glistened red beneath the dirt. He had his father's charm all right. She rubbed his head playfully.

"So where's your brother?"

Albert screwed up his face,

"He's down the road playing kick about wi' Arthur and Gypo."

Emma winced,

"I wish you wouldn't call him that." Gypo wasn't the child's real name it was Peter. The family was Irish, and in their neighbourhood, the Irish immigrants were all thought of as tinkers and gipsies, even though most of them weren't. So that's what the other kids called him: Gipsy or Gypo for short. Albert shrugged,

"He dun't care."

"But I do and I'm your mam...and it's 'doesn't.'" Emma considered whether she could have Mrs Feldman teach them to speak properly as well.

"What does it matter how he speaks, Mam?"

Surprised she hadn't heard the door open, Emma looked up to see Jack tugging off his boots by the kitchen table.

"Because I want you all to have a chance to do better for yourselves. Better than me at any road."

Jack looked even taller than he had this morning. This recent growth spurt had made him look long and lanky. His trouser legs were too short and his shirtsleeves were well above his wrists. How on earth was she going to afford to buy him new ones?

"It's not like we've got much choice here, Mam," Jack put his boots by the back door and washed his hands in the sink. He smelled of sweat and coal dust.

"We owe the Feldman's more than I dare think," she said, on reflection. Not only was Mrs Feldman tutoring her younger children for a pittance but Mr Feldman had given Jack his current living. She was not certain what she had done to deserve such kindness but she was grateful for it all the same. So what if Jack was only delivering coal, for the time being? He was artistic like Jacob, so maybe one day... Emma put the thought away. After what his father did it was unlikely the potteries would even look at Jack.

"You get that shirt off and I'll heat a bit of water so you can have a proper wash. You too, Bert," she added, slapping Albert's grubby hand as he reached out to move a pile of clean laundry. "And I wish you'd stop growing," she said to her eldest. Jack shrugged again.

"Sorry, can't help it," He pulled off his shirt and parked himself on the only kitchen chair not piled with laundry baskets. Emma put the kettle on the stove.

"What's for tea?" asked Albert when his stomach growled loudly. Emma rubbed her hands over her face.

"Bubble and Squeak," she said after a minute. The ageing spuds would stand that and there was just enough cabbage to make it decent. "Sorry, it's a bit late."

"Don't worry about it, Mam, you've got a lot of work this week." Jack offered graciously. Emma took another look at Albert's filthy limbs.

"Bert, go fetch Harry, no doubt he's as mucky as you. I reckon you both need a good scrub down. Jack gets it first mind," she added, dragging the tin bathtub out from the pantry. The metal clunked on the dusty stone floor as she set it in front of the stove where it was warmest. Albert groaned,

"Awww, Mam, do I 'av to?"

Emma shooed him out the door, telling him to find Gloria whilst he was at it. She picked up a basket of finished laundry from a kitchen chair. As she carried it through to the front room she looked again at the letter that had been sitting on the dresser since a little after breakfast. The paper was crumpled and the long dried ink had smudged where something had dripped on it on its long journey. She picked it up and ran a finger over the scrawled writing.

"I almost forgot," she said turning to Jack and handing it to him, "something came from your father, would you be a love and read it to us after tea?"

"Course, Mam," he answered, but he was looking at her with an odd expression on his face.

"What is it?" Emma asked cautiously, not altogether sure she wanted to know.

"Don't look so worried, Mam, I've got some good news, but I want to wait 'til everyone's here."

2

Emma looked into the mottled ancient mirror on her washstand, tugged the pins from her hair and shook it loose. Her hair fell in long waves over her shoulders. It had been golden blond once, but now it was the colour of faded straw. She rubbed her head; even her roots ached tonight. The day had begun like any other but the new moon had found a hole in the clouds as evening drew in and brought with it news that had changed everything. She adjusted the stool beneath her and peered at her own reflection. The bloom of youth had left her long ago with the birth and death of her second child, but her skin was still smooth and her cheeks had always had a natural blush that gave her a healthy glow even in the darkest moments of winter. People had called her pretty when she was young and she hoped, at thirty-six, she could still make that claim. She set her elbows on the washstand and pressed her face into her palms. Could she pack up everything and begin a new life on the other side of the world? Her mind raced with everything and nothing. Spreading her fingers she looked herself in the eyes.

"You have a lot of thinking to do, Mrs B," she whispered.

She rose, made her way to the bed and looked down at the angel already sleeping there. Pink lips softly parted. Hair spread in a dark cloud around her head. For a few moments, Emma watched the gentle rise and fall of her daughter's chest beneath the blankets. This decision wasn't hers alone, all of her children had to be taken into account. Carefully, she lifted the covers and slid beneath them. The moment she was settled, Gloria squirmed and snuggled in close. Emma slipped her arm around her little girl's narrow shoulders and kissed her hair. As she closed her eyes the evening played over in her mind.

*

Seven hours earlier

Clattering cutlery and noisy children rattling away to each other. The kitchen was filled with steam from the hot food and the smell of fried potatoes and cabbage. Jack was beaming like a cat with cream, watching them all as they ate. Emma set down her fork.

"Come on then, out with it lad?" she said. Harry kicked Albert under the table causing the younger boy to yelp and kick him back. "Oi!" She said clipping Harry round the back of his head. "Less of it."

"But, Mam, he started it," Harry baulked.

Emma clipped Albert too for good measure.

"I don't care who started it. Now traps shut and let Jack speak, he's got some news for us."

Both boys stopped kicking but there was still a jostling of elbows. Emma threatened a flat hand at them as Jack cleared his throat, set down his fork and swallowed the last mouthful of his bubble and squeak.

"Delicious, Mam," he said, fully aware that he was drawing out the suspense. Emma raised her eyebrows at him. "All right, all right," he grinned, dark eyes twinkling with mischief.

"About a week ago Mr Feldman wrote a letter of recommendation to Mr Barker on my behalf, asking him if..."

"Who's Mr Barker?" Albert butted in.

"He is the foreman in charge of the painters at the potteries," Emma answered quickly. "He used to be your Pa's boss. Carry on, Jack."

"Well, I heard they were expanding the workshop and..." He took a breath, barely able to contain his delight. "You know what I always dreamed of, and Mr Feldman has always encouraged me to go to him if there were something on my mind. So I thought, why not try, I know I can do the job and I think I've proved myself an honest chap."

"Of course you have, son," Emma offered when Jack seemed to pause for validation. "Mr Feldman knows how steady and hardworking you are. Not like...well, you're not your father, anyone can see that."

"Thanks, Mam," Jack took a sip of tea and carried on. "Well, Mr Feldman kindly agreed and put me forward for an apprenticeship, and on Monday we were in receipt of the reply. Mr Barker asked me to visit his office. The appointment was yesterday morning. I attended promptly and took it upon myself to take along a few of my drawings. He looked them over and seemed to appreciate my initiative. Anyway, today I received my answer," he paused again for effect. He waited for Emma to open her mouth and tell him to get on with it, then said with a flourish, "and he offered me an apprenticeship."

Emma dropped her fork. She was up and around the table before Jack had a chance to draw another breath. She pulled him to his feet and danced him around the kitchen table in a tight hug.

"That is excellent news, Jack. How could you have kept it to yourself all evening?" Harry and Albert were laughing at their struggling brother. Emma glared at them and they stopped.

"Mam, I need to breathe." Jack gasped.

"Sorry." Emma let him go and sat back down.

"What ya training for then?" asked Harry.

"Well, Mr Barker was very impressed with my drawings but they don't really train designers, they come from proper art schools, so I shall be a painter. To begin with, I'll just be working on basic things like background colours and borders, but as I get more used to the materials and my painting gets better I'll move onto more detailed artwork, and maybe, one day, when I have proved myself, I can put forward some of my designs."

"Let's not get too far ahead of ourselves," Emma chastised playfully.

"Does that mean you won't be delivering coal no more?" Gloria asked.

"That's right, Glo, no more filthy coal for Jack," his third-person referral was said with great satisfaction.

*

Emma rubbed her cold feet together, partly to warm them and partly because her ancient woollen bed socks were itchy. Sleep was evasive as thoughts bounced around in her restless mind. Gloria sighed in her sleep. Emma opened her eyes and checked her daughter was all right. The child's eyes danced beneath her eyelids and she clutched her rag-dolly close to her chest. Emma stroked her daughter's arm to ease her. Gloria's mouth twitched into a smile.

"Keep dreaming of nice things kiddo," Emma whispered. She looked up at the ceiling. The grey plaster was cracked at the corners. Dim moonlight streaked over the loose curtains sending long silver shadows over the walls. Emma recalled the moment a few hours earlier when Jack had slid his thumb beneath the folds of the battered envelope and pulled out his father's letter.

*

The children sat in silence, eyes wide with anticipation. Emma realised she was holding her breath. She hadn't heard from Jacob in almost a year. It wasn't that there was anyone preventing him from writing. Not like when he had done his six months of hard labour a decade earlier. She had thought the distance might make him forget them, after all not many came back. And though he didn't write often, he usually managed to send something in time for Christmas. Out there he was as good as a free man. Or at least that's the way he told it. He had been one of the last to get transportation to New South Wales, and when his ship had sailed into Sydney harbour they had been turned away. Australia didn't want criminals anymore. They wanted respectable immigrants now. Jacob and the rest of the convicts had been kept on board for a further week until they had eventually been able to disembark back down the coast at Port Phillip. For months she had imagined him to be in some far off place suffering unspeakable conditions, only to discover eight months later, upon receipt of his first letter, that he was in fact one of a new group called 'the exiles.' He had been billeted to an employer. The job came with a bunk to sleep in as well as food rations and a fresh set of clothes. He was restricted to where he could go and was checked up on regularly to make sure he was doing his work and obeying the rules. But aside from that, he could go out in the fresh air, earn his living, save what he could for his own use and basically begin a new life for himself. What never occurred to Emma, however, were the contents of her husband's final letter. She stared as Jack read it out.

"May 30th the Year of Our Lord Eighteen Hundred and Fifty Six. My dearest Emma and loving children," Jack's voice was smooth and calm as he read each word with careful precision. "It was a pleasure as always to be in receipt of your letter. It is good to hear that you are all doing well. As I am sure you know, my sentence will be over in but a few short months, probably already over by the time you are reading this. I cannot tell you how relieved I will be. Whilst Mr Gisborne has been a generous and kind employer, it will be very nice indeed to be free once more to go where I please."

"Is Mr Gisborne the prison officer?" Gloria asked.

"No dear you know he isn't. He's your father's...he is just the man your father has to work for while he serves his sentence."

"Oh yes, I forgot."

Jack ruffled his sister's hair and continued,

"...And not to have to report back to Mr Williams every Tuesday..."

Emma's stomach twisted and her jaw tightened. She leant forwards in her chair and listened more intently.

"Is father coming home soon?" Albert asked, glancing from Jack to her for a second.

"I should think so, Bertie, but if you don't listen we won't find out."

Albert lowered his head and shrugged.

"Just askin'."

"I know, dear." Emma tried to remain patient.

Jack turned the sheet over to reveal more black ink scrawl.

"As you will also recall, I have been saving my earnings for almost six years now and I am most happy to inform you that I have enough put aside to purchase a small piece of land."

Emma's mind began to swirl. What was he saying? Where on earth could he mean to purchase land? There was nothing in these parts that they could surely afford. He may have saved up his wages for six years, but how much could a convict possibly earn?

"I have placed a deposit on a few acres a little north of here near a village called Flemington. It has a pretty prospect and will make a perfectly pleasant home for us all."

A shiver ran from the base of Emma's spine right up through her hair to her forehead. She drew a slow calming breath.

"He's not coming back to us," she muttered under her breath. For a moment she was livid. How would they manage without him forever? On the other hand, they had managed all these years right enough and perhaps he would face less prejudice there. If he came back here would the neighbours accept him and would he be able to find work again? She considered he might be just as much an exile here as he had been over there. So wildly were her thoughts fluttering that she had failed to hear the final lines of the letter.

"Are you all right, Mam?" Jack was looking at her with concern. "Shall I make us another pot of tea?"

"I'm sorry, Jack. Could you read that last part again? From the bit about the prospect."

"Course, Mam," Jack cleared his throat and began again. "Just as soon as my sentence is finished I shall begin work on the house. My dear Emma, if you register as a domestic help and Jack as a labourer then you can apply for assisted passage. There is enough on the money order (enclosed) to cover the remainder and for the younger children."

At this point, Emma's gaze moved towards the extra fold of paper in Jack's hand and she realised that it was not another sheet of the letter. Jack caught her expression and offered her the paper. Numbly she unfolded it and stared; ten pounds. More money than she had ever seen in any one place at any one time. Jack carried on,

"There will be little question of your not being accepted. They are desperate for free women and children to come. By the time you reach Melbourne I hope to have the house ready for you all, for I should not wish you to be here and have no roof over your heads," Emma knew this was an attempt to lighten the news. Did Jacob really expect her and the children to just up sticks and go to Australia, or was this his way of making them feel like he wanted them even if he didn't really expect them to go? She tried to focus on Jack as he finished reading the letter.

"I will continue to work for Mr Gisborne until such time as the farm is up and running but rest assured this new world is a blank slate ready for us to write our own destinies upon. This colony is not a just prison anymore, but a land with an opportunity around every corner. Think of it Emma, new lives for us all. Green land as far as the eye can see. No more smog, but clear blue skies with fresh air enough to make us all brown with health and sunshine. My conscience is cleared of my sins and my debt is all but paid. The very thought of seeing you all again before a year is out brightens my heart and gives me the will to finish my sentence so that we may begin our lives together again here. Have Jack write as soon as you have your passage so that I may know a date to look forward to.

Your loving husband and father, J B."

Emma just stared at the money order. A small hand slipped over hers. She broke her gaze and looked down. Gloria's little fingers looked so delicate against her swollen washerwoman hands, but the child's skin was cracked and red from helping her out. She knew she couldn't let her daughter end up like her. She had to give her and the boys a better chance in life. Harry and Albert were beginning to chatter again.

"We'll get to see those rangakoos and them cookbook birds Pa talked about," Albert said excitedly.

"Kangaroos and Kookaburras dunce," Harry laughed.

Emma raised her eyes to Jack. He was looking at her pensively. Loud voices and young boys laughter rang in her head. Emma felt like running. All she wanted to do was pull up her skirts and run through the streets until her chest burned with cold air and her mind was numb. Her heart was beating hard against her ribs. Eventually, Jack spoke first.

"Will you go?" he asked.

"Will you?" she returned.

Jack shook his head.

"I don't know, Mam. This opportunity at the potteries is better than I could ever have dreamed of. It is all I've wanted since I was six years old. I thought when Pa was arrested that my chance had gone forever, but here it is. How can I throw that away? How can I have that chance in Australia? We don't know anything about life over there. All we have is Pa's fantastical descriptions of strange animals and the weather. You know how he is. He could sell coal to a miner. What is life really like there? What is this new city like? I don't want to be a farmer, Mam."

"I know, son. If your father knew about your apprenticeship... Write back to him. Tell him. Maybe he'll change his mind and come home."

Jack was shaking his head.

"He has already put down a deposit; he's made up his mind. The question is do you go out there and take that chance with him, or do we all stay here together and leave him to live his new life alone."

Emma didn't know what she wanted. The thought of exchanging the smoggy grey skies and damp air for sunshine and the scent of grass was indeed an appealing one. But Jack was right; here they had a life. It might be a hard one, but it was theirs and it worked. Lord only knew what they would have to deal with over there, let alone spending four or five months in the bowels of some god awful ship like rats in a bucket. Even if they made it to the other side of the world in one piece, there were no guarantees that their lives would be any better. She tugged her shawl tighter over her shoulders and got up to wash the pots. She could feel Jack watching her as she bustled about clearing the table.

"Go play in the front room children," she said without turning around. She could feel three faces staring at her; they hardly ever got to play in the front room. "Go on, do as I ask," she added, turning to face them.

Emma watched them go, waiting for the door to close behind them, then took the stack of smeared plates and placed them in the sink.

"I cannot go without you," she said, glancing over her shoulder at Jack. She knew full well that this statement would cause her son a great deal of guilt, but it had to be said.

"Mam, make your decision for you and the kids, not for me. I'm almost sixteen. I can take care of myself now. There are some good lodgings I can take..."

"Don't... Do not even talk like that, Jack. I can't bear the thought of going without you. None of us shall go. That's all there is to it. We shall all stay here and your father can do as he pleases."

"He might be a bit rough around the edges and he has certainly made some mistakes, but you miss him. I see it on your face every time we get a letter. And it's been hard for you here, managing alone. Put me out of your head for a while and decide for yourself and the children. Maybe Pa's right, maybe there are better opportunities for them over there."

"But not for you?"

"All I know is I have an opportunity here and it's a good one."

*

Emma slipped her legs out from under the covers and put her feet down on the knotted rug. Careful not to wake Gloria she slid off the bed and made her way over to the window. In the other bedroom, she could hear one of her boys snoring. The sound vibrated gently through the paper-thin wall. She found it comforting. It reminded her of Jacob. Jacob! She pulled back the curtain and looked out at the narrow alley that ran along the back of the cottages. Dirty walls loomed in the darkness. Shadows cast from one to another. Stinking brick shithouses sticking out into the dusty path every few yards, filled with putrid filth. Her mind raced; dark dingy days and long cold nights. A warm glow in a window across the way. Kind-hearted friends sleeping nearby. Generous neighbours who help her children. A steady job and good prospects for Jack. Jack! The comfort of familiarity. The excitement of the new and different.

Emma rested her head on her hands and prayed for guidance.

3

The door clicked and the bell above it tinkled. The woman behind the counter peered through the small crowd of customers and offered Emma a familiar smile. She returned it with more enthusiasm than she was capable of feeling. Gloria let go of her hand and weaved her way through to the front.

"Hello Ducky," Emma heard Mrs Feldman say to her daughter. "When is your Mam going to send you to learn your letters? I reckon you're about old enough now."

The kindly neighbour meant well but Emma felt two of her children were enough for anyone to have to handle. Although, maybe it was time Harry went out to work anyway. She thought of the money order, folded neatly and placed at the bottom of the tea caddy in her kitchen drawer. She could cash it and use the money for things they need, like lessons and clothes. Gloria was brightly chattering away to Mrs Feldman. The till rang and money clunked. Gradually the queue was diminishing. The woman before her asked for a packet of sugar and a dozen eggs. Emma shifted her stance to ease the twinge in her back and looked down at her battered old shopping basket. The over-cloth was fraying at the edges and there was a hole slowly cracking open in the side of the wicker that would soon render the whole thing useless. She hoped it would last a few more weeks at least.

"How are you today?"

Emma realised Mrs Feldman was speaking to her.

"Aye not bad, same as always," she replied, considering that the latter part was far from the truth. "And yourself? I do hope you and Mr Feldman are both well."

"Can't complain, Mrs B. Now, what can I get you today?"

Emma placed her order and wondered at how Mrs Feldman could always seem so happy. "And please pass on my thanks to your husband," Emma added, "Jack told me about the recommendation, I can't tell you how very grateful we are."

Mrs Feldman gave an embarrassed shrug and said,

"It was nothing more than the boy deserves."

Emma flushed and tried not to look too proud. As she paid for her purchases she noticed Gloria was coughing again.

"You ought to get some mixture for that before it sets in," Mrs Feldman suggested and took a bottle down from the bulging shelf behind her. Emma watched her daughter carefully and agreed to make the extra purchase.

"She's had it for a few days now," she explained.

"Aye well, there's a lot of it going around. Too much smoke in the air if you ask me. It can't be healthy living under them mucky clouds that them potteries pump out." This was from the woman standing behind her. Emma acknowledged the observation thoughtfully. Clean air Jacob had said. She placed her shopping in the basket and covered it over. Gloria took her hand and tugged her towards the door.

"Oh, Mrs B. It's the meeting to discuss the state of The Marlston tonight. Your Jack's coming, I thought you might want to join him."

Emma paused. She'd forgotten about that with everything else going around in her head. She ought to go. A young girl pushed open the shop door forcing Emma to step out of the way and apologise for lingering. She knew the girl; she was the eldest daughter of an old friend, one who had barely uttered a word to her since Jacob's arrest seven years ago. The girl smiled with no recognition.

"Forgive us," she said to the girl and then "yes of course," to Mrs Feldman, "What time?"

"Saint Leonards at seven."

*

The draughty church hall was filled with rows of uncomfortable looking seats. Emma sank onto a stool about halfway down the room. There were already a couple of dozen folks there. Most she knew and a few she merely recognised. Jack was with her. She had been uneasy leaving the young ones alone, but Harry had promised faithfully to be responsible and take care of his siblings. In her mind, however, all she could see was the two boys scrapping and Gloria getting kicked in the head trying to stop them. She almost got up to go, but Jack put a hand on her knee to stop her.

"They'll be all right, Mam. They're good kids really when they want to be."

Emma nodded and smoothed off her skirt for the umpteenth time. Someone walked by her a little too close causing a breeze with the swish of a skirt. Emma shivered and rubbed her arms beneath her shawl. She looked up to see a familiar face. It was the mother of the girl she had seen in Feldman's General Store that morning. The woman gave her a curt nod and took a seat a few rows further forwards.

At the front of the room were seated a panel of men which included Mr Feldman, Mr Oliver; one of the management from the potteries, and an unknown gentleman who stood up to call everyone's attention.

"As some of you may be aware, I am William Stokes. I am here to represent The Marlston Workhouse..." His voice was dry and monotonous. Emma felt her eyes closing and forced them open again. She drew a sharp breath of autumn cold air, shook her head and rolled her shoulders.

Mr Stokes appeared to be defending the running of The Marlston. He even said that the outbreak of Typhus that had devastated the community earlier in the summer had not originated there. The debate was becoming rather heated. Mr Feldman and Mr Oliver were certainly not about to let the speaker get away with his claims. Appalling conditions were being described: Many crammed into very few bunks. Starving children and feverish infants. Half starved men and women working themselves into the grave. Filth, flies, grime and hunger.

Several voices around the room were beginning to call for reform. She heard Jack shout out something. But her mind was too distracted. How easily she and her children could have ended up in that wretched place. When they had been forced to leave the potters cottages they had come so close to it that Emma couldn't bear the memory. If it hadn't been for the kindness of her dear late father, they would have been as much 'wards of the state' as Jacob was. The Marlston was a pitiful place, the likes of which she never wanted to be threatened with again.

At her side, Jack was on his feet. She looked around to see that many others were doing the same. She watched her son and for the first time really noticed that he was not a child any more. He was a young man with his own opinions and his own life to lead. Her thoughts and emotions were in turmoil.

*

Footsteps squelched on sodden ground. A cart clattered past splattering mud over her skirt. The air smelled of rain and chimney smoke. Emma didn't know what to say to Jack. They walked in silence. Jack's breathing was heavier than hers, not from exertion but from the excitement of the evening. There was a fire in his belly. She could see how eager he was to be a part of their community. His head was full of ideas and dreams. Surely he could find the same level of enthusiasm in a land of new opportunities, perhaps even more?

Someone was huffing and puffing towards them.

"Mrs Burns, Jack...Forgive me, do hold up a minute."

Emma stopped and turned to face the gentleman who was rapidly closing in on them. He was tallish, wearing a greatcoat and shoes that shone beneath the flickering gas lamp. As he reached them the yellow glow cast over his face and she realised who it was.

"Gracious, Mr Oliver, is there some way we can assist you?"

The man pressed a hand to his chest and wheezed. Breath plumed into the darkness. Emma and her son waited patiently for a moment.

"You do walk at a pace, Mrs Burns. Forgive an old man a moment to catch his breath."

Emma curtseyed as Mr Oliver doffed his cap to reveal a thinning layer of white hair.

"Well, well," he gasped. "I didn't mean to alarm you. I simply wanted a quick word with Jack here. I hope you don't mind, Mrs Burns."

Emma shook her head and said she certainly didn't mind at all. She was about to step aside a little when Mr Oliver continued,

"I wanted to congratulate him on his apprenticeship."

Realising he was still speaking to her as well as her son she politely thanked him. Jack looked humbled. Mr Oliver was a very senior man at the potteries and well respected by his employees. He offered his hand to the lad and Jack took it graciously.

"Now son, I saw you tonight and I think you have a very strong mind, and I have heard very good things from Mr Feldman about you over the last three years. So I don't think I am being presumptuous by saying that I think you have the potential to go a long way. I know you have always been a little under the shadow of your father's doings. But let me tell you, after everything I've heard of you and after what I saw tonight, I think if you keep going the way you are, you could do very well for yourself."

Jack grinned and thanked the gentleman as profusely as the compliment warranted. Emma's heart was full. For a moment she couldn't speak, tears were welling so much in her eyes and throat. Finally, she squeaked her thanks to Mr Oliver again, and the moment the gentleman had headed back in his own direction, she threw her arms around her boy and hugged him tightly.

"Mam, we're in the street." Jack gently prised her away.

"I don't care. I am just so proud of you." And Emma knew what had to be done.

4

The candle was down to the wick and two tired faces were looking at her with saucer eyes when Emma entered the kitchen. She put the kettle on the stove.

"Betsy!" Gloria mumbled in her sleep as Jack lifted her up from the corner of the kitchen floor where she had curled up. Emma retrieved the dolly from the floor and placed it in her daughter's arms.

"Sorry love," she whispered, regretting not giving them permission to use the front room while they were out. "Take her up to bed," she said to Jack. "I know what she will say anyway," she added when he was about to protest.

"All right," he replied with an understanding nod.

Albert rubbed his eyes with the heels of his hands and yawned.

"You had better light a new candle," she said to him.

Emma missed having gas in the house. When they had lived in the pottery cottages they had had it, but out on the edges of town, where the cottages were tenanted from The Hall, they had to do without. Her father had left her one good oil lamp that she kept in the kitchen but it wasn't bright enough. She wondered what the houses in Australia had.

"Fetch the one from the sitting room, then come back in here," she instructed. "I'd like to talk to you both."

Harry stretched his long skinny arms above his head and shuddered. Of all her children Harry was the one who looked the most like her. The others were all dark-haired and olive-skinned like their father, but Harry had the same fair hair and golden freckles as her. In countenance though, he was rather more like Jacob. He was kind-hearted but too clever for his own good. Albert had his father's charm all right, but he was too transparent and shallow thinking to put it to any ill use. Harry on the other hand was bright to the point of devious. He was cool and collected and whilst he was as studious as Jack, he had not the passionate temperament that kept his heart warm and his morals on a straight track like Jack. Harry was the one she knew she would always have to watch.

Albert returned.

"What is it, Mam?" Harry said as Albert plonked himself on the stool next to him. Both boys were looking a little nervous. Emma wondered what they'd been up to while she and Jack had been out, but decided she hadn't the energy to find out.

Stairs groaned beneath heavy feet as Jack returned. The kettle whistled loudly sending a spiral of steam swirling into the air above it. Emma took the cups and saucers from the draining board, lifted the teapot from the shelf and slid open the drawer containing the tea caddy. Three faces watched on with interest. She knew she looked on edge, and she knew they were aware of her discomfort. After she made the tea she didn't return the caddy to its home, instead, she fished beneath the tealeaves and extracted the money order from Jacob and set it on the table. Dusting it off, she looked from one face to another. The younger boys peered at it.

She hadn't spoken to either of the younger boys about the exact amount, and now they were clearly attempting to comprehend the value. Albert looked up at her and blinked in wonder. Harry clearly understood what he was looking at. He scratched his head and then folded his arms awaiting her speech. Jack was not looking at the money order. He was looking right at her, right through her.

"You've decided then, Mam," he said helpfully.

Emma fidgeted, smoothing out the folds of the money order and picking out the last fleck of tea. Finally, she spoke,

"Not yet. I want each of you to tell me how you feel about your father's wishes. By that I mean, do you want to obey them and spend this money on our passage to Australia, or do you think we should leave your Pa to it and use the money to make our lives a little easier here? This is not a fortune boys but it is a good deal and enough to ease our burden for quite a while, and maybe send you to a proper school for a bit."

Jack began to pick at the side of his thumb. When no one else spoke he offered,

"I know my choice, Mam, but I think Albert and Harry should have their say first."

"Very well. Albert, how about you?" Emma placed her elbows on the table and entwined her fingers together as if in prayer. The boy shifted in his chair. "It's all right, Bertie; there's no wrong or right answer. I only want to know what you want to do."

His eyes were wide and nervous. He parted his lips, screwed up his face as though it hurt, and said,

"It's miserable 'ere, Mam. Pa said it's warm and sunny there and if we 'ave a farm, I can play with animals and stuff and I won't have to go to lessons no more."

Emma almost laughed.

"You would still have lessons, dear, whatever country you live in."

"Oh! But I would still have animals to play with wun't.... wouldn't I?"

Emma smiled at him and said that he likely would.

"Then I want to go there."

Emma nodded. She had suspected this much. She turned to Harry.

"How about you, son?"

Harry looked at her with cool thought. Outside, a city fox screeched and something tipped over. Emma shuddered and wondered exactly what animals Albert would be playing with if they moved. There was an unnatural pause until finally, Harry said,

"Why ask us, you're the one who usually decides everything?"

Emma wasn't sure if this was an observation or a complaint.

"Not this time," she said after a beat. "This decision affects everything, for the rest of our lives and your opinion matters."

Another pause.

"What about Glo?"

Emma shook her head,

"She's never met her Pa and I know she's curious, but she's still very young and you know how she is, she will just want to do whatever I want to do."

Harry couldn't argue with that.

"Fine. Well, I'm with Bert. I reckon we should do it too. If there really is an opportunity around every corner, if we can have a home of our own, a chance to be something that we will never be here, then I want to try it. And if there isn't, well it can't be any worse than here can it?"

Emma nodded calmly and turned to Jack,

"And you? I know what you have here, but think what you could have there. What heights you might reach in Australia. Will you take a chance on somewhere new?"

Jack looked down at his hands then directly at her eyes. He didn't need to say it but he did so anyway.

"I think it's the best thing in the world for all of you, it is a chance worth taking. I think Pa would be heartbroken if you don't go and I think you would be heartbroken to live the rest of your life knowing that. There will be chances for so many things over there, but...not for me. I can't go, Mam. My heart is in this town and I believe I've been given my shot at doing something with my life already, and it's here. But you should go, really, Mam, you should, all of you."

Emma was trying so hard not to cry in front of him, but the tears escaped anyway. She had known how this would go but it had not prevented her from praying that jack would have surprised her and agreed to go too.

"I will be heartbroken to go without you," she mumbled through a tight throat and bubbling sobs.

"I promise to write, Mam."

Emma knew he would too. She took a long sip of tea.

"Then I shall have to find time in this new world to learn how to read your letters for myself then shan't I?"

Her father had loved his only child with all his heart, but he had not felt the need to educate a daughter beyond the realms of housework and basic arithmetic.

Albert and Harry looked at each other poised with excitement,

"Does that mean we are going to Australia?" Both boys burst out at once.

"Yes...Yes, we are.

"Yippee..."

For once their rivalry was forgotten. Harry and Albert were on their feet and dancing about the room together.

5

Early October 1856

Orange flames licked over coal, filling the small room with a stifling hot glow. Heavy dark wood and books encroached on what little space there was. Emma was invited to sit. As she did so, she unpinned her shawl and pressed her cool hands on her burning cheeks. The gentleman before them sank back into a plush leather chair and clasped his hands over his paunch belly. Her heart was beating so fast she thought she might faint. Jack laid a reassuring hand on her shoulder. She was very glad he had gone with her, and even more grateful he seemed so unfazed by the meeting. The lawyer looked at her from beneath heavy dark eyebrows,

"Would you like a glass of water, Mrs Burns?"

Emma flushed even deeper. Her corset wasn't helping matters. She'd had to draw it extra tight in order to fit into her best dress; one she hadn't found occasion to wear in several years.

"Thank you, Mr Grace. That would be most kind."

On the only free wall hung a seascape, so large and dramatic that Emma felt as though the froth might spray her if she moved any closer. Looking at it made her even thirstier so that when the glasses of water arrived she had to force herself not to gulp.

"Now, I understand from your letter that it was Mr Burns' idea to contact me."

It seemed strange to hear Jack referred to as Mr Burns. It felt like only yesterday that he was in short pants and everyone in their neighbourhood still called him Jack. She shifted in her chair and looked nervously at the man as he waited for her to respond. It was difficult to work out whether he was smiling or not. His beard was so bushy she could barely see his lips. Emma took another sip of water and nodded.

"I was advised to speak to an immigration lawyer, sir, and you were recommended to me," Jack's confident voice was calming to

Emma. She began to relax a little. "We do not have a vast deal of money, but our father has sent sufficient funds to cover your bills as well as my family's passage." Emma looked at her son gratefully.

"Indeed."

Emma drew a breath and opened her purse to retrieve the money order. Mr Grace held up a hand to protest.

"No need to show me, Mrs Burns."

Emma put it back in her handbag and snapped the clasp shut again with a sharp click. She covered the clasp with her hands, as though it might make another noise if she didn't stop it.

"You have three children travelling with you?"

"Yes, sir," Jack answered when Emma didn't.

"And are they all under the age of ten?"

"No, Harry will be twelve three weeks from Thursday," she managed to get out.

Mr Grace looked pleased.

"And I believe you were an upstairs maid before you married?"

The fire crackled and a spark flew out. A cinder dropped on the hearth with a hiss. Emma gave an affirmative,

"Mm hmm."

"Excellent, then you will certainly qualify for assisted passage. Forgive the impertinence but I need to know your level of literacy."

With a flush of embarrassment, Emma expressed her regret that she had never learned to read or write.

"I see," he said, his brow furrowing.

"But my boys are all perfectly proficient in the three R's, and Gloria has recently begun her lessons too," Emma added, hopefully.

The lawyer glanced up at Jack, his steely eyes glistening in the firelight.

"That is a bonus indeed." The lawyer began rapidly scribbling away. The nib crunched on paper and ink splattered over his forefinger. He shook his head and blotted his notes. "Must remember to replace this nib," he muttered. "Well," he looked up, "You have the funds to secure an early passage and, alas you cannot afford second class but we should manage a small cabin in steerage."

Emma waited for him to give her the final cost, but he said nothing further.

"When do you expect us to be able to depart?" she asked after a long pause. Emma feared that the longer they had to wait the harder it would get to part with Jack.

Mr Grace pulled out a ledger from one of the shelves and ran a chubby finger down a list of names.

"I should think we could find you a space before the year is out."

Emma had not known what to expect on this front, but the idea that they may leave before Christmas had not occurred to her. She did not know whether to be relieved or terrified.

"I will make enquiries and write to you in due course."

Emma and Jack thanked him and were back out on the street before she had time to take it all in.

*

Two weeks later

"Well, Mam, it looks like you'll be finally cashing that money order." Jack set the letter down on the kitchen table and looked at his mother intently.

Emma glanced at the bill. The numbers she understood perfectly. She folded her arms to prevent her hands from shaking. Goosebumps prickled and her stomach flipped.

"That leaves two pounds and three shillings," she said after a long pause. "You should have that Jack. You can make use of it better than we shall on the ship."

Jack was shaking his head.

"No, Mam, take what's left back to Pa, besides you never know when you might need it."

But Emma refused to take no for an answer.

"Use it to get yourself lodgings or put it away for a rainy day. You might want to get married one day..."

Jack laughed at her and conceded to taking half.

"What if we can't be ready in six weeks?" Emma felt as though her blood was rushing through her body too quickly and her heart would stop.

"No need to panic, Mam. What have you got that will take more than a week or two to settle? And besides, I'm not going anywhere, so anything you forget, I can take care of."

Then it hit her like a mule kick to her gut. Jack was not going with them. She'd always known this of course, but somehow it hadn't felt real, not until that moment. She bit her lip and fought hard to keep composure. In the end, all she could manage to say was,

"You had better write to your father and let him know."

6

About 4 miles north of Melbourne, Australia
December 11th 1856

The man digging set down his shovel and dabbed his brow with a sweat-soaked handkerchief and stuffed it back in his trouser pocket. Jacob looked up at the relentless blue sky and cursed the heat. Then he looked over at his little piece of land and cursed again.

"Why did I decide to buy the bit with no bloody trees?" he grumbled to himself.

Anyone that knew Jacob and looked at the land for more than a minute could have answered his rhetorical question. It was the only bit of land that was flat enough not to require too great an effort. Overhead a cockatoo sailed by and squawked at him as it went. He glanced up at it and decided it was time for some food. He tramped over to the three-foot banksia bush in the far corner of his foundation plot, sank down to the ground next to it and picked up his small bag. Buried inside and wrapped in a tatty piece of cloth that ought to have been cleaner were a chunk of bread and a wedge of greasy yellow cheese. Jacob took a bite of the bread and tried to chew it.

"Urgh," he grumbled, "dry as a bone." He turned over his jacket that had been laying on the ground in a crumpled heap by the bag and fished in the breast pocket for his flask. The whisky would make him more thirsty, but he was damned if he was going to walk all the way over to the brook to get a drink, it was at least five minutes walk. He wiped his brow again and looked at the leathery dark skin on the back of his hands.

"It'll be a wonder if Emma even recognises me."

A bee hummed past his ear as it made a dash for the orange spike of a flower that was just beginning to open on the tree behind him.

"Well better get on if I'm going to make it back to The Flemington in time for that poker game." Jacob popped the last bite of cheese in his mouth and headed back to the piles of wood he had purchased for the foundations.

7

The Journey
December 11th 1856

Day One

Possessions packed up and stowed away. It was a warm day for the time of year and the air was saturated with the stench of fish and salt. The ocean glittered like a million diamonds beneath the shining sun. None of them had ever seen the sea before and the sight of it made everything so daunting. Emma stood on the dockside with Gloria and Jack and watched the vessel roll with the tide. She called Albert and Harry back from the water's edge and took Albert's hand. They stood there together staring up at the great wooden beast they were about to call home, but not all of them. Soon she would leave one child behind. The moment was rushing up at her with blinding speed. The resounding pain of leaving Jack drowned the nervousness and excitement out. The other children felt it too, and for their sakes, she wanted to remain calm.

Jack had been given a few days off to come with them to Southampton. He was doing very well with his apprenticeship already and had taken a room in a boarding house that belonged to the potteries. He wrapped his arms around his mother's waist and rested his chin on her shoulder. Emma gritted her teeth. She was not going to cry. A sailor rushed past them and ran up the gangplank into the heart of the ship. Another was scrambling up the rigging and yet another was peering out from the crow's nest. Dockers were piling up boxes and bundles; others were loading them on board. Boxes, chests, bottles and baskets were everywhere. Emma couldn't imagine how everything that was going on board could possibly fit in along with all of the people as well.

Another family were standing close by. The woman was gripping a battered old bag with both hands. Standing at her side were two children with bright red hair that flopped over their heads in tumbling curls. The girl clutched a ratty old rag doll-like Gloria's in one hand and a small cloth bundle in the other. The boy stood with his arms folded tightly across his chest, his belongings resting at his feet. The children looked to be about nine or ten. The woman was shivering, or perhaps she was shaking. Emma watched them for a moment. The woman gave a sigh then began to make her way up to the gangplank. The boy shrugged at the girl, picked up his sack, and the pair of them followed her. At the foot of the plank was a uniformed man. Words passed between them and the woman fished around in her petticoat for her passage papers. Emma thought she heard her say, 'assisted' and 'steerage' then the man was checking her name against his list and they were heading on board. Emma felt every one of the woman's nerves.

A moment later a smartly dressed man was doing the same thing, he glanced over his shoulder at her as he passed them by. His features were young, smooth and elegant as sculptured marble, and his eyes were a bright azure blue. He gave her a nod and his lips twitched into a gentle half-smile. Then he handed the man his papers and disappeared into the ship. A young couple of considerably better class followed him, then another passenger and another. The time was coming when they would have to board. 'Dear Lord, are we doing the right thing?' she prayed. Overhead seagulls squawked and circled as though they were waiting for Emma to make her move.

*

The bustle of the dockside was beginning to subside. Most of the sailors were already aboard. The man in uniform by the gangplank eyed them with suspicion and took a step towards them.

"Madam, are you for The Cassandra?"

Emma froze. For some reason, she could not make her mouth open and respond. Jack glanced at her and took the liberty.

"Indeed, sir, they are. This is my mother, Mrs Burns."

"Then you had better show me your passage, madam and step aboard. We'll be shipping out just as soon as the last crate goes on board," he gestured towards the diminished cluster of trunks and crates sitting by the gangplank.

"Your passage, Mam," Jack said when Emma didn't move. In her mind, she was making her apologies for wasting their time. In her mind, she was composing a letter to Jacob explaining to him that they would not come after all. But in defiance of her brain, her hand passed the man their papers. Before she knew what was happening, Jack was hugging her and telling her for the hundredth time how often he would write. What seemed like only half a second later, she was standing on the deck looking back at the dockside, looking back at Jack waving at them, hat in the air and calling goodbye. Then the ship was moving and Jack's figure was growing smaller and his arms had become weary so that now he just stood and watched. Waves lapped and wood groaned. *Too late now*, she thought as Harry and Albert broke away from her and ran off to explore. Gloria was still holding her hand and gripping her dolly. She looked down and saw the tears rolling as silent as the gentle waves down her little girls face. She fell to her knees and pulled her in close. Gloria crumbled and hugged her mother tight. Tears seeped through the cloth of Emma's shawl and her body shook.

"It will all be just fine," Emma promised.

*

Emma perched on the end of the bed she would have to share with Gloria for the next four months or so. Above her, the upper bunk creaked with the weight of her two youngest boys. *Five children I have brought in this world, and now I can only protect three,* She thought. She had not stopped thinking about Jack since they came aboard and now she was thinking of her other son too, the one she had not been able to save. She tried not to think of him too often, it was painful to recall the little blue face, his tiny waxy fingers and toes. The infant had died in her arms with not a day's life in his lungs. Emma got down on her knees and prayed for their safekeeping.

8

Day Four

The stale air was filled with a vile stench. Stomachs churned with every swell. Emma tried to bite back nausea as it waved through her once more. None of them had left their bunk in two days. Buckets were filled and emptied over and over. And they were not alone. Seasickness was rife throughout the ship. Only the sailors and a lucky few with bellies of cast iron escaped it. Albert wretched and the sound finished Emma. She reached the bucket just in time. The first night had not been too bad, but then a storm had come in and that was that. The sea rolled and rolled in relentless torture. Waves crashed and wood groaned. Gloria was the least affected. She had only been sick once when the sway was at its highest. She sat now, crying into her dolly and praying her mother and brothers weren't going to die. Emma wiped her mouth with the back of her hand and sank back on the straw-filled mattress. The wooden slats of the bed seemed to dig into the irritable nerve in her back. She flinched and tried to turn over but the movement nauseated her again. The only saving grace was that they had left in winter. Had it been summer, the stale air in the steerage bunks would have been unbearably mixed with the stink. Emma did not know whether she was going to die or whether she just wished she would. She reached out for Gloria. Her daughter took her hand and squeezed it tight.

"Will it be like this always?" the child spluttered.

"Surely not. If it were, no one would do it." Emma hoped rather than believed this to be the truth. More than anything else at that moment she wanted for her children to be as healthy and excited about this journey as they had been when they had first set sail. The boys had run around each deck, petted the sheep in the pens, laughed at the pigs in their makeshift sties, wondered at the array of fowl that had been crammed into cages, stared at the crates of plants and tried to peak into the boxes of dried food and barrels of wine. Now they just lay on the floor, unable to bear being up on the bunk above her. Harry glared at her with malice. Yesterday he claimed he had never wanted to come and this was all her fault. Emma closed her eyes and ignored him.

*

Day Ten

Masts high and sails billowed. Emma stood on deck and breathed in deeply. Salty air blustered through her hair and tugged it loose. She had given up with her bonnet. It was held tightly in her hand and with the other, she grasped the ship's railing. It felt good to be out on deck stretching her legs and easing the pain in her cramped back. Somewhere behind her, she could hear Harry and Gloria's voices calling out to each other, but their words were carried away on the wind to some distant land. Poor Albert was still feeling sick and had preferred to stay cooped up below deck, but the rest of her reduced family were feeling much more like their old selves again. Emma found it hard to imagine how sick they had all been only yesterday, but now, with a turn of the wind, they had suddenly found their seafaring stomachs. Her legs were weak and her body empty but for the first time in days, she had managed to eat some bread and cheese without bringing it right back up again.

"Have ya been unwell?"

Emma spun around.

"Gracious, you startled me."

"Forgive me," the woman standing next to her looked familiar. She smiled, "I only ask 'cause I ain't seen ya up on deck since the day we embarked."

Emma looked at the wind blushed cheeks and copper-coloured hair. She couldn't quite place the face.

"Lucy Matthews," the woman offered Emma a hand to shake. Emma noticed the thin gold band on her left hand. Mrs Matthews followed her gaze, "my husband's already in Australia."

"Mine also," Emma wondered if Mr Matthews had been a convict too, not that she would ever ask such an impertinent question. "Emma Burns," she shook the woman's hand. "Pleased to make your acquaintance." A wild gust blasted at them and sent them both staggering back. "I don't know why this wind is so much less sickening today than it was yesterday..." she began but the wind took her breath and she was forced to laugh and wait a moment to begin again.

"I know, my poor Molly and Alfie were so sick. But I think my father's blood must be in me; he were a sailor. I never gets seasick," Mrs Matthews continued. "I saw ya on the docks afore we set sail, ya got three boys and a girl don't ya?"

Emma realised with whom she was conversing. Mrs Matthews was the young woman with the red-haired children that had been standing near them on Southampton dock.

"Yes, that's right. But my eldest stayed behind, so it's just the four of us travelling." Emma felt her heart twist as she spoke of Jack.

"I'm sorry. I can see 'ow much ya miss him."

Emma could tell she was going to like Mrs Matthews a vast deal. Her accent was harsh and mostly southern but with an odd foreign-sounding twang that made it not at all unpleasant to hear. She had a kindly face with eyes that matched her hair. Emma smiled and admitted that she did miss Jack, very much. Mrs Matthews obliged the confession with a change of subject.

"I heard from one of the crew that they did the last trip in just ninety-three days!"

"Gracious, how long that sounds, but I suppose that is actually quite fast. I must admit I had not quite expected there to be so many of us on-board."

Mrs Matthews laughed,

"I know what ya mean. Two hundred and eighty-five passengers and nine and twenty crew I heard. It do seem quite a lot. But when I were three my father took us to live in New York. There were a good deal more on that ship, and she were no Clipper. She were slower than a slug and about as comfortable as a month in Newgate."

Emma smiled and looked at her new friend with wonder and a little envy.

"You lived in America?" Jacob had once talked of them moving there but nothing had come of it in the end, perhaps if they had they wouldn't have come to this.

The young woman sighed heavily.

"My father died a few years later and my mother just couldn't get on there wivout him, so she took us all home again."

"How long were you there?"

"Near seven year, 'til, I were ten."

"Do you remember much?"

Mrs Matthews swayed with a rolling swell beneath them and took hold of the railings.

"Not as much as I'd like I'm afraid. But I can tell ya; it won't be easy starting out in Australia. My husband thinks it'll be the new land of opportunity, and I'm willing to take a chance he's right, but I know how hard it were for my parents in America, so I ain't expecting no bed of roses."

Emma's stomach churned and for a moment she thought she would be sick again. But then she realised that it was not seasickness that threatened this time, but nerves. Did she really have any idea as to what sort of life they were going to? A child ran up behind them and tugged at Emma's skirt.

"Mam, can I go play with my new friend?" Gloria was clasping the hand of a little girl with bright red curls.

"Aha," Mrs Matthews exclaimed, "I see our daughters 'ave already met...Where's Alfie?" this last part addressed to her child. The girl shrugged. "Up to some mischief no doubt," Mrs Matthews laughed.

Emma gave her consent to Gloria and watched the girls run off together laughing at some private joke. Mrs Matthews rolled her shoulders and cricked her neck. As she did so Emma noticed the seam at her waist was coming away. She looked the woman over quickly and realised that her whole outfit was more ancient than was fit to be worn, her shoes were coming apart and the fabric of her skirt was frayed at the hem. Here was a fellow-creature that circumstance had brought down and thrown her, finally, into this journey of the unknown. Emma's heart warmed with empathy and she hoped they would become friends. Mrs Matthews was saying something.

"I beg your pardon," Emma apologised, "I didn't quite catch that, the wind was blowing so."

"Oh, it is still whipping a gale all right," Mrs Matthews laughed. "I were saying, there's a schoolroom to be set up for the children. My twins' is going and I wondered if ya were sending your lot along too?"

"I thought that sort of thing was only for the first-class passengers?"

"Oh yes. But one of the clergymen in second class saw how many kids there is in steerage and thought it would be a good idea. Keep 'em occupied I s'ppose. Even roped in a proper teacher. Ain't no fee neither."

Emma pressed her hand to her chest in astonishment,

"How wonderful. Yes, yes I certainly would. My boys already have a little learning, but Gloria has barely had more than a half dozen lessons, would that be a problem do you think?"

"Neither of mine could even tell ya the first letter of the alphabet. There's fifty-six children in steerage, I expect there's plenty that's just beginning."

Emma decided that perhaps she could bear this journey after all.

"How do you know all these things?" She asked.

Mrs Matthews just smiled and replied,

"I listens and I talks to people," she casually slid her arm through Emma's then added, "Come on, let's have a wander and see if we can spy on some of them from first class."

*

Day Eleven

"That's him."

Emma felt an elbow jab into her arm. She looked around at her new friend in confusion. Lucy Matthews rolled her eyes at her and leaned in even closer.

"There, look." Mrs Matthews hissed. The reverend conducting the Sunday service glared in their direction. Emma sank down into her chair and shook her head. Albert glanced around at her, as did the woman sitting in front. There was another sharp prod from her friend.

"Who?" She whispered.

Lucy Matthews rolled her eyes a second time.

"The school teacher. See, I told ya he were handsome didn't I?"

Emma peered through the rows of the congregation towards where Lucy Matthews was not so surreptitiously indicating with a nod of her head.

"Which one?" Emma hissed.

The woman in front spun her head around with such speed Emma thought she looked possessed. She smiled sheepishly and mouthed an apology. The Reverend's voice boomed out the final line of his sermon and there was a mass grinding of chairs on the freshly mopped chapel floor. As soon as they were on their feet Emma knew exactly to whom Mrs Matthews had been referring. There, on the front row, was a young man with hair so shiny black it reminded Emma of freshly polished boots. His attire was genteel and impeccably neat, yet there was a little wear around the elbows that showed his jacket had seen better days. He wore a white cravat around his neck that made the darkness of his hair even starker. From her position, Emma could just about see his aquiline profile. His features were smooth and exquisite, as though deliberately sculpted, and his mouth was soft and a deep shade of rose pink. As he sang out the words to All Things Bright and Beautiful, his melodic voice seemed to drift through the congregation towards her. He must have sensed someone was watching for he glanced over his shoulder to reveal the most flawless pale complexion and the brightest blue eyes she could ever have imagined.

Emma fancied she had seen him somewhere before. But since she had scarce left her cabin until yesterday she had barely become acquainted with any of her fellow passengers. Then it came to her, he was the young man who had smiled at her as he boarded the ship in Southampton.

"They say he's a real gent that's fell on hard times." Mrs Matthews said beneath the soar of music. "He were right amiable when I ran into him on deck yesterday evening. He's got the classroom set up all proper and nice like. Ya should take a look."

The gentleman glanced their way again, only this time he caught Emma's gaze and his lips flickered into that same half-smile she had seen at the dock. She shook her head and tried to hide her blush.

"I don't expect my three would appreciate an escort to their lessons, well not the boys at any road."

Mrs Matthews gave her a sly look.

"I were only sayin' he seems a nice sort of chap and thought ya might like to meet him that's going to be teaching ya brood for the next few months."

Emma didn't really feel the need to make such an acquaintance. She had heard good things about Mr Finch from a couple of the other mothers whose bunks were close to hers, as well as from Lucy Matthews. What would a man of such an education as Oxford University make of an illiterate laundress with a convicted thief for a husband? No, Emma could not bear the notion that her past may taint the education of her children. If she was introduced she would, of course, be pleasant, but beyond that, she had no intentions of falling into conversation with a man of such esteem.

9

Day Fifteen – Christmas Day

Voices soared over the waves like seagulls. Behind them, the Bay of Biscay was becoming a distant memory and the calmer seas of the Southern Spanish coast were beginning to settle everyone into a working routine. Now the whole ship was crammed together on deck for a special Christmas service. Harry shuffled over and began to mumble something to Albert.

"Shhhh" Emma hissed.

There was a brief pause then the whispering began again. Emma turned just in time to catch the boys conspiring together. Leaning back she whispered,

"Keep talking and you'll both get a thick ear for Christmas."

Pouting and grumbling, they obeyed. Emma sighed and considered where they might all be next Christmastide. There were not enough chairs for everyone out on deck, so the lower classes were sitting on the floor. The irritable nerve in her back shot a pain right through her hip and the dampness of the recently swabbed decking began to seep through her skirts to her skin. Finally, it came to the last hymn but Emma found she had to ask Harry to help her up.

"Gracious, I must be getting old," she said to Mrs Matthews as the service ended and their boys tore off in search of excitement.

"I doubt that, sleeping in them bleeding awful bunks will get to us all in the end and no mistake."

Emma had been a little surprised by Mrs Matthew's occasional coarse language at first. But she was learning that rough speech and poor circumstances had no bearing on intellect. Besides, there was plenty on board who were far worse. She just hoped there was no bad influence on her boys. They were incorrigible enough on their own.

"I near forgot," Mrs Matthews was saying. Emma turned to her friend eagerly. With little else to do on-board ship, gossip was fast becoming a welcome form of entertainment. The rigging creaked overhead and the sails billowed. Emma shivered but was glad the southerly wind was pushing them along nicely.

"I heard the laundry's struggling to keep up demand, and they charge a pretty penny..."

Emma narrowed her eyes and felt her heart sink. She knew what was coming. Many little enterprises were springing up all over the ship. It had only been a matter of time before Mrs Matthews came up with a scheme of her own.

"I thought we could start our own little laundry, charge half what the crew do and make us a bit of silver to get us through." The sun chinked in Lucy Matthews' coppery eyes. Her lips were half curled into an encouraging smile. Emma glanced at Gloria and Molly and considered the opportunity.

"Well, what do ya think?" Mrs Matthews pressed.

Gloria cocked her head and said,

"I think that would be a good thing to do, Mam."

Emma could hardly argue with that. She patted her daughter's head.

"You're right. After all, this whole thing is all about taking an opportunity."

*

Day Sixteen

A grinding of wood rolling on wood juddered through Emma's bones as she heaved the large barrel into place. If it was this heavy empty, what on earth had it been like full of wine? The mangle scraped across the floor as it was dragged into place in the dingy corner of the luggage deck, where the Captain had given them permission to set up shop. Mrs Matthews stopped tugging at the hulk of rollers and rested one hand on the winding handle. Emma straightened up and stretched her back out.

"There see, it ain't that bad." Lucy Matthews sniffed and cricked her neck.

Emma wasn't so convinced. But, her new friend had been right so far; there was plenty on board who were willing to send business their way. They had even had three offers for the loan of a mangle, and five bundles of laundry were already piled up in her bunk ready to be washed.

"Good thing there's a few drinkers on board, or we might have had to wait for a barrel to be emptied," Mrs Matthews added with a grin. They had already spent several hours scrubbing out the barrel to prevent any staining from its previous contents.

Emma shook her head.

"If the water gets any more rank, even the children will be boozing."

Lucy Matthews laughed,

"Ya ain't wrong there."

Emma looked around at the piles of trunks and cloth sacks that crowded the hold. They loomed and loured, creating dark eerie shadows of peculiar shapes, almost like people huddled together, watching them. Their little corner was about six feet square. It was dark, stuffy and barely enough room for them to stick out their elbows, but it was not altogether unpleasant. They were below the waterline and the chilly ocean kept the room a degree or two cooler than the higher decks, and the gentle groan of the ship was almost comforting compared to the noisy rabble of the animal deck directly above.

"Right then, better get started." Mrs Matthews began to make her way back along the narrow path between the piles of luggage towards the hatch to the upper decks. Emma sighed and followed, almost tripping over a large box of soap. Mrs Matthews had bartered with one of the crew to get it. She wished she could be as savvy as her friend. She shoved the box into the corner with her foot and sighed again.

10

Day Nineteen

Clattering like thunder. Shouting and screaming. Emma looked up at the ceiling with a start.

"What in God's name?" Mrs Matthews stopped grinding the mangle. For a moment the two women stared up in wonder. Above them, stomping hooves skittered and slid from one end of the ship to the other.

"Come on," Lucy Matthews grabbed Emma's hand and then they were running.

When they reached the animal deck Emma stopped in her tracks and slowly raised a hand to her mouth. Before them was a scene of utter chaos: People were everywhere. Sailors shouting and chasing. Sheep bleating and pigs grunting. Pen doors swinging wide and straw strewn over floorboards. Sheep tumbling about like giant balls of filthy wool. Emma didn't know whether to be amused or horrified. Mrs Matthews had no such dilemma. She was laughing so hard so she had to grasp at Emma's arm to hold herself steady. A sheep stumbled past them, a young sailor on its heels, arms flapping and face red with effort. Birds fluttered and squawked; thankfully they were still in their cages. Emma jumped and spun around to find a pig snuffling at the back of her skirts. Then she began to laugh too. A sailor shoved past her, wildly flinging an apology over his shoulder. Another passenger slid on some dung and shot past her. Feet scrambled and arms flayed. He skidded into the hull wall with a thump. Emma ran to his aid and handed him up. As he dusted himself off she saw Mrs Matthews slamming a sty door shut behind a very disgruntled pig.

"Humph! One down." She said as she slid the bolt across. Then Emma heard the giggling.

She knew that laughter as well as her own. From the corner of her eyes, she caught sight of them. Three boys crouched behind a cluster of barrels like thieves in the night. Harry was holding his sides as though they were about to split open and Alfie Matthews was rolling on his back, tears streaming down his face and red hair matted with straw. Albert was the closest to her. Before he knew she was there she had swiped him around the back of the head and he was sitting up in stunned silence. One of the sailors must have seen her do it, for the next moment the three toe-rags were being dragged out by their ears and the focus on the room switched from rounding up animals to yelling at the boys.

Mrs Matthews turned near puce when she saw them. Emma fancied she could see steam pluming from her ears. She grabbed her son and whacked him so hard on the behind that the boy couldn't help but yelp. Tears welled in his eyes and his mother was about to drag him off to their bunk, bawling him out as she went, when a male passenger asked her to stop. Mrs Matthews looked at the young man with arched eyebrows and tight lips.

"Do you not think they ought to apologise to everyone, Madam?"

Emma realised it was the schoolteacher. Most folks on this ship had begun to turn a penny for various trades and services but this man, Mr Finch, was working purely for the improvement of his pupils and had refused thus far to take even a single ha'penny for his efforts. He was looking at her now with an intensity that almost made her look away. She felt the disapproval of his glare right to her core. Now she wished she had spoken to him sooner. What a dreadful introduction she had made for herself. She shifted her stance and scowled at her boys with a look she knew would freeze hell over if she were standing before it. Harry glared back for a moment but Albert hung his head in shame, bottom lip quivering and eyes filling with tears.

"Sorry, Mr Finch," Albert mumbled.

Emma threatened Harry with the back of her hand. The boy lowered his eyes too and followed suit. Mrs Matthews spun her son around to face the crowd and, with hands gripping his shoulders so tight her fingers were white, she forced him to do the same. Mr Finch seemed appeased and his chiselled face softened.

"I think they should be given a good caning, right here in front of us all," this from a sailor who was frantically attempting to shove an extremely reluctant sheep back into its pen. Mr Finch regarded them for a response, first Emma then Mrs Matthews. Emma was ready to concede. She looked at Mrs Matthews and her friend nodded.

Wood whistled through the air and cracked hard on flesh. People watched with ghoulish glee. Each boy was lined up and bent over. A pig grunted and floorboards creaked. The room was tidied now and as silent as could be. Each boy took five whacks and each bit his lip so hard they near drew blood. Only Albert cried. When it was done the shame on their faces made a tight knot of regret in Emma's stomach. Even Mr Finch looked sorry. He gave Albert a gentle turn towards his mother and smiled at Emma with an odd expression that she took as sympathy. Perhaps she should have punished them in private. But it was done now and if it kept them in check for the rest of the journey then it had been worth the embarrassment. As they slunk their way to their bunks Emma watched the backs of their heads and thought of Jack. He would never have done such a thing. Emma felt a tear escape and roll slowly down her face. Hastily she wiped it away with her fingers and tried to forget the tightness that gripped her chest as she thought of her eldest boy.

11

January 1857

Day Twenty-Nine

The further south they sailed the stickier the weather became. The air was stifling below deck. It didn't feel like January at all. In the middle of the night, a baby girl had come red-faced into the world, waking everyone with her arrival cry. Emma yawned. Sweat trickled a thin line down her back beneath her corset. She blew at her forehead and looked for something to use as a fan.

"This heat is unbearable," Mrs Matthews slopped another shirt beneath the soapy water and began to scrub at a shirt collar. Emma nodded her agreement.

"It's not much better up top," she said with a glance at the ceiling. She had recently taken a brief respite and gone outside for a little fresh air. The sun was baking down on them relentlessly and the ship's sails hung limp like dead fish from the masts. The ship had barely moved in days. "So much for that promising wind," she added.

Mrs Matthews wiped her forehead with the back of her hand, leaving a trail of bubbles in her hairline. The soap glistened and evaporated with a tiny pop.

"Calm before the storm," she replied.

"So they keep saying." The 'they' were the sailors, and they should know.

Emma hoped they were right. If the wind didn't pick up again soon she feared it could be next Christmas before they even made it to The Cape. Yesterday they had been forced to commit a third of the fowl to the ocean, half the rest and two pigs had made a veritable feast. Thirst and exhaustion had taken them. The bird corpses had to be disposed of before they festered and sickness broke out. But now their food supply was down and the hope of a new bird colony for Australia was dashed. Emma squirmed in her corset and felt her spine crack. For a moment the ever-present pain eased.

"Suet pudding and boiled ham all right for supper?" It was Mrs Matthews' turn to cook. The two families had joined together in their efforts of late and it was working out rather well.

Emma smiled,

"Sounds lovely," she replied with a cough. The sarcasm wasn't lost. This was one of the three basic meals they had been rotating since setting sail. There was little selection onboard the ship and Emma would be glad if she never ate any of it again for the rest of her life. It was a blessing when fresh fish had been caught, but there was never enough and they were highly sought after. Thus far they had only managed to get it twice. "If this air gets any dryer and dustier I might just choke to death in my sleep," she added.

"One of the gents thinks he can make a water filter. I saw him this morning fiddling wiv a tin bottle, a sponge and some charcoal. Lord knows how that'll work but if he can manage it then I'd be willing to pay him a shilling to make me anover."

"That would be a Godsend indeed," Emma yawned again. "Did you see Mrs Johnson's new baby yet? She's a little peach. Got good pair of lungs on her mind."

Mrs Matthews laughed.

"I can tell it's been a while since ya had a newborn."

Emma agreed,

"I'm not sure I would want to go through that stage again."

Mrs Matthews raised her eyebrows in amusement.

"Better keep your legs crossed and ya drawers up when ya see that husband of yours again then."

Emma blushed and tried not to smile. She hadn't thought of that sort of thing for quite some time. She wondered if she would remember how, or if Jacob would be disappointed in her after such a long time away. Lucy Matthews seemed to read her thoughts.

"Can't wait to see my Alfred again. Six years is far too long to go wivout, reckon we'll be tearing each other's clothes off afore we even get to the house."

Emma's blush deepened. She had never talked so openly with anyone.

Mrs Matthews continued,

"Come on Emma, ya not telling me ya ain't been missing it?"

"I hadn't thought..."

"Sure ya've."

"Well, not for a while anyway."

Mrs Matthews laughed again.

"I reckon your Mr Burns will have. I reckons he'll be eagerly awaiting your arrival and no mistake. And I wouldn't fret if ya worried ya've changed either. He won't care if ya've grown a second head, he'll just be glad to have ya back in his bed. Men are like that."

"Really, Lucy, you are too much sometimes," Emma began to laugh too. That was the first time she had brought herself to call Mrs Matthews by her given name, but now she had dropped the formality it felt quite liberating. Lucy looked at her with delight and Emma wondered if her influence on her friend was as great as Lucy's influence on her.

12

Flemington, Australia
January 9th 1857

A tavern door swung wide and three men tumbled out into the dawn light. One shielded his eyes. Even the thin silvery hue was too bright. A young woman crossed the street towards them. She was pretty enough for the wretch that she was. He knew her and doffed his battered old cap. She was an exile, like them. Jacob smiled warmly and was repaid with a curtsey and a flash of ankles as she swaggered by. He called after her,

"Good morning, madam. Is it not a fine day?" The formality made the woman smirk. She had seen him in nought but his socks more times than she'd had hot dinners these last few years. She turned on her heels to face him and curtseyed again. The look in her eyes could not be mistaken. Jacob's eyes glistened with delight as they met with her ample cleavage. Her breasts pushed up like some sixteenth-century bar matron, inviting him to dive in between them.

"Would you care to take a walk with me this very lovely morning?" He suggested with a twinkle the woman knew well.

"Don't mind if I do, sir." She stepped in closer and slipped her arm through his.

He breathed in the fresh air and hoped the drink wouldn't hinder him.

A few yards down the dusty street and another man staggered along. Not from beer but from the weight of the wooden planks balanced across his shoulders. It was his half-day off and he wasn't going to waste a second. Alf Matthews' sentence was almost done and his wife and children would be there before autumn was out, God willing. He smiled to himself as he pictured the home they would have ready and waiting for them.

13

Day Thirty-Two

There was an eerie stillness. The darkness threatened to strangle Emma as she lay in her bunk. The tiny room was stuffy and even at night the heat was choking. She turned over and Gloria edged away from her. Suddenly her stomach seemed to flip and her head swam. She gripped the side of the bunk and waited. It wasn't her; it was the ship. From nowhere another roll and a lurching sway. Thunder rumbled and echoed around the ship. Gloria stirred and her eyes fluttered open.

"What was that, Mam?" Harry called down from the upper bunk.

"I think we finally got that storm."

Another lurch; so big they all rolled over in their beds.

"You two better come down here. I reckon this is going to get rough," Emma said to Albert and Harry.

A crack overhead so loud it made their ears ring. Gloria curled into a ball like a frightened hedgehog. Harry and Albert clambered down just in time for another wild sway to send them tumbling to the floor. Emma reached out and pulled them all into the bed and hugged them tightly. Others around them were waking and mumbling. Wood creaked and waves crashed at the side of the ship. Above them the flameless oil lamp swung wildly, clattering into the ceiling. Albert wriggled out of Emma's grasp and curled up next to his little sister in the corner.

The ship shuddered and children cried. The steaming stench of sweat and urine swamped the air like a noxious gas. A tilt sideways and everyone screamed. The ship moaned and hurled them back with an almighty crash. Animals stomped, shat, grunted and bleated. Cages rattled and the stink putrefied. Emma pulled a handkerchief she had drenched in raspberry oil from her petticoat pocket and masked her face.

Rolling and rolling, first one way then the next. More thunder, clapping and cracking as rapid as gunfire. Nothing they had experienced in the Bay of Biscay came even close to as terrifying as this. Emma wondered if they would ever see Australia. She thought of Jacob and what he would do when he heard the ship had gone down. She thought of Jack at home and the letters that he had probably already written. A massive swell and they were raised from their bunk. Gloria screeched and curled even tighter.

Someone in another bunk tumbled out of bed with a crash. People were yelling out to one another, and from somewhere the sound of nervous singing drifted through the violence of the storm in the hope of keeping them all calm. Emma stroked Albert's shivering back and joined in.

*

Heated air and seeping smoke. Coughing and spluttering. People clamouring. Emma sniffed, beneath the foulness hummed the distinct aroma of burning wood. Fear shot through her. Without thinking she was on her feet.

"Upstairs, now," she ordered. A wave slammed hard and sent her tumbling into the wall. Her elbow smashed on an iron rail. She cried out in pain but forced her way on. They tripped over people cowering along the corridor and slammed into others fighting to get out. Overturned slop buckets rolled, contents spilt and ran in a vile stream. Emma gritted her teeth.

Bright flames licked at the wood. Inside a bunk, the fire burned and a guilty broken lantern lay shattered on the floor. Bedclothes were engulfed and the wooden frame was crumbling. Men were smothering it fast, stamping on flames covered in blankets, hurling buckets of whatever they could lay their hands on over the raging fire. Emma glanced back through the thickening smoke. Gloria was sucking her thumb and Albert was greener than cabbage. Harry blinked and rubbed the smoke from his eyes. Emma hesitated. The fire was almost out. It was the smoke that could kill them now. A coughing fit gripped her as she battled on.

Hatches battened. Hammering, yelling, banging for help. Fear gripped, then relief as the hatch swung open and a face peered in. There was no time to wait and no chance to explain. A stampede for the surface and Emma was amongst it. She gripped Harry's shoulders and pushed him up the stairs before her. Then Albert and Gloria, and they were all up top.

The Captain was at the helm, hair plastered to his face and his beard dripping wet. Rain poured as though God had ripped open all the clouds at once. Roaring, rumbling, crashing. The sound was ear-splitting. Gloria pressed her hands to her ears. The captain wiped his eyebrows but there was too much water. Emma stared in horror. Someone was yelling but the sound was torn away. A huge wave crashed over the side and dragged a young sailor into the rails. The rope around his waist was loosened. He clung on, but barely. Emma wanted to help him but she dare not move. Her children crouched on the floor at her feet, huddled together waiting for the end of the world.

Screaming, louder and louder. Voices calling out to something or someone, whoever it was they weren't listening. A great droning became a roar through the waves, closer and closer. Emma held her breath. Sailors waved lanterns at the darkness. The rumbling grew louder than the thunder.

A massive crash made the whole ship shudder.

"Emma, Emma!"

Emma turned around but could see nothing through the sheets of rain. Someone grabbed her arm.

"Lucy, thank God you're all right." She flung her arms around her friend and hugged her. "Where are the twins?" Emma frantically tried to spot them.

"I told them to stay below," Lucy yelled.

"What was the crash?"

"We hit that."

Lucy pointed to the port side of the ship. Towering in the darkness was a great black shadow. Steam pumping and billowing.

The steel bow of a steamer had punched itself into the side of their hull.

"Are we going to sink?"

Lucy shook her head.

"I don't know."

A fork of lightning shattered the night sky and for a moment it was bright as day. At their side, another passenger crossed herself and began to pray. Emma saw Lucy's face and the fear in her heart strengthened its hold. Lucy never seemed to be fazed by anything. If she was frightened then what hope was there?

Turning, lurching, thunder rumbled and lightning streaked.

"Get down below," A sailor was staggering towards them waving with frantic urgency. "Get down below."

Emma began to gather up her children.

"How bad is the damage?" she called.

The sailor stopped and said,

"We won't know until the storm passes."

"Then we're not sinking right now?"

He shook his head and began calling out again,

"Get down below."

"There was a fire, there's smoke," she tried to say, but the ship rocked and listed wildly. Emma staggered sideways. Lucy tumbled after her. Gloria slipped from her mother's grasp. Emma reached out. Terror hit her whole body. Gloria seemed to fly sideways, crashing into the railings with a heavy thump. Harry tried to go after her but a wave swept over the side and knocked him back. Emma thrust Albert into Lucy's arms and begged her to get him below. Lightning streaked violet. Electricity charged the air. Lucy stumbled away gripping Albert's hand.

Tears poured down Emma's cheeks mingling with the rain. She tried to pull herself forwards. Arms outstretched, fingers reaching as far as they would go. Children calling, crying. Gloria was slumped on the floor and Harry was crawling towards her. Another wave and Emma was thrust back against the wall of the sail maker's workshop.

Gloria slid further away. Harry was gaining ground, but not fast enough.

A dark figure from nowhere. Strong arms encasing her daughter. Emma stared and clung to the wall as the man scooped up her children and staggered towards her. For a moment she couldn't see his face. Rain whipped and the wind howled. Then a flash of lightning and a pair of piercing blue eyes glinted at her.

"Are you all right?" he called through a rumble of thunder.

Emma gawped.

"Let's get you below, Mrs Burns."

She tried to nod her response.

Harry flung himself at his mother and they pushed forward. The teacher carried Gloria back towards the hatch to the cabins.

*

Air thicker than soup and stench stronger than the Thames in summer. An extinguished fire and soot coated walls. Emma barely noticed the damage,

"Mr Finch, thank you so much," she said for the third time. The ship lurched but with less vigour.

Mr Finch smiled at her and with a quick bow, said it was nothing.

"I think the worst is over now. Will you be all right?"

His gaze penetrated Emma, causing a small flutter in her heart. Then he was gone again, leaving her and the children safely back in their bunk and utterly stunned.

14

Day Thirty-Three

Cool air and gentle sway. Emma awoke and rubbed her back. She was still crunched in the corner of their bunk. Her legs tingled and throbbed as she moved them and her head ached where she had banged it. For a moment she didn't know where she was. She looked around the tiny bunk to find everything in disarray. Their small trunk was on its side and their clothes had been strewn all over the stained floor. She looked up to see a pair of her drawers hanging over the edge of the upper bunk. She wondered how they had gotten all the way up there. Gloria was back in her bed and huddled beneath a blanket. Albert was sprawled on the floor next to her and Harry...

Where was Harry? Emma's heart began to pound, but then she spotted an arm dangling from the top bunk and heard a gentle snort. She got to her feet and felt the steadiness of the ship beneath her.

"Well, we didn't sink then," she said to herself.

Leaving the children sleeping she went to investigate. Picking her way through human debris, she passed the fire-damaged area. On the floor by the charred bunk, amidst the broken glass and battered lantern, were the woman and her son. They lay, lightly covered with a singed sheet and soot grey blanket, shivering in their sleep. She drew a deep breath of smoke tainted air and continued on to the upper deck.

Daylight burned her eyes. Fluffy white clouds drifted by so innocently that Emma could scarcely believe it after the storm of the night before. She leaned over the railings to check that the sea was really as calm as it felt. Not even the smallest sign that anything had ever happened. Emma stared at the sky and let the gentle westerly breeze ruffle her hair. She looked up at what was left of the tattered sails to find them billowing merrily. At least they were moving now. A midshipman was pulling at the ropes and tying them off and the sailmaker was clattering away in his workshop, busy as a honeybee.

"Did we escape danger then?" she said to the midshipman in disbelief.

The sailor shook his head.

"No Ma'am, we hit The Parisien."

"What happened?"

The sailor finished tying his knot and looked at her.

"The storm was so rough, she didn't see us 'til it was too late and we couldn't turn fast enough, and then there's the fire damage. It's all superficial, but we'll have to go into port to get patched up."

Emma opened her mouth in surprise.

"Where?" she said at last.

"Best place is Rio de Janeiro, ma'am, directly west of here. We got blown off course and the wind is still pushing us that way. We should be there in two days."

"Gracious, for how long?"

"As long as it takes. I'd wager two or three weeks."

Emma was stunned. They had a scheduled stop in The Cape of Good Hope but the thought of dry land in only two days divided her emotions, would this be a hindrance or a welcome relief?

"And we're safe to sail there on our own?"

The man nodded,

"Captain thinks so, ma'am."

"And the other ship?"

The sailor shrugged and pointed out to sea.

"She was all right, solid hull like hers and all that steam power; she can just carry on as she was."

Emma shielded her eyes and looked into the distance to see a tiny dot on the horizon as The Parisien chugged away northward bound.

"She didn't offer to help us?"

"Aye, she did, but the captain said there was no need to delay two ships when we could manage alone."

"She's going home?" she asked.

"Aye," said the sailor, "back to France."

Emma stopped to consider what she had said. Was England home now, or was it Australia? She thanked the sailor and scurried below to tell her children the news.

15

Day Thirty-Five

"Land Ho!"

There was a rush to the fore. Emma watched as the children weaved and wended their way into the crowd and she wondered if the boat would tip forward with all the extra weight. She blinked and peered but could see nothing. Then suddenly Lucy said,

"There, I see it, look right there." She pointed onto the distant horizon and then Emma saw it too, a thin layer of darkness just beginning to peek up over the waterline. Soon it would become a shimmering landscape, glittering, green as an emerald necklace, rising and falling. The Jewel of Brazil began to shine and draw them in like a tiding of magpies.

Small islands of lush towering hills sent sweet fragrances toward them on the breeze. The sky glowed pink as the sun began to rise above the horizon and lights twinkled along the waterfront. Ships were buffering, jostling for space. Great hulks of metal with silent chimneys were bobbing away next to elegant wooden hulls and tall empty masts. Warehouses clung to the coastline and houses reached back into the hillsides. Emma had never seen anything so beautiful, nor so big. Lucy watched her expression.

"Incredible ain't it?"

Emma nodded, unable to find the words.

*

Everyone was desperate to disembark. It didn't matter that this was not the country they wanted to be in; it was land. There would be proper food and fresh water and clean spicy air, and not one of them could wait to put their feet on solid ground. The Cassandra was gently pulling into the sweeping bay of the January River and wending her way past the larger ships towards a docking area where she could be mended. Children were clamouring for views of this exotic land, taller ones leaning over the high sides of the ship, little ones lifted onto the shoulders of fathers or brothers. Gloria was on tiptoes peering over the wooden railing in silent awe. Albert was bouncing up and down excitedly.

"Mam, Mam, there's a giant cat in that cage." Albert tugged at Emma's hand frantically.

Emma looked to where he was pointing and expressed her surprise. She had seen pictures of lions but never one in the flesh. This creature was clearly destined for some rich folks' menagerie.

"Poor thing looks half-dead," Emma pitied it as it opened its mouth and gave an angry roar at the sailors who were dragging it down the gangplank of a nearby clipper. "I hope its owners feed it up now it's back on land."

Albert wasn't paying attention anymore. His focus had drifted to the ship they were passing, far bigger than any of the others and crammed with men, dark-skinned men, eyes down and shoulders heavy.

"What are they?" Albert.

"Niggers." Alfie replied.

"What's one of them?" Gloria asked.

"They's people silly," Molly answered, "Ain't ya never seen a black man before?"

Lucy glanced down at her children and then at Emma. Emma bit her lip and shook her head. Albert grinned and waved, one of the men must have seen him because he looked up and waved back. Gloria pulled at her mother's skirt and tried to hide.

"I don't think you should do that Bert," Emma suggested.

"Do what?"

"Attract the attention of those men, you might get them into trouble."

"Why?"

"Look!" Harry tripped over his brother's foot and was about to hit him when Emma stopped him with one of her glares. Harry lowered his hand and grumbled something under his breath. Relieved she had avoided finding an explanation to give Albert,

Emma decided to ignore Harry's gesture and ask him what he was looking at.

He pointed towards the dockside.

"Have you ever seen so many people?"

Emma smiled and ruffled his thick blond hair.

"No, Harry, I haven't."

Crates, trunks, caskets and barrels of wine were stacked on the dockside. Tradesmen were counting off new stock, merchants supervising and purchasing. There were faces everywhere, dirty faces, glamorous faces, black, red and white faces, oriental eyes and exotic clothes. As Emma watched the dazzling rainbow of people she thought how much Jack would have loved to see such a spectacle. A thin pain of regret twisted in her stomach and she wondered how he was doing all alone.

16

Rio De-Janeiro
January 1857

Day Forty-Three

Emma's lungs felt heavy as a damp sponge and her clothes were glued to her skin. She wafted her face with the little fan she had purchased from a market stall and tried to breathe in some real air through the humidity. She had never known heat like this in all her life and if this was what Australia was going to be like, she was not sure she would stand it. Gloria however, seemed unfazed. The resilience of her little girl amazed her. She watched as she skipped ahead down the Rua do Ouvidor, dancing merrily through the narrow street hand in hand with Molly Matthews. Gloria's ringlets bounced frizzy springs and shone in the sunlight. Emma smiled and shook her head contentedly. It was nice to have an afternoon away from the boys, they had been driving her round the bend, running as wild as street rats ever since they had pulled into port. She wondered how Lucy was doing keeping an eye on them all by herself.

A newsboy scurried past and nearly knocked her from her feet. She was about to call after him when he threw a glance in her direction and yelled something in Portuguese that Emma could only presume to be an apology. She paused to catch her breath and looked up at the elegant Hispanic architecture that surrounded her. Rio was a new city and a thriving one. Everything was bright and shining, tall and glamorous, or at least it was in the parts the captain had told them were safe to visit. Folks with more money than she could comprehend occupied the houses and offices all around. A horse-drawn omnibus clattered towards her and she stepped aside to let it pass. From its roof, a gentleman doffed his hat at her and called out a greeting. Emma shaded her eyes and peered up to see a pair of eyes that matched the sky. The carriage came to a halt in front of a tobacconist shop. She was about to move on when she realised that the man was disembarking and coming towards her.

"Mrs Burns. How are you? You are enjoying this beautiful day?"

"Aside from trying to breathe air that's wetter than the sea, we're all doing very well thank you." *Gracious* she thought; *Lucy's quick wit must be rubbing off on me.*

Mr Finch laughed,

"Indeed," his smile lit up his eyes. Emma thought her heart had skipped a beat. She hadn't seen Mr Finch since the night of the storm, not to speak to anyway. She had caught a distant glimpse of him as the crowd of eager passengers had disembarked that first day in Rio, but then he seemed to have vanished altogether. She presumed he had even taken rooms in a hotel, just as many of the better off passengers had. She realised she hadn't actually greeted him.

"Good day to you, Mr Finch," she said, hoping she didn't now sound silly saying hello after her quip about the weather. "You find this heat a little easier to live with than I do I think." She added with a polite curtsey. She raised her eyes to meet his gaze and felt her heart flip over in her chest. This physical reaction took her by surprise so much that she didn't catch what he was saying to her. He paused and asked if she was quite all right. Emma wafted her fan more vigorously and hoped she wasn't blushing too much.

"Oh yes, quite well thank you."

Mr Finch looked relieved and offered her his arm.

"I was contemplating a nice cup of tea. There is a little lovely cafe that resembles a tearoom just around the corner, have you tried it?"

Emma shook her head and then remembered Gloria and Molly. Glancing around quickly she spotted them standing in front of a sandwich board, heads cocked in concentration. Relief and a little guilt flooded through her.

"I'm afraid I haven't had the opportunity," she replied, her eyes still on the girls.

"Well, then you must allow me to treat you to afternoon tea," he must have followed her gaze for he then added, "I am sure the children are partial to a good cake."

Emma turned and looked at him. His aquiline profile was smooth and clean-shaven, an unusual look for fashionable men. His dark hair peeked out from beneath his hat in a slightly erratic manner that made his chiselled cheeks seem softer. He looked at her, his lips twitching back into that warm smile. Emma's stomach flipped a full somersault and she considered the possibility that perhaps Lucy was right; she had been missing the company of a man over the last few years, far more than she had thought.

"That would be most kind indeed, but I am sure we should not impose..."

"Nonsense, I would be glad of the company," he cut in before she could finish.

They were almost up to where Gloria and Molly were standing now and could see the board they were so carefully attempting to decipher. Mr Finch drew them to a stop and spoke to the girls,

"Miss Burns, Miss Matthews, what a pleasure it is to see you. Now, can you tell me what the board says?"

In her fluster Emma had almost forgotten he was their teacher.

Gloria jumped and spun around in astonishment. Molly merely turned her head as though she had been expecting them. Emma lowered her eyes, embarrassed that she could not read the news board herself. She could not even tell if it was in English.

"Latest news on the span..ish and," Gloria was doing very well, "Am..e..ri..can a..ll...i..ance."

"Marvellous Miss Burns, and the last bit Miss Matthews?"

Molly swallowed and added,

"New Y...ork Times, Jan...u...ary tenth eighteen hundred and fifty-seven." The date was numeric but she was pleased with herself nonetheless.

"Very good indeed," he congratulated. Emma nodded enthusiastically.

"But today is January Twenty-Second, is it not?" Gloria said; her face scrunched into a puzzled expression.

"Well, New York is a very long way away, and the news takes a little while to get here," Mr Finch let his smile broaden. "Now, how would you ladies like to join Mrs Burns and me for tea and cakes?"

The response was a resounding 'Yes'.

*

Cutlery clattered on fancy plates. Cups of steaming beverages adorned the tables and sugary scents filled the air. A stream of sunlight cut through the window and lit a path towards an elegantly laid out table of doilies and elaborate cakes. In the centre stood two huge silver samovars chugging away a constant supply of tea and coffee for the discerning customers.

The conversation began in relative generality. There was a polite discussion about the comforts of the ship or lack thereof, and Mr Finch expressed his good opinion of her children's progress in their lessons. Then she had attempted to discover more about him. He had willingly shared fond memories of his late mother and spending summers with her family in Cornwall as a boy, but when she had asked what had led him to become a teacher he had smiled shyly but politely turned the conversation back to her. Emma wondered why a man like him could possibly wish to avoid speaking of himself. She could see nothing artful about him, nothing devious or dark. Quite to the contrary, his expression was so open that she concluded that the only thing holding him back was his honesty. On the other hand, she felt she had damn good reason to avoid mention of her husband and her lowly roots. Yet, despite her best intentions, Emma found herself answering this man's questions freely.

"How old were you when she died?" Mr Finch was looking so deeply into Emma's eyes that she was forced to look away for fear of blushing. He was asking about her mother.

"Childbed fever took her when I was a few days old."

"I am very sorry."

"Why should you be sorry, it is hardly your fault? Besides, my father was all I knew. It's impossible to miss a mother I never had."

Mr Finch smiled slowly.

"Perhaps you're right, but your father, it must have been hard for him."

Emma nodded sadly.

"It was, but I am afraid I didn't really understand him until I had my own children. He stayed so strong, buried so much inside himself that it never occurred to me as a young lass that he was missing her."

Mr Finch's expression clouded in a way that Emma couldn't quite fathom.

"He sounds like a good father, Mrs Burns."

Emma smiled thinly.

"Aye, he was that. Did his best." She replied with a sudden desire to change the subject. She may not have had the luxury of an education, but Emma's memory was sharp as a tack. Once she knew about something it tended to stay with her. She fished around in her mind for something vaguely intelligent to talk about, but Mr Finch beat her to it.

"I understand that you have another son, Mrs Burns."

Emma felt as though a spike had been driven through her chest. Gloria hung her head and stared down at her empty plate.

"Don't blame the children, Mrs Burns," Mr Finch added. "They are just proud of their older brother."

Emma pressed her fingers to her lips for a second and hoped she wouldn't cry.

"Yes, Mr Finch." She replied, amazed her voice hadn't cracked. "Jack. He's an apprentice at the potteries back home." As the words came out her mouth dried and her throat tightened. It was hard enough to think of her eldest boy, but to speak of him made her whole body ache.

"His brothers and sister are very proud of him. He sounds like a fine young man. Maybe one day he will come out and join you?"

Emma bit her lip.

"He is a very good lad, sir, but I doubt I shall ever see him again."

Mr Finch looked mortified. His fingers twitched towards hers but then he lifted his hand to his mouth and pressed them to his lips in prayer form as if to silence himself.

"Forgive me," he muttered without moving his steady gaze from Emma's face. For a moment Emma felt as though she were diving deep into the ocean. She blinked and tried to focus.

"My Jack is very political, she spluttered. "No grand ideas of course, but he does like to get involved in local issues…"

Mr Finch's eyes glinted with interest as she told him of Jack's involvement in the campaign to improve the Marlstone Workhouse. As she spoke she considered what a maudlin choice of a subject she had made, but the topic seemed to spark a passion in Mr Finch and she soon forgot to be nervous or to miss Jack so much. They became so engrossed in the discussion that she quite forgot where they were. All the while their hands edging closer and closer until their fingers tips were lightly touching.

"Ma will be sorry she missed this," Molly said, as she polished off the last bite of jam-smeared scone. The child pushed the plate away and folded her arms in satisfaction, catching Emma's elbow with her own as she did. Snapped back to reality Emma snatched her hands away, pushed her chair back too quickly and knocked her knee on the table leg, causing the small vase of flowers in the centre to rattle dangerously.

"Thank you, Mr Finch, it has been a most pleasant afternoon, but I feel we have taken up too much of your time, and we should be heading back to ship, she babbled. "My boys will be wondering where we are and poor Mrs Matthews must be tearing her hair out by now. My boys can be rather a handful, but of course, there is no need to tell you that, you know already from teaching them, but she will be missing Molly too by now and…." She ran out of breath and swallowed. Gloria was staring at her as though she had lost her mind. Mr Finch tilted his head with another queer expression that Emma could not quite read. She wished that the floor would open up and swallow her whole. What on earth was wrong with her?

There was an awkward pause whilst Mr Finch seemed to gather his thoughts. Emma stood there, unsure what to do next.

"Mrs Burns, you are quite right, it is time we were getting back to the ship, please allow me to escort you." He called for the waitress to settle the bill.

Emma could find no excuse to deny him nor, if she was honest with herself, had she any desire to. She just wished she could pay her part of the bill, not, she suspected, that he would have allowed her to anyway.

*

Hooves clopped and wheels turned over the dusty hard ground. The streets were abuzz with people and carts. As they walked back towards the docks Emma looked at Mr Finch's fresh sun-kissed face and wondered how old he was. Now she had spent an afternoon in his company she realised he might not be quite as youthful as his appearance suggested. There was a hint of laughter lines about his eyes and the depth of his conversation surpassed that of most young men, even well educated ones. Not that she had met so many very well educated ones. As she surmised that he was somewhere in his early thirties she wondered why he was not married. Perhaps he was. Before she could prevent herself, the question tumbled from her lips,

"You are travelling alone, Mr Finch. Do you not have a wife?"

Emma screwed up her face and prayed he hadn't heard her over the din of a passing carriage. She felt him adjust his shoulders and glance at her sideways. In front of her, Gloria was chattering to Molly, oblivious of their conversation. Emma was glad.

"Sadly not, Mrs Burns. Once I...she died."

It was Emma's turn to be mortified.

"Oh, Sir, forgive me, I didn't mean to pry."

Mr Finch looked at her with such sadness that Emma could barely fight the urge to reach up and touch his face.

"Please, don't apologise, it was a long time ago." Despite the sadness, his eyes were warm and kind and Emma found she was smiling back.

"And there has been no one else?"

Mr Finch looked at her for a long moment, then shook his head, "No."

Emma frowned at the sinking feeling in her heart. What business had she to even hope that he would be remotely attraction to her? As he threaded his arm through hers once more and they resumed their walk, she forced herself to think of Jacob, to imagine their new house and new life. Yes, they were going to have a wonderful life, her, Jacob and the children.

They walked on in pleasant silence for a while. Emma noticed Mr Finch's gaze move from one child to the other. She saw a well-hidden flicker of pity cross his face as he noted the ancient frock and the skin and bone arms of Molly Matthews. Emma looked at the little girl. Her sleeves were too short and the fabric of her dress was thin and the hem had been let down more than once. Gloria's frock was old but she looked positively stately in comparison to Molly. She prayed that the Matthews' lives would be improved as much as they hoped they would be in Australia. Emma was about to enquire after Mr Finch's plans once he reached Melbourne when they heard a ruckus. The teacher laid a hand on her arm to halt her, and Emma called back the girls.

"Wait here," he said letting her go and walking with more caution around the last corner.

Emma strained her ears to work out what was going on. People running. Whistles blowing. Voices calling. Men yelling and a there was a woman screaming. Somewhere amidst the commotion, a child was crying bitterly. Then Emma recognised the sobs. She didn't wait for Mr Finch. She tore around the corner, skirts hoisted and ankles exposed. She didn't care; she had to get to him.

*

Bright red face streaked with tears. Emma swept Albert into her arms and hugged him tightly. He was as rigid as a plank of wood. Lucy was on her knees, head hanging down. People were rushing everywhere. A policeman was blowing into his whistle, cheeks puffed out and sweat beading on his forehead.

"I'm sorry, I couldn't stop them. I'm so sorry, Emma," Lucy was sobbing.

Emma had yet to comprehend the situation. She set Albert back and took in his terrified expression. Slowly she looked around. Mr Finch was talking to a swarthy looking police officer, his voice too quiet for her to catch beneath the din of everyone else. A steamer honked its funnel making both she and Albert flinch. Gloria began to cry from sheer confusion. Emma suddenly felt sick.

"Where's Harry?"

Albert cringed and tried to back away from her.

"What the hell is going on? Tell me now or I'll box your ears!" Fear and anger welled inside her so overpoweringly that she felt her head swim. Albert cowered.

"He was just 'elping."

She grabbed his wrist, clamping him so hard he yelped.

Lucy got to her feet and came by her side. She looked over at Mr Finch. He shifted his stance and continued his conversation with the policeman. Emma's chest tightened and for one horrific moment, she thought Harry was dead. Lucy saw the cloud that crossed her eyes and shook her head.

"He's all right, Emma," Lucy said hurriedly. "But they took him away. He...he was..." Lucy began to tremble.

"Who took him...where?" Emma looked around at the crowd. They were growing silent now, staring at her, some shaking their heads, others tutting. Some she knew from the ship, others were strangers, bystanders, there for the spectacle. Mr Finch and the policeman came towards her. Emma eyed them warily.

"Mrs Burns, this is Inspector Mendoza, he would like to have a quiet word with you."

Emma offered him her hand. Then a freight train of recognition crashed into her gut and settled there like a bad clam. She had seen that expression before, seven years ago when they had arrested Jacob. Seven years ago her world had come tumbling down. Her husband, for whom she had given up her excellent position at The Hall, the man she trusted with her life and with whom she had children, had been proven a thief. And not just for taking a penny loaf or a packet of meat, but barrow loads of goods. When they had searched the house they had found jewellery she had never seen before stashed at the back of the wardrobe, candlesticks jammed in a bag behind the shit house and a tin of money, so much money, buried in the back yard. Emma knew that look from a man of the law and she knew what it meant.

With cheeks burning and a searing pain in her heart, she clenched her fists and gritted her teeth. She couldn't look at Mr Finch, and for some reason, he was the only one that mattered. She couldn't bear the thought of his judgement. She wished more than ever that Jack were there with her. He would have put a reassuring hand upon her arm and spoken to the policeman. He would have been calm and collected and helped her take care of it. She forced herself to draw a breath and moistened her lips. She looked the inspector directly in his dark eyes and asked,

"What did he do, sir? What did my son do?"

Inspector Mendoza was obviously used to dealing with harsh situations. His towering form was one of a bare-knuckle boxer and his nose had seen straighter days. His shoulders were wide and his biceps bulged beneath his shirt. Emma noticed the tattoo on his forearm as he reached out a hand to lead her aside. When he spoke his tone was gruff but there was a softness to it that almost made Emma trust him. She looked at his bronze face and waited for him to get to the point.

"Senora Burnez," his accent was thick Portuguese, "Your son is Arry Burnez, no?"

"No… I mean, yes." Emma spluttered.

"He is twelve years old, yellow hair and green eyes?"

Emma began to wonder if Harry was dead after all. She felt many pairs of eyes watching her. She turned so the crowd couldn't see her face.

"Yes," she whispered.

"He is by now at the police station, in our cells."

Emma was not sure whether to be relieved or horrified.

"What has he done? May I see him?"

"That is not possible, Mrs Burnez. I understand your concern but being an English boy, tomorrow he will be sent to the British consulate, they will deal with him there..."

"And then what? He's just a child!" she gasped. The inspector attempted to look sympathetic.

"Earlier today we arrested a gang of smugglers, thieves. Your son was one of them. He was found in possession of stolen property from one of the cargo ships."

Like father like son, Emma thought. She had always known Harry was the child to watch and she had clearly not done a very good job of it. She rubbed her hands over her face.

"There are still some items we cannot account for. We need to search your quarters."

Emma grimaced but stepped aside to let him pass. Inspector Mendoza looked at her calmly.

"Will you show me the way?"

The last thing Emma wanted to do was stand by and watch while the police searched through her family's possessions, but for the second time in her life, she was going to have to face the indignity of it. Not only that, this time they would be confined to the ship for at least two more months with all the same people, looking at them, watching them. No escaping to the other side of town now.

She turned back to Lucy,

"Look after Bertie and Gloria, please. Keep them out of the way 'til this is done."

Lucy nodded. She knew this drill too and Emma felt her friend's sympathy. Emma's only consolation was that at least Lucy wouldn't judge her. She risked a glance in the direction of Mr Finch, but he wasn't there. She scanned the slowly dispersing crowd but he was gone. Emma bit her lip; he would probably never speak to her again. But then perhaps that was for the best.

*

Their little trunk had been emptied of its contents, and their clothes had been thoroughly riffled through. Emma blushed as the stranger handled her underwear. A wave from the incoming tide caught the underside of the ship and made it lurch. The Inspector staggered, not used to being on the sea. He set down the clothing and closed the trunk. They had already stripped the beds and shaken out the sheets.

"Forgive me, Mrs Burnez; I understand how unpleasant this must be for you."

Emma wanted to say, 'do you, do you really?' but instead she lowered her eyes and sighed.

"Is this all you have?"

Emma parted her lips but couldn't speak. She shook her head.

"What else?"

She adjusted her skirt.

"There is a crate, in the storage hold. I don't know whereabouts and I doubt Harry does either. It was loaded by the crew and we haven't seen it since we set sail."

The inspector considered for the moment then made a decision.

"I think we had better conduct a search of the storage room as well, I will speak with the Captain." Emma closed her eyes for a moment and prayed she was dreaming. The Inspector moved to leave, then stopped and turned to face her. He examined her face for a moment, for what she was unsure, and then he said,

"Tell me something, you are a convict's wife yes?" He didn't wait for her to answer. "One of many on this ship no doubt. Why do you all follow these good for nothing husbands to such a desolate land?"

Emma was flabbergasted. She just sat down on the edge of the bed and stared. Mendoza waited for a moment, gave up, shrugged, clipped his heels together in military fashion, and left.

Emma sank back onto her pillow and began to cry.

Four Miles North of Melbourne
January 22nd 1857

Thin blue twilight stung Jacob's eyes as he set down his hammer and rubbed his back. He remembered Emma's bad back and wondered how they were all doing on the ship. He tried to picture the children, all except Jack. A sour taste filled his mouth and he curled his lips. That boy had deserted him, why should he care.

Instead, he thought of Harry and Albert, they had been so small when he left. Harry was all blond curls and big green eyes, running around the house like a little bull, and then Albert, he had just been beginning to crawl, all curiosity. He contemplated whom the boy might look like, him or his mother.

Jacob perused the foundations of their new home and smiled. Then there was Gloria. The child he had never met. He had never quite fathomed where Emma had found the name, but he liked it. There had been descriptions of her when she was born, but nothing lately. He wondered if she would like him. He hoped she would like him. A sinking feeling ran from the top of his head, taking his heart down to his boots.

He took off his cap and rubbed his head as darkness fell. The fleeting moment of happiness vanished into the deep blue haze as he made his way over to where he had dropped his jacket. In the pocket was a flask. He reached down and retrieved it.

Day Forty-Four

The air was acrid with the heavy stench of sweat and urine worse than a bad day at sea. Emma tried not to notice. She pulled out the raspberry oiled handkerchief from her petticoat and covered her mouth and nose. Mosquitoes hummed around her head. She tried to swat them away but their persistence was unending. Her footsteps clunked methodically as she was led along a narrow corridor. The stone beneath her feet was grey and cold, the damp walls were a mouldy shade of green, paint flecked and stained. Emma tried not to let her clothes brush against them. She had hoped she would never have to face another day like this, yet here she was, in another gaol, and this time thousands of miles from home. How desperately she wished they had never come.

"Damn you, Jacob," she muttered under her breath.

The guard stopped before a gate of solid steel. Emma waited as he jangled a crammed bunch of keys and selected one. She was not sure how she had been granted permission to see Harry. Inspector Mendoza had been very clear that she would not be able to do so until his hearing, but then one of the other police officers had arrived at the ship to say there had been a change of plan. Emma could only express her gratitude and had left right away. The lock clunked sending an echo back down the corridor and through the cells beyond.

Tins clattered against the bars and men called out. Leering faces and sweat-stained shirts seemed to swim before her. Emma tried not to look in the cells as she walked past. A hand grasped at her. She looked down as she wrenched her skirts away from it. The fingers were stained yellow and the nails grimy and long. The offender was saying something to her in Portuguese. For once she was thankful she couldn't understand. By the time they came to a stop, she was close to tears. The guard took out another key and opened the cell door. Rust encrusted bars swung back with a grating creak. Emma stared in horror. Cowering in the corner of the pokey dim cell was a small, thin child; yellow hair matted and dark, eyes wide and snot caked under his nose. His dusty shirt was ripped on one shoulder and his feet were bare. Something scuttled into the corner of the cell behind the slop bucket. Emma shuddered. What diseases and sickness lurked here she dared not imagine.

"Where are your shoes?" was the only thing she could think of to say.

The child looked up at her with a blank expression. For a moment she thought he had lost his mind and didn't recognise her. But his expression was of disbelief. A moment later he was running towards her. She opened her arms and took him in, folding them around him and hugging him tightly. Harry sobbed into her breast, tears bleeding through her blouse and dampening her skin. He was muttering sorry over and over.

"It's all right, son, we can sort this out." Emma knew she couldn't but she said it anyway. Harry pulled back and peered up at her with such hope on his face that she felt her heart break just a little further.

"I didn't do it, Mam, honest, I promise, I didn't know what they was doing. I thought I was 'elpin', they promised us a sixpence if I 'elped!"

For once Emma smiled at her son's lapse of grammar and hugged him tightly again. He shifted his stance and a chain rattled at his feet. She looked down to see a heavy shackle clamped around his ankle. He was free enough to reach her and the slop bucket, but one step back and she would be too far away.

"Oh God, Harry, how did you get yourself involved in all this."

Harry started shaking his head vigorously.

"I promise, Mam I honestly didn't know was they were up to. I would never have gone if I'd known they was stealing. I'm not a thief, I'm not like..." He stopped and swallowed the thought.

Emma knew what he meant. Once, a year or two before, she had caught him "borrowing" another child's wooden horse, and whilst he had sworn he was only playing and was going to give it back, she had said it, she had accused him of being like his father.

She spat into her handkerchief and wiped his face clean with it. She knew when he was lying, or at least she prayed she did. Smoothing back his hair she looked at him intently. He was not lying, she was sure of it.

"All right, Harry, I believe you. They're sending you to the British Consulate soon, it'll be all right then." She was not sure how true that was, but what else could she say. That they might make an example of him and send him back to England as a prisoner, or worse send him back here, to this stinking place. The police had found nothing incriminating on The Cassandra and yet Mendoza seemed determined to believe Harry's guilt. She didn't know the penalty for stealing was in Brazil and she preferred not to find out.

"Time to go." The guard rattled his keys to emphasize his point. Emma glanced at him and hugged her boy one last time.

"Try to be brave," she said as the guard stepped further into the cell and tugged Harry's arms away from his mother's skirts. She dropped a kiss on his head and backed away. He stood there looking at her, bound up like a slave. Unable to turn her back on him she walked backwards until she was outside the cell.

Once at the entrance, she looked for the police officer that had brought her there, but he was nowhere to be seen. When she asked the guard where he had gone the man had shrugged and muttered something in Portuguese. And when she asked if someone would take her back to the ship she had simply been shown the door.

19

Day Forty-Five

Glaring sun cut across the dark ceiling, lighting the dust particles that danced in its path. The room was airless and when the heavy door had slammed shut the oak-lined walls seem to close in on her. Emma was sitting on a bench in a small side room at the British Consulate, where she had been asked to wait. No one seemed to know anything about her son or his case.

Footsteps outside. Emma glanced at the door in anticipation. The doorknob turned but then no one entered. She looked up at the grandfather clock in the corner and gave a shaky sigh. She had been there over an hour. A cloud drifted over the sun plunging the room into shadow. She pulled out her fan and wafted her face.

The door opened. Startled, she looked up.

"Mrs Burns," The man was tall and slender with hair so black and skin so pale he appeared as monochrome as a newsprint daguerreotype. Paler even than Mr Finch had been when they first set sail. "We spoke to the guard on duty and he said there was no English boy in custody."

"But I saw him there myself yesterday," she replied desperately. "The inspector said he was to be sent here, today." Emma's head began to swim.

The man fixed a sympathetic look on his face but the expression didn't quite penetrate his eyes. She could tell he thought the same as the inspector; she and her children were just another convict family, tainted and bad to the core. What did one missing boy of that type matter?

"Perhaps there's news back at your ship. I suggest you speak to your captain."

Emma rose unsteadily to her feet and made her way to the door. "Thank you, sir. I shall do that."

*

The clunking of her heels on the hard ground thudded right through Emma's body. She saw nothing and noticed no one as she strode through the city towards the docks. At that moment all she wanted was to be back at home in the poky kitchen of their old cottage, hands stinging from scrubbing laundry and listening to the rain pour down from the smog-filled sky. More than anything, she wanted to talk to Jack.

As she turned onto the dockside she tried to imagine what Jack would say. What he would do to find Harry and fetch him back.

Someone was calling her name. The sound filtered into her thoughts.

"Mam, Mam!" A pair of skinny arms wrapped around her waist and a scruffy sweaty head pressed against her breasts. The force of the embrace knocked her backwards. Stumbling to remain upright she was unable to take in what she was seeing. She pried the child away from her and set him back. Blinking, she rubbed her eyes and stared.

"Harry, oh my dear lord, Harry!"

The boy was shaking violently. She could see the tension in his shoulders and the pink blotches prickling at his neck, just like he used to get when he was a baby and fretting.

"How did you get here? They let you out? Why? I don't understand. Harry, what happened?"

Harry cringed, his shoulders rising higher around his neck. Emma realised she was clasping his arms.

"I don't know, I don't know." He was saying over and over again.

"Oh, Harry. I am so sorry. Forgive me." She pulled him back into her embrace until he stopped shivering. "Come along, let's go back to the ship and you can tell me all about it." Emma's eyes stung with grateful tears as she put a steadying hand beneath Harry's arm and guided him towards The Cassandra.

*

"There was an English man at the goal. I couldn't see who he was but he was a proper gent, all dressed posh. He talked to the guards then he went away. Right after that they came and unlocked me and told me to go home," Harry told her, once he had calmed down.

The boy had been in such a state that she had fetched a fresh bowl of water and gently washed him until the filth of the gaol was quite gone. She hoped to cleanse his mind as much as his body and it seemed to have worked a little. Emma tried not to cry at the bruises and cuts. The wounds would clean but no amount of washing could hide the dark rings under his eyes and the greyness of his pallor. As she helped him on with a clean shirt Lucy popped her head into their bunk.

"Alfie just told me. He saw you coming aboard." She stopped short. Emma tried not to notice the pity in her friend's eyes as she took in the deep welts on her son's back.

"A belt?" Emma mouthed. Lucy nodded and forced a trembling smile.

"I also came to hasten you. Inspector Mendoza is up on deck. He's talking with the captain."

Emma couldn't breathe. The restraints of her undergarments were suddenly strangling her. She pulled out her fan and wafted as hard as she could, but it was all too much and she felt the room begin to darken. An arm wrapped around her waist and helped her onto the bed. Emma bent forwards and rested her hot forehead in her cool hands.

"Breathe slowly, Em. That's right."

The room brightened again and Emma felt her body begin to cool.

"What's the matter, Mam? Are you ill?" Harry laid a hand on her arm. She looked up at him and smiled.

"No, Harry, Mam just got hot and bothered and she fastened her clothes too tight this morning, that's all."

Lucy lowered her eyes with a suppressed smile, leaned in and whispered,

"See, I told ya it were too hot to wear that damn corset. Ya should do what I've been doing and go wivout."

Emma was all astonishment.

"You're not wearing? But I could never tell... you have a better figure than me."

"I doubt that. But now we've lightened the moment, we'd better get up top and face the inspector."

*

Minutes later they were on the upper deck and all around them people had gathered to watch the spectacle. Emma's eyes roamed over the faces until one made her stop and halted her heart. Mr Finch was there, watching her with his intense gaze. His lips quivered into something resembling a smile, then he gave her a nod and turned to walk away. But what astonished her was the conduct of the captain. He was a kind man, that she already knew, but his abrupt manner in speaking with the inspector heightened her respect for him. The moment the conversation ended Inspector Mendoza was striding towards her. She looked at his face, smooth bronze skin shadowed by dark stubble. He stopped before her, towering over her with a tight expression on his face. She shifted her stance and prayed she didn't look guilty of anything.

Harry crept in close to her side. He sniffed and wiped his nose on the back of his sleeve. Emma whispered to him to use his handkerchief but he said he couldn't find it. Lucy rummaged in her coat pocket and extracted a ragged bit of greying cloth, frayed around the edges and embroidered with initials. Harry blew his nose loudly just as the Inspector cleared his throat. Emma cringed and held her breath.

"Harry is a lucky boy, Mrs Burnez. You have very well connected friends."

Emma wanted to ask to whom he could possibly be referring, but before she could, he added,

"Now, keep you and your family out of trouble and we shall remain friends."

Emma could have hit him. She gave him her iciest smile.

"The ship is almost ready, sir; we shall be gone by Friday," she offered.

"So your captain says."

With that Inspector Mendoza clipped his heels together and bowed in a manner Emma imagined was reminiscent of a Roman soldier, and turned away from her. As she watched him disembark she prayed she would never have to lay eyes upon him again.

Day Fifty-One

Clouds were gathering lazily across the sky and the ship swayed gently in its mooring. Emma stood on dockside looking up at The Cassandra's red-haired figurehead considering if the beautiful face was based on a real woman, when a group of sailors bustled past her, chattering with excitement as they scurried up the gangplank. This was the last morning they would see dry land for some weeks and Emma was not sure she was entirely happy about it. She hadn't realised just how claustrophobic she had been on board until she was faced with it once more. She watched as a handful of new sheep were herded aboard and wondered how well they would fare once the waves were beneath them.

Gloria came skipping up to her mother and wrapped her arms around her waist.

"Will we see Pa soon?"

Emma sighed and looked down at her daughters round hazel eyes.

"Not for a while yet."

It puzzled Emma as to why the only one of her children to have never met her father was the one who was most looking forward to seeing him, not that Bert remembered him either. Perhaps it was curiosity. Footsteps, growing closer. It was a man she barely knew and yet without even turning to look, she recognised his gait as though she had known him all her life. They had not seen Mr Finch at all since the day of Harry's release. She had supposed that he hadn't been living aboard. For the past few nights Emma had found herself, not dreaming of Jack or of seeing Jacob again, but lying awake, sensing the empty space on the ship that Mr Finch usually occupied. She wanted to ask him where he had been staying but it was none of her business. If he could afford a hotel room then why should he not take one? Though it did pose the further question as to why, if he had such finances, was he travelling in a shared cabin in second class? She had asked Lucy this very question since she was always up to date with gossip and information, but for once Lucy had been at a loss to explain. Emma felt his presence intensify as the footsteps stopped at her side. She didn't turn to look; she couldn't trust herself not to blush.

"You are all well I hope, Mrs Burns?"

Emma swallowed to moisten her throat.

"Yes, sir, very well thank you."

"And young Harry is recovered from his ordeal?"

She risked a sideways glance and found he was looking right at her. Her heart fluttered. She folded her arms annoyed at herself for being so silly about a gentleman she had no right to think about.

"He was rather shaken by it all, but I think, in the end, it did him a bit of good," she replied as calmly as she could manage.

From the corner of her eyes, she saw Mr Finch was nodding thoughtfully.

"I gave him a penny to fetch us a cake, I thought it would be a nice last treat for the children before we get out to sea again," she added when she realised Mr Finch was looking around for the boy.

The teacher shifted his stance so that they stood face to face.

"Very good notion indeed, Mrs Burns, I should have thought of that myself. We shall be at sea for quite some time again before we reach The Cape."

Emma forced herself to meet his gaze. The kindness she found in his face made her weak at the knees. All she could do was look into those eyes. Mr Finch took off his hat and ran a hand through his dark hair and a tinge of pink flushed in his cheeks.

"Lessons begin again tomorrow after breakfast, I trust your children wish to continue?" He stammered.

Emma opened her mouth but couldn't make the words reach her lips. In the end, she just nodded.

*

The sun had plunged deep into the horizon and left a cloudy sky so black it seemed to suck them in. Many of the passengers had decided to eat supper on the upper deck to celebrate their onwards journey. Lanterns swung and creaked with the ships calm roll. Greasy smells and hot steam were coming from the crew's galley. Sailors were settled amidst the passengers chatting and singing. Emma rested her back against the bosun's cabin wall and looked up at the darkness. Lucy leaned forwards and sunk a knife through the lemon sponge, dividing it into equal slices. She handed a piece to Emma.

A collective 'oooh' was coming from the port side of the deck. Emma broke from her thoughts and glanced over her shoulder. Gloria tugged at her arm.

"Mam, Mr Finch is telling a ghost story, can we go listen, please?"

"Of course, go on, all of you."

Lucy rose too. She wrapped the knife in a rag, shoved it in her petticoat pocket and wiped her hands together. She stopped and looked at Emma, who hadn't moved.

"Ain't ya coming?"

"I can hear just fine from here." Emma didn't feel like seeing Mr Finch. The attraction to him was beginning to bother her.

Lucy put her hands on her hips and gave her a puzzled frown.

"Come on, not afraid of a ghost story are ya?" Lucy offered her a hand up.

"What about all this?" Emma gestured at the dirty crockery. Lucy gathered up the tin plates and placed them by the bosun's cabin wall.

"They'll be here when we gets back."

Reluctantly Emma rose and followed Lucy and the children around the side of the cabin to where Mr Finch and an excitable crowd of people were gathering. Almost instantly Emma became transfixed. The story was engrossing but it was his voice and those eyes flashing in the flickering light of an oil lamp that drew her in. She watched his animation, the gestures; she listened to his emphatic and expressive tones as the tale went on. Slowly Emma became aware of someone watching her. She glanced at Lucy.

"What?" she hissed quietly. Lucy was shaking her head, her eyes glittering with amusement.

"You like him," she hissed back.

Emma was horrified. She tried to deny it but the more she attempted to protest the more ridiculous she knew she sounded.

"Of course I don't, well, I mean, he's a very nice man, but what makes you think I would be attracted to..."

Lucy's lips curled into a wide smile.

"I told ya you was missing it didn't I."

Emma gasped and nudged her friend in the arm.

"I would never..."

But Lucy was laughing now.

"I know ya wouldn't, but that don't mean ya can't look now do it?"

*

Eyelids flickering and her mind racing. Emma turned in her sleep. The dream was pleasant and one that would be repeated: Blue eyes and dark hair, a tall frame and a calming voice. In her mind, she reached up to him. Her fingers traced the line of his cheek as he slowly leaned down to her until their lips met.

She sat upright with a start and tried to picture Jacob. When the image wouldn't come she tried to imagine what sort of man Lucy Matthews had married instead. Was he a tough Irish East-ender, or just a victim of circumstance?

21

Flemington, Australia
February 6th 1857

The woman giggled as Jacob shifted his legs beneath her. He took his hand from her waist and pushed another coin into the pile in the centre of the table. She leaned close and whispered in his ear but he wasn't listening. She wriggled in his lap and for a moment he was distracted. But the cards were against him and he had to keep focused.

"Go get yourself another drink," he said and pushed her off. She grumbled but swaggered off in the direction of the hotel bar.

Outside the sun was beginning to rise. Jacob stifled a yawn and studied the look on his opponent's faces. There were still three of them in and no one was budging. Jacob looked at his pair of kings and considered throwing in. This was his second bluff of the night and he couldn't afford to lose again. He scratched his head and hoped his face was blank enough. He had to push these two to breaking point. Mac put another whisky double next to him on the table. He glanced over for Lizzy but she had found a girlfriend to talk with at the bar. He let his eyes wander over her figure for a minute before looking back at the table. The man opposite raised the stake and placed a note on the pile of cash. Jacob gritted his teeth and dug in his pocket. It was empty. Shit. He looked back at Lizzy and beckoned her over. She saw him eyeing her cleavage and shook her breasts at him. But he wasn't looking at them.

"Lend me your brooch lass?" He said with a hand wandering over the back of her skirts.

She paused. The look in her eyes reminded him of Emma the day he had been arrested. He held out his hand and she conceded. As she unpinned the only pretty bauble she owned he realised he didn't have the heart to take it. Shit. With an irritated sigh, he threw his cards on the table. Lizzy looked relieved as she refastened the pin and Jacob had to hide that his hands were shaking as walked away from the game.

22

Day Fifty-Nine

Emma lay in her bunk and listened to the incessant coughing. They were directly below the hospital room and the stench of sickness was beginning to seep down through the floorboards. They had feared this from day one, and when it had arrived it was in the form of the measles, contracted on land and brought on board by a small child. It wasn't his fault but he had endangered them all. They hadn't known about it until three days ago, no sign, no symptoms, but now there were two cases more and no doubt many more to follow. The poor child above coughed and coughed until it had no breath left. Emma could hear someone whispering to it.

"Sweet Jesus, don't let this evil thing get to mine," she whispered under her breath as the coughing began again.

*

Day Sixty-One

A fretting sea had given the air a pleasant chill. Masts vanished into the misty heavens and the new sails flapped invisibly, clunking against the wood. The hull creaked and groaned beneath them as the ship drifted blindly onwards. Emma stood on the deck with Lucy, peering out to sea through the swirling grey. She held her arm over the side and watched her hand disappear.

"I've seen some foggy days in London, but this is creepier than the lot of 'em put together." The mist caught Lucy's voice and extinguished the sound the moment it was out of her mouth. Emma let the damp air prickle her arm.

"If there's anything out there we shall never see it until too late," she said. "I'm not even sure it's still daylight." Emma shuddered.

"Fingers crossed there ain't no steamers nearby today," Lucy replied jovially. She looked at Emma then narrowed her eyes. "Oh, ya mean sea monsters, rising through the mists. Pa told me all kinds of stories from his time in the navy. He saw some sights on days like this I can tell ya." Lucy wore an expression so serious Emma almost believed her, but then Lucy's freckle smattered face broke into a teasing grin. Emma nudged her in good humour.

"No sea monsters then?"

Lucy laughed,

"You was thinking of Mr Finch,"

Emma blushed.

"I was remembering his story."

Lucy threw her head back and laughed.

"If it hadn't been him telling it ya would have forgotten all about it."

Emma chose to ignore the insinuation and continued with the ghost theme.

"You have to admit, it's easy to imagine monsters rising from the deep through this."

"Don't think I ain't noticed how ya've been avoiding him since we left Rio."

"A great Leviathan swallowing up the ship."

Lucy took the hint and folded her arms.

"Fine, deny it all ya like." She shook her head and curled her lips into a wry smile. "Anyways, I reckons we'd better gets back to the laundry, not that it'll dry in this."

A cry from down below, a wail like someone's heart had been torn out. An invisible sailor called down from the crow's nest to see what the matter was. Emma stared up into the foggy void. She shivered as the woeful cry from below came again. People began to scurry about. Lucy grasped Emma's hand. A jagged iceberg of fear formed in Emma's gut as she realised what must have happened. One of the sick children must have died.

*

Lucy edged her friend towards the hospital room where the crying grew louder and more distraught. A woman was sobbing and fretting as much as the ocean outside. A board beneath their feet shifted and cracked. The sound seemed to echo down the corridor.

Ahead of them, the door to the hospital room clicked open. As they reached it, the dark wood swung back and the physician came out. Emma opened her mouth but the words stuck in her throat. The doctor shook his head sadly and gently closed the door behind him, shutting away the sorrowful scene.

"Esme Marx," he said, answering her unspoken question, "the measles brought on pneumonia."

"Oh, God! Poor little mite. She were only seven." Lucy wiped the tears from her eyes with the back of her hand.

"Is there anything we can do?" Emma watched the physician's expression darken. She swallowed the urge to pack up her family and row them all off in a lifeboat. He shook his head.

"Just keep a close watch on your children, Mrs...Burns, isn't it?" Emma nodded,

"Harry's had it already." She wasn't sure whether she was asking a question or making some kind of statement.

The doctor paused then offered her a comforting smile.

"Then Harry should be just fine, not many children catch it twice. Just make sure you come straight to me if you see any signs of a fever, a cough or reddened eyes." He was talking to Lucy too. "We are a long way from help and with limited comforts. Things like this can be more severe out here."

Behind the door, the crying continued. Emma had lost a child once herself. She may have only had her baby for a few hours, but she felt the pain just the same as if she had spent a lifetime with him. Her mind flashed to Jack. What had she been thinking, to drag them all away from their home and abandon her lovely eldest boy, and for what, an endless and vile journey to a strange land? Emma felt sick, and then a thought struck her. The woman had another child. They should all be together.

*

"Enter."

Though it felt inappropriate at that moment, the sound of his voice still gave Emma a shiver of pleasure. As she pushed open the door she was greeted by the sound of chalk scribbling on slate and the vision of two dozen silent children with their heads down in concentration. The room smelled minty sweet, like humbugs. It was a surprisingly pleasant aroma. For a moment she stared, for one thing, she couldn't recall the last time she had seen her children so quiet.

"Mrs Burns," Mr Finch was looking at her with curiosity.

"What a pleasant surprise, how may we help you?"

Emma realised her mouth was open but she had yet to say anything.

"Forgive the intrusion, I...We...Mrs Matthews and I..." she glanced over her shoulder and found that Lucy had not followed her into the room. She swallowed and carried on, "...came to collect Matilda Marx, her...her mother needs her company." Emma felt tears sting her eyes. Realisation clouded Mr Finch's expression.

"Ah, yes of course. Mattie, please go with Mrs Burns."

The child pushed her stool back with a grinding scrape and twirled a dusty blond ringlet around her fingers. Emma's gaze locked with Mr Finch. If she hadn't known better Emma would have sworn he was fighting back tears himself. Emma held out her hand to the child. The girl slowly walked towards her and slipped her cold clammy fingers into Emma's.

"Take care of your Ma now, Mattie." Mr Finch's voice cracked as he spoke.

With a shaking hand, he unscrewed a large sweet jar on his desk, tipped out a stripy sweet into the palm of his hand and popped it into his mouth. The action seemed automatic, then, he looked at the jar and back at Emma as though unsure whether offering her one would be quite the correct procedure under the circumstances. Emma saved him the dilemma, she bobbed a curtsey and with a chest so tight her head was light, led the little girl from the room without another word.

*

As dusk fell the sea fret wrapped a prickly damp blanket around them as the crowd gathered on deck. Mrs Marx and her remaining daughter were huddled together at the captain's side, clasping each other. The mother was all cried out. Her tears had dried and left her with a well of despair in the pit of her stomach so deep that Emma could feel it just by looking at her ashen face. Emma glanced around. Figures rose like a dark forest from the swirling mist. She couldn't make out the nervous faces but the tension in the air was sharp as a butcher's knife. She was not the only parent whose sorrow nestled awkwardly over the top of a deep-seated fear. Lucy slipped an arm through hers. Emma smiled gratefully. She looked at the children, watching for the signs. Harry was staring at his feet, the twins were twitchy and restless and Molly kept scratching at her neck. Albert was gritting his teeth and grasping Gloria's hand so hard her little fingers were white. They were not sick or nervous, they were just sad they had lost a friend. Albert was trying so hard not to cry that he was shaking. She moved to rest a hand on his shoulder but faltered, afraid the gesture would make him worse.

As the captain said a short prayer two sailors carried the corpse to the side of the ship. Esme was neatly swaddled in a grey blanket. She looked so tiny and thin. A plank stuck out from the ship like a splinter. Emma watched as the sailors placed the child's body upon it. The ship lurched and pushed it back towards them. Emma bit her lip and she heard Albert gasp. There was a shuffling of feet and someone close by cleared their throat. The sailors gave the corpse a push and it finally slid down the plank and disappeared into the dense mist. Emma breathed out in relief. A heavy splash echoed through the foggy twilight and her heart felt as though it had fallen into the ocean along with the child.

The mother's composure shattered and she let out a despairing cry. Another woman grasped at her as she ran forwards lunging over the side, calling her daughter's name. One of the sailors caught her and held her back. Emma choked in a cry and Lucy began to weep into her handkerchief.

"How are you, Mrs Burns?"

Startled Emma clapped her hand to her throat and spun around.

"Oh, Mr Finch!"

"Forgive me." His expression broke from the stony setting to one of concern. He stepped back a little, "I didn't mean to..."

Emma washed over with relief. She found it comforting to see those lovely eyes. Later she would wonder and worry about why that may be, but at that moment it was all she could do to prevent herself from falling into his arms and sobbing.

"I only wanted to see if you're all right." He swayed back on his heels and shook his head. "Such a dreadful thing when a child dies, it affects everyone, especially in such a confined situation as this." He had clasped his hands together behind his back as though restraining himself from something. Emma felt the now family urge to reach up and touch his face. Lucy edged away, dabbing her face dry and forcing a smile.

"Good evening to ya, Mr Finch. Come along children, let's go play a game and try to cheer up."

Emma was unsure whether to go with them. Mr Finch bowed at Lucy but turned back to Emma before she had a chance to make her escape.

"I'm very sorry that we have had little chance to converse since...Rio," the hesitation was one of clear deliberation. Whether he was thinking of the tea and cakes they had taken together, the dreadful moment when Harry had been arrested, or when the boy had been returned to her, she was unsure. She nodded. There was an awkward pause before he carried on.

"I am pleased everything was settled in Harry's favour." He was looking away at some distant speck in the mist. Emma watched his eyes flicker towards her and away again. She wondered if he was regretting having started the conversation.

"I think the captain made a good case for us with the Inspector," she said after another silent beat that felt like several minutes. It seemed impertinent to make any reference to the mysterious stranger that had also spoken for Harry. Mr Finch let out the tiniest exclamation; so quiet she was not entirely certain she had heard anything at all.

"I'm very glad to hear it," he said.

"Harry is a good lad really," she offered, "he just sometimes gets...distracted," *and he has a little too much of his father in him*, she added in her head. A smile crept over Mr Finch's lips and he turned to face her.

"He's just a typical twelve-year-old boy," he said with genuine conviction.

Emma narrowed her eyes. She had been convinced he had been horrified by her son's behaviour and possibly even her abilities as his mother.

"Do you really think so, Mr Finch?"

A sailor walked by and bid them good evening.

"Yes, I do," he replied when the young man was gone. "I don't think you have anything to worry about with any of your children, Mrs Burns. The boys are steady lads and Gloria is a lovely hardworking girl."

Emma was staggered, she had never doubted her daughter but not in a month of Sundays would she have believed her youngest two boys could be considered 'steady lads'. As she allowed Mr Finch to escort her back to her bunk, she thanked him at least twice for his efforts with them and had to bite her lip to stop herself from asking him to stay awhile.

23

Day Sixty-Three

Daggers of sunlight cut through the portholes piercing the dingy darkness. Emma was pacing back and forth in her bunk whilst the doctor pressed his hand on Albert's forehead for the second time. He had already examined the boy's tongue, peered down his throat, pulled down the lower lids of his eyes and searched his back and stomach for any signs of a rash. Albert was shivering yet sweat soaked his hairline and the nasty cough he had developed overnight was now racking his body to the point of vomiting. The physician gave him a gulp of water and stood back. Emma knew what was coming. She dug her knuckle into the small of her back and waited for the man to speak.

"I'm sorry, Mrs Burns, it's measles. But remember, most children recover just fine. Please try not to fret too much."

Harry came scuttling into the room with Lucy and the twins in tow. Lucy stopped in the doorway.

"Oh God, Emma, is it...?" Lucy gasped. There was no need to reply. Lucy's face was ashen as she said, "he'll be fine I'm sure of it, a little fighter like him."

But Emma was unconvinced. Albert had always been the sickly one and if any of her children were going to come down with measles, she had known it would be him. And now she was terrified that he wouldn't make it to his ninth birthday.

"You had better keep the twins away." Emma's voice cracked in her dry throat as the doctor scooped Albert into his arms.

"I'll take him up to the hospital room," he told her.

Albert lifted his head to look at her, but it was too much effort and he slumped back into the doctor's chest. Emma pressed her fingers to her lips. She desperately did not want her little boy to know just how afraid she was. Lucy stepped aside to let the doctor pass.

"Twins had it when they was two," Lucy was saying, "I'd forgot all about it. They 'ad so many things when they was little. Wiv more than a dozen kids in the 'ouse bringing stuff home, anything one got they all got, quicker than fire through a warehouse. I remember when the eldest Grogan girl..." Lucy stopped.

Emma felt she was looking at her friend through a veil and her voice was echoing around her head as though her skull were a large empty room. Suddenly she was in a tight embrace, her face pressed against Lucy's shoulder. Someone was crying. It took Emma a moment to realise that the sob came from her.

"There, there now, don't fret, Em, if my twins can pull through living in a place like we had, then your Bert will be just fine, onboard a ship or not."

Emma drew a breath and pulled herself together. She stepped away from Lucy and smoothed down her skirt.

"Forgive me." She cleared her throat, "I don't know what came over me." Emma felt her cheeks burning hot as a stove; it wasn't like her to crumble.

Lucy seemed to read her mind.

"Any mother would be just the same, I know I would."

Harry was sitting on the bottom bunk with Gloria huddled in close at his side, both watching her with a wary expression.

"It's all going to be all right." Emma reached out a hand. But, to her surprise, it was Harry who reached out and took it.

"Shall we go sit with Bert, Mam?"

Emma nodded and asked Lucy to look after Gloria for a bit. Harry stood and led Emma past the other bunks towards the hatch to the upper deck. People looked around as they went by. She tried to ignore the sad shaking of heads and uneasy smiles.

*

Day Sixty-Five

The room was filled with coughing and the sickly stench of illness. Emma felt her eyes close and head droop and for a minute there was silence. She jerked awake and rubbed her hands over her face.

Albert was sleeping, thankfully. It was the first time since they had brought him up to the now crowded hospital room that he had rested peacefully. Emma leaned forwards and gently laid the back of her hand on his forehead. She kept it there for a moment and contemplated whether his fever was a little better. Albert turned his head away and mumbled something incomprehensible. Emma straightened up in her hard wooden chair and rubbed her aching back. In the next bed lay a little girl, Amy Reynolds. She had been brought in that morning. Her face was red and her eyes puffy; she didn't seem to be coughing too much but she looked so weak Emma could have cried. Amy opened her eyes and winced. It was dark in the hospital room, measles made the eyes sensitive to light so all the portholes had been blacked out with cloth, but even the thin flicker of a candle was hurting the little girl's eyes. Emma got up and blew it out, plunging their side of the room into darkness.

Emma stood there for a moment and tried to breathe through the stuffy air. The room was not big, meant for six people at most, but somehow they had managed to squeeze in more beds until there was twice that number, so close together there was barely room for a chair between them. Eleven beds were filled now, rickety metal frames and straw mattresses wrapped in coarse blankets that itched. Most of the parents had brought up their own bedding from storage in an attempt to make their little ones more comfortable.

There was a creak at the far side of the room and the door swung open. The dim light from the corridor burst into the room, casting long shadows over the floorboards making the beds look like gravestones. Albert groaned and another child cried out. For a brief moment, the frame of a man was silhouetted in the doorway, and then the door closed behind him. Emma assumed it was the doctor and turned her attentions back to Albert.

Footsteps clunked lightly and stopped by the first bed. There was a hushed conversation between the man and the patient's mother; then the steps began again to the next bed and then the next in turn. Emma and Albert were at the other side of the room in the far corner. Albert stirred as the man drew closer. She took her son's hand and squeezed his cold fingers.

The man was close now and his voice was audible. With surprise, Emma swung around as she realised this was not the doctor but Mr Finch. She was not sure why she should be so astonished to find him visiting; most of these children were his students after all. Feeling heat rise in her cheeks and her heart flutter beneath the constraints of her corset, Emma was glad of the darkness. She closed her eyes for a second and inwardly chastised herself for allowing such desires to bother her, especially at such a time as this. Yet no matter how much she didn't want to, she couldn't prevent it. Perhaps it was precisely this situation that was the cause, she needed comfort and Mr Finch was a kind and understanding gentleman. It was surely only natural for her to feel warmed by his presence. Emma was telling this to herself as she heard the squeak of his heel on the floorboard. Emma breathed out slowly. As he took the two steps to the foot of Albert's bed she turned to face the teacher.

"Mr Finch, it's very good of you to visit."

There was a pause and Emma wished she could make out his expression through the darkness.

"Mrs Burns. How is Albert? We do all miss him in class."

Emma swallowed,

"He seems a little better today, thank you."

There was a sigh of relief.

"That is very good to hear, very good indeed."

"I don't want to presume he is getting better just yet though, sir. The doctor says there can be good days and bad."

Mr Finch shifted his stance a little. He was close enough for Emma to take his hand. Instead, she grasped Albert's fingers tighter. Albert flinched and she realised she was gripping too hard.

"Of course not, Mrs Burns, but I am sure Albert is going to be just fine." Mr Finch's voice was so calm and convincing Emma could have believed anything he told her. The ship swayed to starboard and he was forced to step sideways so that his legs were right by Emma's side. She closed her eyes and tried not to imagine touching him.

"Gosh, they weren't kidding when they said these roaring forties would push us along," she said in an attempt to distract herself. She forced a laugh. They had hit the infamous air current yesterday.

"Indeed. The captain thinks we could be in The Cape of Good Hope in less than ten days if the wind keeps as it is."

Emma thought she could see a glimmer of a smile on Mr Finch's lips. He stepped away from her and sat down on the bed next to Albert.

"Did you hear that, son? We shall be at The Cape very soon and you will be outside on dry land playing again."

Son? Emma had not heard a man refer to any of her boys as such for so many years it made her heart ache. A ball of guilt gathered in her gut as she thought of Jacob, eagerly awaiting their arrival. She looked at Albert's pasty little face, straining to see his teacher. She must put these silly fancies aside and concentrate on their new life.

"Really, Mam?" Now he definitely looked a bit perkier.

Emma smiled and raised Albert's fingers to her lips.

"That's what the sailors are saying and Mrs Matthews too, and you know how clever Mrs Matthews is with..."

The door to the room slammed open and a figure staggered in, a child in their arms. Emma watched, pitying the mother that clung to her sick child, knowing how she felt as Mr Finch rushed to her aid. The teacher gathered up the little girl into his arms and set her down in the last free bed by the door. It was only when the woman thanked him and sank to her knees that she realised it was Lucy Matthews. Emma was at her friend's side before she had time to put another thought together in her head.

"Oh, my dear, not Molly? But I thought she'd had it?"

Lucy was crying into her petticoat and gasping for breath. She must have carried the child up from the laundry room where the girls were helping out in Emma's absence. Lucy shook her head.

"Oh, Emma, I'm so sorry, she just passed out. I thought it were the heat, but then I saw the rash."

Emma's blood went cold. She straightened up and went to the bed where Mr Finch was settling the unconscious child.

"I'll fetch the doctor immediately," Mr Finch didn't meet her eyes as he stepped aside for her to see the child.

Emma was not afraid, or worried, or panicked, there was no horror or desperation, just icy numbness reaching from the tip of her head to her toes. Even the pain in her back was gone. She just stood there, watching, looking down at her little girl.

Lucy began to unlace Gloria's boots, easing them from her feet.

Mr Finch returned with the doctor, his small leather bag of instruments in one hand and an oil lamp in the other. He handed Mr Finch the lamp and said something to him. Emma didn't hear. The room glowed orange, light dancing over the bed and the child in it. Gloria didn't move.

The doctor walked around the bed, checking the child, shaking his head. Still, Gloria didn't move.

In the adjacent bed, a boy was coughing violently, his father trying to soothe him. Somewhere else in the room another child was whimpering, no doubt the light was hurting his eyes, and Amy Reynolds was calling out for her Ma. Gloria was still.

"Gloria never gets sick," Emma heard herself say.

The doctor stopped and looked at her. Emma waited whilst he formed his sentence.

"I am afraid it is measles, Mrs Burns, and it has taken quite a hold. Your daughter has a light frame and conditions aboard ship are never the best...the food unvaried..." Emma sank on to the bed and rested a hand on her daughter's bare feet. "But as you say, she has a strong constitution. Try to stay positive. Try to make her eat and get as much water into her as possible. I'll fetch her some tonic."

"Mam?" Albert called.

Emma looked over at where Albert was lying across the way, in the dark, neglected. She raised her shaking hands and placed her face in them. A hand rested on her shoulder. She looked up expecting to see Lucy; instead, it was Mr Finch. His eyes were brighter than ever, glimmering golden turquoise in the lamplight. He held her gaze, and through the pity, she was sure she could see the same longing for her as she felt for him. She stood so quickly he was forced to stumble back.

"Forgive me. My son is calling," was all she could manage to say.

"Of course. Mrs Matthews and I will stay with Gloria whilst you tend to him."

Suddenly Emma didn't want him to stay at all. She wanted to be back in her little cottage, smoke billowing from the chimney and kettle whistling on the stove, having never laid eyes upon Mr Finch. All she wanted was for Jack to come home from work and put his boots by the back door and take the laundry tub out to the garden to be emptied.

"You have been kind enough already, Mr Finch, it must be time for your class to begin, please don't trouble yourself here when you're needed elsewhere. Mrs Matthews and I can manage."

A flicker of hurt cut across the teacher's face but no sooner had it come than it was gone again. He gave her a polite nod and said,

"Then if I am no longer of use here, I shall bid you good day. Ladies, Doctor Morten."

Emma's heart dropped into the pit of her stomach. Amidst everything else, she had offended the kindest man of her acquaintance.

24

Day Sixty-Six

The stale air was dry as sandpaper. A cold compress was pressed to the child's head to bring down the fever, yet still, it burned. Emma rolled her shoulders and rubbed at her back. It had been the longest night she had ever endured, longer even than the night she had given birth to her poor lost boy and watched him slowly fade away in her arms. Gloria twitched a little and Emma stared and hoped, but the child sank back into a deep slumber, not moving, nor dreaming. Emma sighed and glanced over her shoulder to where Albert was settled. The candle flickered on his side of the room brightening a small circle of light over the side of his face. She realised he was awake. He was watching her. He raised a weak arm and waved.

"Bertie," she breathed as she rose and made her way over to his side.

"Gloria still bad?" he croaked.

Emma waited for him to cough but he didn't. She nodded sadly. "Yes, love."

"Will she be all right?"

Emma wished she dared reassure him, but she couldn't lie to him.

"I don't know," she admitted. "She's very sick. But you are feeling better?" She felt his forehead and found it cool as a healthy boy should be. She gasped in relief.

"I don't feel funny anymore, just sleepy."

Emma smiled through her tears.

"Then better get some sleep lad, you'll be better quicker for a good rest."

*

Day Sixty-Seven

Joy and despair crashed around Emma's chest as though she had a bull behind her ribcage. On one side of the room, she had one child laughing brightly with the little girl in the next bed. At the other side of the room, she had another child burning with fever, still and unconscious, just as she had been for the last two days. Emma didn't know how she was supposed to feel.

Albert and Amy were not the only children to be feeling better. One child had even been sent back to his family that morning, leaving an empty bed. The door creaked open and Emma looked around.

"Oh, Harry!" She was so glad to see him that she grabbed his arm the moment he was close enough and pulled him onto her lap.

"Mam! I'm too old for that."

She looked at him with a playful expression.

"You're not too big to give your Mam a hug now are you?"

Harry struggled free, but not before she planted a kiss on his cheek.

"Mrs Matthews sent me to fetch you away," he said wiping his face where Emma's lips had left a deliberately sloppy mark. "She said you need some fresh air."

It was true; Emma hadn't left the sickbay in almost two days. How could she?

"Tell Lucy, thank you, but I'm fine just now. I need to stay with your brother and sister."

"I'm all right, Mam," Albert called cheerily.

"Bert! You're alive then!" Harry grinned.

"Can't kill me off that easy," Albert said before sticking out his tongue at his elder brother. Amy Reynolds giggled and Harry bounded over and flopped down on his brother's bed with such gusto that Albert nearly bounced off.

"Careful, Harry, your brother isn't fully recovered. And keep it down. There are still sick children in here who don't want loud boisterous monsters like you two waking them up," Emma hissed. Amy giggled again. Emma fancied that Albert was going to turn into rather a lady's man in another few years.

"Your boy's right, Mrs Burns, you ought to take a walk outside, just for a few minutes. The fresh air will do you good."

Emma turned to Mrs Jackson, perched by the next bed.

"I'll keep an eye on Gloria for you, and that lot," she gestured with her chin at Albert and Harry. Just for a few minutes," she urged.

Emma looked at her neighbour's tired face, dark bags hung below her eyes like pouches of tea and her shoulders were slumped forward with the weight of the world on them. Mrs Jackson's daughter was as sick as Gloria. Emma presumed she must look just as haggard.

"Very well then, but only for a minute or two. Then maybe you would like a few minutes?"

Mrs Jackson tried to smile.

*

Bright sunlight pierced her eyes and cool air burst into her lungs as though she had never breathed before. Emma blinked up at the hazy sky and drew a long deep breath. Far on the distant horizon, a black spot bobbed over the waves. Emma squinted and tried to see what it was.

"Frigate." Archer, the sailmaker put down the sheet of fabric he was darning and shielded his eyes to look at her.

"Good lord, how can you tell from here?" Emma squinted harder. She could just about see that there were masts and not steam pipes.

"The shape. Been at sea since I was thirteen, Mrs Burns. Seen everything that's out there a hundred times or more."

Emma liked the lyrical lilt of Archer's welsh twang.

"How are young Albert and that lovely little girl of yours? They've got the sickness I heard."

"Albert's doing very well thank you, back on his feet in no time I should say, but Gloria is still..." Emma bit her lip.

"I'm very sorry to hear that, but she's a tough little thing. I expect she'll be getting better soon enough."

Emma rubbed her arms as though she was cold, but the day was warm and the sun was making her face tingle. Archer retrieved his torn sail and set back to work.

"Mam, Mam!"

Startled Emma spun around to see an ashen Harry hurtling towards her.

"Mam, come quick!"

She didn't stop to ask why or what; she hoisted the hem of her skirts over her ankles and ran. Her chest was so tight she could barely think, and the boning of her corset was digging into her ribs harder than a knife. Harry was down the hatch and running along the corridor so fast Emma couldn't catch him. Oh, God! Her mind could form no other thought than the image of her poor little girl dead and gone in her bed, passing away without her mother at her side to comfort her. Emma paused to catch her breath, resting her hand against the wall and gasping for air.

"Mam, hurry!"

Emma reached the hospital room door. Suddenly afraid to look, she slowly pushed it open to reveal the physician and a priest standing at the foot of Gloria's bed, heads bent as though in prayer. Emma forced her feet onwards and entered the room. Doctor Morten shifted his stance in the dim light to reveal Mrs Jackson lifting Gloria's head so she could take a sip of water. Dizzy with relief Emma sank onto the bed next to her child and cried.

25

Day Seventy-Two

The doctor pulled out the last tack from the dark drapes and let the light stream through into the sickbay. Emma sighed and looked down at Gloria. She was still paler than milk but her fever was gone and she had a smile on her face. She blinked and rubbed her eyes.

"Is it too bright? Shall we put them back?" Emma was anxious.

"No, Mam, just have an eyelash."

"Oh, shall I get it out for you?"

Gloria shook her head.

"It's gone now."

Emma looked around the room at the row of empty beds. There were nine stripped and cleaned spaces. The metal frames of the beds had been emptied and mattresses removed to be burned. They were taking no chances of anything coming back. Emma looked at the bed where Esme Marx had been and considered just how lucky Gloria had been. The little girl yawned and stretched her skinny arms.

"Can I get up tomorrow?"

"Yes, Miss Gloria, I think you can. Just for an hour or so though, not too much just yet," Doctor Morten replied as he came towards them. The smile on his face was warm and all the worry seemed to have dropped away in the last twenty-four hours. Only three children remained now, and in another few days they should be in South Africa and all the children would be well enough to disembark. Emma prayed there were no more horrors awaiting them in this next new country. Brazil had been a disaster in so many ways that the anticipation of Cape Town was beginning to make Emma nervous.

*

Day Seventy-Five

The temperature rising and the day felt endless and hot. Emma pushed open the porthole to let some much-needed air into the sickbay. Another child had been dismissed that morning and now only two remained. Gloria bounced on the bed then looked sheepish, she most certainly did not want to jeopardise her temporary release.

"Now don't get too excited. This isn't permanent just yet. And when it is I don't want to see you back in here for the rest of this voyage." The doctor ruffled Gloria's hair, rose to his feet and offered to hand her up. The child accepted with the grace of a proper lady and even curtseyed when she stepped off the bed. Emma laughed.

"Who taught you to do that?"

Gloria grinned at her mother.

"Molly did, she said all ladies should curtsey."

"Well, you had better turn out to be a lady then."

Upstairs children were laughing. Gloria looked up eagerly. Emma took her daughter's hand and assisted her out of the room and up through the hatch.

Once up top Emma could see just how drawn her little girl looked. She smiled at the child and prayed this was the one and only time she would ever have to consider her so fragile. Gloria raised her face to the sun and held out her arms.

"It's so warm."

"We're getting closer to land," Emma replied.

"Really? To Africa? What will it be like, will it be hot and will the men be savages, black as coal and eyes white as pearls?" Gloria twirled around and around.

"Who told you that?"

"Molly and Alfie. They said they had seen men from the Dark Continent in London and they were just like those ones we saw on that ship in Rio." Gloria stopped spinning and found her legs were

117

wobbly. Emma asked Archer if Gloria could rest on his stool for a minute.

"But are the people savages?" she asked again after a moments rest.

Emma scratched the back of her head and formed a reply.

"Well, South Africa is a bit different; there are white men too there. But whatever the colour of their skin I don't think we should think of them as savages."

Gloria cocked her head with curiosity.

"What were those men doing on that ship in Rio? Alfie said that white men like us had captured them and took them to work on farms in hot countries away from their wives and children. That's not true is it?"

Emma sighed.

"Alfie and Molly are just full of stories now aren't they?" Emma was wondering how to continue with the conversation when Harry and Albert came barrelling around the side of bosun's cabin and almost knocked her over.

"Glo!" You're up. Bluddy 'ell you look terrible."

"Harry!" Emma clipped him around the ears a little too hard.

"Ouch! Mam!" He clapped his hand over his ear and glared, but the look he received from Emma made him shrink. "Sorry, Mam," he offered with something resembling actual remorse.

"All right lad, just don't ever let me hear you use language like that."

"Mr Finch!"

Emma froze. All thoughts of slaves and bad language were wiped from her mind, and all Emma could think of was what a dreadful mess she must look after near a week below deck worrying to death. Without turning around she smoothed over her skirts and tried to form a greeting in her head before she just babbled incoherently. She looked up and realised that Archer was watching her with a raised eyebrow and an amused smirk creeping across his lips. She shot him a warning glare. The sailor took the gentlemanly hint and returned to his work.

"How good it is to see you up and about again, Miss Burns," Mr Finch bowed to Gloria who grinned broadly and nodded her head in acknowledgement.

"Thanks, Sir. I reckon I'll be back in class again tomorrow."

Emma took a moment then turned to face him.

"Let's not get ahead of ourselves child," she said, surprised at how calm her voice sounded, "Doctor Morten only said you could come out for a few minutes today. I expect it will be another day or two before you can return to lessons." She shifted her stance uncomfortably.

The teacher doffed his hat and extended his greetings to her and the boys. As he shook Harry's hand, Emma realised he was looking right at her. Instinctively her hand fluttered at her neck and scratched nervously where her frock collar met with her skin. What on earth was the matter with her? She tried to regulate her breathing and suggested that Gloria had perhaps had enough frivolity for one day and that it was time they go back to the hospital room.

"Of course, Mrs Burns, I shall let you alone to get on with your day." With that Mr Finch turned about and headed back in the direction from which he had come, leaving Emma staring after him with a fluttering heart and her stomach doing little somersaults. She had the terrible urge to run after him and begged him to kiss her.

"Urgh!" She grumbled under her breath. Harry shot her a glance as though he had heard. She decided to pretend not to notice and told the boys to go play before he could question her.

"Do I have to go back yet?" Gloria screwed up her face as Emma took her hand.

"'Fraid so love. More tomorrow." Gloria looked up at her as they made their way back to the hatch.

"So, why do white men do horrid things to black men?"

Emma stopped. She had hoped that conversation had been forgot. With a deep sigh, she said,

"Some bad men do, but not people like us..." Unable to think of an appropriate explanation or anything else aside from her ridiculous desire for Mr Finch, she suggested Gloria ask her teacher to explain when she returned to class. Mr Finch, she was certain, would be a far better job than she.

26

Day Seventy-Eight

Waves crashed against the jagged cliffs. A moist green carpet of grass coated the dark grey rocks below and white sand shimmered in the midday sun. Ever since they had passed Cape Point everyone had been desperate to disembark. Even the crew seemed glad of the forthcoming respite. There was such a sense of relief. The measles was over and Australia was beginning to feel within reach. Emma stood on deck with Lucy and their children and breathed in the scent of fresh vegetation.

"What date is today, Mam?" Albert.

Emma had to think for a minute.

"Six and twentieth day of February, the Year of Our Lord eighteen hundred and fifty-seven, Mam." Archer, the sailmaker was looking up at the rigging as the last of the sails were lowered and detached. "I shall have a bit of work to do all right before we set out again." He grinned at Albert to reveal a gold front tooth that glinted in the sunlight. Albert stopped fidgeting and grinned back. He was fascinated with the idea of a gold tooth and no matter how many times Emma said he was better off with his own teeth, Albert still wanted a gold one.

"That means we leave again on March first," Harry proudly stated.

Archer smiled.

"That's right."

"What happened to February 29th?" Gloria asked innocently.

Alfie Matthews sniggered and Lucy gave him a firm shove in the back.

"There ain't no February twenty-ninth, silly," he hissed.

"There was last year, coz it was a leap year," Molly replied. "But that's only every four years, Glo."

This time everyone else sniggered. Molly puffed up her chest.

"Ain't that right, mister?"

An excited child scuttled past pointing at the shore and dragging his long-suffering mother breathlessly behind him. Emma smiled contentedly. They were so near to shore that she could already feel the cobbles of a town street beneath her feet. Three whole days of freedom ahead!

"Yes, that's right, Miss."

Alfie folded his arms and sulked.

Flemington, Australia
February 26th 1857

Hooves drummed faster and faster on the dry grass. Hot steaming bodies hurtled past in a blur of legs. The crowd hollered louder and louder. One man, tall with slumped shoulders and tired eyes was yelling louder than the rest. The betting slip in his hand was crumpled from the tightness of his grasp.

Beside him, two gents were yelling for a different horse. A nose crossed the line. Jacob screwed up the betting slip and threw it to the ground with a disgruntled snort. The gents at his side whooped with joy as the first place was chalked on the board by the finishing line. He glowered at them. They looked like migrants rather than convicts, but who could tell these days. He shoved past them and abandoned the track. He had things he ought to be doing anyway.

Cape Town, South Africa

Day Seventy-Nine

The fragrant scent of fruits and spices masked the faint hum of human sweat. Bright flowers were gathered in baskets and a kaleidoscope of dyed fabrics hanging over the stalls to shade vendors from the sun. Emma watched as a young girl examined the bulging ripe fruit on the grocer's stall. She was fascinated. She had seen the occasional person of colour in Rio, usually a labourer on the dockside or those poor men on the slave ship when they had first arrived, but here they were everywhere. There were not many white folks in the market place, mostly just those who worked for them. At first, Emma had felt intimidated but now she was beginning to relax. Lucy had informed her that there was no slavery in South Africa anymore, yet for every white person, there seemed to be a black maid or black man working for them, buying their groceries or running their errands. This girl had the appearance of a maid of some sort. She wore a western-style dress with an apron tied about her waist and her thick dark hair was scraped back into a ball on the back of her head so tight and neat that Emma wished she could get Gloria's curls to look so controlled. Emma had the compulsion to reach out and touch her hair, just to know whether it felt coarse or soft. As Emma watched her weave between stalls and disappear into the market-day crowds she thought back to the conversation she'd had with Gloria about slavery and savages a few days earlier, and wondered what her children made of this place.

Today all the children from The Cassandra had been marched en masse to a service at a local church by one of the chaplains and Emma and Lucy had been given an hour or two to themselves. They were perched on a small wooden bench at the far side of the market place.

"Good God, Emma, how ain't ya dripping wet? It's hotter than hell when the furnace is on full blast." Lucy said with a line of juice trickling down her chin and a mouthful of soft orange coloured flesh. "This is delicious," she slurped.

Emma laughed and sniffed at the fruit they had purchased from a nearby stall. It smelled fresh and sweet and extremely appealing. As she took a bite and let the mouth-watering flavour fill her senses she closed her eyes and began to imagine what Australia would be like. She had not been able to picture anything tangible before. The animals Jacob had described seemed fanciful and impossible and the ebony-skinned natives with their untamed hair and wild eyes had been inconceivable, but now, after Rio and being here in South Africa, she could finally envisage life on a little farm in a small town, where the air is fresh and the sun warmed their skin every day.

"Penny for 'em?"

Emma opened her eyes.

"I was just thinking that maybe this wasn't such a bad idea after all. That maybe Australia might be a good place and the opportunities Jacob kept talking about might actually be real."

Lucy swallowed her last bite of mango and wiped her mouth with the end of her sleeve.

"Ya mean ya came all this way and weren't sure it was what ya wanted?"

Emma shrugged.

"Were you sure?"

"Course I was. What could be worse than the squalor of an East End slum?"

Emma looked at Lucy's bright eyes and the lines of age that were beyond her years surrounding them and tried to imagine how tough her life must have been. Emma's life had been one of difficulty and hard work but she knew it had not been bad compared to some. She wondered what sort of a woman Lucy would have been, had fate taken her down a more affluent and educated path. Not that Lucy ever seemed to mind her lot.

"Leaving Jack was the hardest thing. I still don't know if it was right. My lovely boy, all the way at the other side of the world and all alone." Emma felt the familiar stab of guilt rise in her gut. She shoved it back down her throat with a bite of fruit.

"But you do think ya've done the right thing for the rest of ya, don't ya?"

Emma licked clean her lips and folded the remaining fruit skin over to hide the sticky mess that remained.

"I suppose I must."

"Well, we'll know for sure in five or six weeks when we gets there. Not long now 'til you and Jacob will be back together, and my Alf can have his way with me again." Lucy teased as she took their mango skins, wrapped them in a rag and slipped it in the battered old bag she carried everywhere when they were on land. "So ya better get on with it if you're going to have a fling with Mr Finch."

Emma choked on her spittle.

"Lucy Matthews you are incorrigible. I've told you before; I have no desire to do anything of the sort, with Mr Finch or any other man. I'm a married woman."

Lucy was grinning with a relentless teasing glint in her eyes.

"Suit yourself, Mrs Burns, but a woman has needs and you ain't no exception. And if ya don't believe you're attracted to that man, you're deluded."

"Of course, I see that he's handsome. I would have to be blind not to notice that. But please, let's end this topic, there's nothing between us nor can there ever be."

Lucy narrowed her eyes mischievously but did as she was asked and changed the subject. Emma was grateful to be discussing the morrow's laundry list when Lucy said,

"Mr Finch!"

Emma folded her arms in irritation.

"Lucy, please, I asked you not to discuss him anymore."

Lucy, however, nudged her in the ribs.

"Nah, silly, he's over there," she nodded her head towards two stationary figures amid the moving crowd. "I wonder who the woman is? They seems to know each other."

Emma shielded her eyes. For a moment she wasn't sure it was Mr Finch, but then he turned slightly and the light fell full on his face, making his fair skin contrast starkly against the darkness of his hair and the brown skin of the woman he was conversing with. Emma tried not to stare, for the woman was stunning. Her skin was so smooth and clear, as though she had been polished and her features so perfectly set around high cheekbones. She had a beauty and elegance Emma could never hope to attain. Emma's heart sank.

"And ya ain't attracted to that man?" Lucy half laughed and half pitied. Emma pursed her lips and pretended to ignore her. But she knew the only person being fooled by her feigned indifference was herself, and even that was beginning to weaken. As she tried to think of something else to say she found her eyes wandered back in the direction of the teacher.

"She don't look like no poor coloured," Lucy observed.

Emma tried not to notice how close together the unlikely pair was standing, or that his hand reached out and rested on the woman's arm with such familiarity that Emma could only come to one conclusion. Lucy could see another.

"High-class whore," she said with a smirk. "I don't means to be rude about coloured folks but I ain't never seen one wearing such an expensive gown as that. There's only one way a woman like her can afford to dress like that, and that's by earning on her back."

Emma was shocked and horrified.

"Mr Finch would never...he just don't...doesn't," she corrected herself with irritation, "seem like the sort of man who would pay for the services of that kind of woman." Emma looked at her again. Her gown was indeed expensive; the satin alone must have cost more than Emma's entire wardrobe. Her figure was tall and slender and she carried herself with such decorum that only the colour of her skin separated her from a white society lady. "She just doesn't look like a whore," she added.

Lucy shook her head,

"No dear, the best ones don't. But what else can she be?"

"Perhaps it is possible for coloureds to be rich here?"

Lucy sniggered,

"Seriously Emma, ya really ain't seen much of the world has ya?"

Emma tried not to be offended; for one thing, Lucy was right. Her gaze drifted back towards Mr Finch. The woman leaned in close as though she couldn't quite hear something he had said. The teacher gently bent forwards and kissed her cheek. Emma pressed her fingers to her lips. Then the couple parted and Mr Finch walked away in the direction of the military hospital, leaving the woman standing there alone. She watched the man for a moment as he paused and glanced back. He gave an abrupt wave and continued. Emma returned her attentions to the woman as she tugged a handkerchief from her sleeve and dabbed her eyes. Emma realised that she was crying.

"Well, that was unexpected," said Lucy, getting to her feet and offering Emma a hand up.

Emma was still attempting to make sense of what they had witnessed. She watched as the woman slipped her handkerchief back up her sleeve and headed into the crowd. She was tall and Emma could see her for a good minute or two before she blended away.

"I must admit I wouldn't have pegged him as that type either, but what the eyes can see..."

Emma considered that Lucy's excellent observational abilities usually turned out to be right. Well, what of it? Everyone has their needs as Lucy kept telling her, but no matter how she looked at it, she just could not see Mr Finch with a whore. Nor could she imagine that elegant woman as one.

Day Eighty-One

Barrels rolled, liquid slopped and gurgled. A sailor grunted as another lost his footing and sent the wine vat skidding sideways. Something expletive was spat in the offender's direction and the lad grumbled in return. Emma watched the last of their fresh supplies disappear into the depth of the storage deck and dug her knuckle into the small of her aching back.

Somewhere on the dockside behind her she could hear Harry and Albert arguing. She sighed and turned to yell at them when a figure in the distance caught her attention. She peered through the glaring light. It was hard to tell but she could have sworn it was the well-dressed coloured woman she and Lucy had seen with Mr Finch in the market place. Emma began to walk slowly towards her.

"Mam, where you going?" Gloria asked.

Emma near jumped out of her skin.

"Dear God, Glo!" She looked at the child. Startled, Gloria was all big eyes and half open mouth. "Sorry love, you just took me by surprise that's all."

Gloria blinked up at her mother and then screwed up her nose and shrugged.

"Didn't mean to."

"I know you didn't. Sorry I snapped at you. Can you wait here quietly for a minute? I just need to take a little walk, I shan't be long."

Gloria shrugged again and found herself a seat on one of the anchor posts. Emma tried to smile at her but her head was already turning back to the mysterious woman. For a moment she thought she had gone but then a wagon pulled out from a warehouse to reveal her figure again.

Emma moved nearer, casually meandering along until she could see the woman's features. It was definitely the woman from the market, and she appeared to be giving instructions to a much rougher looking black man. At her side was a small boy. He looked to be about three or four and wore a hat that was far too big for his head. His jacket and short trousers were impeccable to the point Emma wondered if they were brand new on that morning. Even then she couldn't imagine them so tidy and clean. Any of her boys could make a new pair of trousers look three generations handed down in less than half an hour, even Jack. She ignored the painful twist in her chest as she thought of Jack and edged a little closer. The boy scratched at his side and the woman tugged his hand to hold him still. He must have sensed Emma watching them, for he glanced up and looked right at her. Emma pretended to look away but the boy's little face broke into a broad smile, teeth gleaming white. Emma noticed his colouring was much lighter than his mother's.

"Keep still." Emma heard the woman say. The boy gave a quick secretive wave and turned back to the adult's conversation. Emma desperately wanted to stay and listen, but there was too much noise and suddenly the volume of it seemed to rise on purpose. Sailors seemed to be calling out instructions from ships in every direction, carts rattled and children laughed. Emma strained to hear something, anything else, but everything around her seemed to blend together into one big din. Conceding defeat she made her way back to her children just in time to catch Harry's arm before his fist made contact with his brother's chin.

"Boys! What have I told you about fighting?"

Albert's startled face blanched and he lowered his eyes to the ground. Harry curled his lips and mumbled something incomprehensible.

"He started it, Mam." Albert grumbled.

"I don't care who started it, just both of you end it, now!"

"But he said I was a dunce coz I..."

"Unless one of you is dying or has killed someone, I don't want to know. Now apologise to each other and get yourselves back on that ship. We'll be leaving soon."

Albert did as he was told but then mouthed something that Emma understood to be 'I'll get you later,' at Harry. So she clobbered him round the back of his head, grabbed them both by their ears and marched them on board, leaving Gloria to follow, laughing merrily at her brother's misfortune.

*

The masts were full once more. Seagulls squawked overhead and white sails fluttered in the breeze with the promise of good speed for their departure. Archer was looking up at his handy-work with his hands on his hips and a satisfied expression on his face. Emma leaned over the high railing of the ship as best she could and looked down at the African dockside one last time. There were still a few people boarding. This scheduled stop was not only to replenish supplies but also to drop off a small number of passengers, and to pick up a few more. Four families and two of the single gentleman had offloaded, and now the new folks had arrived. Emma wondered what this would do to the dynamics of the ship. They had built up a decent routine on board and she hoped that it wouldn't be disrupted. On the other hand, fresh faces meant fresh conversation and perhaps fresh skills. A figure leaned against the railing next to her.

"I hope she ain't planning on taking our laundry business."

The couple that were currently standing on the dockside, watching as a sailor struggled aboard with several leather cases and a large trunk, did not look at all like they would threaten their business enterprise. Emma glanced sideways at Lucy.

"I doubt it. No one else would be daft enough to start washing other folks mucky smalls, for a few pence or not."

Lucy laughed.

"Hello, look who's over there." She pointed towards an African couple with a small boy. They were swinging the child between their arms as they walked along towards the boarding plank. Emma felt as though her heart had stopped.

"I saw them earlier too," Emma rasped over her dry throat. It was Lucy's turn to look sideways. Emma continued, "I thought they were conducting business of some sort. She seemed to be giving him instructions. They didn't look, I mean, they don't look like they could be husband and wife. She's so elegant and he is too old and rough." Emma could hear the judgement in her voice and despised herself for it.

As they came closer and she could see them more clearly she noted just how much older the man really was. His grey hair was curled tight to his head as though trying not to fall out and his rugged skin was lined and lived in. His complexion was also a shade darker than the woman and at least twice as dark as the child's. The boy was giggling as he lifted his feet off the ground and was swung forwards. Whatever they were to each other, they looked like family. At their side another man was pushing a rickety looking trolley, on top of which sat a rather ancient looking portmanteau with battered corners tipped with metal and several large customs stamps imprinted on the side. Lucy began to surmise that they would soon find out who this woman was after all, when Emma noticed a tall white gentleman walking in close step behind them. Lucy's words became a blur. Emma gawped in horror as this little 'family' drew close to the ship and stopped. The trolley was set down and a sailor came to take the luggage aboard.

"Well, I'd never have expected that." Lucy said with a great interest.

"Shhh." Emma.

"I'm just saying, who would have thought that Mr Finch would have some woman and kid stashed away in Cape Town?"

Emma was desperately trying to catch any scrap of conversation that might drift up from the dockside.

The little boy was dancing about Mr Finch's legs now. But then the teacher bent down and threw his arms around the boy, holding him so tight the child must have been struggling for breath. Emma knew that embrace; it was the same as the one she had given Jack in Southampton. They were not coming on board with him, they were saying goodbye.

She couldn't tear her eyes away as Mr Finch set the boy down and shook the old man's hand with a hearty grip like they were old friends. Then he turned to the woman. As she tilted her head, the sun fell full on her beautiful face. For a moment they stood there looking at each other, and then she was in his arms, sobbing into his shoulder. Emma just managed to catch a few words of their conversation.

"You take care, Mercy. Look after yourself and young William here. And when the time comes..."

The next words were swept away beneath the flapping of sails and a yell from the crow's nest to say all was well to set sail. Emma shot the sailor the sort of glare she usually saved for her children.

"...welcome, all of you," Mr Finch finished.

Emma sighed. Why on earth should she care what Mr Finch did or with who? But hadn't he said he was not married. Hadn't he told her that there had been someone a long time ago, but that she had died? So what was this poor woman to him if not a wife? A mistress he was abandoning? The whore Lucy thought her? And what of the child? She folded her arms and turned away.

Lucy shook her head and tutted,

"And he's leaving 'em behind!"

"For once Lucy, maybe you're wrong." Emma barked. Lucy raised her eyebrows.

"Well, I know ya like him, and with good reason for the most part, but seriously Em, ya didn't think it would come to anything in the end did ya? And this is far better gossip..."

Emma did not wait to hear the rest. She stalked off in search of her children. They would be at sea again shortly and there would be supper to make and entertainment to find. As she stepped through the hatch into the lower decks she considered the irony. She had thought that this last part of the journey would endorse excitement and anticipation, but instead all she could think of was how they were all going to bear being trapped together again for another five or six weeks. *And then what?* Usually Lucy was her ally but now she was as irritated by her friend as she was with Mr Finch. Perhaps all this was just her own fear of the future catching up with her. She stretched out her back and felt a satisfying clunk in her spine.

Drawing a deep breath, she pushed open the door to her tiny bunk and wished she couldn't hear the children playing inside. Never in her life had she wished she could find a moment alone more than she did then. She bit her lip and said,

"Right you lot, what do you fancy for tea?"

Flemington, Australia
March 1st 1857

Cards on the table and notes fluttering in the hot sticky breeze. A pair of gnarled hands clasped a prial of queens. The man opposite rubbed his bent nose and sniffed. A line of sweat made its way down his forehead towards his cheek. Jacob was confident. He slid another silver coin into the pile and looked his opponent in the eye.

"I'll see you." His voice sounded rough as an iron file.

He wiped his hand over his face and spread his cards before him. Three queens smiled up; two reds and a black. The fourth was across the table, supported by her king and nave, but she wasn't strong enough. A slow smirk slinked across his lips. He swept his arms around the kitty and drew it towards his chest.

The looser sank back into his chair as the barkeep handed him a whisky double. He watched as notes and coins were shoved into his opponent's tattered jacket pockets. Then he drained his glass, slammed it down on the table, pushed back his chair so that hard it rattled and strode out into the night.

Jacob ignored the wave of relief that should have told him not to play again.

"Fetch me another, Mac, and a round for the house," he ordered with a smug grin.

There was a general cheer and Jacob contemplated that a few more nights like this could really set him up.

The Indian Ocean

Day Eighty-Two

A thick dark line on the horizon was all that remained of their time in The Cape of Good Hope. All the build-up to their brief stop and now it was over, almost as if it had never happened. Emma yawned and stopped. She could hear water sloshing in the laundry bucket. Lucy must have been up with the lark to beat her to it this morning. She weaved her way through the storage trunks until she reached the little clearing. Lucy glanced up and stopped scrubbing a soapy shirt.

"Emma, I'm sorry. I didn't mean to upset ya yesterday. I was just, well, I don't know, I..."

"It's all right. I'm sorry too. I think the thought of being confined on board for weeks again was just getting on top of me." Emma took a sopping wet smock from the top of the washed pile and began to wind it through the mangle. She still felt a little uneasy this morning but she was not about to lose the best friend she had ever had over a silly argument, especially an argument about a man.

*

Day Eighty-Four

"Wheeeeeeeeeeeeeeeeeeeeeee."

"Gloria, stop that, you're making me dizzy." Emma caught her daughter mid-spin and held her steady. "I know you're bored but please find something a little less energetic to do, at least for a while anyway."

Gloria grinned and battered her long eyelashes at her mother innocently.

"Sorry, Mam. I was being a spinning top."

Emma laughed,

"I can see that. When we get to Australia we shall have to buy you a real one. Now, how about you go fetch that book Mr Finch gave you and read to me."

Emma gave Gloria a nod of encouragement as her daughter contemplated.

"All right," the little girl said after a moment and skipped off.

The reading matter on board, for those who knew how, was somewhat limited, but Mr Finch had brought with him a large trunk of educational and storybooks which he occasionally loaned out to the children. Emma had no idea what this one was, but she was happy to find out if it meant a few minutes of peace and tranquillity. She sat down on the freshly scrubbed deck, leaned against the bosun's cabin wall and stretched her legs out in front of her. She hadn't seen Lucy or the twins yet that morning and the boys were off playing Hide and Go Seek in the steerage deck with the son of the new family who had moved into the bunk next door. The Vischers had joined the ship at The Cape and had a strange accent that Emma found hard to follow sometimes, but they seemed nice enough, and their boy was the same age as Harry. She raised her face to the sky and let the warmth tingle her skin. It was going to be a hot one, but a little while longer in the blistering sun wouldn't hurt and the thought of going back below deck again just made Emma even more tired.

Feet scuffed on wood close by. She looked around. Gloria was coming back towards her with a book in her hands, still skipping.

"Don't you ever get tired?"

Gloria stopped before her and offered her the book.

"Nope."

Emma looked up at her and smiled.

"I thought not. Come sit by me then." She patted the decking next to her and Gloria obliged. Emma ran her fingers over the embossed letters on the front cover. Seeing letters and not being able to understand them made her feel as though she were blind. Gloria shuffled in closer, reached over and opened the cover to reveal a yellowed page of typed print.

"What is it called then?" Emma asked.

"But you can see what it's called."

Emma looked at her daughter in horror. All the times she had asked someone else to read something to her and it had not occurred to her little girl that it was because she couldn't do it for herself. She swallowed hard and took a breath before saying,

"Sadly for me, your Grandpa wouldn't let me learn my letters. So you will have to read it for me, just like Jack did at home." Emma watched Gloria register what this meant. Mortified, Emma traced her fingernail below the first line of words. "Tell me what this says."

Gloria cocked her head and looked at her mother for a long moment.

"But you could learn now?"

Emma opened her mouth to speak but the reply stuck in her throat. She recalled the promise she had made to Jack, but she was too ashamed to ask someone.

"Your Pa offered to teach me a long time ago," was all she could manage to get out. She had refused Jacob several times when they were first married and after a while, he had stopped asking. Now, suddenly, she wished she had swallowed her pride and just done it. Having a seven-year-old suggest she learn to read was far more humiliating.

"I bet Mr Finch would teach you. He's a very good teacher."

"Good Morning, Gloria. You bet Mr Finch could teach your mother what?"

Emma had been so wrapped up in the conversation that she hadn't even noticed anyone approach, and of all people to arrive at that moment, it had to be him. She felt her face burn. She wished the deck would suddenly develop a trap door through which she could drop.

"Good morning, Sir. My Grandpa wouldn't let Mam learn to read and write so I thought you wouldn't mind teaching her."

Emma felt nauseated. She looked around for her fan, not to cool her down but to hide behind. She hadn't brought it out. She scrambled to her feet and tried to think of an excuse to flee, but nothing would come to mind. Mr Finch was looking right at her, inside her almost. He clasped his hands together and waited. When Emma said nothing he offered,

"I would be most happy to oblige, Mrs Burns, if you would like."

Emma's mind seemed frozen, in stark contrast to the hot layer of sweat that burned over her entire body. She tried to concentrate on breathing, but the constraints of her corset were choking her. How she wished she could be as brazen as Lucy and go without it. She wiped her hand over her forehead and tried to moisten her throat by swallowing several times.

"Thank you for the offer but I really couldn't trouble you so." Of all the people in the world, he was the last person she wanted to be her tutor.

"It would be no trouble at all, Mrs Burns; it would be a great honour."

"I have the laundry," she spluttered.

Gloria looked up at her and cocked her head to one side,

"But that's not all the time," she said, helpfully.

Emma felt her heart thump in her chest. Why could she think of no way out?

"We can begin this afternoon if you like, after my class," Mr Finch said with a smile. "Perhaps you would like to come to the schoolroom once the children have been freed."

"See, Mam. I told you Mr Finch would teach you."

Emma wanted to run as far away as possible, in her mind, she was already halfway back to England, back in their cottage with Jack sitting by the fireside.

"So we are settled then?"

"I..." Emma's shoulders sank in defeat. She nodded, "after lunch then."

*

Steaming clothes and soapy fumes were overpowering in the laundry area. Emma rubbed her stinging eyes and pushed her hand into the small of her back. Lucy was shaking her head at her with a disapproving expression.

"You ain't serious, Em? D'ya really intend to spend time alone wiv him, when ya know how he makes ya feel?"

"He is the last person on earth I wish to be alone with, but I couldn't get out of it. Besides, I did promise Jack I'd learn." Emma looked at Lucy. "Come with me, you can learn too."

"Nah, I ain't got the patience for learning." Lucy was shaking her head. "Tell him ya changed ya mind. I know I've teased ya about him, perhaps even encouraged ya, but I just thought ya could fantasize. There ain't no harm in dreams. I never thought you had proper feelings for him until the other day when ya saw him with that woman. I can see where you're going to end up. If ya spend time wiv him, all alone...You're on this ship to join ya husband and start a new life. What happens when ya gets to Australia if ya get involved with Mr Finch?"

Emma bent forward and rested her head against the high arm of the mangle and groaned.

"Why am I being so stupid? I have a husband who I've missed very much, for the last seven years."

"And ya just can't wait to get off this ship and see him, right?"

Emma straightened up.

"I'm afraid that Jacob will be disappointed when he sees me again. That's all this is, just silly fears making me feel silly things about a silly man. It'll be fine."

Lucy raised an eyebrow.

"As you please. But don't you come crying to me when ya realise you're madly in love and it is too late to turn back."

Now Emma felt as though she had switched places with one of the twins.

"I promise you, I am not and nor shall I ever be, in love with Mr Finch," she replied, and she meant it.

32

Day Eighty-Seven

The damp air smelled of humbugs. Rain pattered against the portholes and a dim grey light bathed the room in silver. A mellow glow flickered above her from the oil lamp and danced a merry pattern over Mr Finch's face as he sat waiting. Emma set down her chalk and examined her work. Her letters looked scratchy and thin on the slate but they were not as wobbly as they had been yesterday. Mr Finch slid off the desk where he had been perched and stepped forwards to assess her efforts.

Emma felt a flutter in her chest, but this was from nerves, not desire. Or at least that's what she told herself. This was her fourth lesson in as many days and the first time she had written out the alphabet from start to finish without the need for prompting.

Mr Finch walked around to stand behind her. Emma bit her lip and chastised herself. She was determined to keep her promise to Lucy. He leaned forwards and she could smell the freshness of his shirt, one she had scrubbed clean herself only yesterday. Her stomach flipped at the thought of doing this man's laundry and contemplated which was the more intimate task, hers or his. She glanced up at his profile, his face so close to her that she could almost feel the light pulse of the nerve that twitched slightly in his jaw.

"Excellent, Mrs Burns, now I would like you to write out your name." His breath smelled of the humbugs.

The only thing Emma had ever allowed Jacob to show her was her initial: E B. At least she knew where to start. She dusted off the slate and let her fingers settle around the chalk once more. E, she wrote as steadily as she could.

"Sound it out in your head," Mr Finch encouraged.

...m a. B e r n z.

"Very good, but I believe there are two M's in Emma."

She hoped she wasn't blushing as she scrubbed out the A and completed her first name correctly. As he suggested altering the z to an s and changing to e to a u on her surname, he stepped away and walked towards the back of the room. Emma finished her task and turned to look at him.

There was a globe on a stand in the far corner. He had his back to her, gently spinning it with his left hand.

"Are you all right, Mr Finch," Emma asked tentatively. He stopped, as though he had awoken from some kind of trance. He didn't turn around but simply replied,

"Do you know how far we have travelled on this ship?"

Emma pushed back the chair. The scraping wood grated through her bones.

"I cannot say for sure."

Mr Finch pressed his forefinger onto the globe and halted the spin. She walked towards him, expecting him to say something else. When he didn't, she couldn't help but ask,

"You have lived away from England before?" She knew she oughtn't to ask personal questions. It would only lead to a more intimate relationship. But this seemed a reasonable question under the circumstances, and she was curious. Instead of answering he turned the globe back to Europe and began to trace the line they had sailed, swaying out wide to Brazil and then back across to Africa.

"Soon we shall be in the new world. I've been looking forward to arriving for so long that it never felt real somehow, and yet here we are, drawing ever closer and we shall be there in little over a month now."

Emma was unsure what to make of his sudden melancholy. After a moment she replied,

"The captain says we're getting a great push from the Furious Fifties. Archer told me yesterday that he thinks we will be able to make up some of the time we lost in Rio."

Mr Finch finally turned to look at her. His expression was so pained she couldn't stop herself. She reached up and touched his face. For a moment tears welled in his eyes. But then he seemed to swallow them and took a step back.

"Forgive me. I can be foolish sometimes." He cleared his throat and shook his head.

There was a long pause. Emma fidgeted with her petticoat tie and wondered if she should excuse herself and leave him to his thoughts, but then he said,

"Your son, Jack. How do you get by without thinking of him every second of the day?"

Emma's mind immediately conjured up the image of that little black boy on the dockside in Cape Town and the look on Mr Finch's face as they had embraced.

"I don't. Not a moment can pass without my recalling how he did this or that, or what he would say to something, and not a second goes by without my heart aching to see him again...or feeling guilty that I left him behind."

Mr Finch nodded pensively, his hand fluttering at his side as though he wanted to reach out to her.

"Did you leave someone behind?" She couldn't believe she had found the nerve to ask, and the instant the words were out she regretted them.

Mr Finch seemed to turn to stone. He drew a sharp breath so suddenly Emma flinched.

"More than one, Mrs Burns. I've lived away from my family for so long that sometimes it is difficult to picture them anymore. Yet they remain in my heart and the moment I lay eyes upon them again every feeling floods back, and to leave them again in agony."

Emma watched him intently. His eyes looked grey in the fading light. His jaw clenched for an instant, then he said,

"I have a sister I haven't seen in near twenty years and yet there is always the hope that we shall meet again, but I also have a brother and I fear I have seen him for the last time."

His words faded and Emma's heart broke. She was not entirely certain as to what Mr Finch was implying but the sentiment she understood. Tears rolled silently down her cheeks. If he had truly abandoned that African woman and her son, then there must be such a good reason that it couldn't be avoided.

"Jack was my world, Mr Finch. I understand completely."

Mr Finch seemed to break from his catatonia. He began to fluster and fumbled in his jacket pocket for a handkerchief. As she accepted it his fingers brushed against hers. The touch was as though lightning had shot up her arm to her chest. She opened her mouth in surprise.

"Are you quite well?" he said, concerned. "I hope I have not troubled you too much?" His words were so sincere Emma began to cry again. She apologised and said it was her that was foolish and made a hasty escape.

33

Day Ninety-Six

A haunting sound filtered through steerage with a gentle sway that matched the ocean beneath. As the bow of the fiddle swung high over the strings and past the player's ear Emma closed her eyes. Among those who boarded in Cape Town was a pair of Irish brothers. They had not only brought their violins with them but their passion for music as well. Today was the captain's birthday and this evening they had begun an impromptu concert in his honour. Later they had promised jigs and reels but for now, the tune was soulful and heartfelt. Emma let the sound wash over and soothe her. It had been a strenuous day. There seemed to have been more laundry lately than she and Lucy could handle, and her lessons with Mr Finch, though productive, were also of great effort to both mind and heart. It no longer mattered what he had done in his past or whom he had left behind. All that mattered was their time together. It was not as though they had conversed beyond their lessons, not since that day when he had made her cry, yet there was something unspoken between them, something warm. Emma cracked her back and sighed.

"Mam, can we go up top? The dancing must be starting soon." Albert asked for the third time.

Emma had been enjoying being away from the crowd but Albert was right, there was little point staying cooped up below deck when there were festivities to be found outside. She opened one eye.

"Very well, you all go on ahead. I'll be there in just a minute or two."

Albert shrugged. Harry grabbed Gloria's hand and the three of them were on their way before she had time to even glance their way. Emma closed her eye again and smiled. This was one of the few times onboard lately that she didn't feel claustrophobic and she wanted to enjoy a moment alone. But that was not to be.

"Mrs Matthews, make Mam come up top." Gloria pleaded.

Emma winced as she heard her children career into her friend just outside their door. Lucy clattered into the wall and shooed them away along with her own children. Emma sighed as the door creaked open again.

"I thought you would be out there already?" she said without opening her eyes.

Lucy put her hands on her hips and sighed sharply.

"I was but then I realised you ain't gone up yet, so I thought I'd better come down and make sure everything's all right. Now I see that ya's just moping."

Emma sat up and looked at Lucy with a sarcastic expression. Lucy ignored her and continued,

"For someone who spends an hour a day alone in a man's company, it baffles me that you can then hide from him when there's a crowd."

Emma yawned.

"I was just enjoying the quiet," she sounded unconvincing even to her self.

"Hmmm. I reckons ya just afraid that if I sees you two together I'll be able to tell that you broke ya promise."

Emma winced again and stood up.

"Fine, I shall prove you wrong," she said with a huff.

*

Beneath the star spattered sky, arms were flinging, legs were jigging and hair flying wide. Bonnetless women danced like wild children and men bounded about the deck as though their lives depended upon the rhythm. Albert, Gloria and the twins had joined in with several other children. Harry was sitting on the deck with the boy from the next-door bunk and they were playing some kind of card game with another young lad. In every direction, people were laughing and enjoying themselves. Emma hadn't seen such frivolity on board ship since Christmas night.

Lucy grinned and slipped her arm through Emma's spinning her around so fast Emma almost lost her footing.

"I wish every night could be like this," her friend gasped as the song ended.

The respite was brief. A moment later another jig started and they were off again. As they twirled and skipped and Emma's head became light and giddy. She suggested they pause for a mug of wine. Lucy nodded breathlessly and pulled them out of the crowd to rest against one of the lifeboats. Emma patted her chest and wafted her face. One of the sailors was pouring wine into jugs. Emma was about to make a beeline for him when Lucy nudged her in the ribs.

"There's ya chance, go prove me wrong."

Emma looked around to see Mr Finch leaning against the railings and watching the musicians, the moonlight glinting from the toecaps of his shoes as he tapped his foot to the rhythm. She patted her face to cool her skin and smoothed the front of her skirt down.

"Fine, I shall."

With the brazenness of a hussy, she plucked up the courage and strode towards him. He looked around just as she got there.

"Mrs Burns how are you? Are you enjoying the music?"

Emma didn't bother to formulate a response, she had been rehearsing her proposal from the second Lucy had spotted him.

"Would you care to dance, sir?"

A wry smile crept from one side of Mr Finch's soft lips until it reached the other. He looked mildly taken aback.

"Of course, Mrs Burns. It would be a pleasure."

He took off his jacket and laid it over a nearby stool. He folded back his sleeves and held out his hand to her. Emma hesitated then took it. His hands were warm and soft. She felt the heat from his touch spread through her body and she prayed that Lucy could not see it reflected in her face. She glanced in her friend's direction but found that Lucy had been swept up by the children and was being whirled around like a carousel. Emma smiled gratefully to herself and allowed Mr Finch to slip one hand on her waist into a waltz hold. Emma didn't often dance and certainly hadn't done so for several years. As she rested her free hand gently upon his shoulder her heart began to beat so fast she thought it might break her corset.

This tune was a little slower than the last few and lent itself nicely to a more elegant dance. Mr Finch swept her around smoothly and soon Emma's nerves were all but gone.

As they glided past the children she caught sight of Lucy. Her friend was laughing as she tried to teach young Albert how to waltz. Had she had the inclination to notice, Emma would have been impressed with young Albert's moves; he was graceful and had picked up the steps quickly. As it was, all her thoughts were leaving the rest of the ship behind.

"You're an excellent dancer, Mrs Burns."

Emma looked into his eyes and that was the last time she noticed anyone but him until the music ended.

"Gracious, Mr Finch." Emma gasped as they tumbled away into a quieter corner.

"Do my skills surprise you?" He was hardly out of breath. Emma envied his stamina. She flopped back against the railings and wafted a hand in front of her face.

"I had no idea that we would be so...that you would," she stopped, realising she was in danger of saying something she shouldn't. Mr Finch still had his hand resting upon her waist and she felt him step in closer. Her whole body throbbed and her breath almost abandoned her. His eyes looked deep into her. She had the queer sensation of falling into them. She heard him swallow and felt his breath on her lips. Her breasts lightly touched his chest. Then he stepped back.

"Please, forgive me. I forget myself."

She could feel his hand shaking as he let go of her. If she hadn't been so desperately wishing that he would kiss her she might have thought of a reply. She pressed her fingers to her lips, yet couldn't tear her eyes from his. She shook her head.

"I have offended you," he continued. "I should go."

The reaction was so fast she wasn't aware she had grabbed his wrist until she looked down.

"No, please stay."

For a moment she thought he would not, but then the panic that had risen in his expression began to subside and a flicker of a smile twitched on his lips again.

"Very well." He leaned back against the railings next to her and they began to talk. They talked of her children, of how different their lives would be in Australia. They began to imagine what it would be like there.

"I hear they have animals with huge legs like giant hares that hop so high that they could clear a house," Emma said, quoting one of Jacob's letters.

"And there are birds of every colour, so gay they make your heart sing," Mr Finch added to the vision. She was trying not to look at his face, but couldn't help risking a sideways glance. She found him doing the same to her. She looked away again and sighed contentedly, wishing that the moment could last longer.

"Do you have a position to go to when you arrive?" she asked.

Mr Finch nodded slowly.

"I'm told they are in desperate need of teachers. A good friend of mine went out in fifty-one. He wrote to me a year ago to ask if I would consider joining him. I had nought to keep me in England and I felt I should go where I could be of use, and so I wrote back to say that I would."

Emma wondered why he had nothing in England. He had told her that he had lived away from his family for many years, but did that include parents, aunts, and uncles? Before she had time to formulate any further questions he asked,

"And you, Mrs Burns. It is, I believe, not so common for a woman to join her husband after..." he paused, clearly contemplating the indelicacy of what he was about to say, "...his sentence is complete." He cleared his throat. "I hope you don't mind, but the children, they all talk and I couldn't help but..."

"It's fine, really," Emma assured him. "I'm not ashamed of my husband. He has his failings but don't all men," at this, she flushed. "I mean to say, it wasn't an easy decision but in the end, I felt I should give him a chance. Give us all a chance in the new world."

As her thoughts turned to Jack she felt Mr Finch take her hand and lift her fingers to his lips. She dare not look at him for fear she might just fall into his embrace. There was a long moment of silence. Her hand was still in his. Finally, he said,

"I wish you well for it. Mr Burns is a lucky man to have a woman who shows so much faith in him."

There was something underlying in his tone that Emma couldn't quite fathom. Nor did she have time to think on it further for her friend chose that moment to intervene. Emma pulled her hand away from Mr Finch so quickly he flinched.

"Mr Finch, good evening. I beg a pardon, but I must steal my friend away, our children's getting tired and Gloria's already curled up asleep on the floor."

Lucy was looking at Emma with wide eyes and pursed disapproving lips.

"Good evening, Mrs Matthews. Do accept my apologies, I hadn't realised I had commandeered so much of your friend's time. I shall bid you both good night." And with that he was turned on his heels and gone. Emma stared after him. The moment he was out of earshot Lucy hissed,

"Don't think I didn't notice you was holding hands. Ya have to stop this now Emma before it's too late."

Bugger thought Emma.

"I know, I know."

"No, dear, I don't think you do. It ain't just you, see. It's 'im as well."

Emma pretended not to follow.

"Don't be daft."

Lucy looked at her long and hard.

"That man has stars in his eyes when he looks at you. I ain't never wrong about things like this. But since neither of ya's free, I say back away now, before he really does kiss ya and then who knows where it might lead."

Emma cringed and felt her heart sink.

"Men haven't the strength to think with their heads when their pricks wants something else, and if their hearts get involved there ain't nothing to stop 'em, so it's down to you. Be strong Emma. Or you might have a bun in the oven afore you even see Jacob again, and then what will you do?"

"I would never..." Emma began. "He would never... He's too much of a gentleman."

"That's as maybe. But pricks and hearts have ruined many a woman, and man."

Emma wanted to protest but was forced to concede. She set off toward the children with a sigh.

34

Day One Hundred and Ten

Salted beef and mashed potatoes. Flavourless broth and watery stew. Emma forced down the last mouthful of supper. The same old thing day after day was hard to swallow, even when you were hungry. How she longed for an apple or a bowl of strawberries picked fresh from the fields.

"Mam, when are we going to get there?" Albert whined. Has had been saying the same thing every day for the past week.

Some ships might have made it to the end by now but The Cassandra was still a good couple of weeks away from shore. The delays in Rio had been costly to their journey, and now the winds had dropped once more and the whole ship was growing weary. Emma rolled her shoulders and began to gather up the dishes.

"We get there when we get there," she told him for the umpteenth time as calmly as she could manage.

"I dun't think we're ever getting there," he groaned.

Emma was about to correct his grammar but she hadn't the energy to bother. The days were dragging on longer and longer to the point she was beginning to wonder the same thing herself.

"You'll have to be patient like the rest of us. We'll get there soon. I promise." She tried to sound convincing.

"Mr Finch gave us humbugs in our lesson today, didn't he, Mam?" Gloria said brightly.

Ever since the night of the captain's birthday, Emma had taken to dragging Gloria to her reading lessons with her. It seemed like the best way to continue with her studies without being alone with Mr Finch. And it was working. It certainly wasn't easy to have an intimate moment with a man when there was a bright and somewhat chatty seven-year-old sitting next to you.

"That's not fair, he doesn't give us any in our class," Harry grumbled.

"That's coz he likes teaching just me and Mam better than the big class."

Emma flushed.

"I suspect it's just because that jar of his is running low and he doesn't want to run out. Besides if he gave sweets to all the children all of the time they wouldn't appreciate them, now would you?"

"Why have you gone red, Mam?" Albert asked, eyeing her suspiciously.

Emma plonked the dishes onto the tray and told Harry to open the door for her.

"It's warm tonight is all," she mumbled and scurried off to wash the pots.

She had done very well in shutting off her attraction to Mr Finch or at least diverting herself from the issue. But the confinement, boredom and the heat were beginning to take their toll. They had better see land soon or she might find herself looking into those lovely eyes and falling in for good.

*

Day One Hundred and Seventeen

The dusky sky was streaked with vivid pinks and orange above the glittering ocean. The sun was sinking so rapidly on the horizon that Emma thought it looked like a giant ripe tomato dropping into a large blue bag.

"Look, there, Mam!" Harry.

For one glorious moment, Emma thought the children had spotted land, but Albert was jumping up and down next to her pointing at something silvery just beneath the gentle rolling of the sea.

"What is it, what is it? I can't see." Gloria said, standing on tiptoe and shading her eyes.

"Here." Harry lifted Gloria up far enough for her to see over the side at the very moment a dolphin soared into the air, curled like a peeling apple and dived back below the surface. Gloria squeaked with joy. Then there were more, a whole school of them, leaping and diving.

Emma's smile broadened. They had seen dolphins a few times along the way, whales too. But somehow this time they seemed to be bringing them hope. They leapt again and again. Then a pair of them rose up backwards, as though standing on their tails and cackled.

"They sound like good witches casting a spell on the ship to take us to Pa," Gloria said.

Emma was about to say 'chance would be a fine thing' when,

"Land Ho!" echoed down from high in the crow's nest.

A moment later another call came from the front of the ship. Then everything was chaos. People seemed to be everywhere, scuttling this way and that, trying to spot the distant shore. Emma looked around to see the captain peering out through his telescope and she found she was holding her breath. Then his arm went up and silence fell.

"Ladies and gentleman, welcome to Australia. We're still a few days from Port Phillip, but out there is your new home." There was a sense of relief in his voice that Emma had not expected from a long-serving sailor, but perhaps knowing that every voyage could be your last was in the back of even the best captain's mind. Emma closed her eyes and breathed out a long sigh. Soon they would be off the ship and the temptations of Mr Finch would be gone.

*

Day One Hundred and Nineteen

"I thought Australia was an island?" Albert said.

Emma and her children were sitting on the upper deck with the Matthews and several other families. The Irish brothers were regaling the small gathering with a few tunes on their fiddles and some of the sailors had joined in with the songs. The shanty was bright and cheerful.

"It is dear," Lucy replied.

"But we've been sailing past it for days and days and we're still not there yet."

"Well, it's a very big island. And it's only been two days." Emma ruffled her son's hair and rested her head back against the side of the ship.

35

Port Phillip, Victoria, Australia
April 10th 1857

Day One Hundred and Twenty-One

Steam chugged from the funnels and the masts were empty. They had sailed through the mouth of Port Philip Bay and into the welcoming arms of the harbour some hours ago, but still, they had not docked. Before them, through the myriad of flues and wooden poles of many ships, a city was enticing them in. Everyone aboard was desperate to disembark but the sea was rough and the waves were battering the hull mercilessly, preventing them docking. Emma was feeling sick but not from the waves. It had not occurred to her until now that Jacob would not likely be there to greet them. How would he know the day when they were to arrive? It was not as though they were able to stick to a schedule. All she could hope was that he had been watching out for them, reading the newspapers for notifications. They would have been there a good bit sooner had they not been forced to divert to Rio, so he must be expecting them anytime soon. Emma rested her hand on her stomach and tried to calm herself.

"She's bigger than I expected."

Emma's heart skipped and she spun around.

"Mr Finch, I...Yes, yes. Melbourne looks larger than I expected too." Too afraid to look at his face, she turned back to the view,

"Do you know where you are going to stay tonight?"

Emma shook her head, startled by the question, however innocently it was likely meant.

"Mr Burns will come for you the moment he knows you're here I am sure," Mr Finch added hurriedly, realising the potential implications of such a question. "In the meantime, I've been told the Golden Cross Hotel is welcoming, should you prefer not to stay in the Immigrant Barracks."

Emma looked down at her feet.

"I think we shall be fine in the barracks for a day or so, any bed on dry land and fresh food will be welcome. We can send word to him once we're settled." She fidgeted her stance and began to pick at the side of her thumb. "Mr Finch, you have been very gracious to me and my children," she began shakily. "I trust that you will..."

"Mrs Burns, Emma, please, look at me."

Emma swallowed and bit her lip. The sound of her first name passing his lips was more than she could bear. Slowly she raised her eyes to meet his gaze.

"Emma, I know you're married and I pray with all my heart that you find a good life here with your family, but I cannot leave without telling you how much I admire and care for you. Should you ever need anything, please, do find me."

Emma gulped back a sob. It was as unexpected to her as to him. She pressed her fingers to her lips and fought the urge to throw herself into his arms.

"I..."

Gently he ran the backs of his fingers down the side of her face. Emma felt her knees weaken and the tears roll down her cheeks and over his fingers.

"Please, call me William," he breathed.

Emma nodded but at the same moment, an image of the little light-skinned black boy on the dockside shot into her mind. Had he not been called William also? Then it was true, that lad was his. What of the child's mother? He too had someone else. Gathering her composure she forced herself to step away from him.

"Thank you, I wish you the very best, Mr Finch."

William held her gaze for a moment longer and then gave her a polite nod and was gone from her presence. She watched as he made his way through the excited passengers and disappeared below deck. Emma tried to pray that would be the last time she ever laid eyes upon him, but her heart was not in the prayer and she found that despite her better judgement she prayed that one day they would meet again.

36

Melbourne Immigrant Barracks
April 13th 1857

Long rows of beds were lined up like a workhouse. A child nearby was sniffing incessantly and somewhere at the other end of the room a woman coughing loudly. The scent of human sweat and dirty clothes was almost as bad as it had been on board the ship. Emma scratched at her head and hoped she hadn't caught nits from the scruffy brat in the next-door bunk. Lucy Matthews and her children had been collected yesterday. There had been hugs and tears all around but now they were gone with promises to stay in touch that would probably never come to pass, and Emma had never felt so alone. Gloria was perched next to her on the edge of her bed, swinging her legs more and more violently, banging her feet on the metal bed frame, and somewhere the boys were off playing. She could hear them all the way from the other side of the building. Emma picked up the slate and chalk William Finch had given her at their last lesson and began to write out her name carefully.

The light scrape of the chalk was soothing. She put out her arm to stop Gloria's leg from swinging but it wasn't necessary. She had already stopped. Emma looked at her and realised she was staring at something. She raised her eyes to see what it was.

At the foot of their bed stood a man. His face was ruddy and lined, his beard thick and greying and his shoulders seemed to sink into his back. Emma couldn't speak. The sunlight that streaked through the narrow window behind her was making the man's hazel eyes glint almost cat-like, and there was a single glistening tear trailing a line down his left cheek, vanishing into his beard.

"Emma, oh my god you're here!"

Before she knew what was happening he had scooped her up from the bed and spun her around.

As he set her back down Emma reached out a hand to her daughter.

"Gloria, this is your father.

Part 2

1

Flemington, Victoria
Seven Months Later
November 1857

Thundering hooves thumped at the ground. Emma's heartbeat seemed to quicken. She let the shirt in her hands sink back beneath the suds and stretched her back. As she listened to the horses speeding around the racetrack in the distance she let her mind wander to Jack. She had not seen him in near a year now, so long ago it felt like another lifetime. And yet if it wasn't for the heat and rolling green fields outside the window she could have believed she was still bent over the washtub back in Staffordshire with the potteries pumping out their smoke and the sky grey as slate. She wiped the sweat from her brow and dried her hands on her pinny. Outside a kookaburra cackled at her from the bush by the back door and something scurried over the wooden decking and vanished into the long grass. She shuddered, still unsure whether she liked these new and peculiar animals. Stepping out onto the deck she breathed in the sweet-scented air. Probably a rat, she thought. They were close to the river, and keeping rats out of the house was as much trouble as it had been back in England. Emma looked up at the vast blue sky; so clear it was like looking at a painting. She began to imagine what her beloved eldest son was doing right at that moment. In truth, he was likely sleeping soundly as it was the wee small hours of the morning for him, but in her head, Emma pictured him sitting at his station in the potteries art studio, carefully working the edge of a plate with a beautiful bright design.

"When's Pa coming back, Mam?"

Emma swung around so startled she near fell off the deck.

"Bert, I didn't hear you come out!" Albert, now a good two inches taller than he had been when they arrived, was standing in the doorway wearing a shirt with sleeves well above his wrists and short trousers that were barely decent anymore. She recalled a similar scene when Jack had come into her English kitchen in the same sort of outgrown state. Emma shook her head and considered that little had changed in the past year, save the scenery, the heat, and not having Jack to walk through the door to her. She pushed the dull heartache away and said,

"Friday week. You know that, lad." She sighed and went back into the marginally cooler kitchen. "If it gets any hotter than this I think I shall have to take to my bed and wait for summer to end." She was only half-joking. Albert half laughed in return.

"When will he let me go with them?"

Emma had heard this question a dozen times a week since Jacob had got it into his head to go up to the goldfields. At first, she had pleaded with him to stay and finish the house. Then she had pleaded with him not to take Harry with him, after all, he was thirteen now, he could look for a real job. But it had been battle enough just to keep Albert at home and all the boy could think of was getting a gold tooth like Archer the sailmaker from the ship. She looked at her youngest son and gave him a resigned smile.

"Gloria and I can't do with all the men in the family working away now, can we? Besides you get to go to school instead. Isn't that more fun than endless hours of hard labour with little to show for it?" Emma was finding it difficult to keep the resentment out of her voice. Albert heard it despite her efforts.

"Pa will find gold and then we will be rich and he will be able to build a big grand house, and then you will be glad."

Emma winced. She hadn't meant to sound entirely ungrateful. She knew Jacob had good intentions, but the reality was a pie-in-the-sky dream she was almost certain would never come true, and at what cost was the effort? Backbreaking work panning on the surface, or worse, picking in the depths of the mines risking their lives, and all for riches that would never actually materialise. She recalled the first moment they had arrived at the cottage. Still under the impression the farmhouse would soon be ready, she hadn't minded the sinking sense of reality she had felt when she had seen the size of the tiny temporary kitchen and sat down on the threadbare couch. Jacob had put her off from visiting their land for the first week or so until finally, he could prevent her no longer, and then she had seen it. She had tried to hide her disappointment but she knew he saw it. Despite his failure, he had somehow made her feel as though she was at fault for questioning his intentions. In the years without him, she had forgotten how he could do that, how he could talk that talk and make it all sound like he was right and the rest of the world was wrong.

Jacob had always been a dreamer, Emma had known that from the day she met him and he had told her that one day he would make his fortune and she would be mistress of The Hall instead of slaving away below stairs. But she had loved him for it too. He always could make her feel like she was worth the effort, that the dreams were all for her, even though she knew they weren't and they would never come to pass. Once he had decided they would all move to America. He had a friend who was starting a potteries in Virginia and wanted him to go and be the manager. For a minute she had believed it would happen. She saw the letters come and go between them. But of course, she couldn't read the contents, not then. Now she would know better. In the end, it transpired that this friend has indeed gone to America, but he hadn't the finances to start such an enterprise and had not found the backing to support him either. Whether the friend was as much a dreamer as Jacob or whether her husband had simply imagined the whole idea, Emma would never know. But now, here they were, in a real 'new world'; a young country so far from home, and part of the dream had come to pass. There was indeed countryside enough to run across for hours, there was blue sky as far as the eye could see and clean air enough for all, but where was the house? Where was the independent living of a farm she had been promised, the idyllic life he had planted in the heads of her children? Nowhere in sight. She looked around the pokey kitchen of the little shack they called a cottage and wondered if they would make the rent at the end of the month.

Jacob had purchased some land, that much had been accurate, but the seventeen acres they owned was yet standing fallow, save for a few planks of wood that constituted the foundation of a farmhouse. She and Gloria sometimes walked out there, just to look at what could be, but not a thing had been done in months, nor did she ever imagine it would be. Still, it could be worse. Flemington village was nice; it was pretty, there was a little school, a hotel or two, a small row of shops, a post office with a somewhat irregular postal service supervised by one Mr Price, and they were close enough to the city to make it there and back in a day by pony if needs be. Then there was the racecourse, which seemed a far steadier prospect for enterprise to Emma than the goldfields if only she could convince Jacob, but the only thing at the races that caught his attention were the bookmakers.

As she went back to the washtub and lifted up the dolly she contemplated starting a laundry business again, even though she sworn she would never scrub other folks' smalls again. Albert must have read her thoughts for he said,

"When Pa finds his fortune you can send our washing out to a laundress instead of you doing theirs."

Emma smiled and wished that were true. A twinge in her back made her wince and Albert looked down at his feet as though ashamed of her lot.

"Why don't you run over to Mr Price and see if they have any letters from Jack? We must be due for one soon. You can collect Gloria from Mrs McLeish on your way back."

Albert seemed pleased to escape her company and dashed off before she had time to remind him to wait outside until his sister finished her lesson. She had to admit, she had never envisioned any of her children taking music lessons. But on hearing Mrs McLeish practising, the child had expressed a desire to learn, and the teacher seemed more than happy to oblige, even at a discounted rate. Jacob had insisted he could take care of the bills and Gloria seemed to enjoy the lessons very much, so, for as long as finances would allow, the piano would be learnt.

The moment Albert was out of sight, Emma tugged her frock loose, wafted air down the front of her corset and tried to breathe a little easier. It was true, there could be all four seasons in one day out here, but the last week or so had been one long relentless heatwave. She had contemplated taking up Lucy's ways on-board ship and going without her corset altogether, but such behaviour wouldn't do. If only she had something that could send a breeze through the cottage. As she went through to the sitting room to retrieve her Brazilian fan from the arm of the battered old couch someone passed the window and caught her eye. It was not often someone walked by. Theirs was the last cottage on the street and the nearest neighbours were the McLeish's a good hundred or so yards away. Emma went to the window and peered out just in time to hear a knock. She glanced at the front door with a start and then tried to see who it was from the window. All she could make out was the back of a woman's skirts.

Emma pulled open the door, fully expecting to see a neighbour or perhaps the vicar's wife making her friendly rounds, but as the wood creaked back she thought she would faint.

In an instant, the woman was hugging her so tightly she could scarcely draw breath.

"Emma, oh Emma, ain't you a sight for sore eyes. I can't tell ya how good it is to see ya? How are ya? How ya been? How's the kids? It's been far too long."

Emma gently set her friend back and tried to take in the vision before her.

"Lucy Matthews, what on earth brings you out here?"

Lucy put her hands on her hips, straining over Emma's shoulder to see into the cottage.

"Well you and yours, what else?" Lucy replied. "I was going to send a note but then I just had to come and surprise ya in person instead. I came to invite you all to visit us now the 'ouse is finished. My Alfred is so proud of his work that he wants as many people to visit as he can persuade. Course the first person I thought of was you." Lucy was still trying to see inside, so Emma stepped out of her way and invited her in. She watched as Lucy's eyes scanned around the meagre room. There was no judgement in her expression, Emma knew there never would be from Lucy, but she was embarrassed all the same.

"Would you like some tea?" Emma offered, still not quite believing her eyes.

"Ooh, I'd love one, please. It were a bit of a dusty ride. I brought the pony and I still ain't quite used to riding him. I swear my behind will be black and blue tomorrow. I'll be glad when we can afford a trap."

The only hoof beats Emma had heard had been the racers.

"Where did you tether him?"

"Outside the Rose and Thorn Hotel. I had to go in and ask which house was yours. Didn't see the point of untying him again just for a five-minute walk."

"It's a wonder you didn't see Bert on your way. I sent him to collect the mail," Emma said.

Lucy followed her into the kitchen and settled herself on a stool by the wide-open back door. Emma lifted the tea caddy down from the top shelf and filled the kettle from a large jug by the sink.

"I must get Bert to go to the pump," Emma said as she tipped out the last drop of water.

"Ya've a pump? We've a well out back. It's hefty work drawing, but it's better than nothin' and the waters fresh. You're nice and close to the city too. We're a bit out in the sticks, a good seven miles east of 'ere. It takes a bit of effort to get to, but you're welcome to stop a couple of nights, all of ya of course."

"Oh we could never impose, but I'm sure we would love to visit for an afternoon. Maybe we could catch the post, it's a bit ad hoc but it comes most Thursdays, and then we can walk back." Emma mused that the Matthews' house must be a fair size if her friend was sure they could all be put up, but she felt it impertinent to ask.

"You'd do nothing of the sort; we would love to have ya stay. The twins has been missing your three so bad these last few months. They've been begging to visit since we got ya note with your address. I've felt bad not coming before. But it's been such hard work and such a mess, with bits of wood here and bits of tile there, and no distinguishable room to park in and makes yourself comfy. Everything's been a bit of a blur since April and now it's November and I can't believe how quick it's all gone. Still, it's all done now and the farm is getting going proper too." She drew a breath as her eyes wandered around Emma's tatty little kitchen. Emma felt her cheeks colour and hoped Lucy didn't pity her too much. Lucy smiled at her and carried on. "Anyway, Alf had already started with a dozen sheep afore we got there, now we've got a dozen more and a little flock of chickens that lays the loveliest eggs I ever tasted. I tell ya, Em, I ain't never thought a city girl like me would end up on a farm and enjoy it. It's hard work and no mistake, but I can't say as I don't love every minute of it."

Lucy certainly looked well on it too, her cheeks were rosy and her freckles had blended even more together over her nose and her eyes were bright. She had certainly put on a few pounds and she looked extremely contented. Emma was overjoyed for her friend but she couldn't help feeling a little envious. Hearing all this good fortune and prosperity made her little cottage seem even more claustrophobic.

"So, where's your 'ouse then? I'm assuming it ain't finished yet or you'd have moved in."

Emma drew a slow breath.

"No, Jacob, erm... Jacob has gone to the goldfields." She tried to smile and make light of it. "He and Harry have been working up there since the end of May."

Lucy's expression clouded but she said nothing.

"They've done all right," Emma explained. "A little bit of luck here and there, but not the mother-load as yet." She forced a laugh. "I'm sure it will come any day now though, and once it does he will start on the house properly." Emma realised she was sounding like one of the children. "We can take a walk out to the site if you like." The moment she had said it she regretted it. Of course, Lucy would want to see the land, but it was near two miles and Emma was embarrassed that nothing had been done with it. Fortunately, she was saved by the return of Albert and Gloria as they came bursting in through the front door.

"No letter today, Mam," Albert said then stopped and stared at the lady sitting on the kitchen stool.

Gloria didn't hesitate; she just threw herself into Lucy's welcoming embrace.

"Where are the twins?" she asked excitedly.

"At home I'm afraid. There were a lot of work to do on the farm this morning. I left 'em cleaning out the chickens. Besides we can't all fit on Marvin. Once we get the cart, I promise."

Gloria was grinning from ear to ear.

"Marvin is a pony," Emma explained then added, "Lucy has invited us all to visit them."

"Can we go, Mam, can we please?" Gloria was bouncing up and down. "Do you have a piano; I can play it for you."

Lucy looked up at Emma in surprise.

"No dear, I'm afraid we don't," she said. "I didn't know ya could play?"

"I just started learning," Gloria beamed. "Mrs McLeish next door was a piano teacher in England, but now she lives out here with her husband she doesn't have many students, so she wanted to teach me."

Lucy was very impressed.

"Well ain't you an accomplished young lady now? Too grand for the likes of little old me I fancy," she teased. Gloria giggled and curtseyed.

Emma prayed the lessons could continue. The kettle began to screech so she took it off the stove and capped the fire.

"When can we go, Mam?"

"When ever is convenient for the Matthews'."

"How does Thursday sound?" Lucy offered.

"Jacob and Harry won't be back." Emma felt they ought to wait for them, but then, that would be more than a week and they would only be home for a couple of days at best. She noticed Lucy cast a surreptitious eye around the tiny room.

"Then they'll miss out this time," she said firmly. "Go on Em, it'll be a nice little trip for ya."

"Please, Mam!" Both children pleased at once with big round innocent eyes. Emma rolled her eyes and sighed.

"All right then, Thursday it is."

"Excellent, then it's settled," Lucy grinned.

The children began dancing about together excitedly. Emma smiled.

"That's the day after tomorrow!" beamed Gloria.

"Yes, it is." Emma agreed, finding the joy contagious.

2

Gloria was bounding about the back yard like a joey on its first day out of the pouch. Her chestnut curls glinted with golden streaks from the sun and her cheeks were flushed with a healthy glow. Emma untied her pinny and hung it up on the hook by the back door. Today was November 19th: Jack's seventeenth birthday. Her heart twisted each time she let her mind wander across the oceans and imagined him there all alone. She pictured his face, still bonny with youth, and considered that if she ever had the chance to see him again he would look so different she might not even recognise him. They hadn't had a letter from him in almost a month now and she was beginning to worry. She prayed he was doing all right and that he had received their little package in time. Everyone had written something for him and they had mustered together a new shirt and a pair of socks. Emma shook her head and forced her thoughts onto other things. Today was also Thursday; the day they would see the Matthews' family homestead for the first time.

She called Gloria in and closed the back door behind her.

"Albert, make haste," she yelled up the stairs. He was supposed to be practising his maths, but she suspected he was just daydreaming as usual. As she waited she considered, for about the tenth time, what Jacob would say when he found out they had gone off for a night without him. He hated not knowing what was going on, but then, he wasn't here so what else was she supposed to do, sit around and wait for that pot of gold? Besides, it was a welcome distraction from missing Jack on his birthday. She paused for a moment, recalling the pleasure she had felt when she had read his first letter for herself, without help from one of the children. He had been so proud when he realised she had written back to him in her own shaky hand.

Bang, skip, bang, skip.

"Gloria, please sit down a minute," she said with an exhausted sigh. "You'll tire yourself out before we even get there."

Gloria bounced onto a stool by the kitchen table and folded her arms.

"When are we leaving?"

"Just as soon as your brother gets himself downstairs. The post usually leaves at nine so he had better get a move on."

She had paid for their tickets yesterday with the last few pennies she could spare. Gloria would have to do without her piano lesson next week, but she would tackle that little issue when it came around. She just prayed that Jacob would bring a little more money back with him when he came home.

A pair of feet thundered down the creaky stairs. Gloria looked around with anticipation. Emma put her hands on her hips.

"Finally lad, honestly you will be the death of my patience. Now get yourself out that door."

Albert grinned but did as he was told.

*

"Mrs B, Mrs B..."

Emma paused one foot on the footplate and one on the ground. She looked around to see Mr Price scurrying towards her like a large fat mouse, all big ears and pointy nose. He was holding a battered-looking envelope. Emma's heart leapt. Mr Price stopped and stuck out a pudgy hand containing the letter. She looked down at his reddened sweaty face and wondered what on earth had possessed a man so clearly ill-suited to the climate to up sticks and come to a country as hot as this one. But then everyone had their story here. No one would tell, but everyone surmised.

"From Master Jack, Mrs B. I recognise the hand." Mr Price scratched at his collar and adjusted his waistcoat.

"Thank you. It was very thoughtful of you to fetch it."

"I found it just now as I was sorting the delivery and thought you would want it right away."

"Yes, yes indeed. Thank you."

Emma took the envelope and ran her fingers over the scrawled directions. The coachman leaned down from his seat and raised his eyebrows impatiently.

"Madam we really must leave, I have a schedule to keep you know."

Emma smiled at the postmaster and thanked him again.

"Come on, Mam," Albert said. Emma glared at his impatience, considering it had been he that had delayed them.

Mr Price bobbed forwards into the best sort of bow his round middle would permit and scuttled away again. Grabbing hold of the rail Emma hoisted herself up onto the carriage and settled down for the ride. They would go through another village and past several homesteads before they reached the Matthews' farmstead. They wouldn't be there before eleven, so she had plenty of time to fumble her way through the letter. Carefully she tore it open and unfolded the page.

'*June 27th '57*

Dear Mam and Pa

I trust this letter finds you all well. It has been unseasonably cold today, so much so that I had to put on my vest and winter shirt, but aside from that things are ticking along nicely.

I had a review at the pottery yesterday. Mr Barker said my work was excellent. He inspected my pattern work and said I could move on to something a little more challenging! I've been doing a good dozen or so plates a day lately and today they gave me some chambers to do with roses on the side, so now I get to do a bit of freehand to. It's still following a design but it's better than stencils and a great opportunity to develop my own style. I'm still on piece work but that all adds up nicely at the end of the week, so all in all everything is ticking along nicely.

The Marlston Workhouse project is coming along. There is quite a group of us now. We have been trying to raise funds to get them extra rations but it's hard going. We did manage to get enough to pay for some new bunks for the children's dorm though. I just wish we could get them all proper homes instead.'

"Such a good conscience," Emma smiled.

'On a Brighter note Mrs Rogers, Miss Annie Feldman as was, had her baby last week; a healthy girl they are calling Grace. Mrs Feldman asked me to pass on the joyous news to you Mam, as she was sure you would want to hear. Well, that's about me for now. Love to the children.

Your loving son,

Jack'

Emma always fought back tears when she read her son's words. Part of it was simply the joy of reading them herself, part of it was pride for her son's achievements and finally, there was the jagged pain that sat in her heart. Only time would tell if she had done the right thing for them all, but nothing, not even knowing he was doing all right, took away the guilt or the agony of leaving Jack behind. She also hated that they were so far behind in his life. June was five months past and yet this was the closest she could get to being there with him. Emma closed her eyes and mumbled a small prayer of thanks.

*

"Wake up, Mam." Emma opened her eyes and sighed.

"Matthews' Farmstead," the coachman called again.

Emma folded her letter away and slipped it into her pocket just as they turned off the dusty main road. Beneath them, the springs of the carriage creaked and groaned as they trundled onto a rough dirt path littered with bumpy stones. Emma shielded her eyes and peered through the glare to see a huge house. The wooden slatted walls were bright beneath the sunlight and the windows gleamed and glinted like winking eyes. They made another small turn onto what constituted a driveway and the coach drew to a halt.

The coachman was on the ground before she had time to think. He handed Gloria down and then offered to assist Emma. Albert hadn't waited. He had jumped off the footplate and was belting towards the house before she had even moved. In the distance, there was the light clunk of a door swinging open and then two figures were hurtling towards them like ginger lightning bolts. It wasn't until the children met in the middle that Emma noticed how Alfie was now a good bit taller than Molly. He was lankly and so well tanned she could almost have mistaken him for an Aboriginal, had it not been for the shock of orange hair. Molly looked in exceptional health too, she had not grown so much in height but her body had filled out a little. There was a slight curve to her waist and the beginnings of breasts were protruding beneath her frock. The twins were eleven now and the healthy air and country life suited them. Her own children looked skinny and unfed in comparison. Emma bit her lip and made her way down the gravel path towards them.

"Welcome all of you, welcome," a male voice called.

Emma squinted at the stoop of the house. Standing hand in hand were Lucy and her burly husband Alfred. She had only seen Alf once before, the day he had come to collect his family from the immigrant barracks. She had thought then how handsome and strong he looked but now she could see it even better. His profile was smooth and leonine and his strawberry blond hair was brightened by long exposure to the sun, and his eyes matched the sky. A vision of a different pair of blue eyes danced before her. She gritted her teeth and pushed the image from her mind. Since the moment Jacob had arrived at the immigrant barracks she had determined never to think of Mr Finch again, and she had succeeded thus far, well, mostly.

"Oh Emma, we're so pleased you came." Lucy broke from her husband and rushed towards her, hugging her so tight that she stumbled backwards. Emma laughed and set her friend back but Lucy hadn't missed the look upon her face.

"What is it, Em? Are ya all right? Ya, look like you've seen a ghost."

Emma plastered a smile on her face and allowed Lucy to lead her up the steps to a small table that had been set out on the stoop.

"Nothing dear, just taken aback by how grand this all is." She felt her eyes sting with tears as she saw the freshly baked bread with jam, a large jug of fresh lemonade and glasses laid out on the table. "How lovely," she said, "you really shouldn't have gone to so much trouble just for us."

Alfred pulled back a chair and invited her to take a seat.

"All Alf's work," Lucy said running her hand over the smooth surface of the table. "He got real good at carpentry whilst he was...before we got here."

Emma looked at the table and chairs with admiration and wondered what skills exactly Jacob had acquired during his sentence. Panning for gold surely couldn't count.

*

A shimmer of moonlight cast silver streaks across the room. A gentle breeze hissed cooler air through the cracked open window. Emma sighed and stared at the freshly whitewashed ceiling. A faint scent of freshly shorn wood lingered in the air. Something fluttered outside. She glanced in the direction of the window and rubbed hands over her face. She couldn't sleep. It was the first time since childhood that she had slept alone. First, there had been Lilly the housemaid she had shared with at The Hall, then Jacob, and then Gloria. Even now, when Jacob was away, her daughter shared her bed. But tonight, at The Matthews Farmstead, Gloria was sharing with Molly, and the boys were together down the hall. Mr and Mrs Matthew were sleeping soundly next door. Emma was alone. She spread-eagled her arms and legs and felt the full width of the bed. She wriggled, puffed up the feathers in the pillow, turned over and turned over again. It was no use. She just couldn't settle without another warm living creature lying beside her.

An owl hooted close by. Emma kicked off the thin sheet, kneeled up on the bed and pulled back the window drapes. She watched as the heart-faced bird soared over the lawn and dived down at something. There was a screech from the ground as the owl landed its prey and whooshed off to a comfortable spot on the chicken coop roof. Emma couldn't take her eyes away from the creature, so elegant and yet ghoulish as it gobbled the poor mouse in its beak. They seemed to stay that way for a long time, its eyes glinting at her through the darkness as though he was watching her too. For a moment she had the compulsion to wave at it, but then realised how silly that would be. Instead, she tilted her head. It responded by doing the same. Emma gasped and smiled. After a few more moments she was about to look away when it suddenly took flight and came swooping towards her. Emma sat back on her heels and stared as it landed lightly on the outside window ledge. Part of her wanted to click the window shut so it couldn't come inside, and part of her wanted to open it wider and invite the bird in. Torn between reactions, she just continued to stare at the bird. It blinked its huge dark eyes.

"What do you want?"

The bird turned its head right around for a moment, looking at something behind, then turned back to her with even more intensity.

"Is there something out there?"

The bird looked up at the sky. Emma followed its gaze. Looking up beyond the trees stars glittering like white paint splattered across the black expanse of the universe. Emma's mind flashed back to the ship, and she could hear the voice of William Finch echo in her head. The night of the captain's birthday; the music that filled the air, the heat that had flooded right through to her soul as his hand had taken hers. The feel of his soft lips on her skin as he kissed the back of her hand made her weak at the knees, even now.

Forgetting the owl Emma stared out at the galaxy. Then she saw it. Right there, stars bright as lanterns; the Southern Cross. She had looked for it with the children before but had not quite managed to make it out. She had supposed her imagination was lacking, but now that she could see it she was astounded it had been missed. The owl clicked his beak, reminding her he was there.

"Look what you made me do. You made me think of William Finch," she chastised the bird. It blinked at her slowly and then with a sudden wild flutter it was gone, across the lawn, over the trees and into the endless sky.

Emma flopped back onto the bed and screwed her eyes tight shut. The twist of longing deep within her was biting at her harder than she could have anticipated.

"I'm just lonely," she said to herself. "Bloody Jacob, bringing us all the way out here only to abandon us for another pipe dream. Bloody goldfields. Bloody owl!" She muttered. When she finally fell asleep she dreamed of William Finch.

*

Emma awoke to the sound of retching from down the hall. For a moment panic rose in her chest; disease, illness, the fear had never left her since they had been on the ship. Out here they were little better off than they had been in the confines of the cabins. Finding a doctor to come out at short notice was near impossible. She was terrified it was one of the children. She hurriedly got out of bed. But then she heard Alf tell his wife to sit for a minute and take it easy, and the realisation hit her. Lucy had not put on weight from the country living; she was with-child. How had she not realised? She dressed and made her way to the kitchen where she found Lucy perched on a stool with a glass of freshly drawn water, and cooling herself with the fan Emma had bought in Rio.

"Why on earth didn't you tell me?"

Lucy looked up at her with a grin.

"We wanted to wait 'til I passed three month, but I should have known you would figure it out."

"How far along are you?"

Lucy lightly rubbed her hand over her belly.

"I reckon about ten weeks, but I think I'm already starting to show." To demonstrate the point she stood and smoothed over her corsetless frock. It was impossible to tell but Emma smiled and agreed. "Alf is over the moon. We ain't told the twins yet but I reckon they'll be just as excited."

Instinctively Emma touched her belly and felt a twinge of jealousy. She was only thirty-seven and her monthlies still came as regular as clockwork. There was no reason to think she wouldn't have another child. But the empty ache in her womb was not enough to convince her that it would be a good idea. Despite her natural desire, Emma prayed her own childbearing days were behind her. They could barely afford to keep the five of them as it was, another mouth would tip them over the edge. Besides, she had done with endless dirty napkins and late night feeds.

"I'm so pleased for you, both of you," she said hugging her friend tightly and giving Alf a nod of approval.

"Pleased about what?" Molly careered into the kitchen, closely followed by Gloria.

Alf looked at Lucy. She shrugged and her husband said,

"Your Ma is going to have a baby."

For a moment the girls just stood there staring, then Molly clapped her hands together.

"Alfie, Alfie come quick, we're going to have a new sister."

Alfie and Albert stumbled into the kitchen looking rather dazed and bleary-eyed. Emma could sympathise, though she suspected their lack of sleep was from talking or playing some silly game all night rather than the restless thoughts and dreams she had endured.

"Your Ma is going to have a baby," Alf offered when the boys didn't respond. Alfie nodded and rubbed his eyes like a small child, for a moment taking three or four years off his age.

"Good, another man about the house," he said eventually.

"No, another girl." Molly was adamant.

Lucy rolled her eyes at Emma and laughed.

"Oh Lord, I can see this little bundle is going to cause no end of arguments 'til it gets here."

*

Two days later

As the post chase clattered away from the farmstead, Emma settled into her seat for the ride. The carriage hit a hump in the road sending a pain shoot through the damaged nerve in her back. Emma winced and hoped the journey wouldn't be too arduous. She was overjoyed for Lucy and Alf but all their happiness only served to make her even lonelier. How could she be so with three, well two, boisterous children tearing around the house and filling it with noise? Yet there it was, sitting like a lead weight in her gut. She had never felt like this in England, why was it so different here? She would have to talk to Jacob when he came home.

3

A dusky blue hue hung over the cottage interior. Emma felt her head nod and her eyes droop for the umpteenth time. She blinked awake and rose from the kitchen chair. Instinctively she reached to the top shelf for the tea caddy then remembered they were almost out and she hadn't been able to afford to buy anymore. A floorboard creaked above her. She glanced at the ceiling and listened for a moment. It was only Gloria turning over in her sleep. The long hand on the wall clock clicked on to nine. Emma glared in the direction of the front door but there was still no sign of Jacob and Harry. They were usually home in time for tea. She looked at the neat pile of clean dishes on the drainer and decided to go to bed.

*

A rattle and a clunk shuddered through the house. Emma woke with a start. She sat bolt upright and held her breath. Footsteps on the stairs. Her heart raced as she watched the bedroom door handle turn with a creak.

"I thought you'd be asleep."

Jacobs's dark form loured in the doorway. Emma pressed a hand to her throat to calm her nerves and frowned. A chink of pinkish light sliced over the bed and outside the neighbour's cockerel crowed from their fence.

"Where the hell have you been?" she hissed. "It's almost dawn."

Jacob sat down on the end of the bed. Emma watched his back hunch over as he heaved off his boots and socks.

"They found a new seam yesterday morning, a big one. Me and some of the lads went down to assess it before we left. It made us late leaving but it was worth the wait. I reckon it is going to be a good little earner."

"You went down the mine? But you promised you would only pan. Tell me Harry didn't go with you?"

Emma heard the edge in her voice, sharp as broken glass. Jacob shook his head. She took a breath and tried to sound calmer.

"Promise me you won't start going down the mines regular."

Jacob didn't reply. He tugged off his jacket and hung it on the hook on the back of the door. As he turned she could see the tiredness on his lived-in face. He was still thin as a rake, despite her attempt at feeding him up, and his shoulders sagged heavier than ever. The early morning light made the lines on his face seem like deep crevices and dark rings were cast beneath his eyes. He had been handsome in his youth, but hard labour and the hot sun had made an old man of him at forty. Emma didn't like to consider how hard it had been for him, nor that he had brought it all upon himself. She reached out a hand to him as he walked slowly towards her.

"Where's Harry?"

"In his bed, I should imagine. He followed me up the stairs." Jacob stopped to unclip his braces and unfasten his shirt. He shrugged it off, letting it fall to the floor. Emma cringed. No matter how much she swept, there was always a layer of dust everywhere. But what did it matter, his shirt was filthy. Jacob only bothered taking the clothes on his back to the goldfields. Once upon a time, he had been a proud man, clean clothes as often as he could, always a pressed shirt and iron-creased trousers. Not now. She watched as he unbuttoned his trousers and slipped them off to reveal himself to her, as naked as the day he was born. This, Emma, had taken a while to get used to. He had never slept naked in his life before he left England. Not even in their first days of marriage. But the heat here in summer made him irritable during the night and so at some point over the past few years, he had grown accustomed to sleeping nude the moment the weather turned.

He crawled over the bed towards her. She shuffled aside and lay next to him as he sunk down into the creaky old bed. He smelled of sweat and must. He wrapped his arms around her and pulled her in so close she could feel every inch of him. For a moment she wondered if he wanted to take her, but he was snoring into her hair before she had even formulated an excuse. It wasn't that she had lost her desire for her husband, he was still attractive despite the extra years on his face, but if she didn't want another child she was going to be very careful about when she let him have his way.

*

Nibs scratched a dark inky scrawl across the cheap lumpy paper. Albert was sitting at the kitchen table writing out a passage of the Bible. The teacher at the school thought his writing was a little behind the other children, so Emma had set Albert and Gloria a practice task. Harry was slowly reading out the words to Bert. He was growing impatient, especially since Gloria had already finished hers and gone outside. Emma looked at the cracked black leather bible with its foxed yellow pages and noticed there was a long slit in the cover. The beaten-up little copy of the New Testament that her son held in his hands was the same one his father had been given for his confirmation. She hadn't known Jacob then, they had met when she was eighteen and working at the Hall. He still went to church then. He had been charming and respectable. The first trait had persuaded her, the second had persuaded her father. Within a year they had been married and she expecting Jack. They had been happy. She would never have guessed in a thousand years how they would end up.

Harry felt her stare and looked up.

"What is it, Mam?" His lips curled. "You're not going to get all sentimental are you?"

Emma shook her head and turned away so that the children couldn't see her tears. She picked up the dishcloth and began to dry off the breakfast pots. You couldn't swing a cat in the poky kitchen in their rickety rented cottage. But things could definitely be worse.

Heavy footsteps came up behind her and a pair of hands grabbed her waist. Jacob spun her around and tugged her pelvis against his.

"The children," she hissed.

She struggled against him in embarrassment as he kissed her. He laughed and the boys groaned and complained about the spectacle. This was something else Jacob would never have done before, not in front of the children. Emma blushed furiously. She pushed him away and told him to sit so she could fix him breakfast.

As she boiled their last two eggs and Jacob looked over Albert's handy work, she took a chance,

"I need to buy food," she said, as casually as she could manage. Jacob paused.

"Don't you have anything left from the housekeeping I gave you?"

The money Jacob had given her three weeks since was barely enough for a fortnight and the last of it had gone on the tickets for the post chase to the Matthews'. Emma bit her lip.

"Food isn't cheap."

"That must mean 'no'," his tone was even harsher than she expected.

Emma dare not turn around during the moment's silence that followed.

"Well, don't you want this then?"

Emma was confused. She turned around to see Jacob holding out a grimy hand containing a small pouch and a cheeky grin. Cautiously she took it from him and pulled at the strings to reveal a cluster of coins, enough to keep them for a good month, probably more.

"There's a small fortune in here," she spluttered. "Where did you get it?" She hadn't meant to sound so accusatory. She prayed he hadn't noticed. If he had, he chose to ignore it.

"We found a couple of good nuggets. I put some in the bank as well."

Emma was bemused. She looked at her husband's weatherworn face and wondered if she had heard right.

"Bank?"

"I opened it eighteen months or so ago when I was saving for the house. We just haven't had a lot to put in it lately."

Emma scratched her head and tried to comprehend what he was telling her. She had never had a bank account before; it seemed like something only rich people did. She shook her head and blinked.

"How much do we have?"

Jacob shrugged.

"Not a lot. Most of it went on the land and then there was your passage. I reckon there will be more soon enough though."

The small rise of hope in Emma's heart sank down again. There wasn't anything to get hopeful about then.

"You mean when you start on that new gold seam in Bendigo?" There was that sharp edge in her voice again.

Jacob's back stiffened.

"I told you, we will get sorted. This gold is the best thing that could have happened to us, Emma, and don't you forget it."

Damn it. She needed to tell him about the visit to the Matthews' and making him angry was not the way to go about it. She decided to wait until later. It was not that he had anything against the Matthews exactly. He just hadn't been keen on hearing how she had made such close friends in his absence, nor would he like to hear that she had gone somewhere without at least asking him first. Perhaps she should have sent a note to the goldfields. Well, it was too late for that now.

She set one of the eggs in the eggcup before him. He picked up a spoon, cracked it in one smart pat and sliced off the top. As he dipped a finger of half stale bread in the yoke, Gloria bounded in from the outside deck where she had been playing. Jacob looked up at her and his expression melted.

"Pa, you're up!" She threw her arms around his neck and hugged him. Emma had been thrilled at how well Jacob and their daughter were getting along. She had been afraid there would be trepidation, perhaps even fear in the child, and Jacob, only used to sons, would not know what to make of her. But they had taken to each other instantly. She was Daddy's little girl all right, just the way Emma had been with her father. Emma was pleased of course, though she couldn't help feeling a little jealous.

Gloria noted the breakfast he was consuming and said with a broad, proud smile,

"Don't you love those eggs? They came from the Matthews' farm."

Jacob swallowed and set down his spoon. Emma winced and felt her heart rise to her throat. Gloria's eyes grew wide as she read her mother's expression. Emma gave her an 'it's all right' smile.

"I was going to tell you just as soon as you got home, but then it was so late and you were so tired."

A flock of rosella swirled into the tree by the back door, squawking and cooing. Emma rubbed at the nerve in her back and swallowed.

"Mrs Matthews called here on Tuesday last and invited us all to visit."

Jacob nodded thoughtfully.

"Well, Harry and I shall be back in Bendigo in a day or so but I see no reason why you and the children shouldn't go."

Emma was relieved thus far.

"The invitation was for last Thursday, the nineteenth. We knew you wouldn't mind us visiting such good friends so we..."

"You went without telling me!"

Harry closed the bible and placed it on the table. From the corner of her eyes, Emma saw him gesture for Gloria and Albert to follow him into the front room. It was a room they barely ever used just as back in England. She waited until she heard them close the door.

"Please don't be angry Jake. We thought you would be happy for us to get out and about. You know how hard it has been out here. How lonely it is." The moment the words were out she regretted them. It was not that Jacob would ever raise a hand to her, she had no fear of that, but she knew how he liked to be in control. When he was in prison there was nothing he could do or say, but now they were together again, he needed to be 'the man again' as he put it. He had dark moods before he went to gaol but something had happened to him out here, prison, the voyage, hard labour or perhaps even their absence. Whatever it was it ran deep and dark. It was as though he was trapped in quicksand. She watched his fingers twitch to his waistcoat pocket and prayed that there wasn't a flask in there. He saw her watching and stopped.

"I'm not angry, Emma. I want you all to be happy here."

Emma held her breath and waited.

"I know you don't want me and Harry to go away, but it's for your own good, for all our good. When the gold comes right we shall have the best life you can ever imagine."

At least he wasn't chastising her. She wondered if she should protest, tell him that it wasn't his fault, but she couldn't lie. For one thing, he would see through her and that would make it worse. Besides, she hadn't come all this way for him to be still absent.

"We were without you for seven years at home and now we have shift for ourselves again here."

"This is your home, Emma!"

She hadn't realised what she had said until his response.

"I didn't mean it like that. It's just hard to call anywhere home except the place I grew up." Emma could feel the tears building up behind her eyes. She had never been a cry-baby but of late she found tears stinging her eyes more and more often. Her voice cracked and she turned away from him. She heard a scrape as he unscrewed the top to his flask and gulp back the contents.

"You never used to drink, Jake. I wish you could let me in, tell me..."

"I never used to do a lot of things. Life is different out here!" his lips were white and his fists curled. Emma carried on regardless,

"Then why did you send for us, why did you stay? You could have come h...back to England."

"And do what? Walk down the street as if nothing happened. Endure all the whisperings and mutterings behind our backs. And who would employ an ex-convict. How would I have done all that, Emma? I would have been more an exile back there than out here." He was on his feet pacing back and forth.

This conversation had been coming for months, and that now it was upon her Emma found she was relieved.

"We could have moved somewhere else, started again." She knew this was a futile thought but it needed to be said.

"No, Emma, I did the only thing I could have done for us. Yet all I have done is make you miserable," his voice cracked.

Emma risked looking at his face. His pallor was ashen and his fists were shaking, but not from anger.

"I should have released you, let you think I was dead." He slumped down onto the stool and rested his head in his hands.

Emma pressed her fingers to her lips. This was not the result she had anticipated. She had imagined anger and frustration. These had been the reactions she had witnessed before when she had asked if she could take a position at one of the hotels when she had suggested Harry take an apprenticeship, and especially when she had suggested they move into the city. But this time the blackness in him was turned solely upon himself. Perhaps it always had been. She looked at the broken man before her and wondered what had happened to the swagger and confidence of the person she had married. His whole body was shaking. Slowly she reached out a hand to him. As her fingers made contact he flinched. Quietly she crept up beside him. He moved his hands and looked at her. The moment their eyes met threw his arms around her waist and pulled her close. His head pressed against her stomach like a hurt child, wracked with sobs. Emma was astounded. She tried to raise him to his feet but he grasped all the tighter. Gently she began to stroke his hair. She tried to speak, but words failed her. All the thoughts she'd had about William Finch, all the wicked desires that burned inside her stabbed like a thousand swords at her heart. How could she ever have betrayed this man, so defenceless, so in need of her love and loyalty? At that moment Emma resolved to give every ounce of strength she had to Jacob.

4

December 24th 1857

Wood smoke drifted in on the breeze. It crept under the door and through every crack in each window. There had been a fire in the bush. The intense blaze of the sun in that perpetually blue sky had dried out everything. The flames had swept over the fields and raised trees to the ground leaving them as charred and twisted as burnt out matchsticks and the earth crisp and black. Thankfully it had not come close enough to be a threat to the village, this time. But it was a concern she had never thought of until now. Jacob had said they should keep a barrel of water by the back door, just in case, but she was constantly refilling it as it kept evaporating.

Since the day he had broken down and cried out his heart, Emma had not been able to do enough for her husband. She had waited on him hand and foot. She had not argued when he had said that he and Harry were going down the mine, and they had not yet gone back to the Matthews' farmstead despite a further invitation. But today was Christmas Eve and finally, they would all get to meet again. This time Jacob and Harry were coming too. Emma was delighted and the children were as excited as if they were going to stay with the queen.

Emma folded Jacob's extra shirt into the basket and placed it on top of the boys' change of clothes. With the palms of her hands, she squashed them in, then laid the clean kitchen cloth over the top. Glancing at the big trunk in the corner of the bedroom she wished she had somewhere to unpack its contents, but the cottage had already come with the essentials and so there wasn't any use for their own things until the farm was ready- sometime never. The clasps to the clothes trunk had been broken during the storm at sea, so it had been put to use as a linen chest. Emma set down the basket on the lid and put her hands on her hips. As she looked around she considered how glad she would be to see the back of this tiny room for a few days. This cottage didn't feel like home, no matter how much she tried to make it so.

"Ready, Em?"

She turned around to see Jacob leaning against the doorjamb, arms folded and looking a little too intensely at her figure.

"I see what you're thinking, and we don't have time."

Jacob shrugged.

"The children are out in the yard and we have a good half hour until the post chase comes."

Emma sighed,

"Yes, love, but also a ten-minute walk, carrying the bags."

Her husband looked at her with puppy dog eyes and Emma conceded with a raise of her eyebrows. The moment he saw her expression change he was over by the bed and pulling her down beneath him. As his lips met hers and his hand slid up beneath her skirts Emma groaned. She hadn't really believed that she had been missing a man's touch, despite all her dreamy thoughts of Mr Finch, not until the first time Jacob had taken her again anyway. She arched her back and tried not to cry out as his tongue curled around hers and his fingers probed deep within her. She closed her eyes and saw that beautiful face. She didn't mean to picture him. She intended to enjoy Jacob. But she couldn't stop herself. It had become a habit of late. In her mind, she was running her hands through a shock of thick black hair and he was looking down at her with those bright blue eyes. She tried to open her eyes but the lids stayed closed. She tried to replace his face with Jacobs but the image wouldn't shift. Jacob began to mutter things she could not repeat, touching her, sliding inside her until she could hold back the cry no longer.

"Oh, William!"

Emma froze; her back a sudden twist of agony and her heart banging against her chest so hard she thought it would break her ribs. How could she have said such a thing? She bit her lip and held her breath.

Jacob shuddered over her with an animalistic grunt and collapsed on top of her. He began to kiss her neck tenderly but as he felt the contortion of her body beneath him he rolled away.

"Emma? Are you all right? I thought you had...What did you say?"

Emma breathed out slowly and tried to focus.

"Nothing, I just, I did, but then my back! The nerve." This wasn't a lie, the pain was excruciating. But she wasn't sure which was worse, that or the guilt.

"Here, let me...." He helped her turn onto her stomach then gently began to rub the small of her back through her corset until the tightness and pain eased.

"Oh, Lord! We'll miss the post. Help me up." Emma was too flustered to be grateful. She didn't know what she was more panicked about, not getting to the Matthews or that Jacob would realise she had called out another man's name. Either way, it seemed prudent to make haste to meet the post. Jacob knew nothing of Mr Finch and she was certain the children didn't know his given name, but Lucy did. Her friend would not give her away, but one question, one comment about the teacher and her expression might.

Emma slid slowly off the bed and bent to wipe the sticky wetness from between her legs, but the moment she did her back went into some kind of muscle spasm. The pain made her gasp. She gritted her teeth and forced herself to straighten up and retrieve the basket from the top of the linen chest.

"Don't be daft, lass. Let me and the boys carry everything." Jacob ran a hand over her back and patted her behind. Emma tried to smile.

"Children! Time to go!" she called, just as Albert appeared at the bottom of the stairs.

"Ah good, Bert, take one of these baskets. Your Mam's back is playing up, so be a good lad and carry it for her. Your brother can take the other."

Jacob was watching Emma carefully. She couldn't make out whether it was out of concern, or confusion. She decided to presume the former and hobbled down the stairs.

5

Matthews Farmstead
December 26th 1857

The scent of fresh grass mingled with the delicious smell of dinner. The sun hung low over the horizon like a giant precious stone. Emma rose from her chair on the deck and stretched her back. This was a life she could get used to. Lucy had shooed her out of the kitchen and put Molly and Gloria to work drying the pots. Emma felt odd sitting outside with the boys but she was glad of the rest. Christmas day had been a manic affair. The children had been running around since dawn, for once allowed to be as wild as they liked. Animals to feed, the pony's barn to sweep, eggs to collect, sheep to herd and the new escapologist of a goat to chase. Not to mention breakfast and then dinner to cook. Lucy had hit the nail on the head when she had said their new life on the farm was hard work but worth every second of it. Emma felt a hand touch the side of her skirt.

"You all right, lass? Your back still bothering you?"

She turned away from the sunset and looked at Jacob.

"Aye, but not so bad as yesterday." She smiled and took his hand. He seemed not to have noticed her little slip up the other morning. "What a lovely place you've got here, Alf. I know I've said it before, but you really have made a good life for yourselves." She felt Jacob's grip tighten on her fingers. She looked down at their hands and then up at his face. His lips were pressed into a thin line. For a moment he held her gaze, but then turned to Alf.

"You shall have to tell me your secret, sir. We'll be starting on our own little farm soon enough and a few tips on animal husbandry wouldn't go amiss." There was something not quite honest in his voice that none but she would have detected. Emma narrowed her eyes at him until he smiled broadly, released her, stretched out his legs and placed his hands behind his head. "Yes, Alf Matthews, you've made right good here."

At first, Emma had been a little envious of the Matthews' prosperity. She knew Jacob might be a bit jealous too, but it had not occurred to her just how keenly he would feel it. She bit her lip and chastised herself. She would have to reassure him. She didn't get the chance.

"How goes it in the goldfields, Mr Burns?" Alf asked.

Emma sighed. They had stayed away from the subject thus far, but it could not be avoided completely.

"Aye, not bad. We've been working on a new seam, a pretty deep one at that. Money's coming in nicely now."

Alf was nodding with interest.

"Now don't ya be getting any ideas, husband. There's too much work for us here to spare ya." Lucy pulled back a chair and settled herself next to him. Alf laughed and kissed her hand.

"I ain't leaving you again, Mrs Matthews, especially not now you're in the family way." He reached over and patted her belly. Lucy beamed, but Emma caught the glance fired in her direction. Emma looked at her husband. His eyes were like dark holes, his inadequacy pecking at his thoughts.

Later, as Emma was tucking Gloria and Molly into bed, she noticed Lucy was watching. Emma pulled the window too so that insects couldn't fly in and let down the drape. The child yawned and snuggled into the feather mattress, the drawstrings beneath creaking as she moved. Emma kissed her forehead and gently untied the pretty new ribbons she had been given for Christmas and laid them on the small bedside table. When she was done Lucy blew out the candle next to her daughter's bed. Molly smiled up at her mother and shuffled away from Gloria's hot body. Lucy glanced down the hall, past the other three bedroom doors and into the open space of the living room where Harry and their husbands were settled for the remainder of the evening. Moving closer to Emma she whispered,

"Your Jacob, I don't think prison done him well. He seems jumpy and well, I noticed that flask he keeps in his waistcoat pocket. He weren't always like that were he?"

Emma shook her head and led her friend into the room she was sharing with Jacob and closed the door.

"Trust you to see right through the skirts and see the corset. He was always a dreamer and hard to settle, but now, now, it's like he's someone else altogether. I try to make him feel strong and in control, but I just can't quite reach him. He gets in such dark moods; ones where he can't talk to anyone and his eyes seem like there are demons behind them. And then the day before yesterday..." Emma explained what had happened in the bedroom. Lucy raised an amused eyebrow at her.

"What if he finds out about William Finch," Emma said desperately. "I think it would kill him to know I had feelings for another man?"

"Ya don't think he'd be angry then?"

Emma rubbed a hand over her mouth and shook her head.

"Of course he would, but I think there would be more anguish than wrath."

Lucy pursed her lips into a wry smile.

"Then be grateful of that bad nerve in your back and forget about Mr Finch once and for all."

Emma couldn't help but laugh a little. She breathed out in relief.

"Thank you, Lucy. I don't know how I would have got on this past year without you."

An owl hooted outside. Lucy went over, pushed the window as wide as it could and leaned out to shoo it away. Emma stopped her.

"Leave it. It's not doing any harm and it's quite beautiful when you watch it."

Lucy turned back to her with a light laugh.

"Fine, if ya like, but don't blame me if he keeps ya up all night hooting."

"I thought you'd be glad of a mouse catcher. We get no end of rats near us. If you don't want him, send him our way."

Lucy shrugged and pulled the window too.

"I suppose he does do some good, but he's a noisy bugger and it keeps making me dream queer things."

Emma thought of the dreams she had last time she was there and cringed.

6

Flemington
Late January 1858

It was a dingy summers day with a chill in the air. Emma pulled her shawl around her shoulders and shivered. Yesterday had been blisteringly hot, yet today felt like she had slipped back to England. She thought about Jack and how cold he would be in Staffordshire. It was funny how she still thought of the seasons as being all wrong. How could it be January if it was summer?

Outside the children were taking advantage of the extra energy the cooler air had given them and were tearing about the yard playing tag. Emma went to the kitchen window and watched them for a minute. She smiled at their laughter and wished Jacob was home to share it. In the front room, the clock clunked past the hour with the grinding thump that constituted a chime. The long ocean voyage had damaged the poor thing and she hadn't been able to afford to have it mended. She counted six clicks and decided she ought to make a start on tea. She opened the bottom cupboard door and dragged out the stew pot.

*

There were four full bellies at the table and one full plate. Emma shooed the children out of the kitchen.

"Go play in your room 'til your Pa gets home." Beneath the smile, she masked a grimacing frown. Jacob had a meeting with a chap at The Rose and Thorn Hotel. When she had asked him what it was about she had received a muttered response that included the words 'building materials.' Emma wasn't convinced it was anything of the like, but she had decided to give him the benefit of the doubt. 'I'll only be on hour,' he had assured her. That was at noon. Emma placed Jacob's untouched plate on top of the cooling stove and draped a dry cloth over it to keep the flies off. Just as she began to pile the dishes in the sink and put the kettle on to heat some water, the front door clicked open.

"Tea ready, Em?" Jacob slurred.

Emma rolled her eyes. She might have known he'd come back when he got hungry.

"On the stove," she replied coldly, continuing to clear up.

"Pa, Pa, how was the meeting, do we have new things for the house?" Gloria had appeared at the top of the stairs. Jacob stumbled into the bannister as he made his way to the kitchen.

"Let your Pa eat his tea, then he can tell us all about it," Emma called, hoping they would start a game and forget about asking again.

Jacob slumped into a chair at the kitchen table and looked up at her with glassy eyes. Emma sighed and handed him his plate. He glanced at the empty spaces and the dishes in the sink.

"You didn't wait?"

Emma shrugged.

"The children were hungry."

"Well, that's nice in't it. You couldn't hang on ten minutes for your husband."

Emma bit her lip.

"It's nearly eight o'clock, Jake! You're a lot more than ten minutes late."

She felt Jacob's glare on her back as she picked up the screeching kettle and added the boiling water to the cold already coating the dishes.

"So, how was the meeting?" She added, attempting to sound chirpy. She wouldn't get it out of him by provoking an argument. Jacob belched and a stench of alcohol drifted over from the table. Emma pursed her lips.

"Good tea this," he said with a sniff.

"Who were you meeting?" she tried again.

"Couple of gents, about the house."

Emma scowled.

"Long meeting," she commented.

"They invited me to stay for drinks. It would have been rude to decline."

Emma winced as the nerve in her back cramped. She stretched forward a little and tried not to let the pain show.

"And did we get things for the house?"

When Jacob didn't answer she glanced over her shoulder. He looked up from his now half-empty plate, a fork piled high with mash potato paused by his mouth

"Not sure yet."

Emma sighed and conceded. She could tell she wasn't going to get anything more out of him tonight. She set a pan on the narrow drainer, hung the scrubbing brush over the nail its the shelf and took off her pinny.

"Wash your plate when you're done," she instructed.

Jacob watched her leave the room.

"Where you off?"

"Laundry to fold upstairs," she replied, for once glad to have a pile of washing to deal with.

7

Mid-February 1857

Another sleepless night. Emma's back was driving her to distraction. She abandoned her bed and her sleeping daughter for the confines of Jacob's old wing-chair in the front room, and Jack's new letter.

'September 4th 1857

Dear Mam and Pa

Everything is going on all right here. Yesterday I went to the Marlston with Mr Oliver and two other chaps from the potteries.'

Emma's chest puffed with pride. Her eldest boy was so conscientious and certainly a doer and not a dreamer like his Pa. She wondered what Jacob thought of Jack. He never really talked of him and when any of them mentioned him Jacob would get irritable and change the subject. She supposed that he must see the stark contrast between them.

'Mr Feldman was meant to come along too, but Mrs Feldman is laid up with a bad cold so he had to stay and look after the shop.'

Emma reminded herself that she must send her old friend her best regards when she wrote back.

'We were to assess the improvements and make sure the place is being kept spick and span, to avoid any further outbreaks of Typhus.'

Emma shuddered at the thought.

'The place was cleaner all right, but still overcrowded and the male side, in particular, was still in desperate need of improvement. And there are so many children in there. It would have made you so sad to see it, Mam.'

It made her sad even to read it, and for the third time too. Such things always reminded her how close she and the children had come to going in there. Had it not been for her father's lease on the old cottage, she shuddered to think.

'As for me, work is ticking along.'

As always, she tried to picture him, paintbrush in hand and concentrate on his face.

'I seem to be doing all right and getting along nicely with the other lads and lasses. We all went for a drink at the Quacking Duck after work on Friday, so that was nice.'

Emma smiled and wondered if he had made any particular friends.

'Well, I'll write again soon.

Love, your son, Jack'

She sighed and slipped the letter back into its battered little envelope. The sun was just beginning to peak over distant fields lighting the clouds with a silvery glow. No point going back to bed now. *Might as well start with the cleaning,* she mused. She drew in a long breath of cool air and wondered when her husband might return from the fields. Her housekeeping was dwindling and she was missing Harry.

8

Early March 1858

Wheels rolled and rattled over the bumpy cobbled ground. The trap was small and uncomfortable and the pony seemed to be more interested in other traffic and people walking past than paying attention to his mistress.

"The suspension is terrible; it can't be good for the baby," Emma said for the third time.

Lucy took her eyes from the road and looked at her. Emma instinctively reached for the reins. Not that she knew how to drive a pony and trap. Lucy laughed at her.

"I did much worse than this when I was carrying the twins, now relax and enjoy the ride."

As she said this, they hit a loose cobble with one of the front wheels, sending the stone hurtling out backwards and both women bounced hard on the wooden seat. Emma reached up for her hat and held it down.

"Thank goodness it's only nine miles," she grumbled. They had already done a good eight of them. The Matthews had acquired the trap a month ago and Lucy had already driven it into Melbourne twice previously. Yet this knowledge didn't make Emma feel any easier.

"We could've brought the children ya know. They could 'ave sat in the back, a bit snug when we've got the bits in, granted, but they would've enjoyed the ride."

Another bump. Emma slid sideways in her seat and was almost spilt out.

"Yes dear, very snug," she said, not sure whether to keep hold of her hat or grab onto the side of the cart. "Maybe next time."

The children were at the farm with Alf. Lucy had collected Emma, Albert and Gloria yesterday for a night or two. Jacob and Harry were away at the fields, again. Today Lucy had a meeting in the city and they needed a few supplies. Emma hadn't been into Melbourne for months. As they approached the centre, the streets felt narrow and claustrophobic, and yet in truth, they were wide and spacious. She had certainly gotten used to country life. In the distance smoke pummelled the sky, sending spirals of grey upwards. It reminded Emma of home and for a moment she was transported back to the heavy smog, clinging to the Staffordshire skyline, choking them with factory fumes. Emma pictured Jack, still there, sitting at his station in the potteries, head down and paintbrush in hand.

"Penny for 'em."

Emma glanced at Lucy.

"I was just missing Jack is all."

"Ah. I'm sure ya do, but I don't think that's what's really botherin' you is it?"

Emma's shoulders sank and she shook her head.

"Jacob's drinking is getting worse and I daren't even ask about his gambling. And all that time in the mines is making Harry look like death warmed up. He's so pale and skinny. But Jacob won't listen, and Harry does what his Pa wants. What kind of wife and mother am I to drive her husband and son to this?"

"That ain't true! You've been trying to persuade Jacob to finish the farm or sell the land and move to the city. It ain't your fault he's having none of it. You're doing ya best for ya family." They turned onto the main thoroughfare, "We's here now so we'd better find somewhere to park. The wool chap is in the Merchant Exchange over there." Lucy gestured with her arm, tugging the reins sideways so that the pony snorted and stamped his feet in annoyance.

Lucy jumped down. Emma watched with disapproval as her friend smoothed her skirts over her now very visible bump.

"I do wish you would take more care."

Lucy laughed.

"In a few weeks I'll be too big to do anything, so I'll do as I please whilst I still can."

"Well, just don't do anything that'll make you sorry later." Emma joined Lucy on the pavement and helped her tie Marvin (the pony) to a lamppost near the corner of Flinders Street. Emma was not sure what the general etiquette was with parking one's trap in the middle of Melbourne city, but she was pretty sure it did not involve just tethering it up at the side of a busy street. Deciding not to argue Emma noticed a small haberdashery in a row of shops across the way.

"I'm just going to pop over there while you take care of business," she said. "I've been thinking it's time to teach Gloria to sew and she needs a new frock."

Lucy nodded.

Emma crossed the street, hopping over a steaming pile of fresh horse manure and narrowly missing another. She had been quite surprised by the size and scale of Melbourne. In only twenty-two years, the whole area had gone from being open fields to a thriving city that had just risen up from nothing. There were factories, gas works, a theatre, banks, the post office, merchants' hall, shops, houses and now villages like Flemington were sprawling out from it like spiders legs into the outlying areas, and of course, there was the prison. Emma tried not to think about those sorts of things. She pushed open the door to the haberdashery and stepped inside.

Heavy dark shelves were piled high with a rainbow of fabrics. As Emma made her way over to a selection of light coloured bails she noticed the two women behind the counter were staring and whispering. Emma glanced over her shoulder. They were not looking at her, but a woman on the other side of the shop. Whoever she was had her back to Emma and was looking over a book of patterns.

Emma watched the white-gloved hand gently turning the pages and then she realised why the women were staring. This girl was Aboriginal. Slivers of dark skin peeked out between her cuffs and gloves as she moved and at the back of her neck beneath the roll of thick dark hair. She had never seen an Aborigine wearing western clothes before, and certainly not in the city. In fact the only natives

Emma had ever set eyes upon before were a small group that congregated beneath a tree at the edge of their village during a rainstorm;' sheltering like cows' Jacob had said. She hated that he could see people that way. It seemed even worse to find such opinions coming from an ex-convict like him.

The women behind the counter were debating which of them should go and serve her and which would get the nice English woman instead. Emma suddenly pitied her and was about to go over to talk to her when the woman looked around.

Emma froze. This was no Aboriginal, this girl was coloured. And she had seen her before. The woman's flawless skin was as much aglow in the dim lights of this shop as it had been under the African sun. Her beauty was astounding and her eyes were warm like melted chocolate. Emma put her hand to her throat. She could have saved the girl the humiliation from the shop girls by greeting her; after all, she did know her by name. Or at least she hoped she remembered it right. But they had never actually met, let alone been introduced. Emma was suspended between propriety and kindness. The girl offered her a polite smile and turned back to the pattern book, saving her the trouble of deciding.

Finally, the argument between the shop girls was settled and the younger of the two stepped out from behind the counter and towards Emma. The other forced a smile and offered her assistance to Mercy. Emma couldn't help trying to listen to the other woman's conversation. Indeed so got so distracted that she almost purchased the wrong fabric for Gloria's new frock and clean forgot to ask for a few scraps for her daughter to learn her stitches on. She did at least remember to buy the thread and a new set of needles. She was trying so hard to hear the address that the African woman gave for her delivery that she even gave the shop girl the wrong money. She left the shop in a fluster. Irritated at herself, as much for not having introduced herself to Mercy as the mess she made with her purchases.

*

"Did you see who that was?"

Lucy was walking across the street towards Emma, who had taken a spot standing by the cart to wait for her. It had also afforded her a chance to watch for Mercy leaving the haberdashery, which she did just as Lucy emerged for the wool merchants. Emma glanced back at Mercy as she walked elegantly down the opposite side of the street.

"That woman, I could swear that's Mr Finch's doxy from Cape Town. I'd swear it on my baby's life."

Emma sighed.

"You shouldn't say such things about your baby Lucy, nor do we know if she's a doxy. But you're quite right. That was her. Here in Melbourne. We can only presume that Mr Finch is not so heartless after all. Perhaps she was always going to follow on later." Emma didn't quite know how she felt about all this. "And she gave her name as Mrs Finch in the store, so they must be married," she added.

Lucy rolled her eyes.

"Don't you go defending him? And she's not likely to admit to being a whore is she. She's bound to say they are married." She cocked her head at Emma and narrowed her eyes. "Here, ya didn't speak wiv her did ya?"

Emma shook her head,

"No. I didn't know what to say. I...It's just that...urgh! She folded her arms, cross with herself for even caring. "I should only be thinking of Jacob and the children, not some silly school teacher."

Lucy looked as though she were about to tell her to forget Mr Finch and his doxy but then thought better of it. Instead, she suggested they take tea somewhere and sit down for a minute to catch their breaths. Emma was going to protest at first, but she did have a few spare coins in her purse. It was a nice feeling to think she could afford such a luxury for once, so she agreed.

*

The tea trolley clattered and the steamer whistled. The sweet sugary scent of meringue filled the small cafe and made Emma feel warm inside, but as she watched the waiter set down the teapot her memory stirred once again. This time she thought of the tearoom in Rio, where she had looked into that man's beautiful eyes and almost lost herself. She stirred her tea rather too vigorously and Lucy placed a hand over hers to stop her.

"Good lord, Em. That girl really 'as rattled you ain't she?"

Emma didn't want to admit it. She really must get a grip of herself. Lucy changed the subject.

"Alf and me 'ave been trying to decide on names for the baby."

Emma smiled and took a sip of tea.

"And did you agree on anything?"

Lucy grinned and laughed.

"Well, the twins say they wants to call it Ernest if it's a boy and Grace if it's a girl. But Alf likes Tobias…"

Emma allowed Lucy to continue about the baby while she concentrated on devouring the meringue. The pleasure of being away from home and eating delicious things was beginning to make Emma feel much more relaxed, until the moment when Lucy paused. It was only for an instant, and at first, Emma presumed she was simply taking a breath, but as she glanced at her friend's face she realised that something outside had distracted her. Emma turned to look out of the window. Just across the street was Mercy Finch. She looked left and right then stepped out into the street and made her way across the road. She raised her elegantly gloved hand and waved at someone standing with his back to the window. Emma turned further around and tried to see whom it was, but the writing on the glass masked his face. Not that it mattered. His countenance gave him away. She would know that man anywhere. For one horrifying moment, Emma thought they were going to come inside. Lucy reached out a hand and rested it on Emma's arm.

"I'm sorry, we had no way of knowing they would be in town today too. Perhaps we should go before they sees us."

Emma agreed and was waving to the waiter to fetch the bill when Lucy sat back and shook her head. Emma looked around just in time to see Mercy take William's arm and the pair of them walk away. Emma felt as though her heart was stuck so high in her throat that she could barely swallow the last bite of meringue. As Lucy emptied the dregs of the teapot into Emma's cup and dropped in an extra sugar cube, she was overwhelmed by a sense of foreboding. She couldn't quite put her finger on what it was, but seeing them in town had set something in motion, and she was not sure she wanted to know what it was.

9

Flemington
April 1858

The whistle of an axe and the smell of freshly dried grass drifted up to Emma's bedroom window. She sat bolt upright and looked out at the rising sun. It was early, very early. She glanced at the empty dent in the bed where Jacob had been, sank back and closed her eyes again. She knew she wouldn't get long to lie in. It was Sunday and there was morning service to attend, but for now, she savoured a few minutes of quiet solitude. Outside she could hear Jacob talking to someone as he chopped firewood. He and Harry had finally made it home from the goldfields yesterday afternoon, for a few days anyway. The conversation seemed tense. Emma tried to discern who's the second voice was. She had presumed it one of the boys, but the tone was too deep. Curiosity getting the better of her, she knelt up on the bed, peered through the window into the yard.

First, she looked at Jacob and Harry, then towards the fence at the end of the McLeish's garden. Through the silvery hue, she could see no one else. The voice spoke again but this time with a croak that slipped it back into a child-like drawl and to her great surprise Emma realised it was coming from Harry. She stared down at him. His shoulders were still as skinny and narrow as a boy's. He was as tall as her now, that she knew, but when had his voice begun to break, when had he made this step toward becoming a man? He would be fourteen in a few months; she should hardly be surprised. Had it been creeping on so slowly that she hadn't noticed, or was this a painful symptom of his repeated absences to the fields? The stints at the mines were getting longer and longer. This last time, they hadn't seen Harry and his father for a month complete. Emma was about to wave at them when she heard Harry say,

"Promise you'll stop seeing her Pa, or I shall tell Mam."

Emma felt the blood drain from her face. She wanted to turn away but somehow she couldn't. She gripped at the window ledge and leaned back so they wouldn't see her watching.

"You will do no such thing lad. You will do as I say or feel the wrath of my belt on your backside. Don't you go thinking you're too grown-up for that? Besides she means nowt to me, she's just some floozy I knew from before you came out here."

Harry's voice tightened so much Emma could almost feel the clenching of his jaw.

"She's a floozy all right and I've seen you with her more than once. Mam didn't follow you all the way out here to have you shag some trollop behind her back."

Emma tried to swallow but her throat was so dry she almost choked.

"I'll not have you use vulgarities like that at me boy." Jacob slammed his axe into the wood so hard the trunk beneath the firewood cracked. Harry stood his ground.

"Ha! Language like that is all I hear down that bloody pit, and you're the one who makes me go there."

"You spent too much time alone with your mam. She's been a soft touch on you boys. If I'd been around you wouldn't dare talk to me like this. I am your father and you will do as I tell you." His fists were clenched and his face turning a disturbing shade of purple.

"If you had been around!" Harry's was half laughing and half shouting.

Emma winced, praying the neighbours couldn't hear. She ought to go down and break it up, but she decided it would only make things worse.

"And whose fault is it that you left us? You're the one who pilfered and thieved."

"So you could have better things."

"Don't even try to make out your bad ways were for our benefit. I know what you were like back home. Don't think Jack and I didn't know about your gambling. I might have been young but we always knew what you were. Always full of tall tails and fancy dreams, but underneath you were throwing our bread money on the card table."

A low growl came from somewhere in Jacobs's chest like an angry dog.

"Then why didn't you stay in England with Jack then." he spat. "You could both be pompous little traitors together."

Emma gasped. She slapped her hand over her mouth and gritted her teeth. She had no idea until that moment what her husband really thought of Jack's decision. Is that really why her eldest boy hadn't wanted to come? And what of Harry? Why had he not sided with Jack? Why had they not tried to talk her out of going? Life had been hard on them out here but this was the first time she truly regretted getting on that ship.

Harry must have sensed she was there for he flashed a glance at her window, set down his axe and rubbed his face with a guilty twitch. Emma collected her shawl and headed downstairs.

Soft steps on creaky floorboards. Heart on edge and mind racing. As Emma entered the kitchen she considered what she should say. Should she confront Jacob and admit what she had heard, or just act as though everything was normal and see where things headed? When she reached the back door she heard the resident kookaburra cackle. Emma looked at his fat white and brown head peeking out from the half-naked tree branches and made up her mind.

"Good morning boys, good morning, Gordon," she said as brightly as she could manage.

"You named the bird?" Harry seemed relieved to see her.

As Emma forced a laugh, warm air plumed from her mouth into the frosty autumn morning.

"Gloria did." She clasped her shaking hands in an attempt to steady them. What good would it do to make a scene now? It would be better to keep a calm head and think things over for a while.

10

Hooves thumped on the hard ground sending clumps of dusty grass flying out behind a blur of brown bodies. The whiff of manure and human sweat lingered in the autumn air. People all around were yelling excitedly. A crowd of well-dressed gentleman and elegant ladies jostled. A tall woman nearby was peering through binoculars. Sunlight chinked off the brass and caught in Emma's peripheral vision. She looked at the crisp lavender dress and wide-brimmed hat trimmed in lace. It was straight out of the latest fashion books on display at the haberdashery. Emma looked down at her own rather ancient gown and felt even smaller. In front of her Gloria was screaming at the top of her voice, but the name she was calling blended into the cacophony. Emma could not distinguish who was shouting for whom, nor tell which horse was which. She shielded her eyes, peering into the distance as the horses thundered across the far end of the track and swerved around the bend. With a sigh, she wondered what Jack would make of all this.

Jacob was gripping his betting slip in his fist as though afraid it might blow away and 'Come on Dark Fury' was bursting from his lips with increased urgency. He wouldn't let her see how much he had placed. 'Ten to one sure thing' is all he had said. She cringed at the thought of how much might ride on the back of that damn nag. Albert was gripping his little sister's hand and they both grew more and more fevered as the horses caught sight of the finishing post. Harry seemed to be the only other person present that looked less than enamoured with the day's activity. He was standing still as a statue, hand raised to shade his eyes like a soldier saluting.

"Shift your arse." Jacob's voice boomed close to her ear.

Emma tried to ask which one it was but there was no response. She looked back at Harry; his shoulders seemed to stick out beneath his shirt and his blond hair was lank and dull. She was too afraid to ask what the matter was. Her once wild little boy, full of life and cheek, had become increasingly quiet since Rio but now he was practically a stoic. Emma reached forwards and rubbed his arm. The touch made him flinch. He looked around but didn't hold her gaze. This melancholy certainly was becoming a deep concern for Emma. Whether it was the trials of his arrest, working down the mine, or spending too much time with his father didn't matter. Even his freckles had faded and his skin, unlike his siblings, was as light as if he was back in England. Her heart twisted at the thought of Jack in Staffordshire all alone and decided she was not going to lose another son. She had to do something to keep Harry at home with her in future.

"Come on Dark Fury, Come on!" Jacob bellowed close to her ear.

The volume of the crowd rose to a roar, thundering in her ears louder than the hoof beats. The names of each horse crashed against her eardrums all at once. Jacob was yelling and the children were screaming. Harry's face brightened for a moment. Emma looked at the finishing post in time to see two long noses dip past the line. Then there was silence. All eyes looked up at the large slate board down by the betting stand. Murmurings rumbled all around.

"Who won?" Emma said. Jacob didn't move. His eyes fixed on the slate, his breath held.

"We don't know, Mam," Harry explained. "It was on the line. Dark Fury and Parson's Choice." He looked nervous. "They have to wait for the steward's enquiry, see, down there." He pointed to a cluster of men in top hats and grey tails. At her side, Jacob removed his cap and dabbed his handkerchief over his sweat-slick brow. Emma's skin prickled as though someone had walked over her grave.

People in the crowd were beginning to call out for a decision. One of the stewards glanced over his shoulder towards them but then hunched back into the conversation. Minutes went by. Jacob began to waft his face with his betting slip. Emma could feel him shaking. He reached into his jacket pocket and pulled out his flask. She watched from the corner of her eye as he unscrewed the pewter lid and took a long swig. It was whisky, but she didn't know where he got it. Lord knows they couldn't afford to buy any. She had asked Harry a while back but he had just said it came from one of the other miners. Moonshine she presumed and strong stuff at that.

There was some movement at the other side of the track and one of the officials, a tall lanky man with grey hair and a long face like one of the horses, took a chalk from the book-maker and raised his hand to the board. The crowd fell silent once more. Emma heard Jacob swallow. Next to the 'No 1,' a name emerged: Dark Fury.

Jacob swayed back a little in disbelief. His face was as grey as the steward's hair and his lips white as paper. Half the crowd erupted into cheers. Others booed and hollered. Gloria and Albert began to dance about as though it was Christmas morning and Harry's shoulders sank with relief. Suddenly Jacob began to dance too. He clasped Emma's waist and spun her around like a top, crashing her into the elegant woman with the binoculars. She tried to apologise as she sailed past and for a moment or two she was caught up in the joy.

When her husband finally set her back down she could see the utter relief in his face. Emma sighed and decided she would have to find out just how much this race might have cost them. Over the last week or so she had thought long and hard about whether she and the children should leave Jacob and return to England, but the thought of another long sea voyage, just to go back to scrubbing laundry in smoggy Staffordshire was equally as repellent as staying here. What she would have to do is find a way to take charge and make things work in Flemington.

*

"Why can you not just be happy I won?" Jacob ground out.

"That's not the point. We did not come all this way, only for you to gamble our livelihood away again."

For the last hour, Emma had been trying to pry some information from her husband; Jacob was having none of it. He was increasingly evasive and Emma was about at the end of her tether.

Upstairs the floorboards creaked. She glanced at the ceiling and prayed the children couldn't hear everything. She had already asked how much money they had in the bank and been refused. She had asked if there was anything left from the gold they had found in that seam a few weeks since and had been refused. She had also asked him where he got the moonshine and once again been refused.

"Then go back to England woman," he spat. "I know you hate it here. I should never have made you come." Jacob was standing by the back door, arms folded and brow pressed into a deep scowl. He looked like an insolent child. Emma rubbed a hand over her face and drew a breath.

"You did not make us come here, Jake. You asked and we made a choice. We came for you."

"And now you hate it. It was a mistake."

Emma began to pace back and forth. She scratched at her hair and loosened the pins to relieve the headache that was forming. Lucy had warned her how hard it would be.

"I never expected a bed of roses, but I had hoped we would at least have our own house," she barked.

Jacob stamped his foot hard, sending a small shock wave through the warped floorboards that rattled up the uneven legs of the kitchen table. Emma flinched.

"You don't know what it was like here all these years without you. You don't know how hard it was, what people I had to deal with." His voice was harsh as broken glass but his eyes were filled with pain.

Emma wanted to scream at him, to say, 'I know how you got by. With some floozy,' but instead, she swallowed the words down and took a step towards him. He backed away into the door. "Then tell me. Please," she added, trying to sound calmer.

Jacob shook his head and for a moment Emma thought he was going to punch the wall. But he straightened his shoulders into a stiff line and pursed his lips.

"Hell! It was hell on earth. Whatever did I do that was so bad?"

Emma tried to prevent her guffaw but it was too late. The snort, however quiet, was heard.

"You think what I did, slipping a few plates under the table, selling a few cups on the side to make ends meet deserved this?" He flung his arms wide and presented the shabby little room as though it were a gaol cell.

"And what of the jewellery you fenced and the money you embezzled? It was hardly your first conviction, Jake."

"You think I deserved the stench and the sickness, the starvation, the beatings? You think I was no better than the murderers and thugs I was chained up to on that ship."

Emma stopped and looked at him.

"No Jacob, of course not. But you did what you did and you got what you were given. We can't change that. But you can change what you are now. You can stop drinking and gambling and start making a real life for us." Emma stopped short again before she mentioned the floozy.

"You mean like the perfect Matthews, with their perfect farm and their perfect children." The words hiss out so vehemently Emma stumbled backwards. She took a breath and forced herself to continue.

"They're not perfect. But Alfred has tried. He made changes to his ways. He made it work."

"And I haven't tried?"

Emma gave an exasperated sigh. Whatever she said it was going to come out wrong. Jacob was watching her with dark eyes flashing so cold the glare sent a shiver up Emma's spine.

"Today is not the first time you've frittered our money away," she pressed on. "And I see the way poor Harry looks at you, the way he looks so afraid you might break his neck if he says no to you. Stop going to the goldfields, stop trying to follow a dream to a quick fortune and find a real job." She ignored the shaking fists Jacob had clenched at his sides. "You were a good painter, you could do that again. You could finish the farm, or we can sell the land and move into the city. You can get work at the potteries." The words poured out faster and faster until Emma ran out of breath. She stopped and blinked away tears.

Jacob suddenly slumped against the door and sank down, lower and lower until he was seated. He reached for his flask. Emma slowly walked towards him and sat down at his side. She raised her hand to take the flask from him but he shoved her away, his elbow connecting hard with her ribs. Gasping and startled she jumped away from him. For the first time in her life, she was at a complete loss at how to treat him. Jacob's eyes grew wide. It was an accident she knew.

"It's fine. I'm fine," she tried to reassure him, but he began to shake violently, hunching his shoulders and crunching up his legs to his chest like a defensive hedgehog.

"I'm sorry, I'm sorry, I'm sorry," he kept mumbling over and over until Emma was afraid he would never stop.

There was a creak at the kitchen door and a scuff on the floor. Emma looked up to see Harry standing before them. She wanted to wrap her arms around her husband, to tell him everything was going to be all right, but she dare not attempt it. She looked up at her son. Harry looked so small standing before her, so afraid, just like he had that day in the prison cell. They had never told Jacob about that, they had all sworn never to mention it again. She got to her feet and threw her arms around her boy and sobbed as though she were the child. How the tables can turn. Harry rested his chin on her shoulder and stroked her back. She hadn't meant to cry, she hadn't thought she would, but once she began she struggled to stop. Harry led her away, through the door and into the pristine front room. To her shame, this was the first time Emma had not wished that Harry were Jack. Behind them, they heard Jacob slam the back door and step out into the night.

"He'll be all right, Mam. When he gets like this it is best to let him be 'til his head clears of drink."

Emma was horror-struck. How many times had her boy had to deal with his father in such a state? She tried to ask him but Harry evaded her and simply said,

"It's all right, don't you worry about it, Mam."

With a guilty pang in her gut, she vowed never to underestimate or think ill of Harry again.

Hymns rose into the rafters like doves in the ark. Emma felt as though the notes were bursting from her heart and trying to escape their captivity. She noticed Jacob kept glancing sideways at her. The tune came to an end and the Reverend bid them take a seat.

"What's wrong with you?" Jacob hissed.

Emma nudged him gently and gave him a 'shhhh' glare. But there was no malice in it. Today she was feeling strong, as though she could deal with anything and everything was going to be just fine. Jacob shook his head at her and settled in for the rest of the service.

*

When evensong came to an end Emma and Jacob rose to leave. As they wove their way through the people towards the door Emma heard someone call to them. She stopped and turned around.

"Mr and Mrs Burns, how very good it is to see you this evening."

Emma had never been introduced to this man before but she had seen him about the village. She grabbed Jacob's hand and held him back.

"Forgive me for the intrusion," the man said. "Mr Mason at your service." he doffed his hat and bowed. "I am to be headmaster of Flemington National School."

Emma curtseyed and Jacob cocked his head suspiciously.

"Very pleased to make your acquaintance, sir." Emma smiled and shook the hand that had been offered to Jacob. "There's to be a new school here?"

Mr Mason smiled broadly,

"Oh yes indeed. You have not heard then? Well, well, never mind. I shall tell you now." Mr Mason was clearly proud of the venture. "The old school has been very good, but with such a rapidly growing population a much larger school was needed."

Emma found his enthusiasm contagious as he explained about the lessons and classrooms.

"That sounds wonderful, sir."

Gloria had stopped by her parents but the two boys had already gone out the door into the churchyard. Emma put her hand on her daughter's back.

"Gloria this is your new headmaster."

Jacob glared. Emma felt his arm tighten around hers. Gloria lowered her head suddenly shy. Mr Mason chuckled and smiled down at her.

"And shall we have the pleasure of all your children?" He looked back at Emma and then at Jacob. "I believe you have three?"

Emma opened her mouth to reply but Mr Mason carried on.

"Do forgive me for approaching you like this. I simply saw the opportunity. Carpe Diem as they say."

Jacob seemed to soften suddenly.

"You shall have two new pupils," he said.

Emma blinked in surprise. She had not been sure he was going to let any of them attend.

"My son Albert will be joining his sister," he added. "Bert," he called. "Come and meet Mr Mason, he's your new teacher." When he realised they had already left he sent Gloria to retrieve them. A moment or two later they were all standing together in the middle of the church aisle.

"Good evening, sir," Albert said quietly as Mr Mason greeted him with a hearty handshake. Harry stood next to his father wearing a cool, unreadable expression on his face. Mr Mason weighed the lad up with a glance.

"And you, Master Burns, will you be joining your brother and sister?"

Harry fidgeted his feet and shot a sideways glance at Jacob. Emma wondered if this was another sore subject Harry had broached with his father while they had been away.

"Harry is thirteen, sir. He works at the mines with me," Jacob explained with a pat on Harry's back. Harry rocked forward slightly and gritted his teeth.

"Ah. I see. Very well." Mr Mason was looking at Harry carefully. After a moment he added, "If you change your mind, Master Burns, there will be a class for older children too. Thirteen is certainly not at all old for education."

Mr Price the postmaster was edging slowly in their direction. Emma could see he was eager to speak with Mr Mason so she politely suggested it was time they take their leave. Harry gave the headmaster a quick bow and turned away with his father, but Emma noticed that he glanced back over his shoulder more than once before they reached the door.

*

The following day

The clock on the mantle clunked past the hour. The chime may not have worked but the hands continued to tick with remarkable accuracy. The sound of the cogs creaking reminded Emma that it was winding day. She rose from her seat by the fire, retrieved the key from behind the clock and slid it into its slot. Upstairs there was a thump that shuddered through the ceiling. Harry glanced up. Emma called out.

"Play nicely, children."

The response was a resounding,

"Yes, Mam."

She rolled her eyes at Harry. Today had been a reasonable day. Jacob had been bright and seemingly calm, but tomorrow he and Harry were set to head back to Bendigo. She gave the key one last grinding twist and felt the springs tighten. Putting it back in its safe little place she decided to broach the subject of Harry's education one last time.

"Harry, I saw you at church last night, the look on your face when you spoke to Mr Mason. I think you would rather like to go back to school for a while?"

Ignoring the chill that clouded Jacob's expression Emma turned to her son and waited for him to form a response. He was sitting opposite Jacob on one of the hard wooden chairs from the kitchen.

The house had not come with enough seats so they had to switch things about when it suited. The lad leaned forward and rested his elbows on his long skinny thighs and looked up, first at Jacob and then at her.

"Actually...I...I've been thinking that I might like to look for an apprenticeship. I'm not a child anymore and I'd like a better future than..." he stopped, his eyes flickering toward Jacob.

Emma felt a rush of pride. This was not the little tearaway boy she had seen huddled like a tethered pup in a Brazilian gaol. This was a young man who had grown up and thought about how to better himself. Perhaps that nasty little experience had done him some good, or perhaps dealing with his father's moods was the cause. Emma tried not to imagine the latter. She risked a look at Jacob.

Her husband rose from his battered old wing chair and began to pace back and forth, his lips pressed into a thin line and his face slowly turning puce. In an instant, he had gone from gentle to enraged.

She had tried so hard to reach him since the day at the races, but he seemed to have closed up like a clam. The thing that had startled her most, however, was just how much he really did drink. Since then he had stopped hiding it. Harry hadn't seemed at all surprised, and when Emma had worried that she had made it all worse, he'd said,

"No, Mam. This is how he always is. You just don't normally see it."

She wasn't sure which was worse, that she hadn't noticed, or that it didn't make him drunk enough for her to notice. He hadn't been like this in England. She watched as he passed her by, hands clenching so hard his knuckles were white and his jaw so tight the muscle in his cheek twitched. For all his old faults when she married him, Jacob had not been a drinker. He may have been a dreamer but his temperament had been level and placid. He certainly wouldn't have so much as threatened violence at anyone, let alone one of his boys. Right now the look upon his face was so unnerving she could have believed him capable of anything. He spun around to face her, so close she could feel his breath on her hair.

"You and the boy ganging up against me. I see how it is!" he hissed in her face. "You two have cooked up this little moment between you, to force me into a corner. Do you think I can't see how you all despise me?" He was standing so rigid he was shaking.

Emma raised a heel to take a step back but then something in his eyes made her stand firm.

"No Jacob, we haven't. All this hatred and mistrust, it's all in your mind. Why can you not see that we chose you? We came out here to be with you."

Jacob's stance weakened for a fraction of a second, then he curled his lips into a sneer,

"No! No, Emma, don't you try to make this out to be my fault."

Emma tried to make sense of him.

"What do you think we're blaming you for?"

He shook his head and turned his attentions on his son. Harry flinched as Jacob raised a fist, but his hand was shaking so violently that Emma almost reached out to touch him.

"And you, boy, you think the life I've made for you is inferior? You want to abandon me for some fancy apprenticeship you'll never have the brains or courage to finish. You're too wilful to come to anything lad, just like your mam and Jack."

Harry looked at Emma for support and at that moment she knew they were about to win. She gave an encouraging nod at her son.

"I do have the brains for it, Pa, and the will to finish." As Harry spoke he seemed to grow an inch taller and for the first time in her life, Emma decided that he more like her than Jacob. "If I can be half what Mam or Jack are then I shall be very glad indeed."

It took all of Emma's self-control not to throw her arms around Harry and kiss him.

Jacob couldn't speak. He just stood before them both growling like an angry dog. Then with no warning he marched from the room, grabbed his jacket from the bannister post and slammed open the front door, making the wall shake.

"Do as you will. I'm done with you," he bellowed and was gone down the road.

Emma moved to run after him but Harry caught her arm.

"Leave him, Mam. It's just the drink. He'll calm down after a day or two down the mines. He'll be back soon enough, you'll see."

A thousand emotions were swirling through Emma's gut. She leaned on the doorjamb and gasped at the cool autumn air. She stared down the inky dark street until she could no longer hear his footsteps. Harry patted her shoulder gently.

"Come on in, Mam. Sit down for a bit, I'll make you a nice cuppa."

Emma bit her quivering lip.

"You have turned out well, my lad."

12

Autumn leaves rustled on the breeze and the Kookaburra in the tree was cackling at something, or nothing. Emma pulled up a chair to the kitchen table. Jacob had been gone for nearly a week without a word. When she had seen Mr Price waving at her from the post office door that morning, she had thought the note would be from Jacob, but to her far greater pleasure, it was from Jack. This letter had taken a little longer than usual and she had been more than grateful to finally have it in her hands. Upstairs she heard a gentle snore. It was nice to have Harry at home again. With a contented sigh, she slid the sheets of paper from their envelope and settled down to read.

'October 10th 1857

Dear Mam and Pa,

Your parcel arrived today containing my birthday gift. I cannot thank you enough; you didn't have to go to so much trouble. And a perfect fit too,'

Emma smiled to herself. The shirt she had sent Jack for his birthday had been a good size larger than would have fitted him before they left; yet she had still been concerned that it would be too small.

'And the socks are just the ticket now that winter is coming on. I hope you don't mind that I didn't wait until my birthday to open it. Patience is not my best virtue as you know!'

Emma gave a light laugh. How modest he could be. Jack was one of the most patient people she knew, always waiting for things to happen and come right, how long he had been made to wait for his apprenticeship for one thing and his work with the Marlston Workhouse; that must require a vast deal of patience. The candle on the kitchen table flickered and Emma felt goosebumps prickle her arms. She set the letter down for a moment and went to close the door. As she reached outside for the handle she noticed a Kangaroo watching her in the distance. It was a big one, tall as her she fancied.

It flicked its ears and bounced off towards the river, vanishing into the twilight haze. Emma never ceased to be startled by such sights, especially when her mind had been back in England. It all just heightened the sorrow of being so far away from Jack. She rubbed her shoulders, pulled her shawl tighter and went back to the table.

'*I have some news from the cottage. Them that took it...*'

Emma rolled her eyes at his slip in grammar once again. It was the third time she had read through this letter since its arrival that morning, but she never could get enough of reading Jack's news.

'*...Them that took it are moving out again. The lady didn't take to being so far out at the edge of town and now the cottage will be available for let again. So I went up to The Hall myself and asked if they would see fit as to let me have it, after all, it was Grand-Pa Drake's for fifty years and then yours after him. My apprenticeship is meagre pay but the rent is low and I know if work hard and I am careful I could get by.*'

Emma wondered if they had taken pity on him and offered him a reduced rate on account of his family having abandoned him.

'*Well, they said they would have to consider it very carefully and they would need a letter from Mr Barker at the potteries to prove my contract, which of course I got the very next day and took right over. Finally, after three days of waiting, today I was in receipt of the answer. I am to have to the lease from December first, just as soon as the tenants have quitted it. Can you believe it, me back in our little cottage! It will be quiet without you all here with me, but I know I shall feel closer to you just by being back there with all our memories.*'

Emma dried her eyes with an already damp handkerchief. It was hard to imagine any other young man of seventeen, sixteen as he was when he wrote those words, taking such a sentiment. To know exactly where he laid his head at night and at what table he took his meals was a great comfort to her. Though the consideration of how well he could cook for himself was rather a worry. At least he knew how to do his own laundry; he had watched her do it often enough.

'*I saw Mr Feldman yesterday. He called by the boarding house with the coal delivery. His regular man is off with the gout so he was making the rounds himself. He said to send you all his best regards and to tell Mam that Mrs Feldman always misses their chats in the shop. He said she misses tutoring*

Harry and Bert too, though lord knows why she would miss those little terrors. :)'

Here Jack had drawn a little smiling face as if to prove he was only teasing. The front door clicked. Emma looked up. For a moment she had expected to see Jack walk in with his old boots on and smeared in coal dust. But it was just the wind catching under the ill-fitted doorjamb.

'Well, I have gone on enough for this time. I shall write again soon, hopefully from my old spot at the cottage kitchen table.

Your loving son,

Jack.'

Emma drew a long contended breath and ran her fingers over the scratchy black letters. She was still very slow at reading but the pleasure it brought her had been worth every moment of effort and endurance. Her thoughts drifted to Mr Finch. It had been several weeks since she last laid eyes upon him, walking down the road arm in arm with his beautiful African wife. Annoyed at herself for thinking of him, she folded away Jack's letter and placed it safely in the bottom of the tea caddy with the others, beneath the thin layer of muslin and the little pile of tea. Soon she would have to find somewhere new to keep them, for there was almost no room for the tea now. Shaking her head, she locked the caddy and placed it back on the top shelf. Making her way up the stairs to bed she determined to put Mr Finch out of her mind, only to find his face filling her dreams not half an hour later. She thumped the pillow and growled,

"For goodness sake, woman, stop being so daft!" She grumbled into the darkness.

13

A pair of heels clicked back and forth across the wooden floor. Emma had been too nervous to sit since dawn. She was pacing about in the front room and glancing at the clock for the umpteenth time in five minutes. They should be back any time soon. Mr Price from the post office had kindly given Harry a letter of recommendation and when Alf Matthews had found out that he was going to the city in search of employment, he wouldn't hear of letting the boy go off on his own by the post chase. He had arrived with the lark in the pony and trap and dusted off the bench for Harry to sit down so that he wouldn't mark his new clothes. Emma had splashed out half her housekeeping on a pair of well-fitting new trousers and a crisp white shirt for him. Gloria might have to miss a piano lesson or two later in the month but it was for a good cause, and she had been a good little sport about it.

Emma clasped her hands together and tried to still her racing heart with a long slow breath in and out. Drifting in over the breeze she could hear Gloria playing a pleasant little tune on the McLeish's piano. The sound was soothing but not enough. Emma headed towards the kitchen and considered that she ought to make a start on supper, not that she would be able to eat a bite until Harry returned. A clop, clop from the street and Emma was outside in an instant. But the street was empty. She considered going out for a walk. Perhaps she would meet them on their way, but the sun was still high and the day unseasonably hot. She rubbed her face and went back inside.

A grate of a wheel and a creak of wood. Emma bolted to the front door once more. 'It's altogether possible nothing will have come of today,' she reminded herself. She stopped dead in her tracks. This cart was not that of Alf Matthews and on it was not her son.

The horse snorted and shook its sweat-drenched head at her as Emma slowly approached the driver. The two men on the cart bench were rugged and dusty, grime clogging their pores and coating their clothes. The one holding the reins took off his cap and jumped down. The other followed a beat behind. Emma was trying not to see what was on the back of the cart. The bent lump, still as a corpse, hidden under a blanket to protect him from the sun with a mop of dark greying hair poking out at one end. A thin trickle of sweat ran down her back beneath her corset and her face burned like fire.

"Mrs Burns?"

Emma tugged at her collar; her chest was so tight she was fighting for breath. Fuzzy patterns filled her head like sparkling pins and needles. She put her hand to her forehead to try to stop the ground swimming and reached out for the gatepost just in time to stop her knees from buckling.

"Madam, there has been an accident at the mines."

The voice blurred in her head.

"Your husband, he was...he fell, down the shaft."

Emma felt the world slip away from beneath her and everything went dark.

*

Emma awoke with a start. Someone was wafting smelling salts under her nose and another was pressing a damp cloth to her forehead. Mrs McLeish was kneeling on the floor in front of her holding her hands. Emma tried to swallow but her throat was dry as the dusty streets.

"Here drink this," a man she vaguely recognised from the cart outside was offering her a glass of water. Emma sat up and took it. As her vision cleared she looked around. She was in the front room laid out on the threadbare couch. The window was wide open and a waft of warm sweet air drifted in and over her hot face.

"You fainted, dear," Mrs McLeish offered helpfully.

"Jacob!" Emma rasped and coughed. She took a sip of the water and pressed her palms onto her hot cheeks. "Is he…?" She couldn't say it.

"He's in a bad way, Mrs Burns. Reuben and me brought him in and carried him to his bed. We thought he would be better here than out at the fields." The man speaking was the cart driver. Emma didn't know whether to be relieved or more anxious. "Reuben went to fetch the doctor."

Emma suddenly remembered Albert and Gloria. She was about to enquire when she spotted them sitting quietly together on Jacob's chair, faces ashen and eyes wide. They looked so small and young. Emma held out a hand to them.

"It's all right. I'm all right now."

For a moment Albert looked at her with uncertainty, then he slipped off the stool and slowly came towards her.

"I'm sorry love; I didn't mean to frighten you."

Albert threw himself into her embrace and sobbed into her shoulder.

"We thought you was dead. We thought Pa was dead."

"Oh, Bertie, no I'm not dead, see," she patted his back soothingly. "But your Pa has had an accident, so we shall have to see what the doctor says."

The cart driver cleared his throat. She tried to smile.

"He ain't yet awake, Madam. He's been like that since the fall."

"Thank you for bringing him home. It was very kind of you indeed."

Mrs McLeish got to her feet and smoothed down her skirts.

"Perhaps we should give Mrs Burns a moment alone with her family." She led the driver towards the front door.

"Wait, please, what's your name?" Emma called. The man looked back over his shoulder.

"Thomas, Madam."

"Thank you, Thomas."

"Glad to be of assistance, Mrs Burns, least we could do."

Emma laid her head back against the couch and tried to breathe normally.

"Mrs McLeish," she sat up again and felt her head thump. She pressed her palm to her forehead. "Would you mind looking after the children again, just until after the doctor has been?"

"My dear, of course, of course. You just rest until he comes." She began to usher Gloria and Albert to their feet. "Come children, you can have supper with us tonight. We're having lamb stew."

For a moment Gloria just stood there staring, but then, with a trembling lip she did as she was asked.

"You like lamb stew do you not? Of course you do." Mrs McLeish gave Emma a nod.

"You come by and collect them when you're ready, they can stay the night if needs be."

Emma was washed over with gratitude.

"You're too kind but I don't think that'll be necessary. I shall send Harry over when...Oh Lord, Harry!"

Standing in the doorway Harry was stock-still. His expression caught between fear and bewilderment. Alf put his hand on the lad's shoulder and gently moved him out of the way so that Mrs McLeish and the children could go through.

Once they were gone Emma beckoned Harry and Alf inside.

"What happened, Mam? Are you all right?"

Emma pulled herself up to sitting and waited to see if the room began to spin again, thankfully it refrained.

"I had a bit of a shock and I fainted. Son, it's your Pa. Help me upstairs. I need to see him."

Harry slipped his arm around her waist as Emma got unsteadily to her feet.

"We saw the cart out front." Alf offered. "Is there anything I can do? I can send over Lucy?"

Emma was shivering violently but she forced herself up the stairs.

"No, thank you, Alf. Lucy needs to be at home resting in her condition. We'll be just fine."

Alf shifted his stance at the bottom of the stairs and took off his cap.

"I'll wait until the doctor comes if that's all right. And don't hesitate to send for us if there is anything, anything at all any of us can do."

Emma nodded,

"Thank you."

*

Face pale as wax, cracked brown blood caked into his hair. Emma sat on the bed and stroked her husband's hair away from his sleeping eyes. Harry had fetched up a jug of heated water and a clean cloth. The dried blood peeled off in grotesque little flakes as she carefully wiped it away. A salty tear fell from her eyes and dripped onto his cheek, leaving a thin clean streak. For a moment she didn't notice the faint scent of alcohol on Jacob's breath but then when he coughed the fumes rose higher and more potent. Emma paused, horrified, but perhaps they had given him something for the pain.

There was a sharp rap on the front door and then a creak as it was pushed open. Downstairs Emma heard Alf greet the doctor and send him upstairs. She felt like she ought to go down and say goodbye to Alfred and the kind men that had brought her husband home, but she dare not leave Jacob's side.

"Harry, please go down and see them off. I'll call you when the doctor's finished."

As Harry left them alone Emma looked at Jacob's unconscious face and contemplated how peaceful he looked. She was not sure he had looked that content since the day he had met them at the immigrant barracks.

*

Time seemed to be passing considerably slower than usual. Emma watched as the doctor peered and prodded and felt along Jacob's bones and limbs. She flinched, as her husband winced and cried out with pain yet didn't wake. Finally, the doctor stepped back with a sorrowful shake of his head.

"I am very sorry, Mrs Burns. But I see little chance of your husband ever regaining consciousness. Both his legs are broken and several ribs, but what concerns me most is the damage to his head. He has taken a huge blow to his skull and I fear the brain cannot recover from such a severe injury."

Emma felt the room sway again. She flopped down on the bed and gripped at her throat. She must have cried out, though she didn't know it until a moment later when Harry rushed in.

"I can't tell you how long it will take," the doctor was talking to Harry more than Emma now. "Maybe hours or a day or two; a week at best."

Emma collapsed on to Jacob's chest unable to see or feel.

"I'm so sorry, Jake. I'm so sorry," she sobbed into his filthy shirt. "You waited all that time for us and then all I do is argue with you."

She sensed someone sit down next to her and a hand gently touch her back, but she could not comprehend anything more.

*

Moonlight glinted through the silvery clouds and cast a pale shadow over Emma's face. She opened her eyes and looked down at Jacob. Nothing had changed. His chest was rising and falling in shallow rasps and his eyes danced beneath his eyelids as though he were dreaming. Emma hadn't noticed nightfall, nor had she any notion as to the time. She stretched out her back, sending a shooting pain through the pinched nerve. Wincing she stood and gently leaned over the bed to draw the curtains closed. Her stomach rumbled and she realised she hadn't eaten since luncheon. Poor Harry must be starving. She looked over to the corner of the room where her son had been sleeping on top of the linen chest and realised he was watching her.

"I'll fetch us up some bread and cheese," she whispered, but Harry shook his head.

"I went down a little while ago while you were sleeping. I finished the last slice of the potato pie. I hope that's all right, Mam."

"Of course lad." Emma hesitated, unsure she should leave Jacob for even a minute.

"Go on, Mam, I'll stay and watch him."

She was about to acquiesce when she realised that in all that had happened she had never asked Harry how his day had gone. She settled back on the edge of the bed and looked at her boy.

"Forgive me, Harry. Why don't you tell me your news?"

Harry lowered his head as though ashamed.

"It doesn't matter, Mam. I shan't be going anywhere now."

Emma's heart near broke.

"Please tell me."

Harry began to bite the side of his thumb, just the way he used to when he was little and he was in trouble.

"It isn't an apprenticeship, but they're building a new railway station at Spencer Street, due to open next year. One look at Mr Price's letter and they offered me a porters job on the spot. Because I can read the timetables and I was smart and tidy they said I was just the sort of young chap they are looking for. They said there was plenty of opportunities for a hard-working lad to work his way up and maybe even become a station master one day."

Emma found herself beaming despite the pang of guilt. For a moment she saw Harry dreaming and getting ahead of himself. But now she didn't compare him to Jacob, she compared him to Jack, and she knew he would work hard and attain his goal.

"They want me to start right away; learn the ropes at Flinders Street first. Then I can switch once the new station is ready."

Emma's mind raced.

"Right away?"

"Just as soon as I find lodgings in the city. They gave me the name of a reputable boarding house where some of the other lads live."

Emma tried to take it all in. Jacob stirred and she thought he was going to wake. His eyelids flickered open but there was no spark in them, just the fluttering whites of his eyes. As he settled back again she said,

"That is good news, Son; very good news. You must go, just as soon as you can."

"But what will you do, Mam? How will you manage? I have to stay here with you now."

But Emma was shaking her head; she was not going to let him miss this chance.

"Just as I always have," she said. "I managed on my own with four of you back home and I can manage now with two, even with your Pa like this. Besides doctors are not always right. He might be right as rain in a day or two."

14

The sun beat down on her, bright and relentless. Folks in black gathered together in the heat of a Tuesday afternoon. Emma was numb. Her head felt like a ball of dough, heavy and stodgy. Her eyes were puffy and hurt to close. Somewhere in her chest, her heart was still beating but she could no longer feel it. Lucy was standing at one side of her and Harry at the other.

Looking up at the beautiful autumn day Emma wondered why it wasn't grey and raining. It ought to be overcast at a funeral. The Reverend was saying his final prayers for Jacob Burns but Emma heard none of it. The children were staying with Mrs McLeish for the day and she was wondering how they were doing.

"You all right?" Lucy was looking at her through a thin veil of black.

The Reverend had expressed a preference for women not to attend the funeral, but Emma had insisted upon going. She had not meant for Lucy to come, not in her condition and only five weeks from due, but now she was there Emma was glad of it. She looked around at the small crowd, somewhat surprised at how many people Jacob had known. Mr McLeish was there of course, Mr Price from the post office, the Doctor that had come to see Jacob, Rueben and Thomas from the mines, and several other men she had never met. Emma considered whether they were from the goldfields or other 'exiles', perhaps they were both. Someone at the back caught Emma's eye. She turned to look. The woman was hovering nervously half behind a tree and watching her intently. Emma froze. Was this the floozy? Her first instinct was to march right over there and tell her to get lost. But then her strength waned and all she wanted to do was pretend she hadn't seen her. She turned her back on the woman and clung tighter to Harry.

When it was done and the spade slid into the pile of earth to cover him with, Emma began to walk away. She just wanted to get home, but every time she made a move someone else would come over to express their condolences. She had no notion as to what was being said; she just tried to smile and nod. Then something began to filter in. Two or three of the men she didn't know were talking quietly amongst themselves.

"I heard he was drunk when he fell."

"Well, he sure did like a tipple."

"That poor widow of his, coming all this way for him to up and die on her barely a year on."

"I'm surprised she came at all, more fool her."

"I bet she's on the first boat home."

"That's if she can afford the fare. I doubt there's a penny left."

"Aye, you know how he loved his cards and horses."

"I see she came too."

Emma felt sick. She pressed her fingers to her lips and scurried away as fast as she could, dragging a waddling Lucy along behind her. She glanced over her shoulder to where the floozy had been. Her only small consolation was that she had at least had the courtesy to leave.

"Don't ya listen to them, Em. You knew him better than they did."

She stopped. Images fluttered in her mind. Betting slips in his jacket pocket, not just from Flemington, but years ago. She had always told herself that his debts were not the reason he stole. But she knew it was. And to find out now, that all the while she was in England worrying about him, he was living a life of Riley out here with some other woman and hadn't even had the care to end it after she got here.

"He had his faults and maybe I was the worst of them. Had I been a better wife I would have stopped him years ago. I thought the kids didn't know why he was always late home, but they did, we all did, late-night cards and trips to the races. I should have put a stop to it back then, but look what I drove him to." She almost spilt out everything but the words stuck in her throat. No matter how close she was to Lucy, she just couldn't admit that Jacob had a mistress, nor could she shake the nagging notion that this floozy was not his first. Had she been such a bad wife? She felt such shame.

"Don't even say that, Em. It were not your fault. He were weak is all."

"I think we should go home," Emma said quietly.

Lucy patted her arm.

"Of course. You wait here a minute and I'll go find Alf and tell him to stay with Harry"

For a moment Emma wondered where the Matthews' twins were but then she remembered that they had stayed at the farm to look after the animals.

"Ya know I can stay. Alf can come back for me in a day or two."

"That's kind of you, but… I didn't mean home to the cottage."

Lucy blinked at her, realisation slowly creeping across her face before Emma even said it.

"I meant that the children and I should go back to England." Emma took a slow breath. "I haven't even written to Jack yet to tell him about Jake. I could scrape together enough to buy our passage with the little Jacob had left and just go home. Jack would be so surprised. I know it might seem silly, but I've been thinking about it ever since the accident…" *and before*, she thought. "Maybe it's for the best."

Lucy tugged her arm,

"Emma, please don't make no rash decisions. If that's what you decide then we'll miss ya very much and I won't blame ya. But you sleep on it first; take a day or two, a week even, to think about it. There's still a lot ya could do out here."

"Like what?"

Lucy shrugged; she obviously hadn't thought it through.

"You could come work for us. There's plenty of room and lord knows we could do with an extra hand now the baby's coming." She rested her hand on her now huge bump.

Emma closed her eyes for a moment and pictured the idyllic life they had, the one she'd hoped to find for herself. Then reality crept in.

"But how could you afford to keep me and mine as well?"
Lucy shrugged again.

"I'm sure we could manage."

Emma smiled, glad of her kindness but unconvinced.

15

Four days later

Emptied cupboards and drawers tipped out everywhere. Piles of crockery, pots and pans were stacked like towers leaning across the kitchen table. Emma had already scoured every corner of the living room and bedroom but to no avail.

"Mam, what are you looking for?" Harry asked from the corner of the room. His hands were on his hips and there was a baffled expression on his face.

"If we had a bank account, then there must be a record slip somewhere," Emma offered with an exasperated sigh.

"There won't be anything in it."

"Well, whatever there is or isn't, I need to know if there's at least enough to pay for the passage home." She looked up and scowled at the room.

Harry drew a breath and swallowed audibly. Emma stopped, her hands in the cutlery drawer. Something in her head sent a familiar sharp pain to the middle of her gut.

"Mam, I want to stay here."

Emma felt her head swim. She rested her hip against the dresser and placed the cutlery tray back down on the pile of Jack's letters.

"Don't you do this to me, Harry? I left a son behind once before and I've regretted it each day I live and breathe. I shan't do it again. You will not make me choose between you and Jack. You'll come home with us and that is the end of it."

Harry rubbed his hand over his face and opened his mouth to speak but Emma didn't give him the chance. A thought struck her. She went into the front room, to the small table by the side of Jacob's chair and opened his bible. There was a long slit in the leather cover, narrow and barely noticeable, but just wide enough for someone to slip a single sheet of paper through. Emma tried to pry it open with a fingernail without damaging it further. But she couldn't quite manage it. Carrying the book back to the kitchen she picked up the butter knife from the draining board and carefully slid it through the crack. It was there, she could feel it. She jiggled the knife a little, and then very slowly pulled it out until the sheet of paper poked its nose out. As soon as there was enough to hold onto she tugged at it. To her surprise, Jacob had thought to leave a will. But all that it had said was that everything came to her should she survive him, or their children should she not. Without any bank information, all that was left was what she had brought with her from England, that and a bit of wasteland with a half-finished foundation on it.

The slip in the bible was for the last deposit he must have made, for it was dated only two weeks before his death. Three shillings and sixpence. Not a vast deal, but better than nothing. And then she saw the figure at the bottom.

Emma clasped her hand to her chest and sank onto the nearest chair. She blinked and looked again, reading it slowly three times over. She had yet to have the land valued but with that and this money they could actually buy a house.

"This would pay for the passage home and give us a new start," she gasped. "Or perhaps we could all move into the city after all and then Harry can still live with us," she was talking to herself but addressing the empty chair opposite, where Jacob would have been. "Gracious. It doesn't look like I shall have to start taking in laundry again after all." She tried not to smile but her lips disobeyed. "Oh, Jacob, why couldn't you have made it this easy when you were alive?"

Harry sat down on the stool by the stove and looked at her steadily.

"How much is it, Mam?"

Emma looked over at him as though she had forgotten he was there. She read it out,

"Balance – Seventy four pounds, eight shillings and eleven pence."

Harry just stared open-mouthed for a full two minutes before saying,

"Let's stay here, Mam. Things are just starting to settle in for me. Pa might be gone but I still have the job at the railway to go to. They were kind enough to give me two weeks grace, on account of Pa, but I really do want to take the position. Pa was right about one thing, there are plenty of opportunities here and I like it. Bert and Glo have a better chance than they would back home what with the new school and all, and Gloria would never have learned piano in Stoke. And look at the Matthews, look how well they have done. We can do the same, I know it." His speech was steady and carefully spoken as though he had rehearsed it, with or without the money.

Emma was not so sure. There were opportunities back home too.

"What about Jack?" This was her chance to reunite her entire family. The thought of seeing her eldest boy again was near too much for her to bear.

"Ask the children what they want. You asked us all before. Jack made his decision and we made ours, together."

Emma straightened up and put her hands on her hips.

"Give me time to get this straight in my head, Harry. This," she waved the bank slip at him, "this is a lot to take in. Give me a day or two, then we can all discuss it."

Harry sighed but said nothing more. Emma put the kettle on. She needed a cup of tea. As she reached up to the top shelf to retrieve the caddy the Kookaburra cackled by the back door.

"Don't you start too," she grumbled.

16

Matthews Farmstead

The following week

"Sweet Jesus!" Lucy gaped. "Good God! Em, what the hell ya going to do wiv all that?"

Emma puffed out her cheeks and shook her head.

"Not sure yet. I've only told Harry. The children only know that we're selling the land."

"Why don't you keep it, buy some more? Pay a builder. You could really make something of it?" Alf's Irish brogue was persuasive but Emma shook her head.

"I don't think I could manage a farm all alone."

"And Jacob never said a word about it?" Lucy said, still aghast.

Emma shook her head again and shrugged.

"He always said there wasn't much left. Harry thinks he must have had a couple of big wins lately and not said. Then there was the gold seam they found. I don't know what he would have done with it, but I'm sure glad of it now." Emma did know what Jacob would have done with it: put it on a horse or a card table. Maybe even spend it on the floozy, but she didn't like to admit that.

Lucy glanced at the sun through the window. It was beginning to dip lower in the sky.

"I think we'll have to wait and see how much we get for the land and then decide what to do," Emma added.

"You ain't going home though is ya? Back to grey old England, I mean?" Lucy gave her the kind of look you warn a naughty child with.

Emma shrugged.

"I don't know. I need time to think straight."

"Well, God Bless ya, Jacob Burns. Ya left ya Mrs nice and tidy and no mistake." Lucy grinned. "I'm so pleased for ya Emma, whatever ya decide to do." Lucy tried to hug her, but the vast baby bump got in the way.

As they both laughed Emma decided it was time to ask the children what they wanted to do.

"We really ought to be going, before it gets dark," Emma said.

"Suppose ya must," Lucy looked a little forlorn. "Just promise me you'll think about it a bit more before ya decides to go back to England won't ya?"

Emma promised. Alf scratched his head and pulled his braces back over his shoulders.

"I'll fetch the trap out. You round 'em up."

*

Flemington

The next morning

Three young faces were staring up at her with wide unblinking eyes. Harry was fidgety. He was going to Melbourne by the milk cart that evening and despite his best efforts to be excited, Emma could tell he was apprehensive. She had tried to reassure him but he had dusted her off with a 'Don't be daft Mam'. The room smelled of soap and fried bread. Emma took in the scent for a moment and tried to let the pleasure of a full stomach mask her anxiety.

"Well, Mam. What is it?" Harry asked with a tap of his fingers on the table.

Emma picked at her thumbnail. Echoes of a previous conversation of the same nature hovered in her mind. After a long pause, she said,

"I'd like to know what you would all like to do?"

Harry began to nod slowly.

"Bert, Glo, your Pa left us a good bit of money and we can afford to go home if we like." She tried to push away the image of Jack and the ever-present ache in her heart.

*

The Kookaburra was cackling away amidst the falling leaves of the tree by the back door. Emma was up in the boys' room folding Harry's shirts into a neat pile. She smoothed down the crisp white fabric, freshly starched yesterday and sighed. Finally, the decision was made and the children had gone to school. She pulled a pair of trousers from the closet and smoothed them over carefully. Harry was perched on the end of the bed, arms folded, watching her.

"Really, Mam. I don't need much."

"You're not going to the goldfields this time. You're going to the city. You need clean shirts and trousers." She was fussing and she knew it but she couldn't stop herself, nor, if she was honest did she want to. The change in Harry over the past year was astounding.

"I never dreamt you would turn out so…" she stopped herself. Harry cocked his head.

"It's all right, Mam," he said with a nod of recognition. Emma pictured the ragtag little boy in the Brazilian Gaol and smiled at the smart young man that had replaced him. The clock downstairs make a grinding clunk and Emma's heart seemed to thump with it. Harry got to his feet.

"Cart's leaving in half an hour. I'd better say goodbye to the children."

Before he could get any further Emma had flung her arms around him and hugged him until he patted her back and protested that he needed to breathe. As she listened to his footsteps on the stairs she sank on to the bed and cried.

*

Later that evening

The bent nib splattered ink into a fine spray over the page as Emma's trembling hand began to write. How do you tell your son that his father is dead? If only she knew. If paper were not so expensive she would have screwed it up and begun again. Though she could afford to buy some more now, she mused, but then, just because they had a bit of money doesn't mean they should be wasteful. Instead, she scratched out the word and carried on. Slowly and steadily she formed each letter.

'I am so very sorry to have to tell you...'

She put the pen down and wiped the tear from her eye before it dripped onto the page and smeared her words even further.

'The Children and I have decided...'

Outside she could hear Gloria and Albert laughing at something. The sound warmed her inside. She had not heard them sound so jolly since before the night Jacob died.

'We all miss you very much and wish you were here with us.

Love always,

Mam'

It was the first time she had not signed ' & Pa' as well.

17

The following morning

Wind howled through the streets of Flemington. Emma was forced to hold her bonnet to her head as she battled down the street toward the post office. She blinked the gritty dust from her eyes and considered how Jack would feel reading the letter she had safely trapped in her tatty old purse. As she looked down at it she considered that she could purchase a new one. In all her life she never imagined she would have enough money to buy new things and not have to compromise the housekeeping to do it. It was hard to deny she was better off now Jacob was gone and not just for the money. A gust from the north shoved her back a step as she reached the door and Emma felt duly chastised for her thoughts. She glanced up at the sky and muttered,

"Can you blame me?"

The bell over the door tinkled. Emma was greeted by the chattering of women. The familiar faint smell of gum Arabic and beeswax floor polish made her smile as she took her place behind the group of women and a child. Mr Price looked up at her with a jolly smile, causing one of the women to turn her head. Emma didn't recognise her.

"Mrs Burns, very nice to see you," he said. "Permit me to introduce Mrs Spencer and her daughters." The group turned to face her with curiosity. "This is Miss Adelaide, Miss Olivia, and this," the little girl took a polite curtsey, "is Miss Clara."

Emma smiled and greeted them. The woman who had turned first was the eldest of the daughters. Her features were delicate and her hair beneath her bonnet was golden and bright. Adelaide's smile was tight but pleasant as she held out a slender gloved hand to Emma.

"Pleased to make your acquaintance," the young woman said in a light soft tone. Her accent was clipped and her manner accomplished.

"The Spencers are just arrived from England this last week, Mrs B."

Emma nodded and tried to imagine why they had come. The mother saved her some of the speculations.

"My husband is big in horse racing," she explained. "He has high hopes for the course here." The information was given with genuine pride. Emma's ears pricked up like a horse at the start gate and her mind began to gallop ahead.

"He is an investor then?" she asked, attempting not to sound too keen.

Mrs Spencer seemed less pleased to be speaking of financial matters but she plastered a thin-lipped smile on her face and replied,

"Well, the ways out here are different that's for certain. We shall have a lot to grow accustomed to."

Emma opened her mouth to apologize when the lady continued,

"Yes, Mrs B... Burns is it?" She didn't wait for the response, "Yes he is. My husband was in banking, and now he has decided the opportunities in Australia are too great to resist."

The words reminded her of Jacob's letters home. He had made everything sound so wonderful and adventurous. Despite all their setbacks, she had to admit that he had been right.

"I see, well I'm certain he will do very well," she said kindly and attempting to modify her accent to sound more refined.

Miss Adelaide was looking her over with mild amusement. Emma wasn't sure what had provoked the expression on the ladies face. She glanced down at her black mourning dress, the only one she possessed and could see nothing wrong with it other than being a bit out of date. She would have to make a couple more. She couldn't get through a year with just the one. But so far there had been more important things than her attire to consider.

"How long have you lived here, Mrs Burns?"

Emma sighed. She hadn't meant to and the reaction caught her by surprise.

"A little over a year now isn't it, Mrs B?" Mr Price helped her out. His mousy round face was always rosy even without the heat.

"Thank you, Mr Price. Yes, that's right. We came to join my late husband, last April."

Mrs Spencer didn't miss a beat.

"I am sorry for your loss."

Emma was grateful though unsure how to react to the stranger's kindness. It was the first time she had received condolences from someone who hadn't known Jacob. She shifted her feet and scratched at her wrist.

"Thank you," her voice cracked and the lady looked away quickly. Emma could almost hear the thoughts of her new acquaintances; 'clearly, her husband had been a convict, I wonder what he had done?' Usually, she didn't care about Jacob's former status. There were too many ex-convict families out there to count. But of late there were more and more middle-class immigrants arriving and the unjudged freedom they had first enjoyed was vanishing quickly into hushed embarrassment.

Adelaide and her mother shot each other a knowing look.

"Well, we must be getting along. Papa will be home soon." Adelaide said with a second amused scan of Emma's gown. Emma tried not to blush.

"Yes, yes of course. Very pleased to meet you," she offered with a bitter taste filling her mouth.

"Pleased to make your acquaintance I'm sure." Mrs Spencer said with a swift nod. "Come along girls."

As the ladies wafted out of the post office and away down the street, Emma found herself staring after them. Something touched her arm and she realized she was leaning against the counter. Mr Price patted her sleeve.

"Don't let them bother you Mrs B. They're nice ladies by all accounts, they just haven't quite mastered the lay of this land yet is all." The chirpy little man was looking up at her with his beady black eyes glinting kindly. Emma felt tears welling. She patted her cheeks with the backs of her hands. The postmaster fished in his breast pocket and tugged out a greying handkerchief. As he held it out to her, Emma swallowed hard and held up her hand.

"Thank you, I'm fine now really." She smoothed down the front of her dress. "Mr Price. You are very good to me."

The man cleared his throat and flushed a deeper shade of red.

"A letter for Jack is it?" The change of subject was most welcome.

Emma drew a long breath and blew it out again slowly. She placed the letter on the counter and pushed it towards him.

"I thought it was about time I told him about his Pa." She paused. "And we've decided to stay."

Mr Price blinked at her in surprise. Then a smile lit up his face.

"That is excellent news, Mrs B, most excellent indeed. I'm sure Mrs Matthews is best pleased too. She is such a good friend of yours is she not?

Emma half laughed.

"You know," Emma was unsure why she felt the need to confide in this man. It wasn't the first time either. He just seemed to provoke trust and confession, "at first I intended to pack us all up and go straight home, but the thought of another sea voyage and going back to our old life seemed even more unpleasant than starting again here." She leaned a little closer to him. "Then there's Harry's job and the children have only got thoughts of the new school."

Mr Price put a hand on his hip as he often did when he was listening.

"Mr Burns may have been a dreamer, but he left us some money and do you know, I think we can make a go of it," Emma added quietly, as though someone else might hear. Mr Price glanced about the empty room conspiratorially.

"You know, I don't think Horace will tell anyone," he whispered.

The cat raised his tortoiseshell head at the sound of his name and looked over at them from the far end of the counter where he was curled up as always. Emma laughed. Horace stretched out, shuddered right through his body then curled back up and closed his eyes again. Mr Price shook his head at him.

"That is by far the fattest, laziest cat I have ever know."

"Did you bring him from England?" Emma had never considered this before.

"I'm afraid I did. Poor thing hated being captive on the ship but he was a good mouser when he was young and there were plenty of rats to keep him entertained. He doesn't like the weather here though. Too hot. He just lies around and sleeps most of the time; hardly ever goes outside." The cat began to purr, or snore, Emma couldn't quite decide which. "But then he's an old man now. You know it's nearly nine years since we left London."

"Gracious. And you never wanted to go back?"

Mr Price shook his head again.

"After my Pat died, I just had to get away from England, and the thought of being back there on my own! No, no, I would never go back." He patted her hand again. At first, Emma had been wary of Mr Price's affectionate ways. But over the last year, she had grown rather fond of him. He talked a lot about 'his Pat' and in the beginning, Emma had presumed that it was his wife, but he had never denoted Pat's gender, and she had long suspected that Pat had been a man. When the notion had first occurred to her she had been a little shocked. But, whoever Pat had been, Mr Price had loved them very much, and what could be wrong in that?

"Why Australia?"

Mr Price shrugged,

"Australia was the first passage available. I lived in the city for a while. Worked in a couple of the hotels, then came out here in '54 to run this place."

Emma mused at fate.

"Funny how things turn out. I'd never have thought I'd end up here, not in a million years," she said, looking around the impeccably neat little post office.

"What do you think you'll do now that you're a woman of means?" Mr Price was half-joking. Yet, she was well aware it was a decision that needed to be made.

"I was wondering about the racecourse," she replied. "Perhaps an investment? Jacob loved racing, albeit for the wrong reasons," she rolled her eyes at him. "But," she lowered her voice again, "I'd feel less guilty with my inheritance if I invest in something Jacob might have enjoyed."

Mr Price gave her a sympathetic smile.

"You know, I don't think you ought to feel guilty in coming into a bit of money from that husband of yours."

Perhaps he was right about that, but Emma felt guilty all the same.

"What about the empty shop next door?" Mr Price continued. "It's been sitting there waiting for someone like you."

Emma laughed at her friend.

"Now what on earth sort of shop could I run?" *Not laundry!* She thought. "I think I'm better off putting the money into something already established and run by someone else, someone who knows that they're doing."

Mr Price raised an eyebrow and looked as though he were about to protest but thought better of it. In the end, he just said,

"You do as you see fit Mrs B. You know what's best for you and yours." But there was something in his tone that Emma couldn't quite put her finger on, almost as if he already knew what was to become of her next.

18

Melbourne
May 1858

Satin draped walls shimmered beneath the sunlight that was beaming in through the exceptionally clean windows. Outside the clatter of carriages and the hum of voices drifted up to the second floor of the English and Scottish Bank. Emma wriggled in her chair to relieve to tightness in her back, though, she noted, it was not as painful as usual.

"Your husband did just enough work on the foundations to make the land legally yours so…" Mr Crane's voice was rather monotone and mixed with the muggy afternoon Emma was finding it hard to keep awake.

"I'm sorry, I don't quite follow. You mean if he hadn't laid the foundations we would have lost the land?"

Mr Crane began tapping a fingernail on the desk rhythmically.

"Land purchased in…err…such a manner as your husband was able to do must be improved or returned to the Crown," whether he meant to or not, he sounded patronising.

Emma felt her face flush. It hadn't occurred to her that any restrictions might apply. Jacob certainly hadn't divulged them. *Well, thank heavens he at least got as far as a bit of digging and nailing down some wood*, she thought.

"The sale should be quite straight forward." He cleared his throat and appeared to be forming a further thought.

"What about the racecourse?" Emma asked when the pause lasted a little too long.

"Mrs Burns, we always prefer to keep our new families in Australia, and we would very much like to see you invest in something local."

A fire was crackling in the small fireplace making the room stuffy and hot. Emma wafted her hand in front of her face and tried to smile.

"You know, there are plenty of opportunities here, even for a woman in such a position as yourself."

She really didn't care for his tone.

"You could keep your land and run a small farmstead perhaps. Or take up a little business in town." His gaze was wandering over her ancient bonnet and old fashioned mourning dress with some distaste or was it pity, Emma couldn't quite tell. She was beginning to wonder where this conversation was heading.

"I was conversing with Mr Sinclair only last week about such things."

Emma presumed this was someone else at the bank.

"But the racecourse is a bit of an old boys' game, Mrs Burns. I am sure you are aware of that. Your husband was a frequent visitor to the tack I believe."

Emma felt her face grow even hotter.

"I'm not sure they would be too keen on a woman as an investor," he finished flatly.

Emma's had requested this meeting to discuss her financial options, but now she was beginning to feel like she was just as much of a dreamer as Jacob.

"What if you were to make the proposition on my behalf?" She knew she was grasping at a proverbial straw. The banker shook his head. The sympathy of his expression seemed genuine enough, but that didn't change the outcome.

"I know many of these men personally, Mrs Burns. I deal with them all the time. I am quite certain that a woman of... a woman would not be taken seriously, nor would they be keen on any anonymous partner. And erm…how do I put this…the money you have, even with the sale of the land, whilst it is substantial to you, is not a vast deal to them. Please say you follow me, Mrs Burns."

Emma appreciated his honesty but that didn't stop her heart from dropping to her feet. What on earth could she possibly do that would be of any use?

Noting her utter embarrassment he drew a quick breath and asked,

"What did you do in England?"

She sank further into the hard wooden chair and tried not to cry. Thankfully he waited patiently for her to reply. She dare not look him in the eyes when she said,

"I was a housemaid before marriage...and then…a laundress after my husband..." Emma suddenly saw herself, not as a businesswoman, but on her hands and knees scrubbing floors at one of the hotels.

Mr Crane cleared his throat in acknowledgement.

"You can sew I presume?"

"Tolerably well."

"Hmmm."

"Clearly you can read and write,"

This perked her up a little. He could not have made such an observation before she set out for Australia.

"How is your arithmetic?"

"Good, I believe," she replied with a nod.

Mr Crane interlaced his fingers and bent them back with a satisfying crack.

"The railway will be coming this way in the next year or two and the village is expanding rapidly. There are a few houses to be built near the new school and a row of shops."

Mr Price's suggestion drifted back to her.

"You might consider what interests you; what sort of occupation you could best apply your skills to." Mr Crane rose and moved towards the door. Clearly, the meeting was over and Emma was even further from knowing what to do than she was before it began. She thanked him for his advice.

"If you're certain you wish to sell the land then I shall make arrangements accordingly. I shall contact you once we have a purchaser. Perhaps by then, you might have come to some conclusions."

"Thank you," she said again. "Please, proceed."

As Emma left the office she sighed. Even with a bit of money, she was still just a laundress and an ex-convicts widow.

19

Matthews Farmstead
June 9th 1858

Dusky pink light streaked across the dawn sky with a frosty chill. A scream bellowed through the house like a banshee. Emma awoke with a start, heart pounding from the shock. She waited a moment in case she had been dreaming. It came again, loud and clear. Somewhere in the house, someone was rattling pots and she heard the outside door clang as someone hurried out. Emma was already off the bed and pulling her shawl around her shoulders before a voice at her bedroom door called.

"Mrs Burns, it's Ma. The baby's coming!"

Emma pulled open the door and looked at Molly, all wide-eyed and stark awake. She glanced down the hall to see Albert and Alfie hauling a bucket of water in through the back door and Gloria lighting the stove to heat it. She and her two youngest had been staying at the farm for the past few days to help out until the baby came. The children had been told what to do, instructed until their ears near bled. There was no midwife out here and the nearest doctor was five miles away. By the time he could be fetched it could all be over with, so Emma and Lucy had made extra sure that things could be taken care of with no help at all.

"Where's your father?"

"Already on his way to the village," Molly replied.

"Good."

Emma splashed icy water over her face from her washbasin and quickly dabbed herself dry again.

"Go hold your mother's hand," she told the girl. "I'll be there in just a minute."

Another scream. Emma flinched and scurried to the kitchen to make sure the other children were boiling the water and warming the linen.

"Very good," she said with her hands on her hips. "Now Gloria, fetch that bowl and come with me. Boys, just keep up the good work. We'll let you know if and when you can help."

Emma pushed open the door to Lucy and Alf's bedchamber. Lucy was on the floor, crouched on all fours, panting like a dog. Molly was now sitting next to her white as a sheet. Emma glanced at Gloria and saw the same startled fear in her eyes.

"Girls, you can go help in the kitchen, me and Lucy will be all right in here 'til the doctor comes." Molly looked nervously from her mother to Emma. A mixture of relief and disloyalty clouded her face until Lucy said,

"Go on love, too many cooks will only spoil the broth." As she gripped her stomach and cried out Molly was on her feet and out the door, pulling Gloria behind her.

"I ain't never having kids!" Emma heard her say as the door closed behind them.

Lucy laughed through the pain.

"Well if this don't make 'em both keep their knickers on and their legs crossed 'til their wedding nights, nothin' will!"

Emma looked at the soiled bed sheets and back at Lucy. The blood-smeared fluid was tinged yellowish green. Emma was certain that was not a good sign. With a thump of trepidation in her gut, she began to tug off the bedding.

"I'll put some clean linen on the mattress so we can get you back onto the bed."

Lucy howled again, face contorted and red as a beetroot. Emma dabbed a cloth into the washbowl and gently wiped her friend's sweat-soaked forehead.

"Come on, let me get you up." She threaded an arm around Lucy and they tried to stand, but Lucy's legs wouldn't take her. She sank back into a squat and heaved deep into her pelvis. When the pain eased Emma asked her to sit back so she could take a look, and when she did she was even more concerned. Lucy was full ready to give birth but there was no sign of a baby's head. She gently felt Lucy's stomach, pressing and feeling for the baby inside. Something didn't feel right. Emma pressed the back of her hand to her lips and drew a breath. She had pushed five infants of her own into this world and delivered her neighbours youngest when the child came too fast to get help. But the child she had lost; her waters had been tainted like Lucy's. The pain had been unbearable, far worse than any of her others, and he had been breech. The help she had received then had come from an angel of a midwife who had turned the baby and got her through. Though not the child. Anyone else and she may not have escaped with her own life. Emma was not sure she was capable of doing the same for Lucy.

"What is it?" Lucy suddenly looked stricken with fear.

Emma sat back and took a moment to compose her answer.

"Baby's breech. I need to turn him."

Lucy grabbed at Emma's hand as another wave of agony gripped her belly. She heaved again.

"Don't push," Emma said with as little fear as she could manage. "I know you want to, but please try to resist or I shan't be able to get the baby right way up." With a shudder, Emma recalled the agony of feeling the baby turning inside her and murmured a quiet prayer. Lucy was watching her through a grimace. "I'm sorry Lucy, but it's going to hurt."

Lucy gritted her teeth and panted.

"Typical a child of mine should try to enter this world arse first." She tried to laugh but the pain was making her head light. She slumped back. "I got through twins, I can get through one that's upside down," she breathed.

Outside the door, she could hear whisperings. Emma realised one of the girls was going to have to help.

"Molly, please come in. Your Ma needs you."

*

Time seemed to tick on yet stand still. Emma had tried for several minutes to guide the baby around so that the head was facing down, but the child refused to move and Lucy was in agony. Her friend was growing increasingly anxious and the contractions were coming so close together. She glanced at the clock on the mantle; it was a quarter after nine. Alf had been gone near two hours, surely he and the doctor should be back soon.

Lucy hunched over and screamed.

"I have to push."

Emma nodded stiffly.

"Argh!" Molly winced. She was holding her mother's hand and her fingers were turning blue. They had managed to get Lucy back onto the bed, though she was kneeling on all fours with her forehead on pressed into the pillows. Emma scuttled around to see how far they were getting. What she saw left her unsure whether to be relieved or terrified. There, crowning between its mother's legs was the baby's bottom.

"All right, another big push. Deep as you can."

Molly peered around to take a look and turned a light shade of green. She tried to pull away but Lucy hung on to her as though life depended on it, and it might have. Emma hoped Molly wouldn't be sick or faint. She could do without that as well. But the child just stepped back and concentrated on her mother's face. Lucy contorted and screamed so loud the nightstand rattled.

"Good, that's very good," Emma assured her as the baby's bottom slid further out to reveal a pair of thighs and lower back.

Emma reached over and gently tugged a tiny leg loose. First one, then two. The baby hung there, dangling as though on a noose. Emma clenched her jaw and tried to breathe slowly.

"Again Lucy," she encouraged. "It will all be over soon."

Lucy obliged but the baby wouldn't budge any further. The shoulders and head were wedged inside.

"Come on baby, help us out here," Emma whispered. She glanced up at Lucy. Her friend was pale and exhausted. She flopped forward, plating her face fully in the pillow and gasped. It had not been a long labour thus far but the intensity was immense. Another contraction wracked her. She hoisted herself up onto her elbows, puffed out her cheeks, and with the loudest scream yet, she pushed.

"Come on!" she hollered.

Emma felt something give and a squirt of blood-spattered her arm. Poor Lucy had torn but the extra space released the child. Emma pulled as carefully as she could. One shoulder, two, a chin, a nose, ears, out! The infant fell into her hands.

Emma gasped, tears streaming down her face. She used a bit of string to tie off the cord.

"Molly, pass me the scissors."

The girl's hands were shaking so much she almost dropped them. Emma smiled up at her and severed the cord. Lucy gave a last shuddering push and the placenta slid out in one healthy piece.

"Thank God," Emma breathed.

The next few moments seemed to happen in some kind of distorted, slow motion.

A gush of blood. Lucy was bleeding and badly. Lucy collapsed onto the bed and rolled weakly over onto her back. Blood streaked down her thighs and began to soak through the bedding. Emma told Molly to press a clean cloth against the tear but she couldn't make out if that was the source or if the bleeding was inside. She placed the baby on a clean linen cloth, but the tiny, perfect child hadn't moved. Not a flicker of life, not a breath of air entered her lungs. Emma wiped the mucus from her face and mouth. She picked her up and turned her over in her hands. So small. So delicate. She patted her back. Nothing.

Molly was sobbing. Blood soaked through the cloth fast as water. Emma blinked tears from her eyes. Fanatic she begged,

"Please baby, please!"

A whisper from the bed. Emma looked up. Lucy was trying to sit, skin waxen and as grey as an English sky.

"What is it?"

Emma was unsure if Lucy wanted to know the gender or why the infant was so silent. She tried to respond but words stuck in her dry throat. She rubbed the baby's back. Nothing. She stroked her head. Nothing. She tipped her upside down, nothing.

"Oh, God," Molly murmured.

Emma cradled the baby in the crook of one arm and helped Molly press another cloth against her mother. She watched in silent horror as the new cloth turned from white to red in a matter of seconds.

She didn't notice the movement at first. It was only when something pressed against her breast that she looked down again at the baby. There was the tiniest little cough. Large blue eyes, dark as midnight blinked open and a pair of sturdy little legs kicked out. The child screwed up her tiny face until it was wrinkled like a prune and wailed, so shrill it made the sheep bleat out in the yard.

Emma kissed the child's head and sobbed.

"Ma, Ma!"

It wasn't over. Molly had dropped the dirty cloth and was cradling her mother's limp head. Lucy's eyes fluttered open for just a moment. Long enough for Emma to show her the child. Then she sank back, eyes closed.

Molly was hysterical, crying and wailing louder than the screaming infant. Emma grabbed a cloth for the baby and called for Gloria to come and take her. But when the door swung open it was not Gloria that entered the room; it was a young woman, skin dark as cocoa. Emma gawped but there was no time to think.

"Doctor was out with a sick man." Alf gasped from the doorway. He was staring at the gory scene, white as Lucy. "This is Mercy, she's a midwife," he stammered.

The woman didn't hesitate. She didn't pause to remove her bonnet, tie on a pinny, nor even push up her sleeves. She just tugged off her gloves, handed them to Alf and was over to Lucy in less than a heartbeat. Emma watched, unable to move. Thoughts of every kind raced through her mind until she was giddy. Mercy removed the bloody cloth and pressed down hard on Lucy's belly. Lucy groaned and writhed. Emma realised she had been holding her breath and gasped. Time seemed to have stopped. Even the sheep outside were quiet. Lucy's chest was barely moving. Emma dared herself to reach over and touch her. Lucy shuddered, breath shallow and lips blue. Slowly the blood flow eased. Mercy never flinched or retracted the pressure. Finally, the bleeding stopped. Emma sank on the edge of the bed.

"Forgive me," Mercy said, her voice smooth as velvet. "There was no time to waste." She took the last clean cloth and wiped Lucy's brow. Lucy's eye fluttered open and her lips quivered into a shaky smile. "She has lost a lot of blood," Mercy continued, "but I have seen worse. I'm sure she'll be right as rain with a week or two's rest. You did very well Mrs..."

"Burns, Emma Burns." Emma's voice crocked. "The baby was breech," she volunteered.

"Then you did extremely well, Mrs Burns, and you too, Miss Matthews. Now would you be a love and fetch your mother a fresh glass of water and something sweet to eat," she said to Molly.

Molly was too much in shock to ask questions or judge this dark-skinned woman. As she left the room in dumbfounded silence Mercy turned her attentions to the infant.

"May I take a look?" A smile warmed her face, lighting up her eyes and suddenly Emma knew why William loved her. Gloria passed the fretful infant into the woman's welcoming arms and watched as she gently pulled back the cloth from her face. The child cooed and gurgled as the midwife counted her fingers and toes, checked her hips and shoulders for dislocation and finally waved her hand in front of the baby's face to make sure she could see. Finally, she looked back at Lucy and then over at the ashen Alf and said, "You have a perfect daughter, Mr and Mrs Matthews. Congratulations." Mercy got up and laid the child in her father's arms. "I shall give you a minute with your wife and daughter, sir, then I shall be back to tidy up." She turned to Emma, "Perhaps a nice cup of tea?"

Gratefully Emma accepted and led Mercy to the kitchen where three children were seated anxiously around the table and Molly was pouring honey onto a slice of bread. As they left Alf and his wife alone with their new baby she heard Lucy say,

"I think we should call her Emma."

Emma swallowed a sob and went to wash her hands in the water bucket.

"You fed all the animals?" she said to the children. She knew they would have, it was part of the daily drill, but she knew not what else to say. Alfie said Marvin had been put back in his barn too. Molly excused herself to return to her mother. Emma nodded gratefully and sat down next to Albert.

Sunlight shone through the kitchen window lighting dust particles into glowing dancing flecks. She looked out to see the sun burning high in the sky and noticed it was only just gone noon. Despite the difficulties it had been a fast labour. Her stomach rumbled and she realised she hadn't eaten anything yet. Gloria got up and refilled the kettle, clearly trying not to stare at their guest.

Mercy was, as she had been in on each occasion Emma had seen her, impeccably dressed. Her hair was swept neatly beneath the trim of her hat. Her dress was not of the most expensive fabric but the cut was the height of fashion and the vivid colour was a cobalt blue that complemented her complexion perfectly. Her hands were already scrubbed clean. She took off her hat and untied her cape and folded it over the back of a chair before sitting down. Albert and Alfie were both gawping like fish needing air. Emma flashed them a glare. Albert closed his mouth and Alfie said,

"Ain't we seen you before?"

Mercy smiled at him kindly.

"I should think that is possible. My son and I are living with my brother-in-law a few miles from here. Our paths could easily have crossed."

Emma considered that Mercy's command of the English language was better than that of the children, and they had been born in England. Alfie shook his head.

"That ain't it," he narrowed his eyes. "I think we saw you in Cape Town. Ya came to wave off the ship when we left. You was with Mr Finch."

Mercy's full lips curled back into a broad smile.

"Gracious, you do have a good memory for faces. I am afraid I did not see you that day. But then I was not at my best." She took a hesitant breath. "It is Mr Finch with whom we are living."

The kettle began to whistle on the stove. Gloria went to finish her job. It was at this point that Mercy's words struck Emma. Had she not just said that she was living with her brother-in-law, not her husband? And now she had said she was living with Mr Finch. Emma was attempting to formulate a question when Mercy added,

"John, my late husband, was your teacher's brother. You were very lucky. Mr Finch is an excellent man and an excellent teacher. Did you enjoy his lessons?"

Emma was struggling to comprehend what was being said. The children were agreeing with Mercy and beginning to enthuse about their time on the ship.

"I wish Mr Finch could teach us now."

Mercy sat back with a satisfied nod.

"Gloria isn't it?" she asked, turning to the little girl.

Gloria nodded.

"Well, I can let you in on a secret if you like?"

All three children leaned forwards eagerly.

"Well," Mercy leaned forwards too and said in a stage whisper, "You will be having lessons from Mr Finch again, very soon. Mr Matthews told me you live in Flemington, is that right?"

Emma felt her heart skip a beat. Gloria confirmed Mercy's information.

"The new school in Flemington will be open before the year is out and Mr Finch is going to be one of the teachers." Mercy smiled.

The only thought rushing through Emma's mind was that Mr Finch was going to be teaching her children again, in her village, and very likely living close by. She was not certain her heart could stand it. Mercy's face fell.

"I am sorry; I did not mean to intrude. I am sure the current school has been most proficient, or if you prefer to teach your children at home. That is of course a most excellent manner of education."

Emma felt sick. She wiped her hand over her mouth and took a sip of the freshly poured tea.

"Not at all, Mrs Finch, not at all. I am merely tired from the morning's events," she managed to say.

Mercy's smooth features returned to a smile.

"Oh, I am glad. He really is such a good person. He has been so very kind to us. Poor man, he had been so looking forward to visiting us when the ship called in at Cape Town, only to find that John had taken seriously ill the month before he arrived. Had the ship been delayed any longer, he would have missed him altogether. Yet all he could think of was looking after us. He made sure the best was done for John, and promised that there would always be a home with him, for my son and me, should we need it. Then when my father died a few months later, we decided to accept his invitation."

"You're moving to Flemington then?" Albert asked.

Emma still hadn't quite grasped the situation.

"Yes, soon after Michaelmas we hope."

Emma shook herself from her stupor.

"I'm very sorry for your loss," she offered. "My husband passed away recently also."

"Then please accept my condolences. You will understand how much I miss John then." Mercy looked melancholy for just the smallest of moments, but no sooner did the tears prick at her eyes, she pasted a smile back on her face.

"Indeed," Emma did not wish to admit it, but she was not sure she did miss Jacob all that much. She may have loved her husband, yet there was a sense of relief that far outweighed her loss. *Another thing to feel guilty about*, she thought.

"But one must get on with things I suppose," Mercy added more brightly. "And William has done his best to make it easier for us."

Emma wanted to ask how a woman such as Mercy had ever come to be Mrs Finch in the first place but restrained herself. That would be a very impertinent question. Mercy finished her tea, set down the cup and rose.

"I shall tend to Mrs Matthews and then I had better be running along home, it is quite a walk and my son does fret when I am away too long. He doesn't seem to be able to get used to all the strange animals here, poor lamb is terrified of kangaroos," she said with a smile and a shake of her head.

Emma considered this a queer notion indeed when she thought of all the strange and exotic animals that came from Africa, but then, she supposed, it's what you are used to at the end of the day.

"Thank you again," she said.

As she watched Mercy make her way back down the hall to Lucy's bedroom, she wondered what life was going to throw at them all next.

20

Flemington

A few days later

Emma rubbed her eyes and blinked. The room was growing dim and the day was almost gone. Outside she could hear the children playing, taking advantage of a cool winters evening. She went to the kitchen dresser and yanked the drawer. It always stuck fast halfway and she was forced to shove her knee under the base to hold it up as she pulled. It juddered open. She took out a fresh candle, lit it and placed it in the candlestick on the kitchen table. As the small yellow flame flickered into a bright little light she picked up Jack's letter and read through it again.

'28th January 1858'

It was small comfort but at least their seasons coincided, even if the dates were six months apart.

'Dear Mam and Pa
I hope this letter finds you all well.'

Emma felt her stomach tighten. How many more letters would there be addressed to his father?

'Everything is going along all right here. The cottage is doing well. Though I think it misses you as much as I do. The fire still smokes, the back door still creaks no matter what I do and the kitchen is still the warmest room in the house.'

Emma laughed. She was pleased she could finally picture him back in the cottage.

'But I love being here again. I am pleased you left me Grand Pa's oil lamp. I think it would be very dim with just candles. Do you have gas in your cottage? How is the new house coming along?'

Emma glanced at the candle at her side and considered that she could actually afford to buy a new lamp now, or two, or even three for that matter. She had not mentioned the farmhouse in her letters for months, not since she gave up hope of it ever getting finished.

I hope next time I write back I can tell you about a real new house, she mused. "Just as soon as I can figure out what to do," she said out loud.

'I am very sorry to have to pass on sad news, but old Mrs Wheeler at number three passed away last week. The funeral was on Friday. Her eldest son came to clear out the cottage today so it is all empty now and ready for a new tenant. They were kind enough to give me her set of cutlery as they had no use for it, and I only had the one fork and knife.'

That was kind indeed; they could have got a good bit of money for a cutlery set. Emma suddenly felt guilty for having taken most of theirs with them.

"It was a short illness that took her, but she was a grand age so one should be thankful for that."

So much death. Emma took a moment to remember the old woman. Mrs Wheeler had lived two doors down all Emma's life, watching her grow up and then bring her own children into the street after Jacob was sent away. She was one of the few people that had not judged them or gossiped as Emma had dragged her bag of belongings up the road, heavily pregnant and three children in tow. Mrs Wheeler had come over and helped her open the door and settled her in. She sighed and returned to the letter.

'On a brighter note, I have some news of my own to tell you too. I have met a girl! You would like her Mam. I wish you could meet her. Her name is Marjorie and she is the prettiest girl at the potteries. Mr Barker took on two new girls just before Christmastide and one of them is Marj. She is sixteen and has the loveliest black hair I ever saw.'

Emma smiled to herself. Only a boy in love could talk about a girl's hair.

'We have been walking out together these past three weeks. It might be a bit soon for me to be mentioning her to you. But I couldn't resist. She is kind and sweet and she wants me to meet her Ma and Pa next Sunday after church.'

Emma felt her heart brighten again, just as it had the first time she read the letter that morning.

"I do hope she's as nice as you think, son," she said to herself. "Don't go getting distracted by a pretty face and a bit of charm."

'Well, I shall tell you how all that goes in my next letter.

Bye for now,

Your loving son,

Jack.'

Emma folded the letter and put it back beneath the cutlery tray with the others. The tea caddy had become too small for the letters and the tea. She tried to picture Jack standing before her, but the image wouldn't come. Frustrated she closed the back door to keep out the evening flies and began to prepare dinner.

21

Late June 1858

A long winter's day reminded her of home. Emma rolled her shoulders and rubbed at her back automatically, then realised it wasn't hurting at all today. Droplets were running down the kitchen window in tiny waterfalls. She peered out into the dank afternoon and strained to hear the sound of the distant piano, but the rain was beating like a thousand small drums and the soft music was distorted.

"Mam, I'm cold. Can we light the stove?" Albert whined.

Emma looked around at her son, seated at the table with his slate and chalk. He was working on the list of sums she had set.

"Sorry lad, we're almost out of wood, there's no delivery 'til Tuesday and there won't be any more worth collecting in this rain either. We need what we've got to cook supper. Go fetch the blanket from your bed and wrap it around yourself."

Albert did as he was told. Emma shivered as he pushed back his chair, sending a further draft around her legs. She wrapped her shawl tighter but it wasn't enough. She rubbed at her arms then folded them tight. Albert ran back down the stairs, making the walls shake from his thunderous footsteps.

"Careful, you'll fall through if you stamp any harder."

Albert grinned and scuttled back into the kitchen, blanket over his shoulders and flapping out like a cape behind him. The clock in the sitting room clunked past four. Emma pushed open the door and contemplated which room was warmer. Sitting on the mantle was her father's clock, just like it had back in their old cottage. She ought to get the chime mended now she could afford it. She went into the room and looked around at the few nice things they had brought with them from home. A small footstool with horsehair padding and faded green damask cover, the brass tacks catching in the grim silvery twilight. The beautiful plate Jacob had painted for her as a wedding gift; the pink roses still as bright as the day she had unwrapped it. Then there was the brass candlestick, the redundant coal-scuttle and matching poker that sat on the hearth, and finally the clock. Everything else in the room had come with the rental. She perched on the edge of the battered old wing chair and ran her hand over the cracked brown leather. Jacob had said it was his home comfort between stints at the mines.

"What you doin', Mam?"

Emma looked around with a start.

"Just thinking we need some new furniture." She patted the sunken seat next to her and ignored a wave of guilt. She didn't want to think of Jacob's death as fortuitous and yet no matter which way she considered it, if he was still alive the money would have been gambled away again by now. Not to mention the lighter feeling in the house without his dark moods and drunken rants.

"Come sit here with me and show me your sums," she said, sitting in Jacob's chair. "There's room on here for two and it'll be warmer if we sit close."

Albert was ten now and beginning to show signs that he was growing up. Hugging his mother had recently become something he was reluctant to do, claiming he was not a baby anymore. For a moment he hesitated, pulling a face that reflected this notion. But then the child in him took over and he bounded back to fetch his slate then shuffled his narrow body in next to her. Emma wrapped one arm around him and took the slate with her free hand.

"Very good, Bertie," she observed as she ran her eyes down the list of sums. "Very good indeed. All correct."

Albert beamed at her,

"Mr Finch will be pleased."

Hearing the man's name made her stomach flip.

"I'm very certain he will, but the new school doesn't open for months yet."

Albert ran a finger through the chalked numbers, leaving a long smudge through the centre of the slate, and then poked at his mother's side with the dirty end of his digit. Emma pushed him away playfully.

"Filthy child. I shall have you for that." She began to tickle him. Trapped as they both were in the width of the wing chair the struggle was limited. Hands everywhere, bodies squirming. Her fingers reaching and tickling until he cried for mercy. Tears streamed down his face as he gasped through breathless laughter. His hands clawing out, attempting to tickle her back. Finally, they both sank back, exhausted. Emma looked at him fondly. He was not so grown up yet. Albert caught his breath.

"But they're moving in before that."

Emma looked blank.

"Who are dear?"

Albert wriggled further back into the chair.

"Mr Finch and Mercy of course."

Emma felt her heart thump.

"What do you mean? How do you know that?"

"Well, Glo and I saw them in town yesterday when we went to fetch the eggs and milk."

Emma blinked and attempted to compose herself.

"You did? Why didn't you tell me?"

"I am telling you." Albert looked at her suspiciously, "why?"

Emma began picking at the side of her thumbnail.

"No matter. So where were they?" She tried to sound casual. Outside the rain began to ease and a chink of light shot through the clouds overhead and sliced through the window. She would have smiled had she not been so preoccupied.

"Well, they was in the General Store. They had a boy with them."

Emma didn't even notice his grammatical slip.

"That'll be Mercy's son," she said.

"His skin is paler than hers."

Emma ruffled Albert's hair.

"Well, his Pa is Mr Finch's brother. He would have had white skin like Mr Finch, so the boy a mixture of his Pa and Ma."

Albert nodded thoughtfully.

"Does that mean the Abos would be whiter if they could get white Pa's too?"

Emma pressed her fingers to her lips. She was not keen on the tangent in conversation but she couldn't help admiring her son's logic.

"Yes, lad, it does."

"Good, then maybe we can make them all white and they would be like us and they won't be a problem no more."

Now she was horrified.

"Bert! Don't you think like that! Aborigines are people just like us."

"I heard a man in the General Store say they were just like rats and he had to shoot at one to keep him off his farm only last week."

Emma got to her feet quickly and turned on her son.

"I never want to hear you say such a thing ever again, do you hear me!"

"But I was only saying what the mister said." Albert's Staffordshire accent seemed suddenly stronger. Tears were welling in his eyes. Emma drew a breath and crouched down before of him.

"I know. I'm sorry. But I mean what I say. I never want to hear you call any person, no matter what colour their skin, any such thing again. People are not animals." *Even if some behave like it at times,* Emma thought, recalling the men in the Rio prison, leering and yelling like rabid dogs as she had walked past.

"But they live out in the bush just like..." he stopped himself.

"Or how they live," she added firmly.

"But the man said they were on his land."

"Those people have lived here for thousands of years. We're the ones who came and took their land. We can't expect them to just go away and never come back without complaint. The man that was shot at probably used to live there and was just used to walking about wherever he liked."

Albert looked pensive for a moment. Emma waited for him to process the information. She tried not to think too much about the way the Europeans had charged in and set up camp in this colony. Each time it crossed her mind her skin prickled and a sick feeling settled in the pit of her stomach. When she had been reading Jacob's letters it had been so very far away and so incomprehensible. When he had talked of farmers shooting at the wild men or described the broad nose and bare breasts of the old woman who kept straying onto his employer's land, it had felt more like tall and exotic tales than reality. But now she was here living as one of the invaders she felt no better than a slave trader or plantation owner. Her mind snapped back to Mercy Finch. How must she feel, a black woman far away from home living in a white man's world where the dark-skinned locals were banished and shot at. How odd must it be for her? Especially when she considered what South Africa had been like until so very recently. Would she fear for her own life or feel as though she were a persecutor herself? Her parents must have been slaves before the abolition; in fact, she had likely been born a slave herself. Emma couldn't bear to think of it.

Albert finally parted his pursed lips and said,

"So we are the bad men? Just like the men who captured the slaves on that ship and sailed them to Rio?"

Emma didn't wish her son to feel ashamed, yet she couldn't permit him to grow up believing that other men were unworthy of civility.

"Yes, son," she said. "But so long as you behave with respect and treat all men with kindness, then your conscience will be clear."

This seemed to satisfy the lad, so Emma turned the conversation.

"So, you spoke to Mr Finch?"

Albert nodded.

"Mercy saw us first. She waved and came to ask how Mrs Matthews is doing. She said she goes over once a week to check on her, but had to miss this week on account of the fact they were coming to Flemington to move into their new house."

Move to Flemington, now! Emma felt her thighs begin to cramp from crouching and sat back on her heels. *Had she not said around Michaelmas?*

"Gracious, did they say where they are going to be living?" Her voice sounded tight.

"I didn't ask."

The front door rattled. Emma looked up in surprise. For a moment she thought it would be Jacob and Harry but of course, it was only poor, soaked Gloria returning from her piano lesson. The child wiped the water from her eyes with the back of her sleeve. Her ringlets were plastered to her face and her dress stained dark with rain.

"Gracious you only came twenty yards and look at the state of you. Come and get dried off." Emma said, taking off her shawl and holding it out for Gloria to wrap herself in.

"Do we have a visitor?" The child glanced around and listened for noise in the kitchen or out in the dunny.

"No dear, why?"

"You're in the sitting room. We only sit in here when Pa is…"

Emma smiled sadly.

"I felt like a change," she said. "Go get those wet clothes off and put on something nice and dry." As Gloria vanished up the stairs, Emma turned back to Albert for one last question. "Did he…they…both seem well?"

Albert shrugged. Emma cocked her head and raised her eyebrows in a manner that said, 'not good enough, I want an answer.'

Albert shrugged again,

"Yep."

"You did ask them if they were well?" she said archly. "And I do hope you told them we have been to stay with the Matthews for a few days and that Lucy is doing much better."

Albert cowered a little but promised that he had. Emma was not sure exactly which part he had not done but decided to leave it at that.

22

Matthews Farmstead
August 1958

The stove was burning and the whole house was warm and cosy. Everywhere smelled of soap and wood smoke. Emma listened to the giggle of young girls and smiled contentedly. She enjoyed being at the Matthews home, for it was just that, a real home. She set down the spud knife and looked out into the yard. Alfred was working under the shade of the porch; hammer in hand, thumping at nails. He was making pig huts, three of them for the new arrivals. Emma watched him wipe the sweat from his brow with the cuff of his sleeve and decided she had better fetch in the laundry.

"Ya really didn't have to do that." Lucy entered the room from the hall, wriggling bundle in her arms. She was still weak but never one for giving in to rest, she had been up and about not three days after the birth. She had conceded to allow Alfred and the twins to do more work and when the Burns family visited she had come around to letting Emma help out more.

"Least I can do," Emma said looking from her friend to the pile of chopped potatoes. She wiped her hands on her piny and outstretched her arms. "Aunt Emma's turn for a cuddle."

Lucy handed over the baby, sat down on one of the kitchen chairs and plonked her feet on a small footstool.

"Good to see you again, Mrs Burns."

Emma was busy looking at the tiny pink face and large blue eyes of the baby. She glanced up. Mercy Finch had followed Lucy into the room and was standing in the doorway looking as elegant as ever. Emma marvelled at how a woman could look so impeccably neat even when working.

"And you, Mrs Finch?" Emma desperately wanted to ask after William but didn't wish to sound too eager. "Your family are well?"

Mercy replied to the affirmative.

"I hear you're moving to Flemington very soon?" The baby sensed Emma's tension and squirmed, screwing up her face ready to cry. She jiggled her up and down.

"Yes, indeed. As a matter of fact, William is there today, opening up the house."

Emma felt her face flush at the sound of his name. She hoped Mercy couldn't tell. The young woman made her way over to Emma and stroked the child's face gently. Emma watched the slender dark fingers and noticed that the palms of her hands were much paler than the backs, almost as white as her own. She wondered if that was the same with all folks of colour. Since she hadn't been in a position to be so close to a black person's hands before, she had never had the opportunity to observe. It occurred to her that and aside from the birth when her attentions were on nought but Lucy and the baby, Emma had only ever seen Mercy wearing gloves. Mercy noticed her looking and took a step back.

"You know, I really ought to set out. It is already past four and I must get home."

Emma felt flush with embarrassment and tried to think of something else to say. Lucy was the one to rescue her.

"Ya more than welcome to stay for some of that tea you brought, perhaps a bite of bread and jam to go wiv it? Homemade with damsons from that bush out there." Lucy pushed the footstool away and got to her feet.

"Damsons indeed? Where did you get the plant?" Mercy had raised her eyebrows with keen interest.

Lucy shrugged,

"Alfred bought it from a man at the docks, they'd brought 'em out from England."

"Gracious, and they survived the journey! Well, how lovely." Lucy's face lit up with a thought.

"Why don't ya take a cutting? Ya could be making your own jam next season."

Mercy pressed her hands together in a clap.

"How very kind you are Lucy. I would like that very much. Perhaps just a quick cup," she added as Lucy was already filling the kettle.

Emma kissed the baby's head and watched as Lucy smeared jam over several chunks of bread and popped them on plates. They were not very delicate but the jam really was exceptionally tasty. A minute later the kettle boiled and the most delicious scent filled the kitchen.

"Ooh ain't this lovely." Lucy sighed.

"Mmm, very nice." Emma grinned.

"Did I not tell you it was good tea?" Mercy said.

"Where'd ya get it?" Lucy asked through a mouthful of jammy bread.

"Imported from China. I used to get it in Cape Town, then a few weeks ago I found a supplier in Melbourne." Mercy looked delighted her tea was such a hit.

Lucy poked her head out the door and hollered for Alf and the children to come in for a cup. But Alf yelled something in return that they couldn't quite make out. Lucy got up and went outside to find out.

"William is keen to get a kitchen garden going at the house. I have never done anything like it before," Mercy said as she set down her cup.

Emma hoped she didn't look too flustered and attempted to change the subject.

"How did you come to be a midwife?"

Mercy looked at her with a little surprise.

"Well, my mother was what you call a midwife and her mother before her. I have been delivering babies and tending mothers since I was nine years old," she explained.

Emma wanted to ask her if she had been enslaved. The question burned on her lips.

"You...I mean...were they..." She couldn't say it.

"Were my parent's slaves? Please do not be afraid to ask. I would prefer frankness than fear."

Emma would have pressed her fingers to her lips had she not been holding the baby. Instead, she caught her breath and nodded.

"Yes, they were. But there was no one to look after such matters as birthing for us. Masters were rarely interested in our lives or cared enough to fetch assistance. Unless the child was theirs."

This made Emma jolt. She knew of such things of course, but she had never stopped to think of them. Nor was she allowed time to contemplate that matter now. She chewed on her lip as Mercy continued.

"And we preferred to take care of our own. I was born in slavery, Mrs Burns, as you may well have guessed. Abolition came when I was very young and my parents were fortunate to have a generous master who offered them proper positions. But babies will still come and midwives are always needed, so after a time my mother left her post and began to make a meagre living on her own. And when I was old enough I started to help her out. When she died, I took over." Mercy was looking right into Emma's eyes as if she knew what further questions were on the tip of her tongue.

"That is how I met my husband, Mrs Burns. John was a Minister in a white neighbourhood bordering my own. We were both called out to attend the same girl, I to deliver the child, and he to pray for them both. The girl was the housemaid." Mercy paused to allow Emma a moment to process the information. Emma could feel her cheeks burning.

"The mother was in difficulty. It was too late by the time they sent for me. There was nothing neither God nor I could do to save her. We were lucky to save the child. And yes, he was mixed blood."

Emma reached out a trembling hand and touched Mercy's arm. Mercy let her lips melt into a kind smile.

"I didn't mean to pry. I just...I was curious." Emma said helplessly.

"I do not mind. It is entirely understandable. I am aware that I am an unusual sight in this country. Aside from the indigenous peoples, I have yet to set eyes upon another black woman since leaving Africa."

Emma shook her head.

"How does it not bother you that people like me stare and ask questions, or worse? I saw you in the haberdashers in Melbourne a few months since, and the women in the shop, they...their behaviour was appalling."

There was a creak on the stoop. Emma glanced towards the door but no one came in. Mercy drew a long breath.

"One grows used to such behaviour."

Emma was horrified.

"But you shouldn't have to."

Mercy shrugged.

"Where I grew up there was far worse to worry about." She looked as though she were about to add something else when a sudden ruckus erupted in the yard.

Hooves stamping and tramping. Boys shouting and laughing. Emma and Mercy glanced at each other and headed for the door. The sight that met them was both ridiculous and hilarious. Spindly legs galloping about like a gambolling foal. Hooves clattering on the deck, then sinking into the damp ground sending mud flecks flying. The goat had broken out of its pen, again. Alfie and Albert were chasing it around the yard as it bleated and snorted, taunting them with its ingenuity. Lucy was laughing at them so hard she had to hold on to the wall for support.

"Alf, go 'elp 'em," she gasped, gripping her side.

Alfred set down his hammer and went in to assist, but he was laughing so much himself that he was barely any more use than baby Emma-Louise would have been.

The goat reared its hind legs and bucked at Alfie, showering him with sodden bits of grass and narrowly missing his shins. Albert pounced from the side but the creature shot out of his way, leaving him skidding along the ground on his belly. He rolled onto his back and gasped for breath. Emma's mind flashed back to the ship, to the day the boys had set all the pigs and sheep free from their pens. The chaos that ensued then had not been quite as funny as it was now, but looking back she couldn't help but grin. Then Emma recalled the hiding Mr Finch had given the culprits. How the sympathy in those eyes of his had pierced right into her soul. She turned to Mercy who was watching with a delighted grin on her face. She found she was eager to know more about this woman and John and William Finch.

"Mam, Mam, did you see me! I caught the goat." Albert bounded over.

Emma laughed.

"Yes dear, I saw you. Very good work."

"Very clever," chipped in Mercy. "Well, I really had better go before the pony decides it's too late to set off for home and digs his feet into the ground." With that Mercy bid them all farewell, leaving Emma with far too many questions and thoughts.

*

The following day

It was a long, slow afternoon. Emma finished scouring the stove and dipped her hands into the sink. The water stung as it seeped into her cracked skin. She looked down at her reddened hands, as sore and overworked as they had been back home and on the ship. This time, however, it was her own fault. All day she had been finding things to clean. She imagined the little two-up-two-down cottage hadn't been so spotless since it was first built. She had swept the floors and scrubbed them, then cleaned the kitchen from top to bottom. She whipped the shelves, cleaned the sink and had even scoured the back of the stove, twice. It was not as though she had not done all this yesterday and the day before, but today she just kept on scrubbing long after any tiny marks and stains had vanished. It was either that or she sat out on the stoop and let her mind wander.

She withdrew her hands from the sink, dabbed them tentatively dry on her pinny and went to the front room. Her footsteps echoed through the empty house. So often she had felt the desire to be alone before, especially on the ship. But now Harry was away and the children were at school. It felt cold and lonely. Jack's face popped into her mind and she wondered what he would suggest she do with the money. It had been plenty long enough for her to decide now. She looked at the clock on the mantle; ten minutes past two. There was almost an hour before the children would be home, and even then Gloria was going to Mrs McLeish for her piano lesson. Emma considered that she ought to start paying the full rate now they were better off. With a quick scan of the gleaming floor, she decided to take the option of the stoop after all. Despite the cold winter air, the sun was bright and pleasant.

She grabbed her shawl and a chair from the kitchen and lifted it through the back door so that she could sit facing the distant river. From the tree, the Kookaburra laughed at her. She looked up at its fat striped head, set the chair down and walked towards it.

"So you think it's funny, do you? Well, you try to decide what to do with Jacob's money then." The bird nodded making Emma laugh back at it. "Fine, come on then Gordon, tell me your thoughts." As she came to a stop at the base of the tree the bird fluttered down a branch or two until it was almost level with her. Filled with the urge to stroke it, she raised a hand towards its shimmering blue and black wings but it changed its mind and flew away. "That's right, leave me all alone to decide for myself," she called after it and went back to the stoop.

As the last half an hour of solitude began to tick away, Emma tugged the shawl tighter around her shoulders and closed her eyes. In the distance, she heard the bird cackle again but this time she ignored it.

Sleep drifted over her causing her head to nod. She rolled her shoulders and adjusted her position, realising that her back hadn't hurt for a while now. The more she considered; the more she realised that she couldn't remember the last time it had bothered her, a week or two since at least. Perhaps not even since she had found out about the money. She opened her eyes, looked up at the sky and wished she had some of that lovely tea Mercy Finch had given Lucy. There were a few scattered clouds, thick, white and fluffy, like balls of lambs' wool. She watched as they rolled gently by, moulding and forming into discernible shapes. One swirled into something resembling the shape of a teacup. Then the idea hit her. She knew what she was going to do. Tomorrow she would make a new appointment with Mr Crane and as soon as she could, she needed to speak with Mercy Finch.

23

A week later

Gloria was skipping from one room to another with a wide grin on her face and Albert was standing in the living room with an expression of disbelief. Emma could empathise with both emotions. The cupboard doors were new and hanging perfectly straight. The floorboards were smooth and didn't creek. There was one large bedroom, a second of decent size and a smaller box room. The fireplace was clean and soot-free. Downstairs was the pantry and a kitchen almost as big as the living room. There was even a moderate drawing room. This was no palace but compared to any home they had lived in before it may as well have been. Mr Crane was holding a selection of paperwork.

"The deposit is already arranged. All you need to do is sign and it's yours, Mrs Burns."

Gloria stopped skipping.

"You have to sign, Mam. Please say we can live here, please."

Emma smiled, joined Mr Crane by the front window and looked down the street. Naked branches swayed in the swirling breeze, hillocks of crispy brown leaves gathered beneath. Her heart raced with anticipation.

"It is a long commitment you're making here, Mrs Burns. We do have other parties interested in the property, but I understand fully if you're not ready to..."

"I am ready, Mr Crane. Please show me where to sign."

Mr Crane sniffed with satisfaction, flipped through several sheets of paper, and then placed it on the window seat. Emma watched as he extracted a small bottle of ink and a pen from his briefcase and filled the nib for her. He seemed to take an eternity. Drawing a sharp breath she tried to steady her hand as she carefully wrote her name at the bottom of the page.

"And one more here." The banker drew a slender finger over a space in the centre of the next sheet and waited patiently for Emma to finish. When she had, he blew on the ink and looked directly into her eyes. "Well, Mrs Burns. I'm very pleased with your decision. I'm certain you and your family will do very well here, very well indeed."

"There is only a small community here, I do hope it's enough," she said, suddenly more nervous than she imagined.

"With the passing trade from the goldfields and the racecourse, I'm certain a little business like yours will only go to draw even more visitors to Flemington, especially once the railway comes. There's talk of a grand annual racing event to be held here, one to rival the Doncaster St Ledger and the Epsom Derby they say. If that transpires, as I believe it shall, then there will be more people here than we can imagine."

"I hope you're right, Mr Crane." Emma stepped back and pressed her hands together as though in prayer.

"The money from the land sale will transfer to your account by the end of the week. That will be more than adequate to keep you whilst you get things going."

"Thank you."

"Is it ours now?" Albert.

"Yes, children, it's ours."

Mr Crane took a key from his coat pocket and handed it to Emma. Gloria squealed with glee and began to skip around the living room.

*

A Fortnight Later

A rat beneath the deck and a spider's web glinted with frost in the bush. Emma was going to be glad to see the back of the rickety little cottage. She put her hands on her hips and smiled.

"Come on, Mam, Alf is here with the cart," Harry called from somewhere in the house.

She was standing on the back stoop looking at the back at their temporary home for the last time. From the tree by the back door, the Kookaburra was watching her with its shiny round eyes.

"Goodbye, Gordon. I hope you like the next tenants."

The bird cackled and fluttered further up through the spiky branches to the top of the tree. Emma turned and went back inside to find Harry and Alf Matthews dragging a crate of cooking pots out through the kitchen towards the front door.

"Thank you for coming today, both of you."

Harry looked over his shoulder at his mother.

"Of course we came, Mam."

"Well, it was good of Mr Grayson to give you the day off. You will remember to give him my thanks?"

Harry laughed at her.

"Of course, Mam. Don't fuss."

"Mam, I can't find Betsy," Gloria called from upstairs.

Emma rolled her eyes and went up to help her look.

"Where did you have her last?"

Gloria shrugged. Mrs Feldman had given Betsy to Gloria when she was only a year old. She was a raggedy thing made from scraps of fabric and a knot of red wool for hair, making her look rather more like a rainbow than a doll. But Gloria had loved her and kept her safe as well as if she were made of china. When Emma entered the bedchamber she found the child pulling things back out from the linen chest and throwing them over her shoulders.

Emma knelt down on the floor and began to refold the discarded blankets.

"Just stop and think for a moment."

Gloria did as she was asked. Her mouth twisted this way and that and her nose scrunched up. Finally, she exclaimed,

"I remember!" And she was on her feet and off downstairs before Emma could protest. "Found her." Came a cry a moment later from the front room.

Emma shook her head and began to repack the chest. The last item she retrieved from the floor was a shirt, one of Jacob's. Picking it up she went to the bed and smoothed it out over the empty space where he used to sleep. She closed her eyes and pictured him, not as she had last seen him, laid out for the undertaker, but as he was when they had first married all those years before. The bright-eyed young man with smooth features and dark hair falling about his face, playfully teasing her and calling her to bed, grabbing her around the waist and pulling her down beside him.

"Just the two chests from in here now, then we're ready to go."

Emma spun around.

"Sorry, Mam didn't mean to startle you."

She looked at Harry through a stream of tears. Crying over this place was the last thing she had expected to do.

"It's only a house, Mam. You didn't cry when we left England."

Pressing her fingers to her lips Emma shook her head.

"Sorry," she croaked. "It's not the house."

"Pa?" Harry hesitated, unsure how to comfort her.

Emma dabbed her face with the back of her hand and smiled. Whatever else Jacob had been, he had still been her husband and there had been some happy times.

"It's just that this is the last place I'll be able to picture him. Once we leave, the memories will all be kept elsewhere."

Alf arrived to take the trunks. Emma composed herself and watched as they removed one chest then the other. Once the room was clear she looked at the naked walls and dusty floor. The shabby furniture and vacant drawers looked unloved and sad. She took one last look around and closed the door behind her.

24

Emma raised her eyes to the timber rafters and shivered. This small and rather rudimentary structure was far removed from the little parish church she and her family had attended back home, but soon there was to be a new church of Saint Thomas'. The foundations had already been laid and work was in progress. She sighed and looked forward to the day it opened. Perhaps then she would feel like they were in a proper town and not just some queer little backwater in the middle of nowhere. Emma sighed silently. She just couldn't concentrate on the service today. All she could think of was Mr Finch; wondering how she would feel when she saw him again and hated herself for it. Jacob was barely cold on the ground.

The hymn ended and the congregation took their seats. The cold pews were hard and uncomfortable and every time she sat on one for more than a few minutes Emma felt her backside going numb and she was afraid it would set off the nerve in her back again. Risking a glance over her shoulder she scanned the faces behind her. So far she had not seen the Finches in town. For a moment she was transported back to the ship, to the first time Lucy had pointed him out at Sunday service. How strong and upright his stature, how elegant his profile and how well his voice had carried, smooth and tuneful. She told herself she was likely idealising the moment and tried to concentrate on the pastor's sermon.

There was a sharp prod in her ribs. She glanced sideways at Harry and realised everyone was bent forward, hands together. Following suit, Emma said the lord prayer and then quickly muttered,

'Dear Lord, let me feel nothing when I see that man again.'

*

The damp ground had splattered her hem with specks of mud. Emma lifted her frock a couple of inches to step over a large puddle. It had stopped raining sometime during the night but the storm had been heavy, it would take a few days for the ground to dry out. The children were a little way ahead. She took one final glance at the last dregs of the dispersing congregation and sighed with relief, the Finches hadn't been in church today. Perhaps she could get through another week before she had to face William again.

"You all right, Mam? You seem a bit in the clouds today?" Harry was home for the day.

Emma glanced up at him. She could swear that every time he visited he was taller.

"I was just thinking how grown-up you all are now," she lied. "Look at you, working away in the city with a proper job, and if you don't stop growing soon you'll pass six feet. Albert is above my shoulders now too, and even Gloria's catching me up. Before I know where I am you shall all be grown and off with your own families, and then it'll be just me."

Harry laughed at her,

"Well, you can't keep us as children forever."

A new and disturbing thought occurred to Emma. She stopped and looked at her son with cool reflection.

"You don't think Albert or Gloria would go back to England, do you? I mean, one day, when they're older. You don't think they will leave us and go back?"

Harry let a slow smile curl over his lips and settle in his grassy green eyes.

"No Mam, I don't. And I certainly won't leave. There are plenty of opportunities here. Just like Pa always promised."

Emma nodded, but now she had had the thought it was going to nag at her.

"Besides, if they did you could go with them," Harry added.

Emma shook her head,

"I think not," she smiled, "I have a good feeling about this new venture. Pity your Pa couldn't have been right about more things," she sighed. She looked at her boy again as they walked on and considered how much he had grown in the last twelve months, in mind as well as the body. "You know, you're turning out to be a really good lad, Harry." She was about to say something else, something along the lines of how far he had come since the incident in Rio, but then she noticed the crestfallen look upon his face and realised he had already thought of it. Deciding to change the subject she asked whether he had time for tea before catching the milk cart back to Melbourne when she heard someone call her name. She looked around. A small brown and white dog came careering across the road towards them. His eyes were bright and his fur looked freshly brushed. Emma wondered who the owner was when, to her horror, she saw William Finch, Mercy and her little boy coming towards them from the opposite side of the street. William and Mercy were swinging the child between them, just as she had watched Mercy and her father do in Cape Town. The boy was giggling, squealing and grinning like it was the best fun in the world.

Emma's throat went dry. The puppy stopped and yapped at her ankles playfully. Harry bent down and petted it. In front of them, the children had stopped and turned back. Emma didn't know where to look or what to say, so she crouched down next to Harry and fussed the dog.

"Mrs Burns, what a pleasure to see you again," Mercy was saying as they drew up next to her. Emma knew she should stand and greet her friends, but her legs felt unsteady and her heart was beating faster than a racehorse. The dog licked at her fingers.

"His name is Frank."

She looked up at last, but only as far as the child speaking.

"Oh, that is a good name. Did you choose it?"

The child grinned broadly, revealing teeth white as china. Emma smiled.

"And what do they call you?"

"Billy if you please." Billy dropped a bow so low he almost bent in half. Emma pressed her fingers to her lips and relaxed a little. Thank heaven for the charm of a child. She stood up and forced herself to look, first at Mercy,

"Forgive me, how are you, Mrs Finch?"

Mercy smiled as warmly as ever.

"Very well indeed, thank you."

"I was very sorry to hear of your husband." William's voice seemed tight.

"Thank you, you're very kind." Emma did not wish to think of Jacob at that moment. "And you're settled into your new home?"

Mercy took the hint and obliged the conversational diversion.

"Almost, but there is much to do when one moves to a new house, as you must know very well. And you, how is your new home?"

Emma was desperately trying not to look at William. Her gaze flickered towards his chest. His jacket was buttoned and a starched white handkerchief was peeking from his breast pocket. She wanted to touch it.

"Very good, thank you. Still much to do." Emma echoed Mercy as she finally raised her eyes to William. If God had heard of her prayer, he had chosen to ignore it. Instantly her cheeks flushed. Looking right into her were those eyes, clear and infinite as a summer sky.

Emma was paralysed; she could neither do nor say anything. She just stood there, watching his perfect lips move, yet not hearing anything but the rush of blood thundering through her head.

"Mam?" Harry was glaring at her. She realised Mercy had asked her a question.

"How would you like to join us for tea tomorrow afternoon?" Mercy repeated, turning to her brother-in-law. "If that is all right with you, William?"

Several thoughts seemed to crash around Emma's head simultaneously. She couldn't possibly sit in the same room as this man, certainly not with her children present. Surely they would see her attraction to him instantly and then they would know she had betrayed their father.

"Oh, we couldn't possibly impose, not until you're properly settled," Emma stuttered at last.

"Aww, Mam." Gloria and Albert groaned at the same time.

Mercy glanced from Emma to William with curiosity,

"Well perhaps so. Another time then," she said after a moment's consideration. Emma knew she suspected something was afoot.

"It was good to see you again, Mrs Burns." William's voice was cool and clipped, and he avoided her gaze. Despite herself Emma desperately wanted him to look at her again.

"Do give my regards to Mrs Matthews if I do not see her first." Mercy was allowing Mr Finch to lead her away. She reached for her son and took his hand. "I do hope to see you again soon," she added, but the last couple of words were swept away as Mr Finch's pace quickened. The puppy, still enjoying the pettings of children suddenly noticed its masters had gone and shot off after them.

"Tea would've been nice, Mam. Why did you decline?" Harry asked.

A prickle of guilt skittered up Emma's spine and settled in the nape of her neck.

"I just thought it was intrusive when they're only just moving in," she said a bit too hurriedly. "As Mrs Finch said; another time." Emma hoped her voice didn't sound as shaky to Harry as it did to her. She ignored him as he eyed her with suspicion. Over the distant hills, grey clouds were swirling and gathering for another onslaught.

"Come along, before it rains again," she said, reaching for Gloria's hand.

There was a crack of thunder. Perhaps Mr Finch had simply seen the rain coming and that was why he had hurried away.

25

September 1858

The smell of fresh paint still lingered in the sitting room. The only thing missing from their new home was her father's clock from the mantle. That was still at the menders. Emma took off her bonnet and shawl and set the envelope down on the small table. She was savouring the moment, delaying just long enough to build the anticipation. Taking the poker from its hook by the hearth she lit the fire and gave the wood a good stoke before finally sinking into her cosy new chair and retrieving the letter.

'March 1st 1858
Dear Mam and Pa'

Emma felt a sharp pang of sadness. Jack may not have seen his father in nearly nine years, and their relationship may not have been a close one, but she still hated to think of him reading the news of his death all alone. She drew a sharp breath; determined nothing was going to spoil the moment.

'I hope this letter finds you all well. Everything is ticking along nicely here.'

All his letters began the same. It was comforting and predictable. Pride made her smile. Jack was going to turn eighteen in a couple of months. His gift had been bought and sent long before she knew of the money, but it was lovely to imagine that next year she could afford to buy him something better than just another new shirt. If she thought he would take it, she would send him his passage, and not in steerage.

'Spring has finally come. Everyone was beginning to think the sun had forgotten us, but today it is warm outside and the crocuses are blooming in the pottery garden. Everything is well with Marjorie and me. We have been stepping out for two months now. Her folks live on the other side of town but I have dinner with them every Sunday and they seem to like me. I wish you could meet them, especially Marj. I let her read your last letter. She is fascinated with how life is in the new continent. She likes to learn new things.'

For a moment Emma's heart leapt. Maybe this girl would one day persuade Jack to join them in Australia. But then the notion faded away.

'*Life at the potteries is going well. Mr Barker is very pleased with my work and thinks I will be ready to move up to a permanent position sooner than is usual. Marj is enjoying her work too. She is still on borders of course but her work is far better than the other new apprentices.*'

Emma smiled. *Of course, he thinks she's the best*, she mused. It was nice to picture her boy in love.

'*I saw Mrs Feldman yesterday; she had her granddaughter with her. She's a bonny lass, never stopped smiling. Mrs Feldman said to be remembered to you as always and sent her best regards on behalf of her husband as well.*

That is all for now. I shall write again just as soon as I have more news,

Your loving son,

Jack'

Emma yawned, put down the letter to read again later and wondered what he would make of her new venture. She hoped he would be proud of her.

26

A chorus of crimson rosella twittered in the trees outside. Emma had risen some time ago. Today was opening day. A swirl of excitement and anxiety fluttered in her stomach. Perched in the window seat fully dressed and ready to go Emma looked down at her gown. It was black. She considered whether it would be inappropriate to abandon the mourning clothes for a nice cheery colour. It had only been four months since Jacob's death, not even half long enough to come out of mourning. Yet it felt wrong to be opening the business in such a drab state. It wasn't exactly welcoming to be greeted by a widow in black. But, after a moment of consideration, she decided to remain as she was. Everyone in Flemington knew her and what had happened to Jacob. It would be shocking if she suddenly started wearing even grey or dark blue so soon. She pushed open the window and peered out at the street. The cool spring air met her face with a pleasant tingle. It still felt strange to be living on the first floor, but it was nice to look down over the world. It made her feel as though she had finally risen above the damp days of England and taken control of her own life. And with three separate bedrooms, she felt as though she could breathe for the first time. Below, a woman was waiting outside the post office for Mr Price to open up, squalling baby balanced on her hip. Other than that the road was empty. She glanced at the brightening sky and smiled at the prospect of a sunny day.

"Well, Emma. No point sitting about on a day like today," she told herself as she made her way downstairs to the kitchen. The new life was going to take a bit of getting used to. From now on her time would be divided. Aside from when she was cooking or baking, she would either be upstairs with her children or out front with her customers, *presuming I have any*, she thought as she lit the oil lamp in the pantry. Immediately a yellow glow flickered to life, dancing over the rows of eggs, milk and flour and glinting against the jars of

Lucy's damson jam. She lifted the cloth from one of the cakes she had baked yesterday evening and prodded the top gently,

"Perfect, if I do say so myself," she said with a satisfied smile as she replaced the cloth.

Nervously she made her way across the kitchen and opened the door to the shop. The sight that greeted her made her heart skip even faster. Everything looked beautiful. Pristine white cloths adorned every table. The samovar and the large coffee pot shone in the morning light as it cast its fingers through the drapes and reached out to the back of the room. Emma weaved around the tables and imagined them all surrounded by people, eating, drinking and chattering away. She made her way to the front door, turned the key in the lock and pulled it open so that the bell above tinkled its happy greeting. Emma looked at the little wooden sign that hung on the handle but left where it was. From the moment they had moved in the drapes had remained closed on the shop floor. Today she went to the centre of the window and swept them open. As she did so a young couple on a morning stroll stopped and looked in. The gentleman gave her a polite nod and doffed of his hat. Emma waved back contentedly.

*

Rushing about, cheeks burning and heart flustered. Doors open and people everywhere. Emma had not expected quite such a crowd, especially not on her first day. Steam puffed and hissed from the samovar and the delicious aroma of tea and coffee filled the air. Gloria scuttled in from the kitchen with a new cake to replace the one that had already vanished from beneath the glass case on the counter. Emma had made five cakes and thought that had been too many, but they were on number three already and it was barely midday.

"Bert, would you clear the table in the window so Mr and Mrs Crane can sit down," she said, tipping another ounce of coffee beans into the pot. Noting the empty water jug, she collected it and went out back for a refill.

"Mam, they're here." Gloria squealed excitedly through the kitchen door.

Emma wasn't sure whether to be relieved or panicked, but when she saw Lucy Matthews, hands on hips and face beaming, she felt awash with calm.

"No need to ask how business is going," she grinned.

"A little too well at this moment," Emma admitted. "I think I'll have to bake another cake and I may need to increase my order for your eggs in future, do you think your chickens can manage another two dozen a week?"

Lucy laughed,

"If not, we'll just have to buy more chickens."

"You might need another damson bush or three as well," Emma grinned. "Why don't you sit down and I'll send Gloria over to take your order."

Lucy ignored Emma's request and joined her by the stove.

"I think ya could do wiv an 'and in here."

"You'll do no such thing..." But Emma's protests fell on deaf ears as Lucy tied a pinny around her waist and lifted the cake bowl down from the dresser shelf.

*

The air was sweet with the scent of baking cake and warm bread. Emma breathed in deeply and allowed a smile to creep over her lips. Mr and Mrs Crane had come from the city especially for the occasion.

"Congratulations, Mrs Burns. I think you have invested very well indeed," the banker had said as he speared his last piece of sponge cake with his fork.

Emma fancied all of Flemington would have been to visit her little tearoom by the end of the day. She could only hope that she had made good impression enough to bring them all back again tomorrow, or at least once a week. Even some of the folks from the outlying farms had been in. Standing by the counter she took a moment to savour the scene. There were seven tables and six of them occupied. Closest to her were three maids from one of the hotels, there were two gentlemen she didn't know next to them, then there were the Matthews twins and Bertie by the door, Mr Price and one of the waiters from the Flemington Hotel had the table by the counter, Mrs McLeish and another lady from the village was next to them and by the window was the vicar of Saint Thomas' sitting with the new school headmaster.

"Hello, Mrs Burns." Emma looked down with a start. The child before her was looking up with a broad grin that revealed a gap where his two front teeth should have been. The puppy in his hands arms wriggled and sniffed in the smell of the tearoom.

"Billy. Well, how very nice to see you." She looked up expectantly towards the door, "I hope the tooth fairy brought you a ha'penny for those."

The child nodded with another more deliberate grin.

"Where's your mother?"

"Coming. I ran ahead."

"Your uncle is coming too?" she asked, unsure whether she wanted him to or not.

"Yep." Billy was looking around the room at the full tables.

"Sit by the Vicar and Mr Mason," she croaked with a nervous twist in her stomach; worse than when she had first turned the sign on the door to 'open' four hours before. "Oh dear," she added, realising the recently vacated table still needed to be cleared. Emma grabbed a cloth quickly and scuttled over to remove the scraped clean plates and empty teacups. She tried to ignore her thumping heart when Mercy and William Finch entered her tearoom a moment later. Mercy was smiling as broadly as her son had been, but William's expression was far less fathomable. The lady didn't hesitate; she came right over to Emma and enthused.

"Oh my, Emma, everything looks so lovely. I take it the tea order came in on time?"

"Yes, yes it did, thank you so much for putting me on to your contact, they were most helpful." All the while they were conversing Emma's gaze flickered away from Mercy and on to William. As yet, he had not said a word. Indeed, Emma thought he seemed almost as uncomfortable as she. Finally, just as Billy dragged his mother away to be seated, he spoke.

"Mrs Burns, I cannot tell you how pleased I am for you." The formality jolted Emma. She pressed her hand to her chest and tried to breathe normally. "This is a lovely establishment; you have done so very well."

Emma watched his fingers interlace and clench together. She opened her mouth to give her thanks but he continued before she had the chance.

"And you look very well if you don't mind my saying. I...forgive me..." his words petered out and his gaze clouded. As he bowed and excused himself Emma found her legs had gone wobbly. Thankfully, or not, the exchange had been overheard.

"Come into the kitchen for a minute, Em. You've been run off your feet, ya ought to take a minute break." Lucy ushered her out of the tearoom and into a seat at the kitchen table.

"Was that inappropriate?" Emma whispered after a moment or two. Lucy cocked her head.

"Was what inappropriate?" Lucy raised an eyebrow innocently.

"He must think I'm such a silly woman?" Emma sighed.

Lucy shook her head.

"Don't be daft. It were all quite proper and no one, not even him will know ya were flustered for any other reason than it's opening day."

"I do hope you're right. I would hate it if people thought me aiming above my station. And with Jacob not long gone either!"

"Dear Lord, Em. Is there any objection ya haven't imagined to keep you from fancying William Finch?"

Emma narrowed her eyes. She had expected Lucy to tell her yet again to forget about him. But when she shrugged, Lucy shook her head and went back to buttering bread. Emma wafted her face with the bottom of her pinny. A moment later the bell over the door tinkled. She took a deep breath and went back out into the chaos to find two elegant ladies standing in the doorway, staring at the din.

"Miss Spencer, how lovely to see you; welcome." Emma looked around at the crowded room. "I'm sorry but we're full at the moment, perhaps if you don't mind waiting a few minutes one of the tables will become free," she suggested, hoping she didn't look too hot and bothered, "or I can get the children to move into the kitchen. Come along children…" she began.

"No, no, there's no need," Olivia said, "It's a pleasant day, we can take a short walk and come back, do you not agree Adelaide?"

"Certainly," the elder sister replied with a faint sigh.

The sisters turned to leave when Mr Finch adjusted his seat a little. He hadn't seen the ladies behind him and the back of his chair clipped Miss Spencer's elbow. He was on his feet and apologising so fast Emma barely had time to register the incident.

"Do forgive me," he said a second time.

Adelaide giggled and graciously accepted. She looked at Emma expectantly.

"Oh, erm…yes. Mr Finch this is Miss Spencer and her sister Miss Olivia Spencer."

"Very pleased to make your acquaintance." He bowed and took the hand Adelaide had offered him. The lady curtseyed.

"We were intending to take tea but I'm afraid all the tables are taken," she smiled coyly.

Mr Finch didn't hesitate.

"Then permit me to invite you to join us."

Mercy looked around to see what was going on.

"This is my sister-in-law Mrs Finch and her son Billy," William introduced his family with all the elegancy of the gentleman he was, and Emma felt her heart sink far below him. There was a moment of hesitation when Adelaide and Olivia eyed Mercy cautiously, but whatever objections had crossed their minds, they were put aside and Adelaide replied,

"How very kind. We would love to."

Emma couldn't move, she just watched, unsure what was happening.

"Do fetch us some tea and two slices of your best cake," Adelaide requested.

A beat later Emma realised she had been addressed again,

"Oh, yes, of course," she said eventually and rushed back to the kitchen.

*

Emma placed the dirty tea things on the tray far slower than was necessary. She was grateful that the Vicar and Mr Mason had vacated. Now she had an excuse to get closer to the Finches table. She leaned in closer so that she could hear better. All around children were jabbering, adults chattering, plates scraping, cups and spoons clattering and outside Billy's little dog was yapping. No matter how much she tried she could not make out the conversation between the Finches and the Spencer sisters. All she could fathom was that Adelaide was laughing and simpering so assiduously at William Finch that she was in danger of looking ridiculous. Mercy glanced over her shoulder and caught Emma's eye. There was a glint of humour on her face and she rolled her eyes. Emma smirked and abandoned her attempt to eavesdrop.

As she made her way back to the kitchen she saw Lucy leaning on the doorjamb watching her.

"Well ain't she just the flirt," she hissed as Emma bustled past.

"And a far better class than me," Emma grumbled.

Lucy raised her eyebrow.

"Ya think a man like him gives a fig about a coquettish little flirt like that?"

Emma shrugged,

"He doesn't seem to be minding."

"Nah." Lucy snorted.

Emma dumped the dishes in the sink straightened her pinny.

"She's young, pretty, well educated and from a good family," she muttered, extracting the last cake from the oven. Lucy put her hands on her hips and sighed.

"Fine, thinks what ya like."

The day had started so well, and now all Emma could think of was how silly she had been to ever dream of William Finch.

27

Late October 1858

Another busy day was done. Emma yawned. The first few weeks of running the tearoom had raced by as fast as a thoroughbred around the track. She had been prepared for the long hours running around tables, but the aching legs and feet she had not considered. She had gone to bed each night with legs and feet throbbing so hard they kept her awake. Yet, to her astonishment, her back was holding up. Still, no matter how exhausting it was, it was better than scrubbing laundry. And now, finally, she was beginning to get used to it. She lifted the baking tray from the stove then clicked open the back door.

"Gracious, spring's definitely here!" Emma said, blowing a loose hair up from her forehead,

"It's even warmer out there, Mam." Gloria came in from the shop. "I wish we had a giant fan that could keep wafting at us all day,"

"If only there were such a thing."

"Maybe I shall invent one."

Emma laughed at her nine-year-old,

"You do that and I'll pay a fortune for it. Now, how many tables do we have?"

Emma glanced at the sky through the back window and decided it must be well past midday.

"Mrs McLeish and her friends just left so that leaves three."

It was a race day and Emma had opened early. She had quickly found that both before the racing started and after it finished her little tearoom was jam-packed. In the three or four hours in the middle, while the horses were running, it was a steady flow of wives that didn't care for the track. She was glad to tempt them with tea, cake and somewhere to go whilst their husbands gambled away their hard-earned money.

"They'll all be back again soon," Emma told her daughter. "I'm just going to pop round to the general store whilst we've got a minute. You'll be all right won't you?"

"Course, Mam."

She had sent Albert out to play kick-a-bout an hour or so since. All he did was get under her feet on a busy day.

Emma glanced at her shawl and decided she didn't need it then headed out through the shop to the street. She had only got five yards when Mr Price came scurrying towards her.

"Good day, Mrs B. Business is looking well," he said with a glance at the tearoom window.

Emma cocked her head.

"Lovely to see you, Mr Price. Are you in a hurry?" Mr Price always appeared to be in a hurry, but today he seemed rather more flustered than usual. He shook his head and caught his breath.

"No, no. I have just returned from the track. I had a lucky bet and decided to quit the place before I got carried away and put another on the last."

Emma smiled at him.

"Very wise, Mr Price. Very wise indeed."

The postmaster suddenly realised the implications of what he had said and looked mortified.

"Oh, Mrs B, I didn't mean to imply your Mr B was…"

Emma shrugged and smiled.

"If I denied he was a gambler, Mr Price, I should be a liar."

Mr Price laughed in relief.

"It has been a lovely day for it. I even saw the Finches there with the Spencers."

Emma felt a lump rise in her throat. She had always done her best not to think of William Finch. But of late she had made an extra effort. She could hardly avoid hearing about him, especially when Mercy and Billy so often popped into the tearoom for a slice of cake. But seeing was a different matter. She had done rather well so far. There had been a couple of moments in church when her eyes had wandered, but ever since she had spotted Adelaide Spencer leaning back and whispering to him at the end of a hymn, she had been determined never to look over at his pew again.

"Oh, I was unaware the Finches liked the track." Emma heard herself say.

"I'm sure I've never heard Mr Finch or Mercy ever mention going before," he lowered his voice conspiratorially. "But if you ask me that young Miss Spencer has set her frilly ribboned bonnet on our young teacher. I heard it was Mr Spencer that asked the Finches along today. That can only mean he's getting in with the family."

Emma was feeling hotter by the minute. She began to waft her hand in front of her face.

"Oh it is rather warm today," Mr Price said. "You look like you need to sit down for a minute. You ought to catch your breath before the races finish and they all come flooding back."

Emma nodded, unsure she could make herself speak.

"Well, I'd better be off and let you get on with it, Mrs B." He beamed at her with his usual jolly charm and doffed his cap. "Good day to you."

Emma croaked her adieu and hurried off to the store even more determined than ever to put Mr Finch out of her mind.

28

December 1858

Trees rustled overhead and a pair of galah swooped in a pink and grey swirl through the branches. Emma looked up and watched as the birds glided away over the roof of the new schoolhouse. Gloria was holding her hand, eagerly awaiting her first lesson and Albert was fidgeting nervously at her side. The gathering was larger than she had imagined. The parents and pupils she had anticipated. But the famous merchant and local investor, Mr Glass, had come along to declare the school open as well as several other local dignitaries and a crowd of curious townsfolk. Emma looked over the sea of faces and fancied that the whole town had come out.

She wasn't looking for Mr Finch but she knew that he would be there of course. She had been rather pleased with the mastery of her feelings over him and was convinced that she no longer cared if he did marry Adelaide Spencer. But when she saw her standing right at the front she felt as green with envy as the lady in question's dress. Adelaide Spender looked particularly fetching in her gown with a matching ribbon tied around her bonnet. Emma felt dull and hot in her mourning dress. The black fabric seemed to draw the sun towards it and hold in the heat. She pulled her Brazilian fan from her purse and began to waft herself. Emma could make out Mrs Spencer and at least one of the other sisters in accompaniment. Adelaide's arm was threaded through that of her father and she was looking up at the podium unwaveringly in the direction of Mr Finch. The gentleman was staring forwards but eventually, his eye was caught and he gave a nod in the girl's direction. An unpleasant sour taste filled Emma's mouth. She looked away and scoured the crowd for Mr Price or someone else she might find as a welcome distraction. A few feet away from Adelaide was Mercy Finch with her young son. She must have felt Emma's gaze for she glanced over her shoulder. The moment she spotted Emma she gave a bright smile and waved. Emma waved back. Mercy weaved between the standing bodies of people and made her way over.

"Mrs Burns how are you? How is business?"

Little Billy was gripping his mother with one hand, hugging his little dog to his chest with the other, and looking up anxiously at all the surrounding folks. The dog snuffled into the crook of his arm, sound asleep.

"Very well, so far. It's only been a few weeks. Hard to tell in the long run."

Emma was watching Billy with curiosity.

"That's wonderful. I am sure it will only get better and better."

Mercy must have noticed the concern on Emma's face. She looked down at her son.

"It's all right Billy. Just a few people that is all." Raising her eyes back to Emma she added, "He does not like large crowds, he gets a little panicked when there are so many people that are bigger than him. I cannot think why, he was never this way back home. I think perhaps it was being cooped up in the ship for all that time. It was a rough journey and we were confined to the cabins for much of it. Now enclosed spaces seem to bother him. I had hoped getting the puppy would help."

Emma nodded sympathetically,

"A long sea voyage is never a pleasant thing. But he's very young, I'm sure he will forget in time."

Recalling his fear of unusual animals she added,

"Perhaps it's just all the changes. Being in a strange land."

Mercy seemed to agree then asked if Emma was going to take a tour of the building before the classes begin.

"I thought I would. I'd like to see where the children will be spending their days," she replied. "Then I'd better get back to the shop. I asked Kitty Arnold from The Flemington to open up for me. She's been asking me for a few hours a week since October. I only set her on last week. I don't know how she'll cope on her own. Besides I can't afford to miss out on the extra trade from these folks when they're done here," She explained, glancing around the crowd and considering how many might require tea and cake in half an hour or so.

"After standing around in this heat, they shall all certainly require elevenses." Mercy nodded. Emma laughed.

"Indeed."

"We came for William of course, but Billy will be attending school himself in the New Year." Mercy looked over at the building with pride. "William has been looking forward to this post for so long. It hardly seems real that the day has finally come."

Billy looked up at his mother with large dark eyes then hung his head low.

"Now Billy, I told you, school is a good thing. You will enjoy it once you begin I am sure." Mercy assured him, but Billy didn't seem convinced. Emma was about to offer some further pearl of wisdom when she felt a tingle in the back of her neck, as though someone was watching her.

Mr Mason was speaking now, telling everyone what dreams had been realised with the opening of this school. Emma tried to listen but as she peered through the rows of heads her gaze met with a pair of blue eyes. William Finch was standing at Mr Mason's side, hands behind his back and head held high. His tailored jacket was neatly fastened despite the increasing heat of the day but his eyes never left hers. He swung back on his heels a little and flinched, for he had not noticed that Mr Mason had stopped speaking and had passed the address on to him. Emma tried to look away. A flush of guilt swept through her. Then she realised that she was standing in a direct line behind Adelaide; she too was in his line of sight. How silly to think he would be looking at her and not Miss Spencer. Suddenly the speeches were over and Mercy was leading her up the steps and into the building. At the top of the stairs Miss Spencer and her father had accosted Mr Finch. Emma tried to hear the conversation as she passed, but they were gone by too quickly.

*

The school smelled of fresh paint and carbolic. Everywhere was pristine. Classrooms were filled with brand new desks and neat rows of benches. On one wall was a large chalkboard ready for its first use. It was not a large school but it had a cheery and comforting feel and Emma was certain Gloria and Albert was going to thrive there. Emma and Mercy were filing across the back of a large classroom with the rest of the parents. The children were already seated at their desks; slates out and chalks in hand. Emma wondered how long everything would all look so perfect before they were covered in smudges and scrapes: the furniture as well as the children. Gloria was eagerly sitting in the front row and Albert was perched on the edge of his seat a row behind. Little Billy cowered behind his mother still hugging the oblivious sleeping puppy.

"Come along, Billy. I cannot think what has got into you."

A boy in the back row glanced over his shoulder and glared at the little boy as he peered out from behind his mother's skirts. The insolent child pulled a quick face at Billy then turned around again as though nothing had happened. Mercy didn't see but Emma did. At the front of the class, Mr Finch had his back to the room, writing his name for the children to read. When he turned around he caught sight of Emma and dropped the chalk. Emma felt her cheeks burn and she was most relieved when the parents were ushered back out. As they made their way through the assembly room to the front steps Mercy paused to let the other folks go on by.

"Let us wait until the others have gone; for Billy," she suggested. Emma agreed. All the while she was watching for the Spencers but they appeared to have already left.

Once they were quite alone, save for Billy, Mercy threaded her arms through Emma's and suggested they walk together back to the village centre. Emma quietly agreed and they set off. After a moment Mercy glanced at her.

"He appears to be the most confident man in the world," she began. "But all men are lost little boys underneath their hard exterior, Mrs Burns, and William is as afraid of his feelings as much as Billy here is afraid of crowds."

Emma was all astonishment. She pictured William Finch with his fearless eyes and strong upright countenance. They reached the corner before the tearoom. Emma stopped and with a shaky voice plucked up the courage to ask,

"Why should he be afraid of his feelings?"

Mercy tilted her head with pity in her eyes.

"He was in love once before."

Emma tried not to imagine him with Adelaide standing at the altar.

"Many years ago, before I met my John. William was betrothed to a girl. My husband and his brother are from a good family, Mrs Burns, more so than you would be forgiven for assuming. However, just as the couple announced their intent to marry, William's father made a poor investment and everything was lost."

That explains the second-class passage, Emma considered. *Not so mysterious after all, just unfortunate and sad.*

"The girl's family withdrew their consent and the engagement was dissolved. But they were young, barely twenty, and he still in his final year at Oxford. They were filled with all the passions and dreams only youth can sustain, and so they eloped."

Emma wondered why Mercy felt the need to tell her all this. Realising she was gawping, she closed her mouth and waited for Mercy to continue.

"They reached as far as the Scottish border where her father caught up with them. She was dragged back to Cornwall and William sent away in despair. John was a few years his senior and by then already ordained as a minister. He took pity on his despondent brother and they boarded a ship together for Cape Town. William was still living with his brother when I first met them. Life in my country is not so black and white as you might imagine, Mrs Burns. Lines can be blurred when hearts are in the right place. William took to teaching the poor children in my neighbourhood and found passion for the work."

"What happened to the girl?" Emma could not prevent herself from butting in.

Mercy's eyes grew dark.

"She was forced to marry another and died in childbirth a year later."

Emma felt tears well in her eyes.

"But William was living in England before he came out here?"

Billy began to tug on his mother's arm. Mercy rubbed his head affectionately.

"Patience little one. Just another minute."

Billy set down the now wide-awake and restless dog and knelt down to play with him. Mercy continued,

"Shortly after John and I married, William was offered a post in an English school by an old friend who had become a schoolmaster. We thought from his letters that he was settled, but then in August of fifty-six, he sent word that he was going to the new world and had chosen a passage that would bring him by Cape Town on the way. I never imagined he could even be tempted to love another woman, until now." Mercy laughed but the pain in Emma's chest was near choking her. She was hot and in desperate need of a seat. She pulled out her fan.

"Oh, dear. Forgive me. I did not mean to distress you in any way."

"Oh, no not at all. It's the heat." Emma lied. "How about that nice piece of cake?"

Mercy looked at her carefully for a moment then apparently decided she would press the matter no further.

"That would be lovely, Mrs Burns. Very nice indeed."

Emma pushed open the tearoom door and let them in. Mercy stopped.

"Perhaps you would permit me to invite you to our home to take tea instead?" Mercy suggested. "I feel as though you are always waiting on us at the tea shop. I would like to repay the effort."

"I really ought to get back…"

Mercy was looking at her in a way that made her change her mind. William wouldn't be there anyway; he was at the school.

"All right, you're most kind."

She allowed Mercy to lead her the short way to her home and into the drawing room where she was invited to sit down. The room was as elegant and impeccable as Mercy's clothes. The windows were dressed in pretty net drapes and lace doilies adorned the coffee table set in the centre of the room. There was a large walnut sideboard with glass doors that bowed into a gentle curve and the walls were a light shade of mint green. The only things that didn't fit with this traditional English style were a large wooden statue of an African man that stood by the window and a Zebra skin rug in the centre of the floor. Emma looked at a painting that hung over the fireplace. It was of a beautiful young woman with hair black as jet, bright blue eyes and fair skin flushed with just enough colour to make her appear in love. Mercy set the tray of tea things on the coffee table and followed Emma's gaze.

"That is John and William's mother. The likeness was taken when she was first married."

"William once told me they also had a sister. Where is she?"

Mercy smiled,

"There are two sisters. Anne married a Scot and lives in Edinburg, but Catherine, the eldest, left for the Americas when John and William were still children. I do not think any of them have ever seen her since. She lives though; there was a letter not six months ago. She married well I believe, to someone connected to the British consulate in Brazil."

Something about this knowledge bothered Emma, but she could not quite put her finger on what. Mercy dropped a lump of sugar in Emma's cup and passed it to her with a shining silver spoon rattling on the saucer.

"I remember William saying that when your ship was forced to dock there he tried to contact her, but she was away from home," she finished.

There was so much information swimming around in Emma's mind that she could barely take any of it in, and it was all drowning in a mire of guilt for even caring to learn more about William. Poor Jacob was still not a year cold. She stirred her tea and took a sip.

The sweet liquid was soothing. She looked into the cup and tried to focus. Mercy sat back in an elegant Queen Ann chair and observed her carefully. Billy was sitting on the floor rolling a solitary glass marble from one hand to the other, the puppy's head going back and forth with it as he watched. The sound was even and smooth.

"Billy, stop that," Mercy told him.

"Oh, he's fine," Emma assured her. She got to her feet, "but I had better get along. I ought not to leave Kitty alone any longer."

Mercy accepted Emma's excuse and rose to see her to the door. As Emma blinked out into the midday sun, Mercy offered one more thought.

"My brother-in-law aside, Mrs Burns, I am very glad you decided to stay in Flemington."

Emma smiled and thanked her for her hospitality.

"Do call me Emma," she added when she reached the front door. Mercy smiled warmly and nodded her acceptance.

As Emma headed down the street, she wondered what Mercy might have meant by that last remark.

29

December 24th 1858

Never had Emma felt so pleased with her lot. She knew she should still be in mourning for Jacob yet she could not help the warm glow that sat in her stomach like a hot meal after a week of starvation. It was not that she didn't miss him but in the last few weeks, everything seemed to have taken a turn for the better and to top it all, Jack's latest letter had arrived this morning like a perfect Christmas gift. She settled into one of the kitchen chairs and slipped a knife beneath the stuck down edge. Jack had applied too much gum and Emma was forced to tear the paper to open it. Finally, she slid out the sheets and allowed a smile to broaden on her lips.

'July 5th 1858
Dear Mam and Pa'

It still bothered her to read the address to Pa as well, especially since the letters arriving were sent after his father's death. She would be glad when Jack would finally know what had happened. Until that was done Emma felt she could not move on.

'I hope you are all well. Everything is ticking along nicely here. Marjorie has had scarlet fever but she's on the mend now. I was very worried there for a while, I can tell you. The doctor says her heart might be weakened, but only time will tell on the score.'

Emma felt that familiar wave of guilt rush through her. Her poor boy; going through that all by himself.

'Her parents have been very good to me.'

The guilt shifted to a pang of jealousy. She was slowly being replaced and it was entirely her own fault.

'Marj and her parents send their best to you all.'

"He's not alone. Well, I have to be grateful for that," Emma told herself out loud.

'We had a trip to the Marlston again this Sunday. I cannot tell you how much has improved. It is still a hell I would not wish upon anyone, but at least it's clean. The new beds are sturdy and as comfortable as can be, and the food even looked better too. Though I can only hope that was not just for our benefit.'

Emma suspected it was, but she was glad all the same.

'Mr Oliver has decided to run for Mayor and has asked me if I would like to assist him. In my own time of course, but I would be a fool to turn down such an opportunity.'

Emma pressed her fingers to her lips. What an honour!

'That aside, everything is ticking along at the potteries so nothing new to tell you there.

Until next time,

Your loving son, Jack.'

Emma fished for a handkerchief in her pinny pocket and dabbed her eyes. Outside the sun was rising and the cake in the oven was starting to smell good. Another hour and her first customers would arrive. Several workers had taken to coming every morning for a tea and bread roll. Often they would be ready and waiting outside the door at seven on the dot. She looked around her lovely big kitchen and wished for all the world that she could see her eldest boy, just for one minute, just to hug him and tell him she loved him, just to show him their new home. She wondered how tall he might be now and tried to envision him standing next to Harry. Emma put her head in her hands and sniffed.

"At least we have the post," she said to the empty room.

30

Mid-January 1859

Adelaide Spencer tugged off her gloves carefully, as though she might break one of her immaculately filed nails on the pale cotton. Emma tried to smile, but the effort was almost too much,

"What can I get for you today, Ladies?"

Adelaide set her gloves on the freshly starched lace cloth and looked up at her hostess. Her sisters were chatting closely together and smirking. Emma pretended not to notice.

"May we see the cake tray please?" Adelaide asked with a glare at her siblings, "and bring along a pot of tea," she added in her tightly clipped English accent.

"Certainly, Miss Spencer."

As Emma turned to leave she heard Adelaide hiss,

"Will you two be quiet? Someone will hear you."

"We know you only wanted to come here because you hope to see Mr Finch walk by."

Emma felt her stomach twist, though she couldn't tell if she was jealous of Miss Spencer or nervous at the prospect of seeing William walk by.

"Shhh," Adelaide hissed. "No, it is not. Why would he come by here anyway?"

"I don't know what you see in him. He's really quite poor, and then there's that nigger sister-in-law and nephew you would have to live with," the elder of her sisters chided. It took all of Emma's strength not to turn on them and defend Mercy. Instead, she forced her feet to take her to the counter to fetch them the cake trolley.

*

Later that evening when everyone had gone, Emma flipped the sign to 'closed' and tidied the drapes. Mr Finch had not come by that afternoon after all, and after an hour of bickering with her younger sisters Adelaide Spencer had gone home disappointed. There was a wicked sense of satisfaction in this for Emma and she chastised herself for feeling it.

31

February 1859

A rainbow shimmered over the rooftops as Emma crossed the road. The ground smelled damp from the rain and the air had a refreshing breeze. She never got tired of looking at the lovely blue and black sign over the window – 'Mrs B's Tearoom.' Narrowly avoiding a puddle she stepped onto the dusty sidewalk and looked in through the window. The workers had already gone on their way and inside she could see just one table occupied. Perhaps she ought to start serving cooked breakfasts to drum up a little more early morning trade. Kitty Arnold waved at her as she approached the door.

"Hey, Mrs, look where you're going." A child careered into her side, knocking her backwards and sending her grocery basket tumbling through the air. She looked around in time to see the boy running down the street, closely followed by another, in pursuit of something. Emma wanted to grab the offender by the ear and give him a good hiding but she knew she wouldn't be quick enough to catch him. She retrieved her basket; grateful the over-cloth was buttoned down.

"Come back Monkey Boy! Don't you dare run away from us," one of the chasing boys yelled.

Emma put her hand on the tearoom door and had pushed it halfway open when she realised what was happening. In an instant, she had spun around, set down the basket, hitched her skirts over her ankles and was scurrying after the children.

"Stop boys! Stop this instant!" She yelled.

They were already far ahead of her. One of the pursuers stopped to catch his breath and Emma gained ground. The little boy at the front glanced back. His dark eyes were wide with terror. They reached the corner of the street.

"Stop," Emma bellowed again.

The boy at the front tumbled over a lump in the ground and crashed to the floor with a crack. He sat back and rubbed at his knees. A trickle of red trailed down his shins. The white boys pounced on him as though he were an out foxed rabbit. Emma caught up with them, along with the little dog that had been trying to keep up with its master.

"Take your hands off him!" Emma grabbed one boy by the scruff of his neck and shoved him aside, then grabbed the other by the nose and pulled him back just in time to prevent his punch from connecting with the head of Billy Finch. The dog yapped in defence.

"Wait until I tell your parents what you've been doing." Emma threatened. She recognised both children and knew she would see their parents in church on Sunday, if not at the tearoom before.

"There'll be no need to trouble yourself, Mrs Burns. I shall take care of this situation."

Emma spun around to find William Finch standing so close she was forced to take a step back.

"That would be most appropriate," she heard herself say, though the words seemed to echo.

"Now get yourselves to school right now, before you're late," William instructed the boys so firmly Emma almost went too. "Go directly to the headmaster's office and wait for me there." William tuned over the watch on the chain of his waistcoat and checked the time. The elegance of his dress rattled a memory Emma had long since lost in the back of her mind.

In her head, she saw Harry, with matted hair and filthy clothes. 'There was an English man at the gaol, he was a proper gent,' he had told her. Emma remembered William's sister in Brazil. Then the image of Harry running towards her on the dockside in Rio and all he could tell her about his release was that the gentleman had spoken to the guards and then they had unlocked his shackles and let him go. Inspector Mendoza's words rang in her head, 'You have very well connected friends, Mrs Burnez.' Someone had done something to get Harry out. She had always presumed it to be the ship's captain but now she thought of it, that didn't make sense.

Another thought buzzed in her mind. A knot twisted in her gut and nauseated her. How could she not have thought of it sooner? How could she have been so blind? Her heart beating fast and her head swimming, she dropped to her knees and gathered little Billy into her arms. The action gave her a moment to gather her composure. The puppy snuffled her skirt and whined. Swallowing several times to moisten her throat she looked up and said,

"Mr Finch, I think I need to thank you."

"No need to thank me, Mrs Burns." William was looking at her bemused. "I saw what was happening…."

"No, I mean for Harry," she interjected. "It was you, was it not, at the goal? Your sister was the highly placed connection… it was you who spoke to the guards?"

A pink tinge flushed William's cheeks.

"Billy, are you all right lad?" he hunkered down at Emma's side. The child nodded through his tears and she kissed his damp cheek.

"There's a good boy." Emma looked at William and gasped when their eyes met.

There was a moment of utter stillness, as though everything around them had vanished. William slowly raised a hand to Emma's face and swept a strand of stray hair behind her ear.

"I did it for you," he whispered.

"Thank you," she stuttered and lowered her eyes. William removed his hand abruptly.

"Well, I think we know why Billy has become so frightened of things now," he mumbled hurriedly. "Those bullies have a lot to answer for."

"Yes, yes I think we do." Emma could barely speak. She risked a glance at his face and found he was still looking at her. He cleared his throat.

"Would you mind taking Billy home, I must get to the school." He stood quickly and placed his hands behind his back.

Emma's heart sank. For a moment she had felt close to him again, as intimate and familiar as the night of the captain's birthday. But then the feeling vanished.

"Of course. Come along, Billy," she replied, her voice cracking. "Let's get you back to your mother and let your Uncle go to his students," she added, lifting Billy to his feet. William gave a sharp bow.

"Thank you, Mrs Burns, your help is much appreciated," and then he was heading down the road at such a fast pace Emma had no time to think of anything else to say. For a moment she just stood there staring after him.

"Can I go home please, Mrs Burns?"

She glanced down at Billy.

"Oh sorry love, yes, yes of course. We can stop by the tearoom and I'll get you a nice piece of Lemon cake to take with you, would you like that?"

Billy wiped the tears from his eyes with the cuff of his dusty shirt sleeve and nodded.

32

A few days later

The wind howled beneath the tearoom door. The ground was sodden and the smell of wet grass was blowing in from the fields. Emma opened the kitchen window for the first time that afternoon. When she had tried to let in some cool air earlier the rain had tumbled in, bouncing over the side of the stove and threatening to deaden the flame. Through the ceiling, she heard her father's clock chime three. With a satisfied smile, she sighed. It was good to hear it chime again. It had finally come back from the menders in Melbourne yesterday. The bell tinkled in the tearoom. Emma waited for a second, half expecting Gloria and Albert to come belting in. When they didn't, she went through to attend to her new customer.

"A slice of your damson sponge and a small pot of tea please."

The woman was a regular at this time of day and always ordered the same thing. Emma suggested she take her usual seat by the window. There were three occupied tables at that moment and at one of them was Mercy and Billy Finch, the little dog sleeping between Billy's feet. Emma watched as the woman walked around Mercy's table, being sure to keep a wide berth. The action pained her. There were those that made no distinction of course, and many women in the area had been grateful of Mercy's expertise over the past few months when their time had come to give birth. Others though were less kind, such as the younger Spencer sisters and those horrid boys in the street. Emma admired how Mercy managed to take no notice. Little Billy, on the other hand, could do nothing but notice. The child hung his head, acutely aware of the shun. Emma prayed that in time he would learn to follow his mother's example or better still, that people would stop judging him.

Emma poured the tea for the woman and set her a slice of cake on one of the new rose painted plates she had purchased. They reminded her so much of Jack that the very sight of them made her want to weep. When she had delivered the order she made her way over to Mercy's table and pulled up a chair to join them.

"Hello, Billy. How are you today? Are your knees better?"

Billy proudly displayed a large pair of scabs and grinned at her to display his newly grown front teeth.

"I cannot thank you enough for what you did the other day." Mercy said for at least the twentieth time.

"It really was nothing more than was needed."

Mercy put her hand over Emma's so suddenly she almost pulled away.

"I see how you look at each other you know."

Emma froze.

"I'm sorry?" she tried to sound as though she had no notion what Mercy meant. She got up and turned to go.

"Please stay for just a minute," Mercy said quietly.

Emma flopped down into the chair again.

"Please do not think William has betrayed you at all," Mercy said quietly. "I can assure you he has never mentioned you by name. But I have seen how you both are when you are near each other." She looked Emma directly in the eyes and smiled her usual kind smile. "I knew he had met someone, he said as much when he was in Cape Town," she continued. "He also said it could come to nothing, so I knew she...you, must be married." Mercy took a breath, clearly struggling with what she was about to say. "He may be a man with a generous heart, but he does not easily let it be touched. I see how you did. I see why he let you in Mrs Burns, but please do not hurt him. He means the world to Billy and me."

For a moment Emma couldn't speak. The pit of her stomach seemed to have fallen away leaving a gaping hole in her chest.

"Oh, please forgive me. That sounded as though I were accusing you of something terrible," Mercy added quickly. Worry clouding her face.

"Not at all," Emma assured her. She drew a sharp breath. She had to ask, "You are warning me to keep away from him?"

Mercy frantically shook her head.

"No, no. I...oh dear. That all came out wrong. I know it is so soon after your husband, but I see how William feels about you. I believe you feel the same, but if you do not then please, just let him down quickly, that is all I meant," she babbled, clearly regretting her choice of words.

Emma felt tears begin to well in her eyes. She didn't even notice when the woman on the table next to them knocked over the cream jug. She just stared at Mercy.

"Believe me, hurting William is the last thing I would do," Emma replied, her voice sounded distant and strange, as though it belonged to someone else. "But Miss Spencer...I thought..."

Mercy shook her head again.

"Oh no. He is just too polite to be rude to her, but I can assure you there are no feelings there. How can he care for her when he is in love with you?"

Emma was astounded.

"Excuse me," the woman at the table next to them was leaning toward them. "Excuse me, Mrs B, could you fetch a cloth."

"Oh, I... yes of course."

Emma hovered, half off her chair. She wanted to tell Mercy how she really felt about William. She wanted to tell her everything.

"Mrs B, the cream," the woman urged.

Emma blinked, shook her head and then scurried away to fetch a cloth.

As she mopped up the spill, Mercy flashed her a smile and an encouraging nod.

*

Later that evening Emma would reflect on the conversation with confusion and trepidation. She wanted more than anything to believe Mercy was right, yet it seemed impossible. And then there was that all so familiar stab of guilt over Jacob that just wouldn't budge.

33

March 1859

The morning was pleasant and the sun beginning to rise. The gas lamp on the counter flickered an orange glow across the tearoom. Emma sat down at a table near the window and took the weight off her feet for a minute. The last cake was in the oven, the jam had arrived from the Matthews' by way of young Alfie on the cart and now she had a few minutes before she opened the doors. She wafted her face with her Brazilian fan. It was looking a little tired, but it was by far the most useful item she had ever bought. There was a tap on the window. Glancing up she expected to see one of the local children playing a joke, or Mrs McLeish passing by on her daily early morning stroll. Instead, the beaming red face of Mr Price greeted her. In his hand, she could see a tattered envelope and the directions written on it were in Jack's hand. She hurried to the door.

"Mrs B, I thought you might like this. It arrived on the first post just a few minutes ago." Mr Price was puffing from having hurried the ten yards from the Post Office to her front door. He put his hand on his hip and gasped for breath. "I really am getting too old and fat, Mrs B," he laughed.

"Do come in. I'll get you a cup of tea," Emma offered.

"Oh, I'd love to Mrs B, but I have to run. I left the door open and there's sorting to do. I'll pop by later if you don't mind. Besides, you'll be wanting to read this." He handed her the letter and scuttled off again. Emma would have enjoyed his company but she was relieved he had gone all the same. She couldn't wait to read that letter. From the sitting room above she heard her father's clock chime a quarter to seven. With a bit of luck, she would get a few more minutes before anyone came in.

'October 18th 1858
Dear Mam'

And there it was, the moment when Jacob stopped being a part of their lives. She pressed her fingers to her lips; unsure whether she was relieved or saddened.

'I am very sorry to hear about Pa. You must know I found it hard to accept what he did to you when he got arrested, but I hope you know that I did love him, as I know you did too.'

A sob escaped her before she knew it was coming. She got up and poured herself a cup of tea from the simmering samovar on the counter.

'I understand why you want to stay in Australia. The children do seem to be doing well and with the new school and Harry's job. I just hope Pa left you with enough to get by on.'

It had felt improper to write about money in a letter, especially before she had known what she wanted to do with it. But now she was settled it was time she sent him something along with a proper explanation.

'Please don't worry about me back here. I have Marj and my job is ticking along well, and then there is my work with Mr Oliver. The election was last week. He won! Forgive me the timing Mam, but I thought you might be glad of a little good news.'

She dabbed away the tears and realised she was smiling.

'He has asked if I would like to work for him two days a week. As he is a manager at the potteries he has said I can work 4 days a week there and two days for him in the Mayoral office if I like. It's only for a year, but of course, I took it. There was a picture in the paper, I enclosed a copy for you.'

Emma turned the letter over twice but couldn't see anything. She picked up the envelope and felt inside. Folded neatly into a small square was a paper clipping. Carefully she unfolded it. There in the centre of an article announcing the new mayor was a daguerreotype of four men. There on the far left was Jack. He was taller than Mr Oliver now and his face had filled out a little, but he was still the same old Jack. Quickly she scanned the last line of the letter.

'Well, I shall keep this one short. I will write again soon.
Your loving son, Jack.'

Tears were streaming down her cheeks as she hurried out into the street and almost ran right into a pair of workers on their way to the tearoom.

"Five minutes," she called as she bolted towards the post office. A weight seemed to have lifted from her shoulders and she felt as though she were running on air.

Mr Price looked up from the counter in surprise. Thankfully he was alone.

"Heavens, Mrs B, is everything all right? You look most...actually you look, happy."

"Oh, Mr Price. I am, indeed I am. Look. This is my Jack." She handed him the news clipping and pointed to her son. Mr Price looked at the cutting carefully, his smile broadening as he read the headline and examined the picture. When he finally looked up he said,

"Very impressive, Mrs B. And he looks like you, taller, but so like you."

Emma could barely contain her pleasure.

'You know, I think I shall go back to wearing colours tomorrow,' she said with a grin.

Mr Price laughed and handed the cutting back.

"About time too. Black is so dreary and you are so bright."

Emma's hand fluttered to her throat.

"Oh, Mr Price, you're too flattering." She would have thought he was flirting had she not known better. "I should get back. Can't keep the workers waiting," she grinned, hurrying back to the door.

"I shall be by later, and I want to see that black banished," he called as she scurried out into the street. But Emma's mind already drifted. For the first time, she truly felt free to think of William Finch.

34

Emma woke with a start. Outside something clattered against her window. She sat up and pulled back the curtains but there was nothing out there, just the hazy twinkle of the half-moon and an owl gliding away. Leaning forwards she rested her head on the cool glass. A small body wriggled in the bed beside her. Gloria had had a bad dream earlier in the night and insisted on getting in with her mother. Emma quite liked sharing her bed with her little girl again. It made her feel as though she was still needed. She looked down at her sleeping daughter all knotted in the blanket. Gently she tugged at the fabric until Gloria's legs were free to move again. The child opened her eyes and yawned.

"Is it morning?"

Emma shook her head,

"Not quite, lass. I just can't sleep. I think I'll go downstairs and start on the bread." Emma had begun doing cooked breakfasts starting at 730, and as well as the tomatoes, eggs, bacon and kidneys, there was more bread required than she could bake of an evening. "You'll be all right now won't you?"

Gloria's eyelids drooped and closed before her mother's sentence was even done. Emma bent forwards and kissed the child's hair then slid from the bed. Tugging on a pair of thin woollen socks she padded quietly down the stairs and into the kitchen. She went to the drainer by the sink and wiped over the small pile of clean plates from last evenings tea and placed them on the sturdy shelves of her new Welsh Dresser. Then she went into the tearoom and pulled back the curtains. The gas lamp outside was bathing the street in a golden glow. The pile of clean tablecloths was waiting for her on the end of the counter. Washed, she was pleased to consider, by someone else. She began to lay them out. As she passed the window she paused to look at her reflection and smooth back her untidy hair. On the other side of the street a man was standing, watching her. She leapt from her skin. Gathering her composure she stepped up to the glass and peered out. At first, she thought it was an early worker waiting for breakfast to start. But then the figure crossed the street towards her. Beneath the flicker of the gas lamp, his face was momentarily lit. It was William Finch. Without thinking any further Emma opened the door and stepped outside. There was a cold damp smell rising from the ground and she realised it must have rained again during the night. She pulled her shawl tight and folded her arms, uncertain what to make of his presence.

"Forgive me, I didn't mean to startle you." His voice was shaking almost as much as Emma's body.

"Mr Finch, I..."

William Finch came to stand before her. He bowed and doffed his hat in a most formal manner. Her heart sank in her chest, so low it made her stomach hurt. She wanted to turn and run but her feet wouldn't move. There was a sweet aroma of cigar smoke drifting up from his jacket and Emma felt herself lean towards him.

"You are well?"

Emma nodded, her voice caught somewhere in her throat.

"You're up very early, is all well?" She asked.

His hands were fluttering together like butterfly wings at his waist. Emma couldn't stop herself. She reached out and gently laid a hand over them to steady him. There was a crackle as her skin touched his and then there was utter calm. All anxiety in both parties seemed to cease instantaneously.

"I couldn't sleep." She offered. The words were barely audible.

"Nor I." His fingers curled around hers, slowly drawing her hand to his chest until it rested against his heart. "Mercy, she...she said...she gave me hope," he said quietly.

Emma gasped.

"I have never stopped thinking of you. Emma, I know I shouldn't say so, but..."

She shook her head, mesmerised by the feel of him. He was watching her carefully. Neither was aware that they were moving closer together until there was but an inch of air between them. She could feel his breath in her hair. Tentatively she raised her head and let her eyes meet his. When they did it was as though time had stopped. An owl swooped low over their heads but neither of them noticed.

A thump and a creek. Behind them, barrow wheels grated on the rough ground. They pushed away from each other as though they had touched a flame. Emma shot a glance down the street. The lad pushing the barrow was from one of the outlying farmsteads. He was humming a tune to himself and minding his own business. But it was enough. She lifted her skirt over her ankles, turned on her heels and fled back inside the shop, locking the door behind her.

Once safely back upstairs she sank into her favourite chair. Had she been dreaming? Whatever had just happened? It must all be a silly dream. How could she look at another man so soon after Jacob? She really must focus on the tearoom and not on daft romantic notions.

*

The following evening

"William and I should very much like it if you would dine with us. Perhaps next Thursday, if it's convenient?"

Emma blinked and opened her mouth. Mercy had called into the tearoom just as she was about to close the door for the night. Emma was attempting to straighten her thoughts.

"Gloria has her piano lesson on Thursdays," she spluttered at last.

"Surely she is finished by seven. Please, do say you will. We should all very much like you to come."

Mercy cocked her head, clearly attempting to read Emma.

"I see," she said with a sad smile. "William is too afraid to ask and you are too afraid to accept," her tone was only a little exasperated. "Procrastination is tiresome to all Emma. If the two of you will not speak for yourselves then I must intervene."

With a lump in her throat, Emma nodded,

"Very well. Thank you."

"Excellent, see you Thursday at seven then," and with that, she was gone again.

Emma stared after her and hoped she had not just imagined the encounter.

"Are we going to Mercy's house for tea?" Gloria said excitedly.

Emma hadn't even noticed she was there.

"How long have you been standing there?"

Gloria shrugged,

"Just got here. We are going to Mercy's for tea though aren't we?"

"So it seems."

35

Matthews Farmstead
March 13th 1859

Two Days later

A lovely autumn Sunday was turning into an even better evening. The warmth of the sun had faded leaving a pleasant hum of heat rising from the ground and sending a fresh scent of grass into the air. The goat was securely tethered, the sheep were in their field and the pigs were snuffling in the mud contentedly. Only the chickens seemed a little less than placid as they hustled and bustled each other to peck at their food. Gloria and Molly were lolling in the hammocks that Alfred had recently strung up across the deck and the three boys and Alf were kicking a pigs-bladder football about on the grass. Today was Emma's birthday and on account of him doing so well, Harry had been granted a full day off so he could go and see his Mam.

Lucy was tilting back and forth in the new rocking chair Alf has made her, the baby gurgling softly in her arms. Emma got up and stretched her back.

"Penny for em, Em."

Emma looked around at Lucy.

"Oh, nothing, I was just watching the boys and thinking how grown-up Jack is now."

"You mean Harry?" Lucy had stopped rocking and was trying to get out of the chair without annoying the infant. Emma shook her head and offered to take the child.

"No, I meant Jack. I can't believe how quickly time has gone since we first received Jacob's letter asking us to come out here. I haven't seen my eldest for more than two years. He was only a boy then, just starting out."

"He was sixteen when you left weren't he?"

Emma nodded.

"I know. But he still felt like a boy to me and somehow I think he always will. The others will grow up before my eyes. I will see them married and have families of their own. But all I'll ever know of Jack is words." She heard her voice crack. "Sorry, I didn't mean to get all sentimental." She dabbed her eyes and sniffed. "Until that newspaper clipping came I was starting to forget what he looked like." She drew a breath and headed for the kitchen door. "We'd better make a start on some tea, or there'll be six hungry mouths complaining."

Lucy followed her in.

"Of course you won't forget Jack." She took baby Emma-Louise back from Emma and placed her in the straw basket she used to cart her around the farm in. "How often do you hear from him?"

Emma took a pinny from the hook by the back door.

"About once a month. I think that's the hardest thing, being so far behind." Emma paused. "Jack could be dead and I wouldn't know it for months."

Lucy had begun lighting the stove. She stopped and turned to look at her friend.

"That ain't going to happen, Em, and ya got to stop thinking that way." Lucy narrowed her eyes. "But I don't think that's all what's on ya mind is it."

Emma cringed. Shrinking into herself, she pulled out a chair and sat down. The sound of laughter filtered in from outside. She glanced at the window and sighed.

"Please, tell me something. How come Alfred has done so well? He seems so straight forward and unaffected, as though prison did him more good than harm."

Lucy smiled and began chopping carrots. Emma got up and made a start on scrubbing the potatoes.

"As bad at it were, it were no worse than what we had to survive in London. The slums were a terrible place, Em. Crowded and filthy no matter how we scrubbed. Always the threat of starvation and disease every day." Lucy tipped the cut carrots into the stew pot and began chopping the clean potatoes. With a sniff, she carried on. "The ship were bad. He ain't told me much about it, but I see how it was in his eyes sometimes when anyone mentions ships. But once he was here, it were like a proper new start. He was lucky to have been an 'exile,' and not in a gaol cell."

Emma considered how Alf and Jacob had been given the same chance, and yet. She ignored the thought and listened to Lucy.

"It's hard here, Em, harsh as you like for them, and always a challenge for us. But nothin' could have been worse than where he came from. His life were much worse than mine. At least I started out all right, even if I ended up as trash, but Alf, he started out as no better than a rat in a filthy back alley. One of thirteen kids, their Ma dead before he were ten and a father that spent more time in the pub than earnin' a penny. No one cared nor gave him a chance 'til he got out here."

"You did," Emma offered kindly. The baby fussed in her sleep. Lucy checked on her, but she was only dreaming.

"True," she answered. "But even I couldn't stop him getting into that fight and knocking that man out."

"That's what got him sent out here? Just a fight?" Lucy had never volunteered this information before and Emma had always been too polite to enquire.

"Like I says, he had a rough life. Fighting were the only way to get by sometimes. One night he hit the wrong bloke is all. He didn't kill him or nothin' and the man were rougher than a jagged rock himself, but Alf beat him up pretty bad. So the peelers made an example of him."

Emma didn't know what to say or think. She looked through the window at Alfred laughing and playing football with the boys. It was hard to imagine him brawling in the street.

"But Alf ain't the type of man to sit down and get sorrowful over himself," Lucy said. She too was watching him through the window. "He's the type to take an opportunity when it presents and do as best as he can with it, and so he has. That's why I love him Em, that's why I married him."

A thousand thoughts rushed at Emma, memories of all Jacob's wild ideas. His charm and his elegant ways, how he never finished anything he started and how his mind was so easily distracted by pretty shiny things and dreams.

"I think I married a magpie," she said with a laugh.

Lucy looked at her as she added the potatoes to the pot.

"Please don't think he was all bad," Emma added hurriedly. "He had a good heart underneath." She opened the drawer to retrieve the cutlery. "Maybe I didn't love him enough. I should have been stronger for him and not let my eye wander. He could get into such dark moods sometimes." Her hands were trembling. A fork tumbled from her grasp, clanging the side of the dresser and clattering onto the floor. As she bent to pick it up Lucy put her hands on her hips.

"Don't you ever think that, Mrs Burns! And I never want to hear ya say such things again."

The use of her formal name made Emma pause and looked up. She felt like a scolded child.

"You loved him all ya could. I hate to speak ill of the dead and I know he were your husband, but he were a useless sort from what I could tell. And to make ya come out here and then just leave you all alone in that tatty cottage like that and carrying on with that doxy all the while."

Emma stared at her, gobsmacked. She had felt bad not talking to Lucy about Jacob's floozy, but she had been too proud.

"I saw her at the funeral too, I knew right away what she were," Lucy explained. Emma sank into a chair and watched her friend. How could she have doubted Lucy? Of course, she would have known and understood.

"And I seen how you've struggled wiv ya feelings for William Finch and it's all because of Jacob. Not many women would have resisted as you have. Not many women would stick by a man like that. You're loyal, Em and no mistake, but I reckons ya needs to put your thoughts of Jacob in the back of the closet next to that bloody black frock ya finally got rid of."

Emma laughed. She pressed her hand over her mouth but it was no use.

"And anover thing," Lucy carried on, though a smile was spreading over her lips too. "Look at everything you've achieved, Em. Look at the tearoom and how well the kids are doing."

Emma nodded, the laughter subsiding. She sat back and sighed.

"I saw him the other morning. Mr Finch I mean," she admitted.

Lucy folded her arms and waited for the rest.

"And now I can't get him out of my mind."

The way her friend was looking at her made Emma nervous. She narrowed her eyes.

"You already knew that didn't you?"

Lucy walked over to Emma and pulled up a chair next to her.

"Mercy stopped by yesterday. She were on her way back from another visit and popped in."

Emma felt her heart flip over in her chest and a sudden sick feeling boiled into her throat. Mercy could only know of the encounter if William had told her, or worse, the farm boy with the barrow had seen more than he appeared and gossiped.

"She said her brover had been acting all out of sorts and dreamy like all day Thursday. She said she asked him what the matter was, but all he would say is that the woman he loved was free now and he didn't know if he was capable of hiding his feelings no more."

Emma pressed her cool hands onto her hot cheeks and tried to swallow the lump that had formed in her throat.

"When she pressed him, he admitted he'd seen ya in town."

"He mentioned my name?" Emma's heart was beating so fast she could feel the blood thumping in her temples. Lucy shook her head.

"Don't be daft. You know he's far too considerate for that. Nah, but Mercy knows it's you don't she? She told ya so."

Emma felt her heart slow a little. She leaned forward, placed her head in her hands and nodded into her palms.

"That's why she asked us to tea on Thursday next," Emma said. "A few days ago I thought it was all right." She looked at the navy blue skirt covering her legs, "but what will the children think, their father is barely cold?"

"It's near a year ago, Em. And we don't choose who we fall in love wiv, nor when. It chooses us. The children like Mr Finch, why would they mind?"

Emma recalled Jacob, crumpled on the kitchen floor sobbing like a small child.

"I know, but I still feel guilty."

Lucy sighed kindly.

"Ya really needs to stop feeling so guilty all the time. If it ain't Jacob, it's the money, if it ain't the money it's Jack or even Harry. It's about time you just forgave yourself and accepted how things have worked out." She took her friend's hand and gave it a squeeze. Emma closed her eyes for a moment, then straightened up and wiped the dropped fork with her pinny.

"I almost kissed him and now we're going over for tea," Emma knew she sounded panicked.

Lucy was attempting not to smile.

"I think ya should call him William now, don't you?"

Emma crumpled. All the anguish turned to hysteria and she began to laugh again.

"Oh dear!" she gasped.

Lucy folded her arms in amusement.

"You're a free woman now, and no one would think ill of ya if ya were to take up wiv a man like William Finch."

Emma's heart skipped a beat and she finally allowed herself to hope.

36

Flemington

The following Thursday

Crisp red and gold leaves littered the street. A boy was sweeping them up into piles. Emma tried to focus her thoughts into some semblance of order that would result in a coherent conversation. Albert pushed open the gate to the Finches front yard and dashed up the path. Emma hesitated, watching as Gloria skipped along after her brother. The scent of late-blooming English roses danced in the air; pink, yellow and white flowers just beginning to fade lined up beneath the window.

"Come on, Mam," Albert called as the front door opened to reveal Mercy and Billy bouncing excitedly around her skirts. The puppy shot out to greet them. Gloria scooped him up and kissed his furry head.

"Emma, children, welcome. We are in the sitting room." Mercy was looking over the heads of the children and directly at Emma, her expression full of encouragement. She let the children pass as Billy grabbed Gloria's arm and tugged her inside.

"Good to see you, Emma. I am delighted you agreed to come."

"Thank you, you look well as always." This was the only thing Emma could think of to say.

"And William has been most looking forward to seeing you," Mercy laid a gentle hand on Emma's arm to bring her inside. "In fact," she added with a hint of mischief, "he has been fussing about all afternoon in preparation."

Emma considered that she would have been doing the same had she not had the tearoom customers to distract her. She followed Mercy into the drawing room where the children had already settled, playing jacks on the floor with the dog fussing about them. William was perched uncomfortably on the edge of an elegant mint green chaise longue that matched the wallpaper. The moment he saw her he was on his feet.

"Mrs Burns, how good of you to come." The abrupt formality clearly amused Mercy and she shot him a, 'for goodness sake' glare. There was a clatter on the floor as the jacks crashed down. The dog yapped. William flinched as though someone had fired a cannon. Mercy laughed at him and suddenly Emma was laughing too. William stood for a moment, somewhere halfway between joining in and confused. Emma saw his face and pressed her fingers to her lips. Mercy shook her head at him,

"Oh, William dear, sometimes I despair." she slipped her arm through his and patted his hand. "Now, please excuse me a moment, I must check on supper." As she left the room, William adjusted his cravat and cleared his throat.

"Please, do sit down."

Emma chose the Queen Anne chair and tried to distract herself by wondering if the Zebra rug went with the rest of the very English looking room.

"Uncle William, please tell us a story." Billy had stopped with a jack balanced on the back of his hand. "Uncle William tells the best stories," he told Emma and the other children.

"We know. He told everyone a ghost story on the ship, and sometimes in class, he tells us stories about lions and ephelants." Albert explained.

"Elephants, silly." Billy giggled.

William looked down at his hands. Emma noticed they were shaking just as much as hers.

"After dinner," he told them.

"Aww, please Uncle William."

"Oh, yes please do," begged Gloria.

William looked at Emma for assistance, but she was too relieved to be avoiding actual conversation to protest. William swallowed so hard Emma could see his Adam's apple go up and down. As he paused to think, Mercy returned from the kitchen.

"Perhaps I should let you get us a maid," she said, patting her flushed cheeks with the back of her hand. She stopped and looked at the expectant faces, all watching William. "What are you all doing?" she said with curious accusation.

"Uncle William is about to tell us a story," Albert said, catching Billy's familial address. Emma blushed as she considered the intimacy.

"How lovely." Seeing the bank expression on William's face, she added, "How about the one about the baby elephant that got lost."

The relief on William's face was enough to make Emma want to kiss him right there and as he started to tell the story she began to imagine herself spending the rest of her life listening to his voice.

*

Cutlery clattered, hungry mouths chewed heartily and conversation buzzed around the table. The evening had been a great success and both she and William had gradually become more and more at ease. As soon as the last spoonful of treacle sponge vanished from Albert's dish Mercy began to clear the table.

"Come along children, I think you can all help me clear the pots and wash the dishes."

Emma was startled by Mercy's eagerness and was about to protest when she added,

"You too, Billy. The sooner everything is cleaned away the sooner you can all go up to Billy's room and play."

William shifted uneasily in his chair and Emma understood. She sat, unable to move or think as the children gathered up the dishes and followed Mercy into the kitchen, leaving her and William entirely alone. For a moment or two, they were silent. Emma listened to Mercy giving instructions to each of the children in order to keep them out of the dining room. Then a chair leg scraped on the floor at her side and William was on his feet.

"Emma," he went over to the window and turned his back on her. Emma felt her heart rise to her throat and the blood pound in her head. Slowly she rose too. "May I call you Emma?"

With legs wobbling like jellied eels, she made her way over to join him.

"Of course."

They stood, side by side, looking out of the window.

"I know you are only just out of mourning, but...please, tell me, Emma, do I have any chance to win you?"

Tentatively she reached out her hand and slipped her fingers through his. The very feel of his skin against hers sent a warm tingle right up her arm into her chest. He turned to face her, took her other hand in his and looked so deeply into her eyes she felt as though she were falling.

"Do you think you could ever love me?"

Emma felt the tears in her eyes spill out and sting her burning cheeks. William's eyes began to widen and his breath quickened.

Emma gasped back a sob.

"I do love you, William. I think I always have."

Before she could even draw another breath she felt his lips on hers. The kiss was warm and soft, gentle at first, then passionate as she gave in to him, arching closer, pressing her breasts against his chest. He wrapped an arm around her, pulling her in tight as though she would fade away if he let her go. At that moment Emma realised she was finally home.

37

Flemington
November 7th 1861

The warm sweet scent of candyfloss and toffee apples filled the air. Carousels and street organs were playing their tunes and children's laughter drifted on the spring breeze. There was an excited buzz around the racecourse as people crowded into the stands or meandered amidst the stalls that littered the edge of the track. Emma was sure she had never seen so many people in Flemington, even when the miners were passing through on their way to the goldfields. It seemed all of Melbourne and its outlying villages had come along to witness this new annual horse race: The Melbourne Cup. She wondered if it really would come to rival the Doncaster St Ledger and the Epsom Derby. There was a thump in the pit of her stomach. She rubbed at the swell of her belly and smiled as the child inside her kicked at her hand. For a moment she considered how things had changed. Only two years ago another child would have been the last thing she would have welcomed and yet here she was, seven months along and she couldn't have been happier. She tried to picture her new baby, all grown and attending the races in twenty years. Would he be tall and handsome like his father, all debonair in top hat and tails, or would she be raven-haired beauty in an elegant gown, hanging off the arm of a fashionable gent?

"Is everything all right my love?"

Emma was startled out of her musing. She slipped her arm through her husband's and sighed.

"Oh yes," she replied.

"Are you sure? Perhaps you should sit down for a little while."

Emma laughed at William's wide-eyed expression. He had done nothing but fuss over her from the moment she had discovered she was expecting.

"Mam, Mam, can Billy and I go on the Carousel?" Gloria was jigging around in front of her. Emma looked at her daughter. Her chestnut ringlets were bouncing like glossy springs down her back and her new dress fitted neatly over her slender figure. At twelve Gloria was caught between childhood and turning into an attractive young woman and Emma was enjoying watching the transition.

"Of course, but you'd better ask Mercy first."

"Mam, Mam," Billy called as he weaved between Mr Price and Mr Grayson to reach his mother. His African accent had faded of late and he had begun to sound more and more like Gloria and Bert. Emma was not sure if this was a good thing but it was sweet all the same.

"Good day," Mr Grayson said doffing his hat as they reached the group.

"You really are looking very well Mrs B." Mr Price was beaming at Emma in his usual jolly way.

"Good day, and thank you," Emma was about to return the compliment when William interjected.

"Perhaps you could persuade her to rest more, Mr Price. My wife insists on continuing to bake and run the tearoom and I can do nothing to persuade her to leave it to the girls. They're perfectly capable of running the shop by themselves." William was playfully chastising Emma, but she had no intentions of resting until she needed to.

"How is the new girl getting on?" Mr Price was as rosy-faced as ever.

"Mary, yes very well. Kitty has turned out to be a good teacher."

"Yes, and yet I still had to drag my wife out the door this morning." William was smiling at Emma with those blue eyes twinkling in such a way she wished they were alone so she could kiss him.

"Well, I just don't like to leave everything to them," Emma leaned on William a little and rolled her left ankle. *Perhaps I could do with resting my feet a bit more often,* she thought.

"I thought the Matthews were coming today?" Mercy had packed the children off with tuppence for the ride and a toffee apple. Emma nodded.

"They are."

"Well, they had better hurry along. There is only a half-hour to the big race."

Emma looked at Mercy, stunning and elegant in a deep purple gown, and wished she could find a nice young man to step out with. It astounded Emma that such a beautiful, gracious and kind woman could still be alone. Yet it didn't seem to bother Mercy, she and Billy had the house to themselves since William had moved in with Emma and the children. Billy was doing better now he was in school and there was plenty of midwifery to keep Mercy busy. And yet… Emma looked around the stands and eyed all the handsome young men in their elegant frockcoats. There must be one of them in this crowd worthy of Mercy. Her eyes fell on the husband of one of her regular ladies. With him were two other men, young, attractive and definitely not convict class. Perhaps she could engineer an introduction or two.

"Mam!"

Emma spun around.

"Harry, my goodness. What are you doing here?"

"For the race. They sent me and the other porters out on the one o'clock train. We've all been given a couple of hours off, 'til the train goes back."

Emma flung her arms around her boy.

"Have you seen Bert, he was going to watch the train come in?"

As she spoke there was a tap on her shoulder.

"Here, Mam."

Emma extended her hug and embraced both boys.

"Are you crying, Mam?"

Emma sniffed.

"Silly emotional, Mam," she said, "It's the baby, it makes me all weepy."

Harry looked her up and down.

346

"Looks like you doubled in size since I last saw you," he grinned.

Emma clipped him lightly around the back of his head.

"You're not too old to go over my knee lad," she laughed.

"Harry is Head Porter at Spencer Street," she said proudly to Mr Grayson. The gentleman was new in town a couple of months since, but she had seen him with Mr Price a few times of late, and now the postmaster seemed even jollier than before if that was possible.

"And this is Albert."

Mr Grayson shook the boy's hand,

"Pleased to meet you both."

"I'm going to work for the railway too." Albert announced.

"When he's a little bit older," Emma added. "He's only thirteen.

"Next year," Albert insisted.

"Perhaps he could start at Newmarket Station, here in Flemington," Mr Grayson suggested with enthusiasm. Bert nodded and they began to chat about the rapidly expanding rail network.

Down at the track horses were beginning to parade, the bright silks of the jockeys shirts glistening in the sunlight. There were people everywhere, laughing and talking, glasses chinking and wine flowing. At the carrousel Billy and Gloria were riding the gaily-painted wooden horses, travelling around and around. The ever faithful Frank the dog sitting close by watching. Gloria waved as they sailed by. Emma sighed.

"What is it, my love?"

Emma looked at William and smiled.

"I was just thinking how Jack would have enjoyed today."

"He seems to be doing very well for himself," Mercy said comfortingly.

"I know. But I'll always miss him. And now he and Marj are getting married, I'll miss my eldest son's wedding and never meet my future grandchildren." Emma felt William squeeze her arm. Something tugged at her hem. She looked down to see the bright orange curls of Emma-Louise. The two-year-old looked up with her big amber eyes.

"'Lo Aunty Emem," the little girl beamed. Mercy scooped her up and balanced her on her hip.

"Don't you look pretty as a picture," she stroked the child's hair and made her giggled.

"Sorry we're late," Lucy called as she and Alf shoved their way through the crowds towards them. "Bloody goat got out again."

Emma laughed, glad for the distraction. Jack was the only thing left in her life that caused her pain. But as William kept reminding her, they had all made the right choices, even if they were a few thousand miles apart.

"Where are the twins?" William asked, searching between the satin draped bodies to find them.

"Down there," Alf pointed to the trackside. "At the coconut shy."

Emma shielded her eyes and peered down. If it hadn't been for the two shocks of red hair she should have found them hard to spot amidst the jostling crowd. William greeted Alf with a hearty handshake as Lucy bustled in closer to Emma and Mercy.

"Ain't never seen a day like this," Lucy shook her head. "Who'd a thought an 'orse race would draw such a crowd."

"Mummy," Emma-Louise reached for Lucy.

"She looks much better," Mercy smiled and handed the child over.

"Yeh, them chicken-spots is just about gone now. Just a few little marks here and there, but I don't reckon they'll scar."

"Oh, that is good news." Mercy was speaking to Lucy and yet her eyes were drifting over to William and Alf. Emma was compelled to follow her eye line. Standing with them was another gentleman. Blond hair peeking out beneath his top hat and pale green eyes glinting merrily as his gaze shifted between the men with whom he was conversing, and Mercy. A slow smile crept over Emma's lips.

"Are you going to introduce your friend, Alfred," Emma said as casually as she could.

"Of course," he replied. "This is our new neighbour, Mr Benson. He's just purchased the plot at the end of our land."

There was an interlude of pleasantries until Emma could resist no longer, "And where are you and your wife living whilst you build the house?"

Mr Benson smiled coyly. The quick glance in Mercy's direction did not go unnoticed.

"I have not yet had the pleasure of finding a wife," he replied. "I only arrived in the colony a month ago with my brother and his family."

"And now you're setting up a life of your own, how lovely." *How perfect*, she thought. Emma tried to suppress her pleasure. "Permit me to introduce you to my sister-in-law, Mercy Finch."

THE END

Historical Note

I have tried to be as faithful as possible with descriptions of places and life, in England, on board ship, and in Australia in the 1850's. The characters, however, are entirely fictional and any similarity to any real persons is purely co-incidental, including those of my ancestors.

My three times great grandmother, Mary Keeling's decision to leave her life in England behind, including her eldest children (who were already grown up), to join her convict husband in Australia is as far as the similarity goes between her life and that of Emma.

Acknowledgements

Thanks to everyone at Abingdon Writers, Gabrielle Aquilina and my dad for their feedback. Thanks to Antonella for her technical help and Carmen for her proofread. And thanks to the anonymous reviewer at the Romantic Novel Association who gave me few pointers and the most lovely review.

About the Author

Liah S Thorley wrote her first book aged 9; it was 15 (school textbook size) pages long and a rather unconvincing ghost/mystery story. Since then she trained at the Italia Conti Academy of Theatre Arts and became a dancer and actor. In 2006 she decided to return to writing and moved to Oxfordshire. She has a Masters degree in History and loves to travel.

Liah is dyslexic and can write faster than she can read, though not necessarily with the correct spelling.

She considers herself a nomad and has lived in the US, Australia, and (for three months) Italy. She now lives and teaches acting on the sunny island of Malta where she intends to stay, probably.

Please visit her website wwww.liahthorley.com or follow her author page on Facebook or Instagram

Also by Liah S Thorley
Hidden Doorways – A time travel romance.

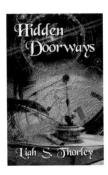

'All Catherine wants is a happy home and a contented life, but Time is a playful thing.'

To her family Catherine is lost in time, lost to her friends and lost to the 21st century. To her she is a young Tudor woman with a new husband, a business to run and no memory of who she really is. But Catherine's life takes a most unexpected turn, in more ways than she could ever have imagined.

Half a millennium in her future is her father. Michael is a professor of physics, racked with guilt for accidentally sending Catherine back in time when she was only six year old. As he determines to find her, he unwittingly sends her though the hidden doorways of history to passions and sorrows on the most unusual of adventures.

ISBN- 978-9918-0-0041-8

Catherine

Hertfordshire – 28th August 1646

A blank page can be a daunting thing, especially when the words one is about to write may endanger the lives of others. Perhaps I should not begin at all. Yet the quill itches in my hand as though being drawn to the ink, and I find the need to record the events of my life overwhelming. In so doing, I can only pray for the safe keeping of those who have shown me great kindness, and for the child whose weight grows heavier in my belly with each passing day.

It is a glorious afternoon. The day is bright outside and the room in which I must sit is filled with light and warmth. But there are happenings out there, beyond these walls that sour the air and strike fear into the best of us. Despite all I have experienced in my twenty-three years of life, I never envisioned that I should face England in the midst of the Civil War, and yet here I am. You may wonder at my lack of foresight on this account and I cannot blame you for it, for surely someone who lived through the events of the last twenty years would have expected such a thing. But there is the rub, dear journal. I did not grow up here. As queer as it may sound, I cannot say for certain from which century I truly hail; I can only say that it was not this. Time, you see, has played games with me, sweeping me here and there and all against my will. I have no understanding of the manner of these actions and never a warning as to where or when I shall go next, only a continual feeling of inevitability that one day I shall be moved on once more.

Perhaps this sounds bizarre or bemusing right now and my story is a peculiar one, 'tis true. But I shall tell it to you, and I promise it will all make sense. I have learned to keep my eyes, ears and mind open over the years. All I ask is that you do the same.

Oxford, 1491

It was the first of the month and the year still held the promise of a good summer. By eleven o'clock the sun was glowing high in the sky. As I approached the heavy doors of St Mary Magdalen's, the sweet scent of damp grass drifted on the breeze and a blackbird serenaded me from the tree by the church wall. Nervous and alone, I paused in the doorway clutching a posy of pink roses. A single thorn remained and stabbed at my palm. As I stepped though the porch into the peaceful cool of the church, a small blue butterfly hovered in the doorway as though about to follow me in, but it changed its mind and fluttered away. I took a deep breath and walked down the aisle towards Daniel More. At that moment my life seemed to be of little consequence to the world, and it never occurred to me that things might not stay as we planned.

When I first met Daniel I had been a mere fourteen years old and he a little over a year more. He was a student at Balliol

College. One morning my father sent me on an errand there: one of the masters had ordered a new travelling cloak and I was to deliver it. I had walked past the building many times and looked out at it from my father's bedroom window most days, but until then I had never set foot inside. With their closed doors and grand stone facades, the colleges were something of a mystery to the town's children. And the men who walked their halls did nought to dispel their unfavourable image, stalking about in their rich clothes, conversing in Latin or Greek and frowning down at the locals. Understandably I was nervous when the door creaked back. The only woman to set foot inside, I fancied. But as I walked across the quad the sun was shining brightly and the elegant architecture seemed not at all frightening.

The porter gave me directions, and I set off down a long corridor. In a room towards the end I could hear voices speaking Latin. My curiosity got the better of me, and I stopped outside the door and pressed my ear to the wood. Thanks to my excellent tutor, Father Thomas, I was able to follow the debate with little effort. So I set the cloak down on the floor and settled into eavesdropping, wishing I could join in.

Suddenly I felt a sharp tap upon my shoulder. I screamed in surprise and whirled round to see a tall man squinting down at me. My heart leapt up to my throat so fast that I jumped back and hit my elbow on the door. It swung open it to reveal a spiky, hard-nosed figure, robed in black, heading towards me. .... *Continued*

Printed in Great Britain
by Amazon